DEATH ON THE PEARL RIVER

A.E. GOLDIN

Pushkin Press
Somerset House, Strand
London WC2R 1LA

Death on the Pearl River was first published by Pushkin Vertigo in 2026

ISBN 13: 978-1-78227-921-1

A CIP catalogue record for this title is available from the British Library

The authorised representative in the EEA is eucomply OÜ,
Pärnu mnt. 139b-14, 11317, Tallinn, Estonia,
hello@eucompliancepartner.com, +33757690241

Designed and typeset by Tetragon, London
Printed and bound in the United Kingdom by Clays Ltd, Elcograf S.p.A.

This book is made of FSC-certified and recycled paper. The FSC-certified
materials meet FSC's standards for responsible forestry, and recycled
materials are used instead of virgin forest materials. www.fsc.org

www.pushkinpress.com

1 3 5 7 9 8 6 4 2

PRAISE FOR *MURDER IN CONSTANTINOPLE*

'Delivers a multitude of pleasures... In this atmospheric, immensely satisfying mystery, Goldin ratchets up the tension... leaving Ben and the reader gasping for breath'
New York Times

'From the tenements of London's Jewish East End to the lush costumes of the slowly declining Ottoman Empire, Goldin brings a long-lost era to life in vivid, evocative detail'
Financial Times

'A zip-along plot, packed full of political machinations, strange deaths and ruinous romance'
Daily Mail

'An inventive story rich in detail that ducks and dives just like its hero. Unputdownable'
Sun

'This fast-moving romp makes for wonderful entertainment'
CrimeTime

'A gripping historical mystery'
Glamour 'Best September Books'

A.E. GOLDIN is a British writer and lawyer. He has worked as a screenwriter for television companies in London and Los Angeles, and has released two albums as a classical pianist. *Murder in Constantinople*, his debut novel and the first Ben Canaan Mystery, was published to acclaim in 2024. He lives in London.

Contents

*The greatest danger, that of losing one's own self,
may pass off as quietly as if it were nothing.*

— SØREN KIERKEGAARD,
The Sickness unto Death (1849)

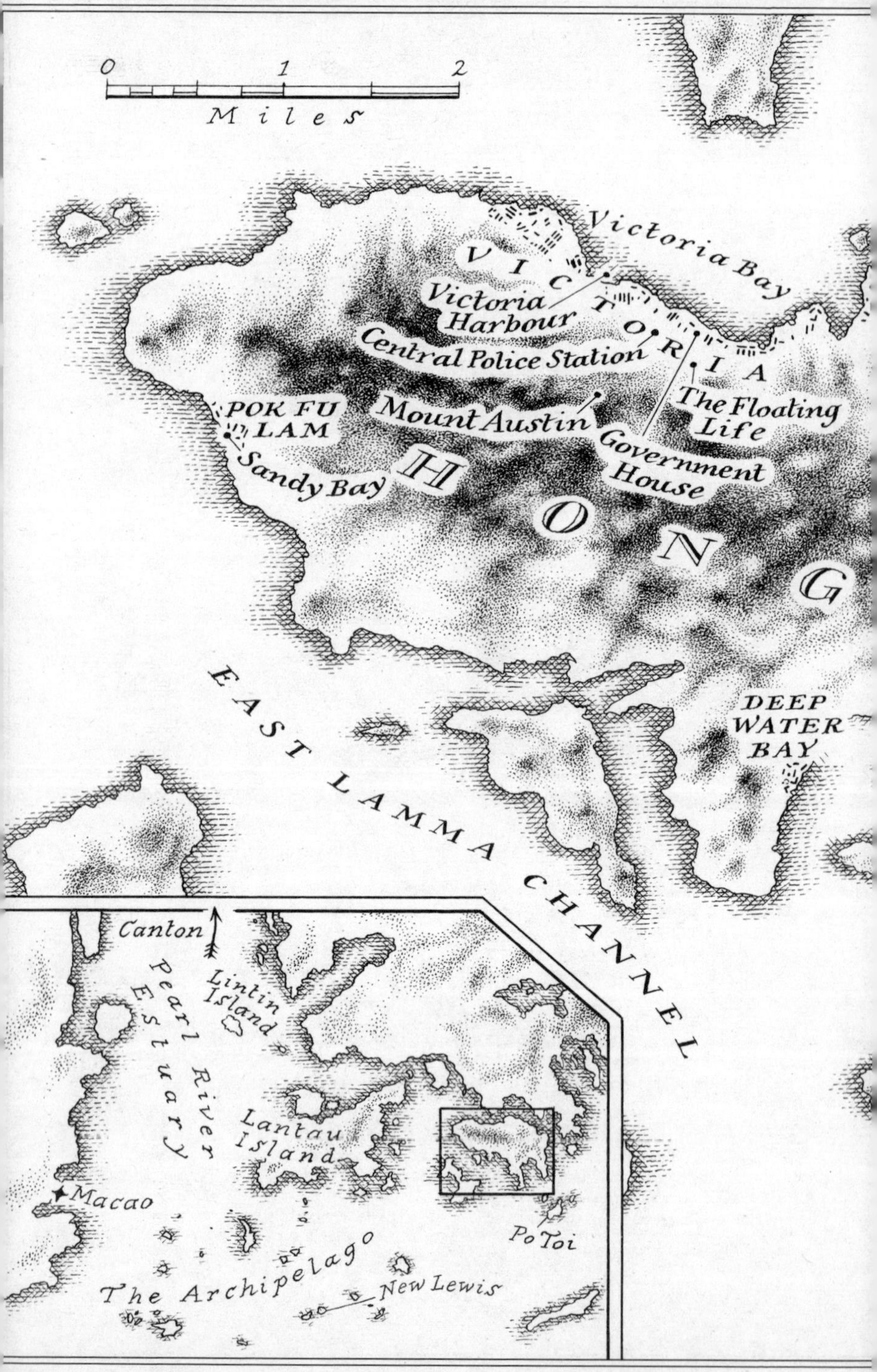

Miles
0
1
2
Victoria Bay
VICTORIA
Victoria Harbour
Central Police Station
The Floating Life
POK FU LAM
Mount Austin
Government House
Sandy Bay
HONG
DEEP WATER BAY
EAST LAMMA CHANNEL
Canton
Pearl River Estuary
Lintin Island
Lantau Island
Macao
Po Toi
The Archipelago
New Lewis

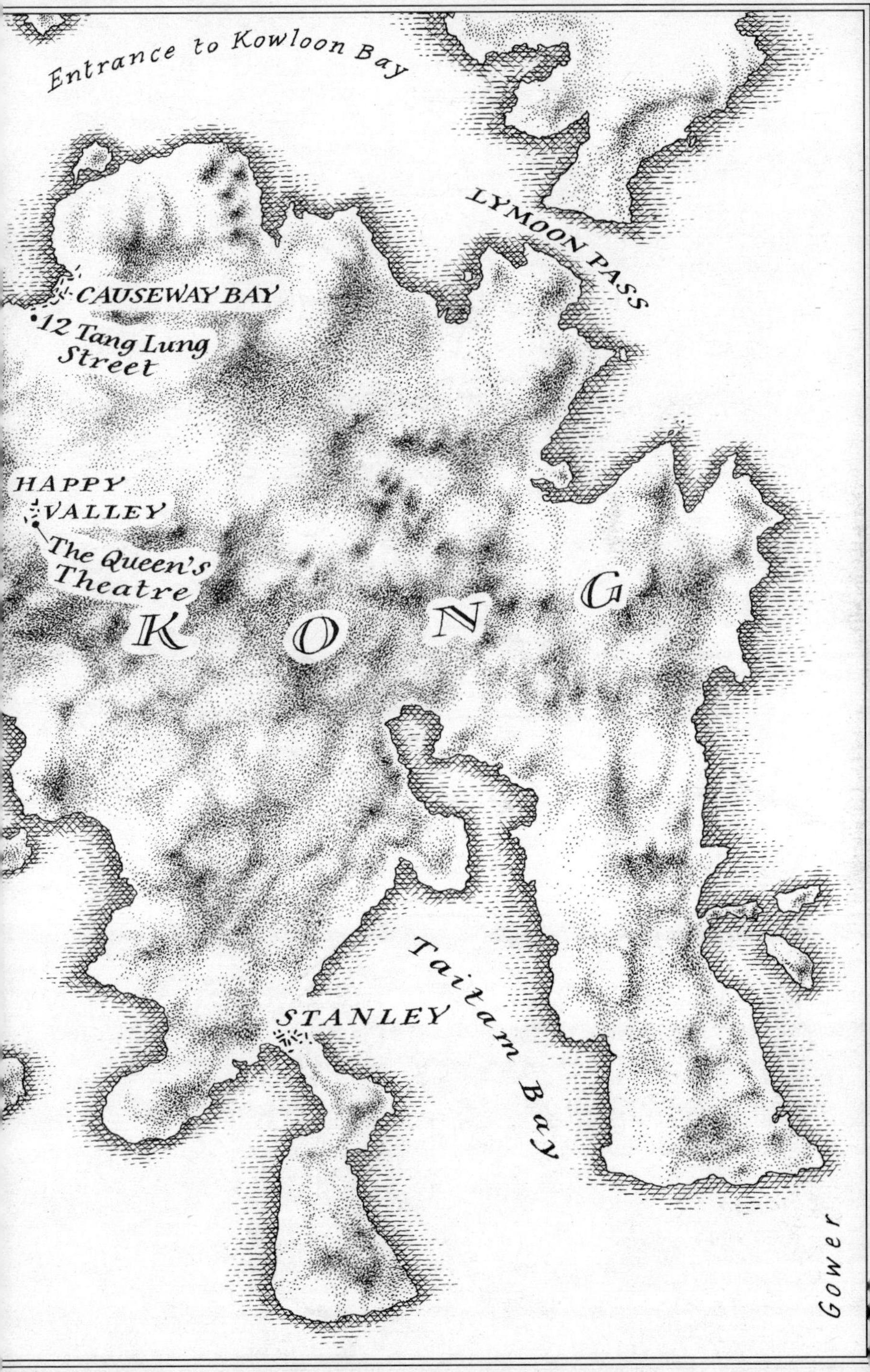

Entrance to Kowloon Bay
LYMOON PASS
CAUSEWAY BAY
12 Tang Lung Street
HAPPY VALLEY
The Queen's Theatre
KONG
Taitam Bay
STANLEY
Gower

In loving memory of my grandfather
Geoffrey Levy – Tzadik ben Eliezer

1

Uninvited Guests

They found him sprawled face down on the dining table. The blood had long since dried, staining the tablecloth deep burgundy. His arms were spread wide, in a crucifix-like gesture, and his face was buried in a half-eaten lemon posset. The cutlery, fine sterling silver, lay scattered across the oak floor, in puddles of Laurent-Perrier and shards of shattered champagne flutes. The candles had almost burnt through their wax and shadows hung heavy around the corpse.

It was an oddly peaceful sight: constables drifting through the stillness as they formed a perimeter around the table, a gentle breeze nudging the windowpanes, the barely stifled sobs of Lady Louisa Ellison. She was huddled with the other witnesses at the far end of the dining room, wrapped in the arms of her husband the Earl of Mansfield, whose right hand was covering her eyes to shield her from the horror.

Two men were standing over the body. On the right, vigorously chewing tobacco, was Sergeant Will Hardy of the Metropolitan Police – his top hat crooked to the right as he fiddled with his specially issued revolver, which he had a habit of keeping in an open holster for easy access. On the left, in a smooth black overcoat and slim-fitting suit, with a neat bowtie nestled under his chin and a thin moustache traced over his top lip, was Detective Ben Canaan.

They stared at the gruesome sight with a detachment not unlike that which was writ large on the faces of the Mansfield ancestors whose portraits were affixed to the walls.

'Did Commissioner Mayne sanction your presence?' Hardy grumbled.

'Not quite,' Ben replied. 'My own superiors sent for me. Don't worry: there's plenty of space on the dancefloor and I'll be sure not to tread on the Met's toes.'

'You're more than happy to cling to our coattails. You angling to join our ranks?'

'I go where I'm told, Hardy. Besides, I wouldn't join the Met for all the money and caviar in the world. Now, what say we turn this chap over and get a good look at him?'

Ben and Hardy flipped the body onto its back, and Ben slipped on his glove to wipe away the yellowish dessert that had congealed on the man's face.

Lying dead before them was none other than Lennie Glass: notorious East End gangster – king of the Isle of Dogs. A man whose casual glance used to strike fear into Ben's heart. Who played with people's lives like a cat with fresh yarn. And now he too had met a sticky end.

Hardy narrowed his eyes. 'You know our dear friend Mr Glass?'

Ben tut-tutted and flicked the cream from his glove. 'I owed him a favour once.'

Ben inspected Lennie more closely. The man's hair was brittle and tangled, as when it is caught in the rain and left to dry naturally. Ben parted his lips – Lennie's pristine white teeth, one of his great prides, were still intact. From the face alone, the pallor of death aside, Lennie could easily have been mistaken for a man at the peak of his powers.

It was below the head where things got messy. His suit, courtesy of H. Huntsman & Sons, was made from the highest quality cotton twill, as Ben could tell from a cursory brush. But it was streaked with mud and punctured with ragged holes, and his bloodstained dress shirt was torn down to the sternum. The front of his right trouser leg was in tatters, exposing his bright-purple silk socks. His shoes, custom-made black leather loafers from Tricker's, were caked in dirt. Ben gave them a sniff. *Horse manure.*

'How unlike Lennie,' Ben said. 'He wouldn't be caught dead looking like this.'

'He has now,' Hardy chuckled.

With his mother-of-pearl penknife, Ben carefully slit the edges of the opening in Lennie's dress shirt to expose his belly. It was drenched in blood and riddled with stab-wounds. Ben wiped away the blood to tally them up, but what he saw made him freeze.

A phrase had been carved into Lennie's belly: *Black Blood.*

'Not just dead,' he murmured, 'Gutted. I take it none of the guests did this?'

'They claim not.'

'So he staggered through the rain in this state for who knows how far.'

'Is that even possible?' Hardy said as he topped up his chewing tobacco.

Ben nodded. Lennie was strong as a bull – he always had been. Obviously the person responsible for this, unlike Ben once upon a time, had not had the dubious honour of working for the man.

But this was speculation. Ben needed something more concrete. He approached the witnesses, who had formed a semicircle by the bay windows. Behind them was a bleak view of the Kenwood Estate – its pastures sloping down to Wood Pond, the banks of birches and sycamores giving way to a pitch-black thicket that swayed back and forth in the breeze.

'Good evening, Detective,' the Earl of Mansfield said in a low voice, as he shook hands with Ben. 'You must forgive my wife: she cannot brook the sight of blood.'

'That is quite alright.' Ben bowed his head and held out a hand to Lady Louisa. 'All will be well, my lady. Fear not.'

There were eight witnesses in all: the Earl of Mansfield and Lady Louisa, the hosts; the Earl's imperious mother Frederica Murray, Countess of Mansfield; Lord Brougham and Vaux, lately arrived from the spa town of Cannes; Sir Alexander Cockburn, the current Attorney General; Westbury, the septuagenarian head steward, and two pages who served as Westbury's under-stewards.

'I daresay,' Ben exclaimed, 'an illustrious crowd, in an equally illustrious venue! Kenwood House is a fine piece of land, my lord. Which begs the question: how on earth does a dead man end up on your dinner table, with his face submerged in what I'm sure was a delicious lemon posset?'

'*My* lemon posset,' Frederica Murray said with venom – and, with a sharp nod in Lennie's direction, 'ruined by this frightful boor.'

Everyone provided much the same account. They had been having dinner at the Earl of Mansfield and Lady Louisa's invitation. It was a quieter affair than the lavish soirées that the Earl typically hosted, though by any other measure a seven-course meal including oysters, *soupe à l'oignon gratinée*, and roasted pheasant with buttered potatoes was far from standard. They were just about to tuck into the famous lemon posset when they heard a commotion outside, followed by shouts of alarm, and the sound of a scuffle.

Then, without warning, the double doors to the dining room burst open and in staggered Lennie Glass. He was wild-eyed and bleeding profusely from his belly, which he clutched tight with one hand. The stewards trailed behind him, Westbury grabbing his arm to yank him back. The guests leapt from their seats as Lennie tore himself free of Westbury's grasp, approached the head of the table, and with his last ounce of strength uttered just one word: 'Seven!' And with that, he collapsed onto the table, letting out a final choke, quite dead.

'Seven?' Ben frowned. 'Seven what?'

'Just seven, Detective,' the Earl of Mansfield said.

'You didn't hear him say anything else?'

'I'm quite sure it was simply the number "Seven",' the Attorney General interjected.

Westbury and his pages filled in the events leading up to this dramatic entrance. There had been a knock at the door – highly unusual at this hour, with all the guests having arrived and the gates to the Kenwood Estate being locked. Westbury answered, expecting perhaps that the Earl of Mansfield had made an impromptu invitation. But he was greeted instead by this uninvited guest, doubled over in pain and sopping wet from the rain shower that had just passed.

'So, by the time he arrived, he was already in a rather sorry state?' Ben asked.

'I was not compelled to *stab* the man myself, Detective, if that is what you are implying,' Westbury said sharply. 'He was begging for help and saying that he had to come inside before it was too late.'

But Westbury was not minded to let Lennie in, not knowing who he was at the time and wondering whether this was all an elaborate con. That said, he was also keen to spare his master the scandal of a man expiring on their doorstep, so he turned to the pages and instructed them to send for a surgeon.

As Westbury's back was turned, Lennie shoved past him and lumbered into Kenwood House. The three stewards pursued Lennie, trying with all their might to hold him back. But Lennie, despite his mortal wounds, had an almost preternatural drive and made it as far as the double doors of the dining room. Hence the fracas heard by the dinner guests.

Ben mulled this information for a moment. He had the ending. But what was the beginning? This was a case where he would have to work backwards to go forward.

He turned to the Earl of Mansfield. 'I assume, my lord, that you own stables?'

The Earl nodded and snapped his fingers at Westbury. 'Take Detective Canaan to the stables and fetch Higgins.'

Westbury led Ben, Hardy and a squad of four officers out of Kenwood House and down a meandering footpath across the pasture to the stables. They found Higgins, the stable master, fast asleep in his annex. He was lying on the floor with his Balmoral bonnet over his face, next to a bowl of beef gristle and an empty bottle of gin. He had the snore of a man who would not be lightly woken. Westbury barked his name, and when he did not stir, Hardy gave him a kick to the backside.

Higgins jolted awake and looked up at the officers blearily. 'Peelers? I didn't steal no bloody gin from the earl, it's mine fair 'n square…'

'Get up, Higgins,' Westbury said, 'and let us into the stable.'

'I'm telling yous, I didn't do nothin'—'

'*Up, you drunk rat!*' Hardy bellowed, hauling Higgins to his feet.

Higgins led them round to the front of the stables and unlatched the doors. Ben held his lantern out into the gloom. The light flashed in the bulbous, unblinking eyes of the earl's prized studs. They were spooked: shaking their manes, whinnying, kicking the ground restlessly.

'Well that's a strange 'un,' Higgins said, pointing to the ground. 'Look.'

A faint track had been trodden into the hay, all the way from the back door, which was splattered with dried blood and hanging ajar.

'Someone must have sneaked in through the back,' Ben said. 'Probably our unhappy friend. Higgins, did you hear anything?'

'Agh, well…' Higgins winced, 'No, sir. I think I may have hit the bottle a little too hard tonight. Been sleepin' sound for hours.'

'But why would Mr Glass come here?' Hardy said.

Ben looked around at the stables, the spooked horses, the trampled hay. 'My bet is that he was looking for shelter. Somewhere to hide, maybe, if he was being chased. Then he realised that he was going to die if he didn't get help. And when Higgins didn't rouse himself he must have figured his best bet was to make for Kenwood House.'

Ben circled round back. Beyond the stables was a pen for the horses; and beyond that, the forests of the Kenwood Estate.

'What's past these trees, Westbury?' Ben asked.

'The outermost edge of the estate. Iron fences running the full length of the grounds.'

Ben turned to Hardy. 'Call your men.'

Within half an hour, the dozen constables posted at Kenwood House by Commissioner Mayne were filtering through the forest, with Ben leading the way. The ember glow of his lantern flickered across the blackened tree-trunks. Shadows leapt in the corner of his eye. An almost sacred hush descended on them, pierced only by the hoots of unseen owls, the wet crunch of leaves and branches under foot, and Ben's steady breathing.

They reached the perimeter of the estate, demarcated as Westbury had described by a six-foot-high black iron fence. Ben peered through the bars, onto the wilds of Hampstead Heath. There was hardly even a moon out tonight, shrouded by banks of grey swirling clouds, and the darkness was impenetrable.

He looked up. Something had been impaled on the spiked tip of one of the iron bars. It was a tattered piece of dark fabric. He gave it a feel. Just as he suspected: *cotton twill* – ripped from a trouser leg.

'Well, that explains how Mr Glass ended up in Kenwood,' Ben said to Hardy. 'Attacked nearby. Some isolated spot on the Heath. The kind of night-time hideaway people use for… illicit liaisons.'

'So he climbs over the fence into Kenwood to escape the killer.'

'Precisely. Hence his lack of care in preserving his clothes. And the killer, whoever it was, did not pursue him into Kenwood. I presume so as not to be apprehended. No doubt the killer trusted that enough damage had been done to render any escape futile.'

'Or the killer wanted Mr Glass to get into Kenwood,' one of the constables snorted. 'Frighten a few aristos, get the police all lathered up. Sends a message, don't it?'

'That's one way to put it…' Ben replied.

He was interrupted by a sound on the other side of the fence: the crackle of twigs. *Careful footsteps.*

Hardy, his back to the fence, spun round and brandished his revolver. 'Who's there?!'

A diminutive figure edged towards the fence, arms raised. 'Commissioner Mayne sent me, Sergeant! Don't shoot!'

Ben lowered Hardy's gun. 'Put it away, Hardy. And close your holster while you're at it, will you? One day it'll fall out and somebody will get shot.'

The figure stepped forward, into the light of Ben's lantern. He looked to be in his early twenties, slack-jawed, with a snub nose and bright blue eyes.

'What's your name?' Ben asked.

'Bertie Cook, sir.'

'He's one of Mayne's lads,' Hardy intervened. 'He runs messages up and down the flagpole.'

'And I've been riding halfway across bloody London for you tonight,' Bertie shot back. 'There's an emergency and Commissioner Mayne has sent for every Peeler he can get.'

Hardy threw his arms up in exasperation. 'We're dealing with an emergency here, boyo. One that Mayne alerted us to in the first place.'

'Well, this has come up and it's… it's really bad, Sergeant.'

Hardy was a bit slow at the best of times, but Ben could tell that Bertie was shaken – and not just from having to ride a few miles in the evening chill. 'What is it, Bertie?' Ben asked.

'It's easier to show you. Come up Parliament Hill and you'll see.'

Hardy left two constables behind to take witness statements at Kenwood House. Meanwhile, Bertie led Ben, Hardy and the remaining constables to the summit of Parliament Hill – one of the highest points in Hampstead, offering a sweeping view of the London skyline.

At this hour, the view would be practically non-existent, save for the few spots of torchlight burning on the rooftops like resting fireflies. But tonight, the blackness was painted igneous orange: a wall of flames and plumes of black smoke pulsing from a tract of land down by the Thames. From their vantage point, it looked like a silent portrait of the apocalypse.

'Where is that, Bertie?' Ben asked.

'Isle of Dogs. Lennie Glass's territory. It's been firebombed. The whole thing is burning to the ground, sir. They're saying there's hundreds of people trapped in there. Hundreds.'

For a few moments, none of them dared move: framed against the distant conflagration like helpless insects, as the realisation sunk in that it was not a murder they had encountered tonight, but a massacre – on a scale that they were only just beginning to imagine.

It took until dawn for the London Fire Engine Establishment, led by James Braidwood, to bring the blaze under control. They made swift work of it, aided by the fact that the Thames was at high tide and could be drained for water.

But for the people trapped inside, it was not fast enough. Ben watched from the perimeter on Westferry Road as the few survivors were dragged from the carnage. They had been burnt so badly that it looked as though their skin had been flayed from their bodies. Ben would try to reassure them as he ferried them into the back of the ambulance wagons, but most were unresponsive – and those that were conscious could only sob and shriek in agony.

This was no accident. The neighbours watching from their windows on Limehouse Causeway talked of gangs of men, dressed in black with their faces hidden behind balaclavas, hurling powder flasks and grenade shells into the warehouses, before escaping by boat and disappearing downriver. Searches were carried out along the banks of the Thames, but not a single one of them could be found.

Once the fire had been beaten back to the water's edge, Ben and his counterparts in the Met, along with Commissioner Mayne himself, were left to pick through the smouldering rubble looking for survivors. They found none. The place had been razed to the ground. Buildings and warehouses where Lennie's gang, the Dogs, had once thrived were reduced to eerily silent ruins. Merchant ships that had come to port for the night were like ghostly husks crumbling in canals now filled with wood, bricks and the bodies of those who tried to escape the flames. The smoke was so thick that it blotted out the sun over the peninsula, and Ben had to wrap a scarf over his nose and mouth just to keep breathing.

Not all that long ago, when Ben had been one of Lennie's dutiful errand-boys, the Isle of Dogs had had an air of invincibility – a Camelot for the legion of wayward boys in the thrall of London's criminal underworld. Now it was a graveyard.

As they proceeded through the docklands, Ben filled Commissioner Mayne in on his findings: the events at Kenwood House, the testimonies of the witnesses around the Isle of Dogs. Commissioner Mayne, never known for his verbosity, summed it up in a phrase as he kicked aside the remains of a timber beam: 'Mr Glass's enemies caught up with him.'

They stopped outside a burnt-out warehouse above the water in the West India Docks. Hardy waved them over to the entrance. 'Commissioner! Take a look at this!'

As they edged their way in, the smoke began to clear. Even the commissioner, who had combed through more bloodbaths than he cared to remember, recoiled at the sight. Corpses lined every inch of floor space: more than a hundred of them piled up, twisted, malformed. Hardy gingerly turned over one with the tip of his boot. It was a woman, scorched coal-black, lying contorted with her arms wrapped over her chest, what remained of her face locked in an expression of open-mouthed terror.

'Chinese,' Commissioner Mayne seethed.

'Migrant workers,' Ben said. 'The Dogs probably had them sleeping here with the doors bolted. Turned the place into one giant furnace.'

Hardy sniggered to one of the constables. 'So! Who do we thank for this?'

'What's that supposed to mean?' Ben snapped.

'What?' Hardy shrugged. 'Lennie Glass? The Dogs? They were scum. They terrorised London for years.'

'These are innocent people – they were probably trafficked here as cheap labour!'

'Yes, packaging Mr Glass's contraband. If you ask me, horrible as it is, whoever's responsible has probably done this city a favour in the long run.'

Commissioner Mayne shut Hardy up with a brusque wave of the hand. 'Quiet, Hardy. Mr Canaan, thank you for your help – it is greatly appreciated. But the Metropolitan Police will handle matters from here.'

'I've been instructed—'

'*Thank you for your help, Detective.*'

Commissioner Mayne turned his back on Ben and made for the exit. Ben looked down at the woman. She was holding something in her arms: a smaller creature, pressed to her chest and charred to the point of being totally unrecognisable, save for the plump hand of an infant child poking out – grasping at thin air for help that never came.

2
Pandora's Box

The Middlesex Club and Epsom were facing off at Lord's. It was an off-season friendly, running into the late hours of the afternoon. It had been a crisp, clear-sky day; now the grass, the lanky players in their whites, and the gaggle of suited spectators on the sidelines were bathed in mellow amber. They lined up for the next innings, Middlesex to bat. Epsom's bowler came loping to the crease and whipped the frayed red cricket ball low towards the batsman. A resonant *thwack* – and the ball was sent soaring outfield.

Ben was watching them from a window five floors up, in the nearby mansion block of Crownley Place. He was leaning on the sill with a mug of lapsang souchong, collar undone, sleeves rolled to his elbows, hair matted to his scalp after his habitual Sunday afternoon bathe. At this hour, if the weather was good, the south-facing window made for an ideal suntrap. He closed his eyes and took a deep breath, listening to those periodic *thwacks* and the cries of the outfielders.

His reverie was cut short by Mendel, a grey Chartreux cat who had a habit of interrupting him whenever he tried to relax by that spot on the sill. Mendel nestled in front of Ben and began flicking his tail in his face.

'Do you mind?' Ben said. 'I pay the rent round here. This is *my* spot.'

Mendel met Ben's gaze insouciantly and went back to sunning himself.

'Alright, you win.' Ben relented and scratched Mendel behind the ear.

His living room was a mess. Newspapers and casebooks were piled on the table. Today's paper was pinned under a bowl bearing Ben's supper – a fine attempt at cream of cauliflower soup. His book collection had long since spilled over from his modest shelf-space to form stacks on the floor: an edition of Kant's *Critique of Pure Reason* that he had picked up in Königsberg, Dryden's translation of *The Iliad*, both volumes of Mrs Gaskell's latest novel *North and South*, and many others. A random assortment of objects lined the mantelpiece, ranging from tickets to Shakespeare's *Henry VIII* at the Princess's Theatre – an ill-judged date – to a Christmas letter addressed to him personally from the Prime Minister, Viscount Palmerston, thanking him for his 'dutiful service'.

He polished off his lapsang souchong and leafed through the broadsheets. They were dominated by two big stories.

The first, unsurprisingly, was the sweeping attack on Lennie Glass's empire. In one night, his entire operation had been crippled – a third of his men killed, along with a hundred and eight migrant workers who had been housed illegally in Lennie's factories. The result was an all-out scandal: criticism of the Met for being caught flat-footed, accusations that the government had turned a blind eye to Lennie's operations for too long, and a power vacuum threatened to be filled by someone even more reprehensible than the late strongman of the docklands. Now there was even talk of an inquiry.

The second was a recurrent theme these days: India. Earl Canning – 'Clemency Canning', they called him – was the new governor-general and had been talking of growing unrest in the territory because of the intensity of farming, and mounting debt within the East India Company as its returns in the Asia trade faced a second consecutive annual decline.

There came a knock at the door: a distinctive triple-rap. It could only be one person.

'Time to avert your eyes, Mendel,' Ben said.

He opened the door and before he knew it, the woman on the other side had leapt into his arms and was kissing him passionately. It was Jemimah Plassey, as petite as she was effervescent, dressed as always to the highest standard of refinement. Today, it was a slim red satin dress in the 'Half' style, the kind worn when out and about in the evening, complemented by elbow-length gloves, her prized silver chatelaine purse, and a red velvet drawn bonnet pinned with a bright-green peacock feather.

'Darling Benjamin!' she exclaimed.

Ben linked his arm around her waist and pulled her closer. 'How did you get into the building?'

'The lovely landlady let me in, of course! Mrs Maudsley. Do you know, I had never noticed that she had a wooden leg! How queer.'

Ben closed the door behind them and Jemimah gave a little twirl as she skipped down the corridor. She sniffed the air. 'Lapsang souchong? I hope you brewed some for me…'

'Of course I did – it's your favourite,' Ben smiled. 'What did you tell Terrence?'

'The usual: euchre at dear Florrie's.'

'And Florrie is still willing to lie on your behalf, is she?'

'Given her staunch dislike of my husband, it is her dubious pleasure.'

She dashed over to the windowsill and scooped up Mendel in her arms to smother him with kisses. Mendel was not altogether pleased, but he knew Jemimah well enough by now to understand that pawing her away would only encourage her.

'Poor baby!' she cried. 'Has Benjamin not been feeding you properly?'

'If anything, he is a little chubby,' Ben replied, hurriedly sweeping away the newspapers to give his living room at least the façade of respectability.

'As any cat should be! Oh, Benjamin, why do you live like the great unwashed? I'm in half a mind to clean the place myself!'

'It's been… a *complicated* few days, Mimi.'

'Ah, yes. This frightful business in the docklands. I hope you steer well clear of all that – what was the delightful Yiddish word you told me? – *balagan!*'

Ben could not help but laugh at Jemimah's peculiarly aristocratic spin on a word that he was more accustomed to hearing from his grandmother. 'I can only imagine the scene you would cause if you used such language at home.'

'Well, Terrence as you know is not a terrific fan of the Jews.'

'Believe me: *I know.* The last time I met the man he referred to me as "another one of those scruffy Hebrews". Not exactly a glowing letter of recommendation.'

Jemimah set Mendel down and he immediately darted out to escape her. She ran her hands up and down Ben's shirt and ruffled his hair into an unruly damp shock.

'You look like a pirate,' she pouted, 'ready to ravish a helpless, unsuspecting maiden.'

'Maybe I am,' Ben replied, 'and I've just encountered a galleon I'd like to board.'

Jemimah's grip around his collar tightened. 'Perhaps I could appease my merciless captor with a gift?'

She removed a small yellow box from her purse and cracked it open: the finest Benares opium. Such a perfect, polished black that it seemed to swallow up the light around it. He held up the block of paste to admire it.

'How long do we have?' he asked.

'Four hours before my driver must carry me off. Else Terrence will get suspicious.'

She gave Ben the selfsame smile that she had first shot him across the hall at Spencer House last September, as she waltzed in the arms of her husband. The flawless impression of an ingénue. Ben had recently returned from Königsberg, vaunted as a hero for having solved the murder of a diplomat in the retinue of Frederick William IV, an episode since hailed as the 'Great Prussian Expedition'. He was man of the hour, and Jemimah – the listless second wife of a far older gentleman whose knighthood and mutton chops did little to make up for his dearth of personality – wasted no time.

Even after six months, that smile had not lost an iota of its allure.

'I'll fetch my pipe,' Ben whispered.

By eight o'clock, the two of them were reclining on the floor by the crackling hearth, a velvet eiderdown draped loosely over their naked bodies. The hours had run away from them and the city beyond Ben's narrow window was invisible in the abyss of the night. Within arm's reach, on a copper tray, was the kit: Ben's stained bamboo pipe, slick from the inspissated oils that had rubbed off from their fingertips; a lit spirit lamp; a white-hot needle that Jemimah had used to pierce, stretch and cook the globules of bubbling opium; a box for the burnt-out residue;

the metal bowl, charred black, blacker than the bodies on the Isle of Dogs.

They lay there in gentle delirium, floating somewhere between waking and sleeping, in a veil of smoke that smelled of jasmine and mandarins. 'Do you like it?' Jemimah murmured.

Ben's hand traced down her tingling spine to the small of her back. 'I love it.'

'It's a new blend. Brinier than your average Benares. I bought it from my Chinaman, Zhilan… the fellow with big coarse fingers… He said they infuse it with a special ingredient.'

'And what might that be?' Ben whispered in her ear. His hand wandered lower.

'Three drops of human blood.'

Ben pulled away suddenly. Jemimah's dark eyes were glimmering in the fire.

'What… He told you that…?'

Jemimah nodded drowsily. Ben's fist clenched. A nauseous knot tightened in his gut. Then she playfully slapped him on the chest and wiped the sweat from his balmy brow.

'Come now, Benjamin, you're too paranoid! It was just puffery.'

'I've seen crazier things.'

'You've seen rather a lot, haven't you?'

'Occupational hazard. I'm a valued servant of Her Majesty's Executive. They send me into imbroglios that only I can untangle. And look what they've bestowed on me in return…'

He gestured to his living room – to the clutter of keepsakes retelling the story of his life over the past year.

'Christmas cards from world leaders. An apartment in St John's Wood, while my family grinds away in Whitechapel. They stow their coins under the mattress. Just last month, I opened an account with Hoare & Co. Even Mendel: gifted to me by the

Comtesse d'Agoult, a token of her appreciation for the Paris job in December. If a few grisly crime scenes are the price, I will happily pay it.'

Jemimah propped herself up with her right arm and smoothed Ben's hair back. He could still smell that trace of almond and rosewater left on her fingers from her hand cream, penetrating the heady aroma of opium.

'Was it that bad, Benjamin? What you saw the other day?'

Her voice and touch were so soothing. It left Ben feeling exposed. He said nothing.

'I can tell that it is weighing on you, my dear. Speak. Better out than in!'

Ben just stared at the ceiling. He felt his lips slowly move, open and shut, open and shut. The voice that emerged felt unreal to him, as though echoing from somewhere far away.

'I've never seen so many bodies, Mimi. There was a mother, clutching her infant – I couldn't even tell if it was a boy or a girl. Its face had peeled off. It didn't have any skin. Just… black flesh, black bone. It didn't even have a chance at life. What must they have been thinking as the building caved in? Were they thinking anything? Or did the world just go dark?'

Jemimah pinched the opium needle between her thumb and index finger, and lightly speared a pea-sized ball of opium. As she held the needle over the spirit lamp to heat the opium, Ben rolled over to gaze into its flickering flame.

'Somehow, Mimi, this feels different. It's as though the rules of the game have changed and can never be wound back. As though Pandora's Box has been opened.'

The opium ball began to bubble and swell, black turning to gold. Without a word, she stuffed the ball into the metal bowl affixed to Ben's pipe, and held the pipe to his mouth.

'And then what?' Ben said. 'Does the fire take the rest of us with it?'

'Deep breath, Benjamin.'

He inhaled. The heat filled his lungs in a flurry of embers. Jemimah stood up, the eiderdown slipping from her slender form, and he closed his eyes, listening to her footsteps patter away.

The next day, Ben returned to Whitechapel. He hitched a ride in a hansom cab to St Paul's Cathedral and walked the rest of the way. Dressed in his signature slim-fitting suit, with his carefully trimmed moustache, he seemed at a glance to belong more to the world of financiers and solicitors milling past the Corinthian columns of Mansion House and the Bank of England, than to the watchmakers and peddlers roaming the East End.

The occasional passer-by would clock Ben as he ambled down Aldgate. Perhaps they part-recognised him as the ruffian who used to saunter along with his fellow Good-for-Nothings. Perhaps they had heard the stories of the boy who had made good; who would come and go, and sometimes disappear for a month without explanation, but always return with money to hand. Or perhaps they were simply wondering what a gent such as this was doing in a dump such as Whitechapel.

But to Ben, it was not a dump. It was home – or, at least, it had been once upon a time. The memories replayed on every street corner: pinching apples at the Goulston Street market on Sunday mornings, sneaking into the Yiddish theatre on Commercial Road to hide from the Peelers, jostling outside Mrs Adler's for a free bagel at the end of the day. Were these people, who looked at him now with suspicion, the very same who told him that leaving had never been an option?

He stopped outside 82 Whitechapel Road, the shopfront of Canaan & Sons, Tailors, and knocked on the side door next to the shop window. He heard his family before he saw them: his mother Ruth crying, 'Somebody get it!'

Ben was greeted by Herschel, known to all as 'Uncle Herschy', though in reality he was just a cousin. He was the same slightly dishevelled sot as always. His thinning hair had been brushed to one side to give the impression of a man in his forties as opposed to his fifties. In his left hand was the latest *News of the World*, a rag that he read more religiously than the prayer-books at Bevis Marks.

'Benjy!' He threw his arms wide and drew Ben into a warm hug. 'I didn't recognise you!'

'Good to see you, Uncle Herschy.'

Herschel looked Ben up and down. 'Wow!' he said, somewhere between admiration and envy, 'That is… a *very* nice suit. I wore the same style once as a young man: I had newly arrived in Buenos Aires—'

'Benjy?!' his mother's voice echoed from the kitchen. 'Is that you?!'

'Yes, I'm coming!' He brushed past Herschel. 'Tell me your story later, Uncle Herschy.'

Ruth was in the kitchen putting the final touches to the chicken soup. Golda, his youngest sister, was intently focused on slicing the pickles and laying them on the chopped liver. As soon as he entered, Ruth bombarded him with kisses and questions.

'How did you get here? You walked, didn't you? I hope you haven't eaten – have you?! Why, Benjy? I've prepared enough for thirty Canaans! And why is that monstrosity still on your lip?'

Ben smirked. Some things never change.

'I took a hansom cab and only walked the last leg. I haven't eaten, because I knew you'd be preparing a feast. And I have kept that "monstrosity", commonly known as a *moustache*, because I happen to like it.'

Ruth did not reply. Her trademark look of light disapproval said it all.

'Would you rather I shave it off?' Ben asked pointedly.

'No, no…' Ruth went back to stirring the soup. 'If *you* like it…'

Ben came up behind Golda and grabbed her by the waist. 'What's our little chef brewing in her cauldron today?!'

'Wait!' Golda cried. She carefully laid down the last pickle slice, scrubbed her hands in the washbowl, and patted them down on her handmade apron – and only then did she scamper over to Ben and jump into his arms.

'You smell like the fat men at shul,' she grumbled, face buried in his lapel.

'That would be the cologne, Golda. But let me ask you something…' He led her out the kitchen. 'Do the fat men at shul give you this?'

He reached into his jacket pocket and removed a chocolate bar wrapped in exquisite yellow paper, bearing the black letters *Chocolat Menier*. Golda's eyes went wide in awe.

'I received a mysterious package from a magical chocolatier in France,' Ben said. 'I was specifically instructed to give you this cocoa tablet. Tell Mama to melt it into your milk before bedtime!'

Ben found his grandmother Hesya in the living room. She was in the same armchair as always, next to the empty place once occupied by grandfather Tuvia, now a shrine to the late patriarch. Ben's sister Judit, the next eldest after him, was kneeling before Hesya, her ginger hair pinned in a circular braid.

Dozing in Judit's arms was baby Esther: Ben's niece, barely two months old. Judit had not wasted any time since her marriage last May to Jack Hauser, Ben's erstwhile partner in crime and the latest addition to the team at Canaan & Sons, Tailors. Esther's premature birth, by about a month, had given the family quite the fright. But since then, she had been in rude health, showing all the signs of a strong and wilful baby.

'Benjeleh!' Hesya whispered, careful not to wake Esther. 'Come give me a kiss.'

Ben kissed Hesya and Judit on each cheek. But his attention was mostly taken up by the innocent creature cradled before him. He caressed her wisps of fair hair with his fingertips and placed the tenderest of kisses on her brow. Slowly, her eyes flickered open. He was afraid she would start crying, but she was perfectly calm. Instead, she reached out to grasp his index finger tight with her tiny hand.

'She's always liked you best,' Judit said. 'Even more than her papa!'

Her papa arrived not fifteen minutes later. Jack had put on a few pounds since getting married, and his once-unmistakeable mop of hair showed the first signs of receding. But the one thing that had not dimmed in the slightest was his breakneck manner: quick on his feet and quicker with his tongue.

'Benjy!' he grinned, bear-hugging his friend, 'Now that's a *macher* if I've ever seen one – waltzing into Whitechapel with Savile Row on his back!' He clocked Ben's shoes and raised his eyebrows. 'And a brand-new pair of Foster & Sons on his feet! If these were the good old days, I'd be asking where you nicked them from.'

'You wouldn't be asking, Jack – you would've nicked a pair yourself!'

'Be quiet, Jack!' Judit hissed. 'You'll disturb Esty.'

'Ach, God forbid I should crack a joke with my oldest friend in the world,' Jack muttered. 'Hullo, Hesya. What've you been knitting today?'

Jack had not arrived alone. No sooner had he knelt to greet Hesya, than the last two members of the family appeared in the doorway behind him. First came Max, Ben's younger brother, clutching a weighty leatherbound book to his chest. He was a skinny thirteen and lately hit with a growth spurt that, in the space of just a year, had left him almost as tall as Ben.

Hot on Max's heels was Ben's father, Solly. His hair had noticeably thinned over the last few months and his habitual cough was sharper – a product of long hours inhaling microscopic fibres in the workshop downstairs. As soon as he saw Ben, it was as though a weight had been lifted from his shoulders, and an uncharacteristically cheerful smile softened his weathered features.

'Hello, boychik,' he said, embracing Ben and placing a calloused hand on the back of his son's head. 'I missed you.'

'I popped in one week ago, Dad.'

'One hour can feel too long!'

Ben reached over to tousle Max's hair. 'That's a hefty tome!'

'De Tocqueville,' Max said proudly, splaying it open to the frontispiece. '*Democracy in America*. First volume. It's a masterpiece of political science!'

'I would've thought you'd be reading the latest Dickens. I've heard it's rather good.'

'*Little Dorrit*?' Max waved it away dismissively. 'Too heavy handed. Too English. It takes someone like De Tocqueville to remind you that there is so much more to the world than this little island!'

Before Max could pontificate any further, Solly summoned everyone to the dinner table. Ruth and Golda carried the food in from the kitchen: hearty chicken soup, chopped liver with sliced pickles, latkes, and roasted parsnip with fried leek and onion. As the family plated up, Solly placed nine thimble-sized silver cups in a line across the middle of the table – one for each person, minus baby Esther.

'I have an announcement,' Solly declared, 'and it requires a special ingredient…'

He opened the cabinet and pulled out an unopened bottle of whisky: Chivas Brothers, Royal Glen Dee, Tuvia's favourite brand.

'Surely not!' Ruth exclaimed, as Solly poured a dram into each cup.

'No, no,' Solly shot back, 'even Golda is allowed a drop, just this once.'

'Did I miss something?' Ben whispered to Jack. 'Has my father been kidnapped and replaced with a fun-loving doppelganger?'

Jack smiled enigmatically, keeping his eyes on Solly as he assumed pride of place at the head of the table.

'You may be wondering,' Solly said, 'where Max, Jack and I were just now. Well, I'll tell you. We were at 110 Fleet Street – the building on the corner of Poppins Court. Once the home of John Carlyle's pharmacy, now untenanted after poor Mr Carlyle closed up shop. But the building is owned by one Charles Halevy, who just so happens to sit right across from me in the congregation at Bevis Marks. We arranged with Mr Halevy to visit the space…'

'Which we did,' Jack chimed in.

'…with a view to making a formal offer to rent the ground floor…'

Then Max: 'Which we made.'

'…and after a swift negotiation this afternoon at Mr Halevy's office, we concluded the deal. Which means that, for the very first time, Canaan & Sons, Tailors will have a second location – not in the East End, but in the City of London!'

The family intoned a full-throated *l'chaim* and knocked back their drams. Even Golda mustered up the nerve to have a taste, though as soon as it touched her lips, she dashed out with a grimace to rinse her mouth.

Solly had the air of a man who had just reached the summit of a mountain. Every disappointment, every setback, every moment of discouragement as he looked over his shoulder at the men who had surpassed him, seemed to drain away like the last dregs of rain before sunshine.

'We have Max to thank,' he added. 'He was the one who spotted the letting, made the connection to Mr Halevy, did his own calculations for the best opening offer. He even contributed once or twice during the negotiations, which I think rather impressed Mr Halevy!'

Ruth was beaming with pride. 'All this business must be making my clever boys hungry. Enough speeches – eat!'

The family dug in while Solly waxed lyrical about their plans for the future. How he would manage the new Fleet Street store, while Jack would take over their Whitechapel operations, with Judit and Max's help. How they would finally be able to hire junior tailors to do the menial handiwork, and a secretary for all things clerical. At last, after two generations of stitching and sewing in dingy cellars by the light of a lonely oil lamp, the Canaans were scaling up.

Ben listened to this outpouring of excitement with a certain detachment. He hardly reacted, except to chuckle or nod in agreement. He was drifting back to some other point in time, at this very table, when the expectation had been on him as Solly's eldest son to be the standard-bearer – and how, so often, he had sought to drop that standard. But now that burden had been removed, and it was as though everyone around this table could breathe again. And Ben, for all the love and camaraderie that coursed through the room, was a mere spectator watching from the sidelines, just as he did from his window over Lord's.

'And you, Ben?' Herschel asked, nosy as ever.

'Me?' Ben said with a thin smile.

'Well, you've spent the better part of a year working in a governmental position of some kind. Every now and then you disappear for weeks at a time – first to Prussia, then to Paris, shorter stints elsewhere. God knows you are handsomely rewarded for what you do. But I don't think you've ever *explained* what that is exactly!'

'Don't bother, Uncle Herschy,' Max said, snapping De Tocqueville firmly shut. 'Benjy is incapable of giving a straight answer.'

'Well, as fellow Canaans, I think we're entitled at least to ask!'

Ben glanced at his father. Solly had locked his fingers together and placed his hands under his chin, and was looking studiously into his half-eaten bowl of soup. His telltale gesture of quiet acceptance, the fulfilment of a promise that he made when Ben first set himself on this path: *no prying*.

Ben laid a reassuring hand on Herschel's arm. 'It's not that interesting, Uncle Herschy. The government sends me out to collect information on various matters of state. The only reason I can't talk about it – not with you, not with anyone – is because of the sensitive nature of this information and the sources from whom I obtain it. I understand why you'd ask: secrecy breeds curiosity. But in this case, it's unwarranted. My life is simply not all that exciting!'

Herschel shrugged and returned to his chicken soup. There was a moment of silence around the table. Did any of them really believe the former Good-for-Nothing?

After supper, Judit went to put Esther to bed and the rest of the family retired to the living room. Jack, Max and Herschel played several rounds of Brag. Ruth tidied up in the kitchen. Hesya dozed off in her armchair. Ben, meanwhile, excused himself and went upstairs to the attic-room on the top floor, which had once belonged to him.

He had not been inside for months, ever since he moved to St John's Wood with his earnings from the Great Prussian Expedition. He found the bed stripped, the curtains drawn, a film of dust collecting on the floor that sprang into the air with each slow footstep. Boxes lined the walls, full of fabrics, sewing equipment, disused dummies, old mungo that the shop had not been able to sell off. It was quiet – not a homely quiet, but one of abandonment. It was just another attic like the many that went unnoticed in the East End.

He slid the curtains open onto that familiar view of Whitechapel. To the south-east, he could just about make out the skeletal ruins of those warehouses on the Isle of Dogs, protruding like grim monuments over the clustered roofs of London.

'Feeling nostalgic?'

He turned. Solly was standing in the open doorway, hands in his pockets.

'A little,' Ben replied.

Solly closed the door behind him. 'There's something I wanted to give you.'

He removed his hands from his pockets. He was holding a coin-purse.

'Fifteen pounds,' Solly said, holding out the coin-purse. 'To pay you back for the sum you lent last autumn to cover the workshop renovations.'

'That's not necessary, Dad. It was my gift to you.'

But Solly was adamant. He closed Ben's fingers around the coin-purse. 'I will be in debt to no man, let alone my eldest son. I promised I would pay it back. Please accept it.'

Reluctantly, Ben nodded and slipped the coin-purse into his jacket pocket. Solly brushed a loose lock of hair from Ben's fringe.

'Are you alright, Benjy? You seem out of sorts.'

Ben gently pushed his father's hand away. 'I have a lot on my mind right now.'

'There are rumours going around about you. Rubbing shoulders with powerful people. Secret trysts. Opium.'

Solly's gaze was effortlessly penetrating, as though he was staring straight into the corners that his son kept shrouded in shadow.

'I'm not going to tell you what to do, Benjy. All I can give you is my best advice. Just remember who you are. I don't care how much money they shower you with, how glamorous your peers are, how special they may make you feel. You're not one of them.'

Ben bristled. He met his father's gaze with equal conviction. 'I'm serving a useful purpose, Dad. I'm doing something that I'm good at. And I'm making a difference.'

Solly let Ben's words hang, for both of them to ponder.

'Just be careful, Benjy. If it turns you inside-out, then the price is already too steep.'

'I'll be fine, Dad. I promise.'

'That's all I ask.'

Solly made for the door. But at the last moment, he cast a mischievous look back at his son.

'I will say, though: it's a nice moustache...!'

Ben was left to his own devices. He sat on the edge of the bed-frame and gazed out the window at the last light of the day. He closed his eyes, seeing once more the faces of those innocents consumed in the inferno. Their silent screams, their scorched flesh, their hopeless deaths. And the longer he looked at them, the more his despondency hardened into resolve – the more intolerable it became to simply sit by and do nothing.

He bustled downstairs and bade a hasty goodbye to his family. As he strode down Whitechapel, he made a solemn promise to himself: the Met be damned – he was going to get to the bottom of what happened to Lennie Glass.

3

Suspect No. 3

Ben's breakthrough came later that week. He heard through the grapevine that Yanky, one of the Litvak goons who formed part of Lennie's inner circle, had survived the attack on the Isle of Dogs. He was an inpatient at the London Hospital and had suffered life-changing injuries: his right hand amputated, both legs shattered by a falling rafter, riddled with third-degree burns. Even in the most favourable scenario, Yanky would be left permanently maimed, facing decades ahead as a dependent, with nobody to depend on.

Ben found him immobilised in a bed by a window overlooking the Whitechapel Road, in a room with forty or so other patients. His face was wrapped in gauze tinged red from his wounds. Though a little addled from the ether, he recognised Ben at once. After all, the two of them had a history. Back when Ben worked as an errand-boy for the Dogs, Yanky had been Ben and Lennie's intermediary. They had often antagonised each other, but beneath it was a begrudging respect – even when Ben switched to a more honest line of work.

Yanky told Ben everything he knew, though it was not much. On the night of the attack, he had been gambling with other members of the Dogs on the top floor of the opium den Ah Jiang's, when they heard explosions down by the canals. Some two dozen men were filtering through the Isle of Dogs, dressed head to toe in black. Some lobbed grenades into each building they passed, while the rest had drawn pistols and daggers and were cutting down anyone trying to escape.

Yanky hot-footed it downstairs, but it was too late. He was in the middle of the main smoking parlour on the ground floor of Ah Jiang's when an explosion blew him off his feet and brought the ceiling down on him. The only reason he survived was because he was able to wrench his legs free from the flaming rubble, breaking his ankles in the process, and crawl through the wreckage before the smoke got to his lungs. The rest was a blur. The last thing he remembered was slumping over the edge of the canal and waking up in the back of an ambulance wagon en route to the hospital.

As for Lennie, he had not been on the Isle of Dogs all evening. The last Yanky heard, he was in Hampstead – The Spaniards Inn pub, to be precise. The owner, John Chapman, was an old friend from Lennie's adolescent stint in the clink. After they made it out, they would do favours for each other. Lennie would send Chapman the occasional shipment of opium as a 'sweet treat' for Chapman to sell off at a profit. And in return, it had become tradition on the first Friday of every month for Lennie to be treated to free pints at The Spaniards Inn – right on the border of the Kenwood Estate.

'Be honest with me, Yanky,' Ben said, lowering his voice so that the other patients nearby could not hear them. 'Do you know who did this?'

Yanky shook his head.

'You don't have any idea? Lennie had plenty of enemies.'

'I don't know, Canaan. Only thing that stood out about these guys was their armbands. Some gold pattern on them that I'd never seen before. So if it was a gang, they're new. If they're not, it could be anybody.'

'What about Lennie? Did you notice anything strange about him lately?'

Yanky paused. 'Only that… he seemed a bit on edge about things. He was smoking more. Opium, I mean. I think it numbed the stress. But it made him sloppy. I was going to say something, maybe tell him to go easy on it… But I never got the chance.'

'What was going on with him?'

'I don't know. He didn't talk to me about his private life.'

A nurse came over with a bowl of brownish gruel – Yanky's pureed lunch. It was time to go. But Ben had one more question.

'Does the number "Seven" mean anything to you?'

Yanky hesitated. All Ben could see of his face were his blue eyes and the reddened skin of his eyelids, as he stared back through the ragged holes poked in the gauze.

'No, Canaan.'

Ben emerged from the London Hospital onto Whitechapel Road. He could head home and call it a day, but there was no time like the present. He hailed a hansom cab and set off for The Spaniards Inn.

By three o'clock that afternoon, Ben was back in Hampstead. London these days was a frenzy of urban expansion. Every second road boasted some new stucco-fronted townhouse, tanners and breweries and packed pie shops. The High Street, now a constant bustle of mercantile activity, was no different. But up on Spaniards Road, it was like a slice of countryside served with a dollop of bygone rustic charm. On one side, the gates of the Kenwood Estate, where this strange series of events began; on the other, open fields dotted with couples out on bracing February walks.

Ben tipped the cabbie a shilling and crossed the cobbled courtyard outside The Spaniards Inn. A bulldog was curled up by the door, eyeing Ben as he entered. He found the place empty, save for a couple of portly grey-haired drunks dozing in the corner, one of them snoring away with his free hand gripping a pint glass. A teenage boy was sweeping the dusty floors.

'Mr Chapman in?' Ben asked.

The boy looked sheepish. This new arrival was clearly not their average day-drinker.

'Pa!' he called.

A tall fellow with a flat rough-hewn face, broad shoulders and thick fingers emerged from the back room and assumed a towering stance behind the bar. He looked at Ben stonily.

'Bit early for a drink,' he said, in a cockney accent that transported Ben right back to his East End roots, 'but I'll take the business.'

'Not here for a pint,' Ben replied.

'Nah, didn't think you were. Yer dressed too slick. John Chapman.'

They shook hands across the bar.

'Ben Canaan. I'm an investigator. Looking into a case that's caused quite a stir. A murder. Lennie Glass.'

Chapman sucked through his teeth in a show of dismay.

'Mmm, heard about that.'

The quiet shuffling in the background came to a sudden halt. The boy had stopped sweeping.

'I'd be surprised if you hadn't. He was your mate, after all.'

Even as Ben spoke, he was not entirely sure whether Yanky had been telling the truth about Lennie and Chapman's prison friendship. But Chapman's sullen quiet gave the game away.

'And he was here as well, wasn't he?' Ben added. 'The night he died.'

Chapman studied his fingernails. 'I dunno what yer talkin' about.'

Ben pulled up a stool opposite Chapman. 'I'm not accusing you of anything. If you know something and you've got nothing to hide, you'd have no problem answering.'

'I just don't like coppers.'

'Good thing I ain't a copper then,' Ben replied with an amused smile. 'But I am *really* good friends with them. And I happen to know you flog Lennie's opium for an extra bob. Now, I'm only occasionally a betting man, but if I were to wager, I'd say you don't have a licence for that. So I could just tap the shoulder of the next bobby I come across and pass on the information. See how much you like coppers when they're bursting in, hoofing you out and boarding up this fine establishment.'

Chapman looked like he was chewing a hornet. But, finally, he relented.

'Lennie was 'ere, alright. But I didn't have nothin' to do with what happened to 'im.'

Chapman took Ben through his story. Lennie came in, as usual, on the first Friday of the month, at about six. He was unaccompanied – he never came to The Spaniards Inn with henchmen. The evening passed as it always did: Lennie getting hammered, chatting to the locals, playing five-card draw. Chapman had even commented to his wife Sarah, who ran the pub with him, that it was nights like this that made all the stress of running the place worth it.

Then something strange happened.

'It was probably around seven, seven-thirty,' Chapman said. 'The place was heaving. And these three men come in, and they make a beeline for Lennie. Now, Lennie, he seems to recognise them, and he goes all serious. They sit together at a table in the corner over there on the right and they chat on their own, secretive like.'

'Did you know these men?'

'No, no. But they were Chinamen, all three of 'em. I remember sayin' to myself, "Well that's mighty odd: damn Chinaman has never set foot in my pub – and now we've got three at once?" Then, after about twenty or thirty minutes, the Chinamen get up and leave with Lennie, and 'im not even sayin' a word of goodbye.'

'Just like that?'

'Just like that! Lennie didn't look happy about it neither. Two of 'em had their arms locked on either side, practically marching him out. The other was pressed real close, and I know what that means: I'll bet he had a gun or a knife pressed against 'im, I'm sure of it. I don't know what happened to Lennie after he left – but last I saw 'im, it was with them three.'

'And you didn't do anything?'

Chapman shrugged. 'What was I gonna do then? We know what Lennie was like, the kinda business he got up to. I didn't fancy sticking my nose in and gettin' it chopped off.'

That was the last Chapman saw of Lennie. But his son Pete, who had been listening to his father give his account, was able to fill in the gaps. He had been playing fetch with their bulldog Grady in the courtyard, when he saw Lennie being frogmarched out by the three men. He kept to himself and pretended to look the other way as they passed him, but he overheard Lennie muttering under his breath – a threat of some sort, about what he would do to them when this was over.

But the men kept their lips sealed. The two glued on either side of Lennie led him across Spaniards Road and disappeared into the thicket of beech trees on the edge of the Kenwood Estate. Meanwhile, the third man peeled off to the right to head further up Spaniards Road. As this man disappeared around the corner, Pete noticed the silver barrel of a revolver at his hip.

'I was suspicious,' Pete said, 'so I peeked round the corner to get a proper look at him. All I saw was him about ten yards ahead of me, getting into a hansom cab that was waiting on the kerb. I heard him tell the driver an address as he got in: 4 Hopkins Street.'

Ben recognised the name. That was in Soho, right by Berwick Street Market – a cesspool of prostitution and petty crime.

'What did he look like?' Ben asked.

'He was young, clean-shaven, about twenty-five or so. He had round glasses with what looked like a wire frame. Short black hair, cut real close to the scalp.'

'And the other two? Did you see them again?'

'Not after they packed off with Lennie. My mum called me inside and I didn't come back out. Didn't want to get involved.'

Ben had everything that he needed. He got up and reached out to shake with Pete and Chapman. 'I won't mention the opium, by the way.'

Pete, better mannered than his father, was quick to accept – Chapman less so.

'You're too kind,' Chapman said as he folded his arms over his chest. 'Now get the bloody hell out my pub.'

Ben was only too happy to oblige. Thanks to Pete Chapman, he would be heading across town to a decidedly seedier, less bucolic locale in the West End. But not before a detour to police headquarters at 4 Whitehall Place. He tipped off Sergeant Hardy that he had a lead – the third man, whom he had dubbed *Suspect No.3* – and would need a few constables to tag along, both for protection and to make an arrest if needed. Hardy was delighted, no doubt anticipating that he would take the credit for Ben's clever find.

By five o'clock, as the sun dipped under the horizon and the chilly February gloom set in, Ben was striding down Hopkins Street flanked by Hardy and a detail of six constables – two for each of their targets. It was a dingy side-street, deserted save for an elderly Chinese man wheeling a mobile food stall selling roasted peanuts.

Ben pushed open the front door of the building, onto a grimy corridor. The wood panels were rotting and the thick fermented odour of damp clung to the air. They knocked on the door of each apartment – greeted by prostitutes and their pimps, lonely men down on their luck, an impoverished single mother looking after three unruly children. But no sign of Suspect No. 3 as sighted at The Spaniards Inn.

Ben climbed to the fourth floor, while Hardy and his constables scoured the floor below. It was at the top of a tapering stairwell, with just one door. He put his ear to the door. He heard light footsteps and creaking floorboards.

He knocked. The footsteps stopped. Then a long silence.

'The police are carrying out a search!' Ben announced. 'Open up!'

He waited, ears pricked for a reply. But nothing came. Just another few creaks, shuffling feet, the rustle of clothes.

Ben leant over the banister and waved for Hardy and a constable to join him.

'Someone in there?' Hardy asked Ben under his breath.

'I think so.'

Hardy gave a signal to the constable, who brushed Ben to one side and removed his truncheon. '*Police!*' he bellowed, thumping the door. 'Open up now or we'll force our way in!'

Still, nobody answered. The constable thumped again, even harder this time.

'Last chance! Don't make me break down your—'

He was cut short by a volley of gunshots. Wood-shavings sprayed into the air as the bullets punctured small, jagged holes in the door. Muffled shouts of alarm reverberated from the floors below. The constable collapsed in a heap and clutched his arm.

'Get him over here!' Hardy roared.

While the other constables came rushing up to the fourth floor, Ben and Hardy grabbed the constable by the legs and dragged him from the landing onto the stairwell. Another two gunshots rang out, bullets pinging over their heads.

Then a series of dull clicks. Ben knew that sound all too well. The one thing no man wants to hear in a gunfight: *an empty chamber*. If whoever was on the other side knew their way around a revolver, they had about thirty seconds before it was fully reloaded.

Ben surged forward and rammed shoulder-first into the door, knocking it off its hinges. Inside was a bare-bones apartment. The stench of damp was overpowering. The walls were a discoloured navy-green, peeling away in thick wet clumps. A rotting mattress lay on the floor, next to a half-packed suitcase.

Standing before Ben, back to the window overlooking Berwick Street Market, was a young Chinese man of about his age. He was wearing a rumpled brown suit and round glasses. His hair was short, shaved just a few millimetres from the scalp. In his right hand was a revolver, which he was trying to reload. But he was so shocked by Ben's entry and was shaking so violently that he dropped his bullets, sending them spilling across the floor.

He fitted Pete Chapman's description to a tee. *This was Suspect No. 3.*

Hardy lumbered in, reaching for his own revolver. 'Put the gun down!' he barked.

The young man said something in Chinese. Ben could tell that he was terrified. The gunman's feet were rooted to the spot. A feverish sweat had pricked his brow.

Hardy brandished his gun. 'Put it down now!'

The young man dropped his revolver and took a step back. Before Ben could grab him, he spun round and leapt straight out the window, smashing through the glass and plummeting to the street below.

Ben ran to the ledge and leant out. The young man had crashed into a fruit stall and was lying on his side. He was bleeding and his left leg was bent sideways below the knee, but he was alive. As the unlucky fruit-seller started yelling at him, the young man staggered to his feet and limped off.

'He can't get far!' Ben said, sprinting out and down the stairs three steps at a time. 'Secure the apartment!'

By the time Ben rounded onto Berwick Street, Suspect No. 3 had vanished in the crush of Berwick Street Market. Ben shoved his way through the milling crowds until he reached the junction with Peter Street. He looked left, then right. No sign of the suspect – save for a trail of dark blood splattered across the cobbled stones. He followed the trail straight ahead, up an alleyway opposite Berwick Street, marked Walker's Court.

It was dark and quiet. No gas lamps to light the way. Just shadows and gloomy alcoves carved into the brick walls hemming Ben in. He came to a stop halfway down the alley: the trail abruptly ended here.

In the next breath, Suspect No. 3 came lunging at him from an alcove, wielding a Bowie knife. He slashed Ben's right forearm, leaving a deep gash below the elbow. But that was all Ben let him get in. In one deft move, Ben flipped him over and slammed him against the pavement to pin his arms behind his back. Suspect No. 3 yowled incoherently and writhed about, more animal than man.

'Very smart,' Ben seethed. 'You just turned a routine search, which you could have bluffed your way out of, into a rendezvous at the gallows.'

But Suspect No. 3 did not seem to hear, let alone understand him. He kicked out in vain with his one good leg and began sobbing. Hardy, breathless after a somewhat leisurely jog from 4 Hopkins Street, appeared with two constables and hauled the man up.

'Bit late for tears, mate,' Hardy grunted. 'Dump him in a cell.'

The constables dragged Suspect No. 3 away. All the while he kept his gaze unflinchingly on Ben. Somewhere behind the mad moans in his native tongue was a flicker of recognition – as though he had already seen Ben in a nightmare and the young investigator was an unearthly vision come to life.

Ben winced as the pain in his arm hit him and the blood came seeping in rivulets down the grooves of his knuckles. Hardy, meanwhile, lit himself a cigarette and took a long, self-satisfied drag. 'I must say,' he said, 'I think I handled that rather well. Fancy a smoke?'

But Ben was already walking off, his sights set on the shattered window on the top floor of 4 Hopkins Street – and the secrets that lay within.

4

You Are Already Dead

The first port of call was to get Ben's wound stitched up. The police took the liberty of summoning Robert Weston, a short-tempered surgeon at the North London Hospital, somewhat miffed at having been dragged from his wife's goose dinner to an altogether less savoury end of Soho. Gertrude Hawkins, the single mother on the second floor, was kind enough to lend them her living room and washbasin for the task. She brewed Ben a strong cup of black tea, which he took with his one good arm while Weston got to work on the other. The surgeon had neglected to bring ether at such short notice, leaving Ben with no choice but to grin and bear it.

Gertrude was pacing back and forth. Her three children – two boys and a girl, all under the age of twelve – were wide awake from the night's commotion and peeked at Ben in wonder through a crack in the bedroom door. Ben noticed her plain bronze wedding band.

'Where's your husband?'

'Locked up in Marshalsea for four months, the silly fool. I always told him he lived beyond our means. Two pounds owed to the baker, four to the carpet seller…' She gestured to a blackened rug in the middle of the living room floor. 'I got a bleedin' rug but not a bean to my name. Even if he comes back by some magic with cash in hand, we'd be starting from scratch. *Go to bed, you little imps!'*

The children slammed the door shut. Gertrude sighed and ran her hands through her wiry hair. 'I told 'im we should move. This place is trouble through and through.'

'What do you know about your upstairs neighbour?'

'Nought, sir. Not even his name. He hasn't been 'ere long though, two weeks at most. The landlord, Trevor Morgan, he owns the whole building. Got a new tenant up in that garret every month. Usually foreign types. Tourists and whatnot.'

'Did you ever have any contact with him?' Ben asked.

'Just once. I was coming into the building after a long day at the seamstress – I sew there for a few extra shillings – just as he was coming out. He held the door for me an' I said thank you. But I doubt the fellow speaks a lick of English, because he didn't even acknowledge me. He seemed polite enough, if a little shy. Honest to God, sir, he came across as a harmless type! I couldn't imagine…'

Gertrude's impression made sense. The terror in the man's eyes, his trembling hand, his sobbing – this was not the behaviour of someone to whom murder came naturally. Ben had dealt with enough killers to sort the wheat from the chaff. Suspect No. 3 was chaff.

Ben flinched. Weston's needle pierced the sharp edge of the knife wound – a final stitch.

'Sit still, boy,' Weston grumbled.

Gertrude kneeled at Ben's side and refilled his tea. 'Go on, sir, drink up. It'll take yer mind off the pain.'

Weston finished up and hurried home to his wife's cold goose. Ben gave Gertrude one pound as a token of thanks for being so helpful, and wished her the best while her husband served his time in Marshalsea. Then he went upstairs to that lonely garret, now heaving with bobbies, to see what they had found.

All that was left were fragments. Three suits that Ben could tell had been made cheap: bleached calico cotton with unsinged yarns, unwashed and reeking of stale body odour. Pockets carrying a handful of English shillings and Chinese copper cash, a metal-body propelling pencil lined with gold leaf, and a crumpled ball of brown paper that smelled vaguely of sugar and rhubarb. The moth-eaten mattress on the floor, damp with sweat. Weapons in a portmanteau suitcase behind the door: polished steel knives, palm-sized boxes of bullets and gunpowder, and an unlit grenade. A medicine bag too, with a panoply of drugs including unguents for dry eyes, herbal cathartics for joint pain, sulphur disinfectant, camphor for itchy skin, and laudanum pills.

Strangest of all was what they found in the closet set against the far wall. The shelves had been stripped away and in their place was a meticulously hand-carved wooden shrine, like a temple in miniature – columns supporting a curved roof with overhanging eaves, painted a faded yellow, with a robed silver figurine on a black throne. Laid before the figure was a piece of dark fabric emblazoned with the image of a golden snake. Ben held it up and inspected it. As he suspected: it was an armband, just like the one Yanky had described.

Then there were the documents in Suspect No. 3's wallet. He had multiple sets of travel papers, each one belonging to a different alias: *Lee Chunyen, Long Sang, Yang Decheng, Fou Chung*. The stamps showed that he had arrived in London just two weeks ago, and a ticket stub confirmed that this had been aboard a steamship known as *Verulas* that had set sail from Hong Kong. This was paired with another ticket for a return to Hong

Kong, this time aboard the *King Kyrië*, due to depart in three days' time. And, finally, a calling card: sepia-toned paper with two Chinese characters printed in black. Ben tracked down the Chinese peanut seller they had passed earlier that afternoon to have the card translated. The old man drove a hard bargain, forcing each of Hardy's men to buy a cup of peanuts in exchange for his help. According to him, on the card was a single word: *Lǎaohǔ* – 'Tiger'.

Ben questioned the other tenants of 4 Hopkins Street, and each one gave much the same answer as Gertrude. Nobody knew the name of their mysterious upstairs neighbour. Aside from Gertrude, none had shared a word with him. He was largely invisible and over the past two weeks there had been hardly a peep from the fourth-floor apartment. Nor could anyone recall ever seeing two other Chinese men pay a visit at any point since he moved in.

The landlord, Trevor Morgan, arrived later that night, once he received word about what had happened to his latest tenant. He explained that he set the garret aside for weekly tenancies, mostly to visitors from abroad; his broker at Chestertons had arranged one such let to the young man now in police custody. He was eager to set it straight with the police that he had nothing to do with whatever his tenant was caught up in. All Morgan knew about the man was his alias, Long Sang, and that he had ostensibly come for a business meeting in Westminster with an unidentified client.

By one in the morning, Ben had exhausted his leads and it was time to head home. Between his empty stomach, the knife wound, and a walloping headache, he was about ready to collapse. He emerged out the front of 4 Hopkins Street, his injured arm tucked inside his coat. Some of the tenants from the neighbouring buildings lined the pavement, grinning and cracking jokes as they watched the scene unfold. These days, it was the closest thing they got to entertainment. A few of them clocked Ben as he passed by, but there was only mistrust in their eyes. To them, Ben was just another cog in a machine built to grind them down.

It took another hour for Ben to get back to his St John's Wood apartment. He went straight to bed, still fully clothed, and rolled onto his side to stare at the moon through the open window and listen to his slow, heavy breathing. These moments were the worst: when he was alone with nobody to talk to, when it was dark and the shadows took on shapes of their own. All he wanted was to sleep. But it was no good. His arm was on fire, his temples were throbbing, his mind was racing.

He opened the bedside drawer. Inside were the dregs of Jemimah's precious Benares opium. He rolled it in his palm. Just a few puffs would send him off, into that strange cavernous slumber he knew so well. He fetched his paraphernalia and perched on the edge of the bed, the light of his spirit lamp puncturing the darkness. He felt himself leaning back, drifting away from his own body, and his world sank into a bottomless static pool, deaf to the hoots of an owl outside, blind to the light of the moon. For the first time that day, Ben felt at peace.

He was woken the next morning by a knock at the door and a squeaky pubescent voice. 'Mr Canaan? Are you there, sir?'

Ben came to his senses and hobbled to the front door. It was Bertie Cook, Sir Richard Mayne's messenger-boy. He seemed surprised to see Ben so dishevelled.

'What is it, Bertie?' Ben checked his pocket-watch – just past seven in the morning. He had had a few hours of sleep at most.

'Sorry to wake you, sir,' Bertie replied. 'It's just that the commissioner's sent me. You're needed at Whitehall over the chap they brought in last night.'

'I thought the commissioner wasn't overly keen on my involvement.'

'He's asking for you, sir. The Chinaman, I mean. He said he'll only speak to you.'

Ben needed no further encouragement. He grabbed his coat off the rack and threw it on – but Bertie raised a hand of caution.

'Sir, if I may… Perhaps you should freshen up a bit first. Even if just to comb your hair. You might give, erm… the wrong impression.'

Ben caught his reflection in the entrance hall mirror. Bertie was not wrong. He had emerged from an opium reverie, and he looked like it: stooped, red-eyed, hair in disarray. 'Give me a few minutes.'

A fresh change of clothes and a splash of cold water on his face later, Ben set off for 4 Whitehall Place with Bertie in tow. Suspect No. 3's presence had cast a pall of uncertainty over the Met. Ben was escorted to a windowless holding cell where their prisoner was waiting. He was seated at a bare wooden table, his face in chiaroscuro under the lantern dangling from the ceiling. His broken leg had been set in a makeshift splint, but even so Hardy stood on guard just to his left, keeping a close eye in case he tried anything on with Ben.

'Fine morning to you both,' Ben said in a droll tone.

He sat down opposite the suspect. He looked pale and sallow, clearly in tremendous pain. But he was doing his damnedest to suppress it, staring at Ben with renewed intensity.

'Well?' Ben said, 'You asked, I'm here.'

The man on the other side of the table said nothing. He was like a statue.

'Is there something that you would like to tell me? Perhaps an apology to start things off? After all, your antics with that Bowie knife cost me a good night's sleep.'

Ben waited. But still, the man said nothing. Ben looked at Hardy quizzically.

'Does he understand me? Or does he only speak Chinese?'

'That would be Cantonese, Mr Canaan,' the man interjected. His voice was round, with a certain shine to it, and his English sounded studied. 'And yes, I am sorry.'

Hardy snorted. 'Hear that? The murder suspect is sorry.'

'Does the murder suspect have a name?' Ben asked, clasping his hands together and leaning into the halo of light below the lantern. 'And none of this "Long Sang" tripe you fed old Mr Morgan.'

'My name is Bo.'

'And your family name?'

'I have forsaken it. Left it in the dust where it belongs.'

Bo spoke with an otherworldly conviction, the sanctity of a priest executing a sacred duty. His gaze was steady. His hands were still.

'And why did you come to London, Bo?'

The tiniest hint of a smile broke through Bo's stony exterior. 'You know exactly why I came to London, Mr Canaan. The sinner Lennie Glass had to die. It was written.'

'And those people you had slaughtered on the Isle of Dogs? They were burned so badly that they couldn't even be identified. Were they sinners too?'

Bo was silent for a moment. He was sincerely pondering Ben's question.

'We are all sinners,' he finally pronounced. 'Some are just slower to sin than others.'

'Who sent you?'

'*Destiny*.'

Ben could not suppress a scoff. 'Did destiny send your two mates with you as well?'

Ben's scorn washed off Bo like water from a duck's back. He just nodded serenely. 'Yes. We three are emissaries of the powers above. Sent to raze the old order to the ground, reduce it to ash and rubble and embers. And in its place to lay the foundation of a new world, with new names inscribed in its books. The coming storm needs Horsemen to deliver it up.'

'You sound awfully confident that things will go your way.'

'I am. The pieces are exactly where they should be.'

'Including me? Is that why you summoned me here?'

Bo was back to being statuesque. He did not need to say anything. The chill that descended over the room, the slowly tightening knot in Ben's stomach, the unreal presence of this all-knowing stranger, said it all.

'You knew who I was before I kicked down that door, didn't you?' Ben said.

'Oh, Mr Canaan, we *all* know who you are. And we are so very excited to meet you. You are like a spider trapped in a glass, crawling around and around and around. Not realising that you are already dead. You simply do not know it yet.'

Bo placed his hands on the table and pushed himself to his feet. Ben leapt up to meet him, unsure what Bo was about to do. Bo's posture was lopsided from the splint, and he reached out to grab Ben by the lapel and draw him close.

'A black crow will land at your door tonight, Mr Canaan,' Bo intoned. 'And thus the next phase will begin: the crow will peck at your heart until black blood comes pouring out to drown your lungs and bury you in eternal sleep—'

Hardy had had enough of Bo's ranting. He stepped forward to separate the two – but Bo's grip tightened and pulled Ben right up to his face. Suddenly, something in Bo seemed to shift, and a flicker of panic sparked in the murky depths of his wild eyes.

'Benjamin,' he whispered. 'Listen to me: *everything is connected.*'

'That's enough!' Hardy bellowed, shoving Ben away and putting his arms around Bo to restrain him. 'Get back in your chair before I have you cuffed again!'

Bo lashed out and struck Hardy in the face, sending him staggering. Then Bo lifted his arms. By the time Ben saw it, it was too late.

In Bo's right hand was Hardy's revolver, which he had slipped from its open holster. Hardy roared for Bo to stop, but the young man was deaf to him. He was staring at Ben all the while, knowingly, as if in that split second the two were having a conversation which nobody else could hear.

Bo uttered a single word: 'Seven!'

And before either Hardy or Ben could do anything, Bo slid the barrel into his own mouth and pulled the trigger.

In the blink of an eye, Bo crumpled to the floor. Hardy stopped in his tracks, hand frozen in the air in shock, as though reaching for the spot where Bo had just been standing.

Ben could see Bo's lifeless face under the table, turned to some nondescript point in the corner of the room. Torrents of blood came spilling from his nostrils and an exit wound had been blown open on his scalp. His body seemed to deflate as his final breath rushed from him.

Ben looped round the table to stand over Bo. He lay in a heap, legs folded underneath him, his limp shooting arm draped across his chest. His glasses had fallen from his face and lay mangled a few feet away. Ben picked them up with a trembling hand and inspected them: the wire frame bent backwards, the lenses cracked and splattered with blood.

Two constables burst into the holding cell. 'Sergeant?! Are you hurt?'

Hardy shook his head. 'It was the suspect. He… he shot himself… Go, fetch a doctor…'

'He's dead, Hardy,' Ben murmured.

'Well, we need someone to move the body—'

Ben's fists clenched round Bo's glasses. He turned on Hardy and all at once the horror of what they witnessed erupted from him: *I told you to keep that bloody thing holstered!*

He stormed out. No sooner had he slammed the door shut behind him, than the nausea bubbled up to his throat and he doubled over, closed his eyes, let out a ragged sigh.

There was something in his jacket pocket. He reached in and removed a loose scrap of paper. A few lines had been scribbled on it, but it was in no language that Ben recognised – a strange blend of Latin and Chinese script, and signed at the bottom with the name *Bo*. It had not been there when he first entered the holding cell.

One by one, the constables filtered past him, piling into the cell to get a closer look at Bo's body. A human being reduced to a mere eyesore, just another drop of blood in the ocean. Without a word, Ben pocketed the note and trudged off, insensible to the crowd of stunned faces.

Ben received the invitation that afternoon: tea and cigars at Brooks's, the gentlemen's club on St James's Street that had long been an unofficial headquarters of the Whig elite. Membership was almost as hard to obtain as the keys to Buckingham Palace, but it paid dividends. In a single evening, one could secure a wealthy patron, strike up a venture with a merchant tycoon, and win enough at hazard for a deposit on a house – and all while swilling the finest sherry in London. Ever since the start of Viscount Palmerston's premiership, Cabinet ministers would gather here to discuss matters of state and lubricate the gears of colonial governance over cognac and Byron cigars. There was a strict 'No Jews' policy, but special arrangements had been made for Ben courtesy of the man in Number 10: if Ben was a guest of one Herr Gustav Bruckner, Palmerston's right-hand man, then he was to be treated as any other landed gent or made man of commerce.

Ben found Herr Bruckner in one of the gambling rooms, indulging in a game of whist with a group of sozzled peers. Bruckner was an unassuming fellow, with his pince-nez, top hat and slight physique, but he made up for it with shrewdness and charm. A Prussian expatriate and avowed Anglophile, he had an enduring fondness for the quaint, puffy idiocy of the noble upper crust. He was the quintessential eminence grise: while the flashier Lords of State sucked all the air from the room with their pomp and circumstance, Bruckner was content to sit in the corner and take shallow breaths.

As soon as he saw Ben enter, he left his cards and led Ben to a private table by the window. A server came to take their order. Ben was not hungry, but Bruckner nevertheless requested two servings of duck à l'orange and a bottle of Porto Ferreira 1810. His justification? The Treasury was picking up the tab.

'Thank you for your work over the past week,' he said as he tucked into his duck. 'I understand it took a rather sordid turn the other day.'

'It's been sordid from the word go,' Ben replied. 'But orders are orders. I had a sense that something was rotten when I received your note the night Mr Glass was killed, telling me to go to Kenwood House.'

'And the Metropolitan Police?'

'I think my presence is rubbing them up the wrong way. Then again, if it weren't for me, they'd probably still be picking their noses at Whitehall.'

A volley of raucous laughter erupted from the whist table. One of the marquesses was showing off a collection of explicit daguerreotypes – a nubile young woman draping her naked body over a plush lectus. One of his mistresses, no doubt.

Bruckner lowered his voice. 'What did this "Bo" fellow say to you?'

'Apocalyptic babble. Out with the old, in with the new, that sort of thing.' Ben took a sip of port and cleared his throat. 'He seemed to know who I am.'

Bruckner gazed out the window at the people milling down St James's Street below: well-to-do men and women in their finery, swaddled against the February cold. He shook his head and sucked through his teeth in disgust. 'What a mess…'

Bruckner looked grave. Ben knew what this meeting would entail before he walked through the front door. He was only ever invited here and treated to this taxpayer-funded indulgence when Her Majesty's Executive had a new mission for him.

'It's happening, isn't it?' Ben asked.

Bruckner nodded. 'It is significant. I am afraid we are dealing with a danger of a far greater magnitude than we perhaps first thought. I cannot say more for now. But I will need… certain assurances from you, Mr Canaan.'

'Namely?'

'Discretion. Reliability. Absolute loyalty.'

Ben set down his cutlery and looked Bruckner in the eye. 'Herr Bruckner. You know me. You have entrusted me with a solemn duty. I respect it with my life. Tell me what you need, and I will execute it to the utmost of my ability.'

Bruckner's otherwise impenetrable features cracked: a flicker of a smile. He leant over to shake Ben's hand. 'Good man.'

As they locked hands, they felt a bang on the table. One of the peers playing whist had staggered over to them. He looked hardly older than Ben, but was twice his weight, swollen like a gouty foot from a lifetime of luxury, with a thick ruddy beard and locks tumbling down to his shoulders.

'Ah, Viscount Raynham,' Bruckner said, 'I never introduced you to my friend. This is Mr Ben Canaan.'

'Mister?' Raynham slurred. 'Is that it?'

Ben gave a curt nod, and was otherwise silent. Raynham did not like that.

'I say,' he muttered, looming over Ben. 'The boys and I are placing a few bets. I have a wager of a hundred guineas that Dalrymple over there can't give a woman a good rodgering in a hot air balloon by the end of the month.'

Ben glanced at the whist table. The thirty-something chap who was surely Dalrymple, with his finely groomed mutton chops and port-flushed cheeks, gave them a slick grin.

'Best of luck to him,' Ben replied.

'What shall we wager for you?' Raynham dropped a pouchful of coins on the table. 'I say five guineas that you have no foreskin to speak of.'

'Are you angling for a peek?'

Raynham darkened. But before he could be any more indiscreet, Bruckner intervened with a conciliatory hand. 'Right, shall we get you back to whist, Viscount Raynham? Pay us no mind.'

Just as suddenly as he breezed into their conversation, Raynham breezed out. Ben kept one eye on him as Bruckner returned to his seat. Raynham seemed utterly nonchalant, as though he had already forgotten about Ben.

'I'm terribly sorry about that,' Bruckner said with a quick bow. 'Viscount Raynham can say such foolish things when he's drunk!'

'*In vino veritas*,' Ben murmured.

Bruckner polished off his port. 'You are to come to Number 10 tomorrow morning. The PM intends to brief you on next steps.'

'Very well.'

They said their goodbyes and Ben returned to St John's Wood. He did not go out all evening, and he barely ate dinner – just a hunk of bread, fig jam, a slice of cheddar, several cups of tea. He paced and paced, but his mind could not settle on a single idea. Every time he tried to focus on something, the memory of Bo's words in the holding cell would come back to him. That they had been watching him. That the pieces were already in place. That a crow would visit him tonight.

Hour by hour, the evening whiled away into oblivion, punctuated by the chiming of the grandfather clock. Then the rain began to fall until it roared incessantly at his window. At about fifteen minutes to midnight, Ben found himself standing by the lonely light of the hearth, staring at the note that Bo had slipped into his pocket just before he took his own life. What could it mean? And why would Bo plant it on him like that?

Ben turned around to look at the empty room. The gloom seemed to gaze back at him.

'What did you know?' he said aloud.

At that very moment, there came four loud thuds at his door. They rumbled down the entrance hallway and echoed through his apartment. Ben's breath caught. The crow. The black crow.

He went over to his desk and removed a pistol from the drawer, already loaded. Then he proceeded down the pitch-black hallway, towards the tall front door at the other end. He looked through the peephole, but nobody was there.

'Who is it?'

No answer. Tentatively, pistol raised, he edged the door open. But the corridor was empty. Two details caught Ben's eye: a faint trail of wet bootprints running from his front door to the top of the nearby stairwell, and a leatherbound emerald-green book left on his doorstep. Before he could pick it up, he heard a clang rattle up the stairs: the metal entrance gate to the mansion block, five floors down, swinging open and slamming shut.

He sprinted downstairs, but by the time he burst through the front gate and out into the rain, it was too late. The street was deserted. The avenue of oak trees outside Lord's shivered in the wind. Even the gas lamps had been snuffed. His only company out here was a drenched fox, skulking into a bank of hawthorns. Whoever had just paid him a visit had slipped away.

Ben returned to his apartment and inspected the book by the fire. It was heavily ornamented, like an antique folio from a bygone century. He peeled it open. The title page simply read 'BLACK BLOOD', with no authorial attribution. On the opposite page was an elaborate frontispiece with an engraving in the style of Dürer. It showed a crowd of onlookers gathered on the shores of an open sea, in a barren dreamlike world – pointing towards seven blazing pyres that floated in a line over the black waters, forming a wall of fire.

The remaining fifty or so pages of the book were blank, save for the very last page, where a list of names had been carefully written out in impeccable calligraphy:

João Gilberto Lalé

Oberon de Morèse

Geert Van Hook

Lennie Glass

Ezekiel Ormrod

Hokoa

Odysseus Halliday

Underneath that final name was a message underlined for emphasis: <u>For Detective Canaan</u>.

Ben hovered over that last line. Whoever was responsible for this had made it their mission to goad him on. To dare him. This was no ordinary book. It was an invitation.

His finger traced up the page, moving from name to name. 'Seven…' he whispered.

57

5

A New Mission

Number 10 was as sullen and decrepit as ever. The place was steeped in the stench of sulphur. Years of subsidence had left the floors sloped and the walls skeined with diagonal cracks. It was a picture of decay, as it had been since Ben first set foot inside, and not even Viscount Palmerston's fondness for the finer things in life had been enough to prompt a refurbishment. The British Empire may have been awash with cash, but it was not being funnelled here.

Ben was led up the stairs by Palmerston's butler. The grim visage of every past Prime Minister greeted him on his ascent, as though they too were tired of standing on ceremony in their portraits, day in, day out. Palmerston was waiting in the Breakfast Room – a wood-walled adjunct to the grand State Dining Room. The PM was at the head of the small table, digging into a breakfast of kedgeree and coffee mixed with chicory, à la française. Bruckner was to his left, flicking through a thick wad of bound papers.

'A fine morning to you, Mr Canaan!' Palmerston declared. He did not bother to get up. 'I trust you are well?'

'Quite well, my lord,' Ben said with a bow. 'I had the pleasure of Herr Bruckner's company at Brooks's yesterday.'

'Raynham said something rather horrid, I heard.'

'I thought nothing of it, my lord.'

'Still, a pity. His father was a fine fellow. He must be what's left.'

Ben took a seat to Palmerston's right, opposite Bruckner. Only then did Palmerston deign to devote more attention to Ben than to his kedgeree. Prime ministership had grown on him, or rather he had grown into it. Ben could tell from his years as a tailor that Palmerston was filling out his suit, more rotund each time they met. But he had retained that strong aristocratic profile: the face hewn from granite, the aquiline nose, flinty blue eyes hardened by a lifetime in politics.

Even at the best of times, Palmerston was gruff and impatient. This morning, however, he seemed especially waspish. Whatever it was that Ben was being called in for, it was important.

'Herr Bruckner has briefed me on the latest turn of events,' Palmerston continued.

'It's been quite a week,' Ben replied. 'Ever since Lennie Glass was killed, it's felt as though the world is turning upside-down.'

'It has been for quite a while, and well before Mr Glass's untimely demise. As is often the case in espionage, things changed very slowly, and then very suddenly. The Isle of Dogs was simply the straw that broke the camel's back.'

'I'm guessing, then, that this did not begin with Mr Glass.'

Palmerston shook his head. 'Mr Glass's death was merely the latest in a string of murders that we have been trying to keep pace with. Now, a full-blown crisis is brewing.'

It was odd to hear a man of Palmerston's stature invoke Lennie's name. In Ben's mind, the two inhabited entirely differ-ent domains: the underworld and the establishment, the slums and the halls of state. Yet it seemed as though they were more closely involved than Ben could have imagined.

'Forgive me for asking a foolish question,' Ben said, 'but was Lennie Glass not a… well, a reprobate? What interest did the British government have in his dealings?'

'Mr Glass had his foibles, and his enterprise certainly had illicit offshoots,' Palmerston replied. 'But that is only part of the picture. He was far more important than a mere "reprobate". He was an omni-merchant of sorts – dealing with anything and everything, on a vast scale. And though we would not air this out in public, Mr Glass was a linchpin in British trade: crucial to the facilitation and maintenance of Britain's economic interests globally.'

'So,' Bruckner added, 'an attack on Mr Glass is an attack on Britain.'

'And I'm guessing the "string of murders" you mentioned is part of this attack?' Ben asked.

Palmerston gestured to Bruckner, who handed Ben a set of papers. One was an intricately detailed map: the mouth of an enormous river delta on some southern coast, branching off like veins into innumerable tributaries further inland. Islands dotting the ocean to the south and various settlements along the riverbank had been circled in red and marked with names: MACAO – CANTON – HONG KONG.

'The Pearl River Delta,' Bruckner said. 'One of the largest of its kind in the world. Man's gateway to the imperial dynasty of China, known as the Great Qing. The epicentre of the most important and lucrative nexus of trade that civilisation has ever known: *the China trade*. And as we speak, her shores are running with blood.'

Ben leafed through the rest of the papers: a tangle of diplomatic cables, newspaper clippings, letters penned by the governor of Hong Kong, statements from police inspectors and provincial administrators.

'For the past year,' Bruckner continued, 'the region has been thrown into turmoil by a series of killings. All the victims had ties to prominent trading firms that use the Pearl River and the South China Sea as a base of operations – ranging from the firms' heads, to high-ranking partners, supercargoes, merchants, even sailors. Perhaps foolishly, we believed that Mr Glass would be safe in London. It is clear now that we grossly underestimated the extent of the danger. Hindsight tastes bitter on the tongue.'

'And the net result of this debacle,' Palmerston chimed in, 'is a crisis of monumental proportions. The China trade, which Britain is sitting astride, has become a powder keg ready to explode at any time. And with Mr Glass's death, my government has ordered an official inquiry to determine what exactly is going on here and what we should be doing about it.'

Ben had already seen that last piece of news. The papers had been flooded with speculation, especially after it was announced that esteemed Law Lord Montague Wetherton would be heading up the inquiry. Wetherton, from what Ben understood, was a notoriously uncompromising fellow, and not known for mincing his words. Cross-examination at his hands would not be a pleasant experience.

'Do we have a working theory? Culprits? A motive?' Ben asked.

'We have our suspects, but their identities are a mystery,' Bruckner said. 'Clearly a well-resourced disruptor, going to war over the China trade, or indeed seeking to wipe it out altogether. And with it goes the very foundation of the world economy. Not an outcome, you may imagine, we can afford.'

'What do you need from me then?'

'We will be sending you out to the Pearl River,' Palmerston said. 'Hong Kong, to be precise. Your mission is to investigate these killings, identify who is responsible for them, and prevent any further deaths from taking place. Most importantly, you will be expected to write a report on the progress of your investigation and testify before the Wetherton Inquiry in October of this year.'

It was that last instruction that caught Ben's attention. The Wetherton Inquiry, if the opinion of the tabloids was anything to go by, was set to be one of the most momentous political events of the year. And Ben would be standing slap-bang in the eye of the storm, for everyone to see.

'Rather a public-facing task, my lord.'

'For good reason. Her Majesty's government must be seen to be vigorously protecting our national interest in China.' Palmerston raised his teacup to his lips. '*I depend on it.*'

Palmerston was speaking in subtexts, but Ben did not need to be told twice. The PM was due to stand for re-election this time next year. A highly publicised foreign policy embarrassment was the last thing that he needed.

'Your point of command in Hong Kong will be Sebastian Coldwell,' Bruckner interjected. 'He is the superintendent of the Hong Kong police department. You are to take your directions from him for the duration of your stay. It is a matter of necessity: Hong Kong is a wild place, far from the laws of man.'

'And payment?'

'£550. £225 up front, £225 on completion. Six months in Hong Kong, with all expenses covered by the Treasury. Plus the potential for bonuses, if you execute the mission dutifully.'

As was the unspoken rule in these circles, Ben made little fuss of the sums on offer – though a quick mental calculation suggested that this fee alone could see him through the next few years if he earned not a penny more.

Bruckner handed Ben a set of travel documents. A government-issued international pass-card with his details filled in, stamped with the insignia of the Crown and a personalised code: Clearance Level 1A – the highest offered by the Executive.

'You depart tomorrow,' Bruckner continued. 'Pardon the haste. Our intelligence suggests that Bo's accomplices, the two men who helped him kill Mr Glass, are leaving London aboard the steamship the *King Kyrië*, bound for Hong Kong. You are to join them on the *King Kyrië* and tail them to their destination. Your tickets are enclosed. First class, of course.'

'How will I recognise them? I've never seen these men in my life.'

'The documents found at Bo's apartment on Hopkins Street indicate that they will be in cabin 212. Whoever is living in that cabin for the duration of the trip is the target.'

Ben felt some misgiving as he scooped up his travel documents. Bo's ominous words and the eerie invitation that he had received the previous night were rattling about in his head.

'Why not arrest them while they're here?' he asked. 'If you know where they'll be.'

'We were in half a mind to – until this other chap decided to throw the cat amongst the pigeons by getting rather too intimate with the barrel of a gun,' Palmerston said, in his icy, offhand manner. 'There is simply no point in arresting these men when they are so fanatical that they would rather die than talk. This is the first time that these cockroaches have scuttled out into the open, and we are not keen to scare them back into the shadows.'

'Better to follow them back to source,' Ben said pensively.

'Quite. Hence, as you may have observed, we have refrained from saying anything in the press about our suspect's capture and death.'

Ben had not planned on leaving so soon. Under normal circumstances, he would have at least two weeks' notice to get his affairs in order and say his goodbyes. Yet he simply could not dispel that instinctive unease curdling in his gut. It was the glint in Bo's eye just before he placed the gun in his mouth – the strange shift in his voice, as he went from calling Ben *Mr Canaan* to *Benjamin* – the clang of the metal gate as his late-night visitor vanished in the rain.

Palmerston could sense Ben's disquiet.

'The stakes of this operation are extremely high, Mr Canaan. Hong Kong may be a faraway backwater, but as of this moment the most powerful economic interests in the world are in its orbit. As Herr Bruckner no doubt impressed upon you yesterday: we require absolute loyalty on your part. And I promise you this…'

Bruckner produced a wad of cash – the £225 advance payment – and slid it across the table.

'Her Majesty will be indebted to you for your service.'

Palmerston knew the power of his words. He let them settle over the room like the aftershock of a distant thunderclap. Ben thought back to his father's workshop: the grated window specifically, offering a narrow view of the feet of passers-by up and down Whitechapel Road. He remembered that stinging, rudderless feeling, as though each foot was stepping on him. He remembered the hopelessness – that he would never be free, or appreciated, or even noticed.

He pocketed the money. 'I'll need this evening to get my house in order. But rest assured, you can rely on me.'

Palmerston reached out to shake his hand.

'Always a pleasure, Mr Canaan.'

As soon as the money was in his pocket, Ben was galvanised into action. First, he went up to Mrs Maudsley on the top floor of the mansion block, to inform her that he would be absent for the next six months, but would continue to pay his rent in the interim. Next, he dispatched a note to Jemimah Plassey with a request for her to appear at the window of her Belgravia town-house at six-thirty that evening. Then he packed his belongings: a large suitcase for his clothes – a medicine bag for his toiletries – several sets of notebooks and stationery – and the emerald-green book left on his doorstep. He kept his pistol on his person, holstered under his jacket, and his mother-of-pearl penknife folded in his pocket.

Finally, he scooped up Mendel and went to 82 Whitechapel Road. He owed his family a farewell. He arrived to find everyone present except for his father, who was meeting with an architect about designs for the new shop on Fleet Street. So he waited, taking tea at the dinner table and chatting to Max about what they had been reading as of late, while Mendel sniffed at baby Esther in her cradle with cautious curiosity.

Once Solly returned at the end of the day, Ben gathered his family into the living room and told them that he was bound for Hong Kong. He was not at liberty to say why he was going, but the Canaans, deep down, knew that it had something to do with the disaster that had struck the Isle of Dogs the previous week. It was not the first time that Ben had unexpectedly upped sticks. But this time, it felt different. Dread stirred like a restless thorn.

'When will you be back, boychik?' Solly asked him.

'By October, at the latest,' Ben replied. 'I swear.'

'And you'll write in the meantime?' Ruth said, wiping away her tears with a handkerchief.

'Of course. As soon as I reach dry land.'

'I have one request for you, Benjeleh,' Hesya said, leaning forward to clasp his hand. 'Wear the scarf I knitted for your birthday, the woollen one that says—'

'*Honour thy mother and father,*' Ben chuckled, kissing her on each cheek. 'I couldn't go without it!'

'He won't need a scarf where he's going, *bobba,*' Max said wryly. 'I read that Hong Kong is a devilish, humid swamp for half the year.'

'I'll take it for good luck then,' Ben replied, 'Isn't that right, Dad?'

He glanced at his father. But Solly was in his own world, gazing just past Ben at some undefined point by the window, as twilight closed in. Melancholy always seemed to carry Solly away. Like an automaton, he cleaned his glasses and brushed the lint from his trouser legs.

Ben took Solly's hand, and it seemed to drag his father back up to the surface.

'I'll be fine, Dad.'

Solly nodded and squeezed Ben's hand. But he did not believe him.

'Ah!' Ben said, rising to his feet. 'One more thing.'

He returned to the living room with Mendel clinging to him.

'Will you look after Mendel for me while I'm…'

Ben could not get the words out before Golda leapt from her spot on the sofa. 'I'll do it, I'll do it, I'll do it!'

Mendel was looking at Ben with dismay as Golda began petting him, clearly asking in all but words why Ben was subjecting him to this torture.

Ben knelt down and propped up Golda's chin. 'And if you take extra good care of him, I'll bring back something special for you…'

'Chinese chocolate…?' Golda murmured in awe.

Ben tapped his nose. 'Couldn't possibly say!'

The clock struck five. It was time to go. He embraced each Canaan with enough warmth to last him the lonely months ahead. But warmest of all was baby Esther, whom he took in his arms. He held her to his chest, resting her head on his shoulder, and felt the steady, strong beat of her little heart. Maybe, by the time he was home again, she would be able to utter her first words. Maybe she would smile at him like no time had passed at all.

'Goodbye, Esther,' he whispered.

He stored that moment of perfect tranquillity in some quiet corner of his mind. Then he handed her back to Judit, looked round once more at his family – his chaotic, happy, infinitely loving family – and took his leave.

He had one more stop before his departure: 60 Eaton Place – the Belgravia townhouse that was the birthright of Sir Terrence Plassey. The street was quiet at this hour. The aristocrats and ambitious arrivistes who made up the neighbourhood were having supper, and it was not the kind of milieu into which evening wanderers could easily stray. Ben came to stand under a gas lamp directly opposite Number 60, waiting for Jemimah's svelte figure to appear in the window. As his pocket-watch struck six-thirty, he looked up.

As usual, Jemimah was between two and three minutes late. But when she did finally appear, time itself seemed to stop. She was part-silhouetted by the candlelight behind her: an obscure profile lifting a slender hand to the lightly frosted windowpane.

They stood utterly still and utterly silent, connected by an invisible line strung from eye to eye, across the barren evening.

Then Ben gave a little bow, as though closing a modest musical number – a final thanks to a grateful audience. He held his hat to his chest, watching as that shadow of a hand drifted from the windowpane to her mouth, stifling something unseen and unheard.

They held it for one moment longer. Then Ben turned on his heel, donned his hat, and vanished beyond the halo, onward into dark.

6

King Kyrië

It was the coldest day of the year. An arctic wind whipped up the choppy waters of the Thames. Swollen clouds bore down on the spires of London, sprinkling solitary snowflakes across the jagged rooftops of this coal-black city. Ben took in the view from the landing point of the St Katharine Docks: that peculiar blend of ancient and modern – factories and finance houses cheek-by-jowl with the great dome of St Paul's and the medieval turrets of the Tower of London. Steamboats chugged up and down the river, pumping thick plumes of smoke into the barren grey. It was the furnace of Empire, grand as it was grim, and he was leaving it behind.

He threaded through the crush of people lining up to board the *King Kyrië*. It was the largest steamship that he had ever seen, putting to shame even the *Midas* that had transported him to Constantinople in the summer of 1854. The brainchild of Brunel himself, rumour had it, with a capacity of over three thousand people – and she was ready to set sail across the world.

He looked around at his fellow passengers. It was about an even split between British and Chinese travellers. There were hardly any tourists, and certainly no families: only traders, labourers, missionaries, and single men of business in dark suits, carrying leather satchels. Bo's accomplices could just as easily have been on board or right next to Ben without him knowing. He cast an eye across the dock, towards the columns at the western exit, where a bobby was loitering in the shadows. He was one of forty from the Met, posted around the perimeter of the docks – ordered not to engage unless the situation soured.

Ben reached the front. Ramps ran from the edge of the dock onto the deck of the steamship, each manned by a ticket inspector. When it came to Ben's turn, the inspector noticed the executive clearance stamped at the top of Ben's pass-card, and gave him a once-over with his beady eyes.

'Up the ramp and turn left, sir,' he said. 'Steward will take you to first class.'

Ben was greeted on deck by a steward in a red button-up jacket. He was a young chap, scarcely older than Max, sallow and sun-deprived, with tufts of facial hair sprouting from his chin. 'Let me take your bags for you, sir. Which cabin might you be?'

'101, I believe.'

'101! Phor-wee! That's one of the premier suites. I do believe Mr Brunel himself sojourned there when this fine lady embarked on her maiden voyage. You'll want for nothing, sir. I'll make sure of it. Name's Alfie Wellstone.'

Alfie was angling for a tip – or several, if he got lucky. Ben gave him a reassuring pat on the back. 'Nice to meet you, Alfie. Call me Ben.'

A broad wooden staircase took them below deck. From the outside, the ship was a great iron behemoth. But inside, it had the aspect of a stately Alpine hotel, where moneyed elders might retreat to clear their lungs. Banks of candlelight illumi-nated wainscoted corridors and lent warmth to the patterned vermilion carpet.

'Reason for travelling to Hong Kong, sir?' Alfie asked as they passed one of the first-class salons – complete with a Bösendorfer piano, a billiard table, and a fully stocked bar.

'Business.'

'True enough, sir, true enough! Nobody here's bound for a pleasure trip or the like. Business! That's the only reason to go to Hong Kong. Dig for gold and leave instanter.'

They breezed past a neighbour on Ben's corridor: a peevish-looking fifty-something gent with one of those newfangled gold-buckled leather briefcases. He gave Ben a cursory glance wavering on the brink of irritation – the look of a man hollowed out by his trade, leaving a hole only evening port could fill.

'I could've guessed from the surliness of my fellow passengers,' Ben said as they walked on. 'Nobody seems too keen to head off to that corner of the world.'

'And why would they, sir? I hear the mosquitoes alone are enough to carry you half to madness and leave you to walk the rest of the way.'

They entered cabin 101. Two portholes let in a little light and the carpet was ornamented in the Kurdish style. There was a bed carefully made with far too many plumped pillows for a single passenger. To the left was a private bathroom, and on the far side was a Georgian oak dresser, a cherry-wood bureau, and an oval mirror decorated with intricate Boulle work.

'Fit for Prince Albert himself!' Alfie said, laying Ben's luggage by the bed. 'Shall I fetch one of the servants to unpack your belongings?'

'That won't be necessary,' Ben said. 'If you don't mind, Alfie, I would prefer a rather more… hands-off approach during this voyage. I am quite self-sufficient and, if anything, prefer to clean up after myself.'

Alfie bowed his head. 'Understood, sir. If ever you change your mind, let me know.'

'I did have one question, though…' Ben lowered his voice. 'I notice all the cabins on this level begin with the number "one". I assume that's because it's first class.'

'That's right, sir.'

'And any cabin beginning with "two" would be second class? On the floor directly beneath us?'

'Quite so.'

Ben popped Alfie a couple of shillings. 'Thank you kindly, Alfie. Travel well.'

As soon as Alfie left, Ben pulled the curtains shut over the portholes, stowed away his documents, and donned his John Bull top hat. Then he slipped out, locked the door behind him and circled back to the central foyer below deck, where he took the stairs down to second class.

Second class was more akin to a London chophouse: cheap tablecloths, wooden chairs, and the familiar smell of baked fish. Ben blended in more easily with the passengers down here. Most of them were young men like him, though they looked older than their years – like crude sketches of the men they would one day become. Only the missionaries walked about with a spring in their step, buoyed up by the cause that had sent them to China.

Ben loitered at the end of the corridor where cabin 212 was located, leaning on the wall and flicking through his notebook, with his hat tipped over his brow to hide his face. Several young men passed by while he waited, but none entered cabin 212.

Then came a gravelly voice, speaking in clipped Cantonese; and another chiming in at a softer, higher pitch. Footsteps echoed down the corridor. Ben peeked from under the brim of his hat. Two men rounded the corner and walked right past him, close enough for Ben to reach out and touch them. They looked eerily similar to Bo: bespectacled, hair shaved short, dressed in austere brown, as unassuming and slight in demeanour as classical scholars. The only difference was that one was markedly taller, and the other sported a well-groomed chin puff goatee.

They stopped outside cabin 212. The taller man produced a key. They let themselves in and shut the door behind them.

Ben had identified his targets. Now it was simply a question of observing them as closely as he could for the duration of the trip, without being spotted. He retreated to his first-class cabin as the foghorn of the *King Kyrië* rattled the corridors of the ship.

In another life, when long-haul journeys to faraway places were a novelty, Ben might have joined the other passengers on deck to wave goodbye to London, to Britain, to Europe. But he had other concerns now. He sat at his desk by candlelight, leafing with ink-stained fingers through the brown pocketbook that would record his observations for the next six months. Every material detail had its place, from the men's appearance, to the location of their cabin – amidships and, by Ben's calculation, more or less directly beneath him – to the idiosyncrasies of his first-class neighbours.

Spread out on the desk were all the things that he would need on this voyage. A daybook tabulated hour by hour, to record their movements and paint a detailed portrait of their routine. A Cantonese–English lexicon by one Chalmers, that Ben had picked up on Booksellers' Row in Charing Cross, along with a thin book about the history of Hong Kong that came with a map of the island. Then there was the emerald-green book that had been left on his doorstep, with those seven names now etched in Ben's mind. And, lastly, his pistol: an arm's reach away – the barrel turned to the door, just in case.

He pored over his map, marking each significant location per his brief from Bruckner. Hong Kong, the site of the newly founded British colony, was one of the larger islands in a glittering archipelago below the Kowloon Peninsula. Victoria was the main settlement on the island's north-western shores, separated from the southernmost tip of Kowloon by the narrow strait of Victoria Harbour. Running across the middle of the island like a belt was a mountain range, and on the other side of those mountains were a handful of settlements: Stanley, an administrative town named for Palmerston's arch-rival and predecessor in Number 10; Red Hill, a forested summit above Taitam Bay, an inlet of the South China Sea; the granite quarries of Shek O and Cape D'Aguilar; the forts of Chai Wan on the eastern shores, overseeing passage through the channel of Lymoon; and the fishing village of Aberdeen, named for Palmerston's *other* arch-rival.

He could glean very little about how this place came to be. Not one generation past, it was but a barren, sparsely populated wilderness at the mouth of the Pearl River: steaming swamps, desperadoes on the run from the law, yearly monsoons. Then it was ceded to the British in the Treaty of Nanking almost fifteen years previously, bringing an abrupt end to a three-year war between Britain and the Great Qing. In the intervening time, Britain had turned Hong Kong into one of its fastest-growing military and economic outposts. Now this rocky and precipitous island was a breeding ground of factories, ports, naval barracks, racecourses and pubs – the bastard son of an unlikely union between the Anglosphere and the Sinosphere, flooded with thousands year in, year out, seeking to dredge up filthy lucre from its black marshes.

The engines started to rumble as the *King Kyrië* cast off and turned its prow east down the Thames. Ben did not bother to peer through the curtains. He had learned in his year of service to Her Majesty's Executive not to look over his shoulder. People who allowed their gaze to be drawn back in time were always the ones to be caught off guard. And after everything that had happened since that bloody night at Kenwood House, he needed to stay ahead of the game.

Only when he had finished putting his plan for the coming two months of travel in order did he retire to his private bathroom and wash himself off. He lay in his tub, gazing at the ceiling, inhaling plumes of lavender-scented steam. He felt an uneasy twisting in his gut: the feeling that he was being watched, that whatever he was doing was exactly what Bo had wanted him to do.

When he was finished, he donned a dressing gown and went over to the porthole. Just before he pulled open the curtain, he thought of his family. He would have liked to have visited the new shop on Fleet Street before he left, if only to see the look of pride and achievement on his father's face. To breathe in the musty smell of leather in the workshop. To admire the new suits on the rack, the drawers filled with ties, the rows of bowler hats on the wall. To catch his reflection in the full body mirror that had seen practically half the men of Whitechapel.

He parted the curtain. He was met with the pitch-black of the English Channel, accompanied by a soughing night-breeze and the echoes of a cello from the first-class dining hall. He recognised the melody.

'Bach,' Ben muttered. 'Hmm. Could be worse…'

*

They got up at six in the morning, every morning. Ben knew because their porthole was one level below and two towards the bow, and just past six it would swing open like clockwork. The man with the goatee – on account of which Ben assigned him the nickname Chin Puff – would lean out in a white vest to have a smoke. Then he would murmur some incantation in Cantonese. After a week of listening to this refrain, Ben was able, roughly, to identify a word here and there in the lexicon: *father, safety, victory*. A prayer of some kind.

Then they would go to the second-class dining room, usually among the early diners, and would sit in the furthest, quietest corner. The tall one, whom Ben referred to as Longshanks, would sit and read a pocketbook while Chin Puff ate porridge and canned peaches with black tea. Not once did they interact with a single person, passenger or crew. They hardly even spoke to each other.

After breakfast, they would retire to their cabin. Some days, they would never leave, except perhaps to peruse the book collection in the second-class salon – though never actually lifting a book from the shelf – or to pace on deck, typically three loops at the end of the afternoon, as a constitutional. A couple of evenings every week, there would be music and burlesques, and occasional performances by a travelling humorist from the United States, employed by the charterers to keep the passengers entertained. But Chin Puff and Longshanks stayed away, showing no interest in the amenities on offer. Just two ghostly pockets of silence drifting about the ship, unseen and unheard.

Ben made good use of Alfie Wellstone, punting the odd shilling his way in exchange for favours and information. Through him, Ben found out the names under which they were listed on the passenger log: *Francis Lo* and *Kenneth Chen*. But Alfie was sceptical. It was common practice for confidence men and chancers travelling under an alias to combine English first names with traditional Chinese surnames.

Alfie also procured a key to cabin 212, courtesy of Fergus Connell, an ordinary seaman who did the rounds in second class and was Alfie's drinking pal. Like Ben, the two tenants of cabin 212 had instructed staff not to enter under any circumstances, not even to empty their chamber pots. But after four weeks, by the time the ship was looping round the southernmost tip of Africa and sailing headlong into the Indian Ocean, Ben had grown familiar with the rhythms of their life. While they were out for their habitual late afternoon walk, Ben let himself in and put those ten minutes to good use.

Their room had the appearance of being unlived in – no smell, their bags still packed, the beds made. There were only two signs of life. One was an aqua-blue plate on a narrow desk by the door, with a still-steaming cup of fragrant tea. The other was an image in a silver frame by the bed: a drawing in the gongbi realist style, of a man sitting cross-legged against a plain white background. His arms were folded into his yellow robes and he was wearing a guapi mao skullcap. But instead of a face, there was a gold seal of a snake curled into coils and baring its fangs – the kind of graven image found on the doors of an ancient temple.

Ben was careful not to draw too close to the pair. With three thousand people on board and separated by a class, his chances of being recognised were slim. But despite his excess of caution, he did have one close shave in the latter stretch of the trip, as the ship navigated the Sunda Strait between the islands of Java and Sumatra. Ben had ascended to deck to take in the view: the island of Sangiang, with its verdant cliffs and untouched beaches; fishermen in a jukung hauling up a net of skipjack tuna; the shores of the Dutch East Indies widening out into the expanse of the Java Sea. Once he had had his fill, he turned to head back to his cabin – and practically walked straight into Chin Puff. But before Chin Puff could get a good look at him, Ben brushed past with a hurried apology and retreated below deck.

It was night-time in mid-May, some three months after he left London, when the *King Kyrië* reached Hong Kong. The steamer passed across the mouth of the Pearl River estuary, approaching the Kowloon Peninsula from the west. The waters were vast, and the rolling tide splashed with faint traces of moonlight. Barely visible in the oblivion were the sloped contours of isles large and small – Lantau, Coffin Island, Cheung Chau – all mute, mountainous monoliths.

Hong Kong gradually came into view. It was lit up in the distance by sporadic flashes of sheet lightning, casting momentary silhouettes of Victoria Peak, as its knife-like summit pierced the low swirling clouds. The closer they came, the more oppressive was the humidity, the skies bloated with heat and ready to erupt. Then, finally, the rain started to fall, thicker with every wave they crested, and the thunder seemed to bubble up from the bottom of the sea.

The ship entered the Sulphur Channel, hugging the edge of the north-west bulge of the island. The outskirts of Victoria began to take shape: villas reminiscent of a Tuscan country-side built into the rocky outcrops at the foot of Mount Davis. Three lighthouses marked the entrance to Victoria Bay, just one kilometre of water separating the sprawling mainland of Kowloon from this fledgling British colony. The shores of each territory were buttressed as far as the eye could see with stone forts marked out by beacons of firelight, and fleets of gunboats keeping their cannon trained across the channel. The entire peninsula was slumbering with one eye open.

They approached a half-built wharf, lodged into the side of Victoria like a hastily grafted extra limb. The deck started to fill with fellow passengers, ushered forth under rows of black umbrellas. Nobody spoke, lulled into a sombre hush by the sight of Victoria. Its confused jumble of new-build houses and crumbling fishing huts, bunched together in haphazard clusters across the marshy banks. The creaking skeletons of merchant brigs and junks rocking back and forth around the wharf, piled high with cargo. The house flags of those grand, faceless trading firms whose offices formed long congested lines on the waterfront. The thunder, now upon them, cracking open the air itself, matched only by one last boom of the *King Kyrië's* tremendous horn.

The crew threw ropes down to the stevedores on the jetties and the steamer was reeled into one of the last available places on the wharf. Ramps were extended and the engines slowed until they had fallen silent.

Ben stared straight ahead, through the beads of water dripping over the brim of his John Bull. In those brief flashes of sheet lightning, he could make out the faces of Chin Puff and Longshanks, up at the front by the ramps. They were looking at each other with the same grave determination that Ben had seen in Bo's eyes the second before he took his own life.

A whistle blew and the crowds were invited to disembark. Ben marched forth, a suitcase in each hand. He kept his eyes fixed on the outlines up ahead of those two men, blind to everything else, tracing their footsteps into the murky embrace of Hong Kong.

7

The Floating Life

It began with a slow march down Pedder's Wharf. The rank and file of the *King Kyrië*'s sea-weary passengers proceeded up the landing stairs from the ramshackle wooden jetties to the thoroughfare of Pedder's Street. The final steam-launches from Hong Kong to Kowloon were setting off from the wharf: boats bearing the insignias of navigation companies, the decks heaving with exhausted, coal-coated labourers. Fishermen, local Chinese, sat at the head of sampans moored along the jetty, trying to no avail to flog the day's last snapper and snakehead. Pumping out smoke all along the waterfront were godowns, foundries and saw-mills, protruding in a long line over the water like a set of jagged industrial teeth. The place stank of molten steel, rust, and rotten kelp washed up on the marshes.

Ben followed the suspects onto Pedder's Street. Immediately opposite the wharf was the Hong Kong Hotel. Suited smokers sat under a canopy on the third-floor veranda, their faces lit up by smouldering cigarettes as they watched the huddled rain-soaked masses, like tired birds of prey amusing themselves from an unspoiled perch.

Outside the hotel was a cab rank lined with rickety carriages drawn by emaciated horses. The drivers were shielding themselves from the rain under makeshift umbrellas made from bundles of newspaper. One of them, an older grey-haired man with spectacles so rain-spattered that Ben could not make out his eyes, was holding a sign to his chest that read in a looping scrawl: *MISTER CANAAN*.

Ben approached him and offered his hand. 'I'm Mr Canaan.'

The cabbie ignored his hand and went straight for his bags. 'We go Mount Austin. Hotel. English there waiting for you.'

Ben looked ahead while the cabbie loaded up the carriage. Chin Puff and Longshanks had drifted past the cab-rank and were heading east down Pedder's Street on foot.

'You go ahead with my bags,' he said once his luggage was stowed. 'I need to stretch my legs.'

'I not coming back – you late already!'

'That's fine,' Ben sighed. 'You go on and I'll find my own way.'

'What do I tell English at hotel then?!'

'Make something up,' Ben shot back, slipping him a few shillings as a sweetener.

Ben tailed the two men from Pedder's Street onto Queen's Road Central: the main highway running the full length of Victoria. There was no rhyme or reason to this place. Trading houses, magazines, bars and churches were crushed together in one bulging tumour that seemed to spread uncontrollably from the sea to the mountain. The lights were on in the windows of the merchant offices – as true a sign as ever that money never sleeps. The storekeepers and shop-hands, peddling cheap homeware from their narrow nooks, loitered outside the shopfronts and knocked back shots of baijiu to wash away another thankless day. The only signs of luxury were the gentlemen's clubs, with their bronze-plated doors and gold plaques. Distant volleys of gunfire peppered the night. Practice shots from the military barracks further inland? Or a skirmish between rival gangs? Either way, nobody batted an eye.

Chin Puff and Longshanks marched on, with the confidence of men who knew this place well. They seemed to have one destination in mind, paying no heed to the chaos around them. Not to the press offices of Wyndham Street; not to the draped banners strung across the road warning about pickpockets and piracy; not to the sight at the entrance of the naval hospital of a brawl between drunken sailors; not to the vagrants with stained teeth hiding in alcoves from the rain, resigned to another night of hunger.

The ascent up Kennedy Road brought a brief respite. It was more upscale here: a broad avenue, mostly empty, lined with overgrown camphor trees and gated villas that reminded Ben of the estates of his aristocratic employers back home. Yet even this affluent little suburb sagged with a sense of abandonment – a morose silence lingering behind the rain.

At this higher elevation, he could see the full span of the settlement below. It had the aspect of a frontier-town, newly conceived, multiplying with every passing day – half of its skyline under construction, the other half waiting to be built. A few hundred metres north, spread out at their feet, was the Murray Parade Ground: British naval barracks, the contours of its high stone walls traced against the bleak night by banks of lanterns.

And then, just as quickly as they had risen from Victoria, the road wound its way back down into the melee. They were in Wan Chai now: a seedy growth of alleyways populated by pawnbrokers, slopsellers, and low-end casinos for luckless gamblers down to their last penny. And it was there, on Spring Garden Lane, where Chin Puff and Longshanks finally came to a halt.

They were standing outside a three-storey building in the Italianate style, topped with belvederes and a green marble loggia, the Venetian windows shut tight against the downpour. A wooden sign painted with white letters hung above the double doors: *The Floating Life.*

The men entered and Ben followed. The doors clicked shut behind him, snuffing out the pandemonium of Victoria. The ground floor was a series of parlours, each one flowing seamlessly into the next. Men and women of all ages were sprawled on couches of red sandalwood and finely embroidered mattresses. Some took desserts of toffee apples and steamed rice out of lotus leaves, others indulged in oolong tea as they leant over mahjong tables. But every last person had one thing in common: within arm's reach was an opium pipe, still burning with the ashy residue of their last smoke.

It was an opium den, but a far cry from Ah Jiang's. It was clean, fashionable, intimate. The opium-eaters were relaxed and chatted freely among themselves, slipping from slurred Cantonese to drowsy laughter and back again. Golden lamplight cast their shadows against the padded walls, and tendrils of fragrant smoke – the familiar unctuous burn of opium, but shot through with tart hints of tangerine and schisandra – danced over their forms. Attendants in black robes brushed past Ben with silver trays of fresh opium shaped into bricks and bao. Their faces were hidden below ceremonial conical hats, out of respect for the clients.

Ben tracked the men into the final parlour, separated from the others by a bright red door. On the other side was an altogether different scene. Plush divans were ranged in a circle around a dais in the middle of the room, where a woman was dancing to the vigorous percussive strums of a pipa. Her face was painted white. Her eyes were closed. The velvet folds of her white *aoqun* crept up her arms as she wheeled in ever-quickening circles. Ben snatched a glimpse of the underside of her forearm: porcelain-smooth skin, eerily radiant, like a sallow veiled moon.

He looked around at the clientele: old, plump, wealthy-looking men. Thin characterless smiles cracked their wrinkled faces. They were attended by beautiful women, each wearing a different-coloured *aoqun*. The only exception was a man in the front row: a seventy-something greybeard with unruly mutton chops and tinted spectacles, in a suit studded with platinum buttons, and a brooch of a white-gold dove pinned to his lapel. A scar ran from the corner of his lip up to his ear, an incongruous pink streak against his bronze skin, and he watched the dancer with his hands resting on the grip of an ivory cane in the shape of a dragon's head.

With a final jangling thrum from the pipa, the dance came to an end and the audience started to clap – everyone except Chin Puff and Longshanks, who were leaning against a column on the periphery of the dais. The woman got up, linked arms with her fellow dancer and gave a brisk curtsey, before stepping off the stage to join the old man with the tinted spectacles. He embraced her with a kiss to the forehead, that she accepted with a solemn bow.

Then the woman saw Chin Puff and Longshanks. She whispered something in the ear of her elderly companion. He nodded and brushed his hand down the nape of her neck. She responded with a smile and a peck on the cheek. She rose to her feet and glided towards a side door, staring all the while at Chin Puff and Longshanks. They followed her and just like that the three of them disappeared from sight.

They were only gone for a minute. But when they emerged, it was as though they did not know each other. Chin Puff and Longshanks marched out as quickly as they came. The woman passed right by Ben on her way back to her elderly client, and for the first time, he got a good look at her. She was grave, withdrawn, her mind was elsewhere. She took her client by the hand and guided him upstairs to a private room.

Ben was about to leave when he felt an arm drape around his shoulder. It was another one of the working women, flanked by a couple of her friends: a girl to her left carrying an opium pipe, the other to her right a pack of cards.

'Lonely English boy,' she said breathily. 'So wet from rain.'

'All the more reason for me to go dry off,' Ben said, edging away from her.

'We help with that,' she said. Her friend with the opium pipe slipped a free hand around Ben's waist and pulled him back in. 'Our skin hot like flame.'

'Well then, I wouldn't want to get burned! Please excuse me.'

But by the time he was back out on Spring Garden Lane, it was too late. Chin Puff and Longshanks were nowhere to be found – and there was no way of knowing which way they had gone in this crush of people.

Ben sighed. What now? There was no use scouring Victoria looking for them, when he was about as fresh off the boat as one could possibly be. Better to cut his losses and call it a night – after all, his compatriots were waiting for him. So he wove through the evening crowds back to Queen's Road and hailed a horse-drawn cab to take him to the Mount Austin Hotel.

Ben was taken west, through the forests on the outskirts of Victoria, with only the cabbie's shuddering lamp to guide him. Every now and then he snatched glimpses through the Batavia cinnamon trees of Sai Wan – a clutch of warehouses on a bay to the west, circling the dry docks. The higher they ascended, the louder the winds roared, bending the trees and rattling Ben's windows.

'Where is this place?' he shouted to the cabbie over the din.

The cabbie laughed and flashed him a black-toothed grin. 'Up, boy!'

The path levelled out just shy of the summit of Mount Austin. In the middle of a clearing overlooking Victoria stood the grand hotel that would be Ben's home for the summer months. It was a Beaux-Arts pastiche: a shallow imitation of the hotels and public libraries in the central arrondissements of Paris that had formed the backdrop of his spell in France. Its only distinctive feature was its gothic spires, like razors slicing through the moonlight.

The carriage stopped under the porte cochere. A suited doorman in a bowler hat stepped forward and opened Ben's door for him. As Ben emerged, he took a deep breath. It was fresher up here – a soothing scent of dew and freshly mown grass.

He doled out his fare to the cabbie. 'I presume you take British sterling.'

The cabbie dropped the coins into a pouch. 'Even better. Silver get you the good stuff.'

He flashed those blackened teeth again. Then it clicked. That was opium black. By sunrise, every penny would be frittered away on a night of smoke. From British coffers, to Ben's hands, to the pouch of a lowly cabbie, and into the pocket of some peddler of low-quality dross on a street corner.

Before Ben could respond, the cabbie was trundling away. The doorman gestured to the lobby entrance. 'Your company is waiting, Mr Canaan.'

Mount Austin had been built for a respectable crowd. The walnut-brown walls, burgundy carpets and sweet strains of a string quartet gave it the air more of an august library than a hotel on a far-flung island. The guests were similarly civilised: a potpourri of colonial administrators enjoying Madeira wine in damask armchairs; expatriate businessmen closing deals and playing backgammon; and doctors, lawyers, and other members of the professional classes indulging in coffee *à demitasse* after a sumptuous dinner.

Ben was accosted by a stout bespectacled man of about thirty. His full cheeks were red with anticipation, and he had bowed several times before coming within touching distance.

'Mr Canaan!' he declared in a nasal wheeze. 'My goodness. Tremendous honour, first of all. I have heard wonderful things from Herr Bruckner. And for a fellow so young as you…!'

Ben nodded, but kept quiet. The man was nervous beyond belief. His palms were oily and he bounced from foot to foot.

'Oh my, I apologise,' he said, waving his hands about as if to shoo away any offence caused. 'That is not to say that you are inexperienced! I am sure you are *just* the right man to sweep up the mare's nest that we have here on this little island of ours. And it is the privilege of a lifetime for me to assist you, in any way I can.'

'I'm sorry,' Ben frowned, 'but who are you?'

'Ah! How gauche of me. Lionel Fitzjohn. I have been assigned as your aide for the duration of your sojourn on Hong Kong Island. I will, for all intents and purposes, be your go-between – shuttling from your mouth to the ears of Her Majesty's Executive, and vice versa.'

'Right… Well, thank you,' Ben said. 'I trust my bags arrived safely?'

'Oh, yes. They are in your room. Governor's Suite on the top floor, if you don't mind. I believe you have *two sinks*. And complimentary mint crisps.'

'Strike me down,' Ben said. 'I'm being spoiled.'

A bellboy came to escort Ben upstairs to his room, but Fitzjohn waddled after them. 'I apologise for being such a… a damned *pest*, Mr Canaan – but I am obliged to ask: where have you been this evening?'

'Business.'

'What kind of business?'

'*Personal business.*'

Fitzjohn stopped Ben at the foot of the stairwell. 'I should clarify, Mr Canaan: I do not ask to make frivolous chit-chat. It is simply that, as I'm sure you appreciate, I will have to report to Herr Bruckner. Which requires a level of, shall we say… candour on your part.'

Ben narrowed his eyes at Fitzjohn. A harmless little fellow. But he held Ben's gaze. Maybe there was some steel there after all.

'I went to a whorehouse.'

Fitzjohn looked momentarily taken aback. 'Oh. Well. Jolly good! And… *why* a whorehouse, exactly?'

Ben smiled and patted Fitzjohn on the back. 'Have a good night, Fitzjohn.'

The Governor's Suite was as advertised. A double bed, a dressing cabinet, a bathroom with two sinks, and a plate of mint crisps on the mantlepiece. His bags lay in a line at the foot of his bed. A writing desk had been placed by the window, with a thick wad of blank headed paper marked with Her Majesty's royal seal, together with an inkpot, a bottle of Old Overholt Kentucky rye whiskey, and an envelope marked with his name.

Ben prised it open: it was from Bruckner.

Ben popped open the Overholt and poured himself a couple of fingers. Tumbler in hand, he ambled to the balcony and threw open the windows to let the night rain bead his face. Far below was Victoria: a vortex of commerce, drugs and sex – a wasteland at the foot of Kowloon – a newborn writhing in the mud. This nondescript marshy island, around which the whole world was turning, even if people did not know it yet.

Ben knocked back his drink. He had been here for all of two hours, and already he did not like it.

8

A Fine Mess

Ben did not remember falling asleep. The next thing he heard was a knock at the door and Fitzjohn chiming, 'Mr Canaan!' like an over-eager boarding house master. A shaft of sunlight passed over his face and all he could see of the outside world was a diagonal slice of spotless azure, cut across by the occasional gull. The storm had cleared the skies out and summer heat pulsed through the open window. The clock on the wall above his bed read six in the morning, on the dot.

'Are you still drawing breath, my good man? It would be quite the headache if not.'

'One moment, Fitzjohn…'

Ben slipped into a dressing gown hanging on the bathroom door. He opened up to find Fitzjohn, bright as a button, in precisely the same suit that he had been wearing the previous night. Even his reddish hair, finely sculpted with a parting down the middle, was completely unchanged. He saw the Overholt on the desk.

'You wasted no time! I received a bottle too, but I'm saving it, sir – for my Annabelle, when I return to Sussex with a promotion and enough money to expand the farm.'

'Fitzjohn, it is always a pleasure,' Ben said, rubbing his eyes, 'but why exactly are you waking me now?'

'Because…' Fitzjohn said, checking his pocket-watch, 'in twenty-eight minutes and fifty-six seconds, these little piggies are going to market. And, contrary to popular belief, it's not the Hong Kong custom to venture out in a cotton dressing gown.'

'Where are we going?'

'I'll brief you fully in the carriage.'

By six-thirty, Ben had freshened up, changed into a suit, and mounted a carriage with Fitzjohn bound for Victoria.

'We'll be breakfasting with Sebastian Coldwell,' Fitzjohn said as they zipped downhill. 'I assume our employers informed you about him.'

'My point of command, so they said. Superintendent?'

'*Captain Superintendent* is the full title, I believe.'

Ben tutted. 'Oh joy.'

'Careful now, Mr Canaan – your irony is dripping onto the upholstery.'

'I don't tend to get along with the brass, Fitzjohn. I have an ingrained dislike of anyone wielding a truncheon in the name of Queen and Country.'

Fitzjohn said nothing for a moment. Ben knew that pause. A quiet mental note.

'You'll like him. He's an amiable fellow,' Fitzjohn smirked. 'Perhaps a little stiff. War heroes tend to lose their sense of humour. But you have six months to salvage the wreck of his *joie de vivre*.'

It was a half-hour journey to the Central Police Station, at the corner of Hollywood Road and Old Bailey Street. It was a sorry sight: a white-walled adjunct of the only jail on Hong Kong Island, its gutters hanging loose from the eaves after the previous night's squall. The officers inside were a curious blend of

Chinese, English and Indians, in dark blue uniforms with yellow buckles and white slouch hats. Virtually every man stopped in his tracks and stared Ben down as he passed by, stunned to silence. Ben's reputation clearly preceded him.

They found Coldwell on the upper-floor terrace, surveying the parade ground and the high stone walls of Victoria Prison. It was a curious tableau: the Captain Superintendent with his back to them, resting his fingertips on the balustrade; the rank-and-file officers below; and, just on the other side of the parade ground, the very men that Coldwell had put away.

Ben was struck by his handsomeness. He was tall, lean, with white-blonde hair and the first shallow cracks of middle age in his cheeks, lending him a certain gravitas. He stood perfectly upright – as Fitzjohn warned, a little stiff – and he wore an immaculate, if rather tight-fitting dark-blue suit with gold collar pins. Everything about him was disciplined and carefully held together: the appearance of ease, belied by something strained, like a duck gliding effortlessly as its feet furiously paddled below the surface.

He shook hands with Ben and Fitzjohn. 'Good to see you again, Lionel. And Mr Canaan! What a pleasure it is. I trust you had a trouble-free voyage?'

His voice was smooth and honeyed. But Ben detected a familiar twang in the vowels.

'I caught a whiff or two of trouble,' Ben replied. 'But I would have been disappointed had it been otherwise.'

'Best not get too comfortable then,' Coldwell winked. '*Trouble comes in threes*, as we used to say in the Dragoon Guard.'

Ben finally identified the chink in Coldwell's polished accent.

'Where are you from, Captain Superintendent?'

'London.'

'No,' Ben shook his head. 'Where are you *from*, Captain Superintendent?'

Coldwell matched Ben's smile. 'Shadwell. And yourself?'

'Whitechapel. So we're neighbours.'

Coldwell seemed self-conscious. 'I always liked Whitechapel for the music-houses.'

'And I seldom ventured into Shadwell,' Ben replied. 'Too many enemies. I'd have to take the long way round to get to Limehouse.'

'And now here we are,' Coldwell spread his arms, 'on an island in the middle of nowhere, shaking hands. Anyway. It's early. How about some breakfast?'

They retired to Coldwell's office: a pokey back room with a lingering smell of coffee, and cluttered with bundles of case notes, ink-stained ledgers and paperboard boxes. Coldwell's deputy, a young native Hakka by the name of Tsung, brought them coffee, Victoria sponge and a bowl with an assortment of local fruit: lychees, jackfruit, persimmon, longan. But Coldwell was more interested in the coffee. 'Six a day,' he remarked as he breathed in the steam from his mug, 'and yet I sleep like a baby!'

They traded anecdotes about how they ended up in their respective stations. As it turned out, while Ben had roamed the streets of Constantinople, Coldwell had been hunkered down in the trenches on the outskirts of Sevastopol, looking out across the blown and blasted plains of the Crimea. A lowly corporal in the 5th Dragoon Guards, traipsing through fields littered with cannonballs, shattered skulls and carrion. A winter of brutal cold, followed by a summer of unbearable heat. He had led his squad into the frenzy of the Battle of Balaclava, in a campaign to beat back the Russian cavalry. It was there that he earned his stripes, digging up medals from the onslaught with his bare hands.

'I ended the war a colonel,' Coldwell reminisced. 'I had waited all my life to do something special. But by that point, I'd lost almost every man whom I could call a friend. There is one in particular that still haunts me. John Thomas, or JT, as he was known. My lieutenant at Inkerman. He was struck by a stray bullet as we ascended Shell Hill: straight to the face, at an angle that vaporised one side of his head. You would think it instant, but it wasn't. He just… teetered there for a few moments. I saw his eyes – registering what had just happened. JT was an indomitable chap, a man of vim and sheer brute force. Yet in a flash, he looked utterly helpless and afraid. As though he had realised that it was too late, and he was exactly like the rest of them, and there was nothing he could do. And then he appeared to trip over himself, and he crumpled to the ground.'

Coldwell's gaze drifted from his coffee to Ben. Steel sparked in the blue of his eyes.

'Every man is the hero of his own story, Mr Canaan. No one went to Crimea thinking that *he* would be the tally on the chalk-board. But the truth is, human life is cheap as rags and traded with ease. You can take a life one day, and the morning after it will be your turn. You can scour the earth for a reason, but you won't find any. There are simply no rules.'

'Odd thing to say as a policeman, isn't it?' Ben shot Coldwell a skew look.

'Excuse me. Did you ever visit Crimea during your Turkish frolic?'

Ben shook his head.

Coldwell's face creased in a dull smile. 'All the better for you then.'

Ben studied Coldwell. The Captain Superintendent had a near unreadable expression typical of soldiers, chiselled from years of military discipline. But for the briefest moment, a gust sent the curtain billowing up, to reveal a faint glimmer of disdain.

Tsung cleared away their breakfast and the three of them got down to business.

'As Bruckner has no doubt explained,' Coldwell said, 'we've been dealing with a string of quite vicious murders. Not just on Hong Kong Island, but all across the archipelago.'

'I had a brush with the suspects myself back in London. There are – well… *were* – three of them. One is dead by his own hand. I trailed the other two here, but lost them shortly after my arrival last night.'

'In Victoria?'

'That's where I last saw them.'

Coldwell scribbled a note onto a slip of paper and handed it to Tsung, who peeked at it and promptly hurried off.

'The whole of Kowloon is in a true frenzy,' Coldwell said, 'and nobody knows who to trust. This has been going on for the better part of a year and, I am ashamed to say, we have made no progress. The evidence simply piles up like the Tower of Babel.' He gestured to the assortment of paperboard boxes. 'I will have these sent up to your room at Mount Austin. If the PM's word is anything to go by, you're the man to lance the boil.'

'I'll be happy to take a look,' Ben said. 'In the meantime, why don't you set the scene for me? The more context I have, the better.'

Coldwell knocked back the rest of his coffee. 'There have been dozens of killings that we know of. All people involved in some way, shape or form in the China trade. But there are four that form the centre of gravity. The first of them was João Gilberto Lalé, head of the largest Portuguese trading firm in the South China Sea. His ship was besieged last summer, on a return trip to Hong Kong from Kolkata. It was only found a month later, with Lalé and the rest of the crew gored, mutilated, left to rot in the sun.'

Coldwell slid a bundle of papers bound with string across the desk. Inside was Lalé's likeness: a stern-looking middle-aged man with a chinstrap beard, sallow emotionless eyes, and pursed lips that seemed calculated to intimidate.

'He looks like a bit of a bastard,' Ben remarked.

Coldwell shrugged. 'He was not known for his good cheer. Then, two months later, Oberon de Morèse met the same fate. He was Lalé's French counterpart. The House of Morèse, which he founded, is in all but name the representative of France's mercantile interests here in China. Morèse and his immediate family were slaughtered at their home in Macao. Only his youngest daughter Lucile survived – we found her hiding beneath the floorboards at the very spot where her family was executed.'

Ben flicked over the page. No image this time: just a garlanded crest, with a navy green wreath curling around a sword on a sapphire-blue shield, on which was emblazoned the name *Maison de Morèse*.

'Christmas saw a new member join the club: the Dutch industrialist Geert Van Hook. He had gone missing for a week, only to be found strung up in a forest on the China–Vietnam border, near the town of Chongzuo – disembowelled and hanging from an evergreen. And then, not long after, came that quite horrific night at the Isle of Dogs, as you know…'

Coldwell trailed off when he noticed Ben furrow his brow.

'Is something the matter?'

'I know those names…' Ben murmured, whipping out and leafing through his notebook, until his index finger landed on the vital page. 'That's right. Shortly after Mr Glass's murder, somebody left a book on my doorstep with a list of seven names. Those four you just mentioned… they were on that list.'

'And the other three?'

Ben read out the names: 'Ezekiel Ormrod. Hokoa. And Odysseus Halliday.'

Coldwell nodded. 'Same story. Powerful trading magnates. Ormrod is a Yank, I believe. Hokoa is a Chinaman. And Halliday…'

Fitzjohn reached between Ben and Coldwell to retrieve the coffee urn. 'Halliday's one of ours, isn't he?'

'Well. He's a Scotsman. So maybe don't say that to his face. But yes: Halliday's firm handles much of Britain's business in China. So it's not surprising that he's on the list too.'

'Seven targets, seven nationalities…' Fitzjohn mused. 'These killers are on one almighty tour round the world!'

'That must be part of their strategy,' Ben said sombrely. 'The China trade, from what I gather, is a lucrative enterprise – a magnet for every major imperial interest. So, if this is indeed a war on the China trade, then it is also necessarily a war on the world.'

'Which leaves us in a sensitive diplomatic position,' Coldwell interjected. 'We already have the Dutch and the Portuguese breathing down our necks, and if we don't resolve this quickly, it will spiral into a crisis of global proportions. We are new arrivals on foreign soil, at a moment when a great vacuum of power has opened up in the trade. This is a dangerous interregnum, gentlemen. And interregnums breed chaos.'

They left Fitzjohn to organise transport of the boxes of evidence up to Mount Austin. In the meantime, Coldwell had an introduction to make. He took Ben ten minutes down Wyndham Street, then onto Albert Road. Through the green, Ben made out a building in the colonial style, not unlike pictures he had seen of the plantation houses in the American South. Only this one was topped by the Union Jack, and gave onto a sweeping panorama of Victoria Bay and the fleets of steamers ploughing across the choppy waters, framed against the backdrop of the sloping hills of Kowloon.

'What is this place?' he asked.

'Government House,' Coldwell replied. 'Residence of our dearly beloved governor, Sir John Bowring.'

Ben recognised the name. Bowring was infamous back in England, as an ambitious chancer whose lack of scruples was matched only by his lust for prestige and capacity for self-promotion. He had a corner in the *Westminster Review*, which Ben occasionally dipped into for his own amusement, where he told people whatever they wanted to hear in a given month. Now he was a free trader, but before that he was a Chartist, abolitionist, utilitarian, Unitarian, hedonist, internationalist, and imperialist. Every career he had tried before landing on diplomacy – from railways to publishing to Parliament – had ended in failure. Yet Bowring, against all odds, seemed to have a knack for getting his name stuck in people's heads.

'Can we trust him?' was all Ben said.

'He's a diplomat, Mr Canaan. It's his job to lie through his teeth. If he wishes you good morning, I advise you check the time just to be sure.'

They were taken by the staff to the drawing room, where Bowring was holding court before a small delegation of suited elderly men. Bowring was on the creakier side of sixty, with a bulging brow and thinning strands of grey-brown hair. He was shuddering as he spoke, with the intensity of a priest and the oiliness of a salesman on his soapbox.

Ben and Coldwell lingered at the back, watching Bowring's performance.

'That, gentlemen, is why I cannot impress upon you enough, that the British are working tirelessly to resolve this present state of uncertainty in which you find yourselves – indeed, in which we *all* find ourselves. Nobody is a champion of free trade more than myself. I have always stood by the free market and our ability to enrich the civilised people of the world through the magic of commerce.'

Ben noticed pins and badges on the lapels of Bowring's audience. One of them he recognised as the crest of the House of Morèse: the wreath, the sword, the blue shield. These were men of the China trade. And Bowring was limiting the damage.

The Governor's rattlesnake eyes flicked across the room to glance at the new arrivals. But he hardly skipped a beat. 'Now, I know full well the unrest that these murders have wrought on your businesses, on your ability to trade without fear of reprisal from this unseen enemy. But I must urge you, gentlemen: do not kow-tow to the pressure. That is precisely the aim of these provocateurs – to dissuade us from the pursuit of prosperity and industry.'

One of the men rose to his feet and addressed Bowring directly, in a Portuguese accent. 'Governor Bowring, you cannot seriously expect us to trade in these conditions. Our men fear for their lives every time a boat comes to port, every time a shipment passes hands. And these men depend on us for their livelihood. Our firms will be bankrupted if we cannot provide the proper safeguards—'

'All the more reason,' Bowring cut in, 'to stand with Britain as we root out those responsible. Many millions of people depend on us, gentlemen. Not just those who work for us, but those who buy our goods, consume our products, demand our supply. We must not let them down. Or the world's economy itself will turn belly up, and we will all be washed away.'

Bowring fielded a few more objections, then brought proceedings to a close. Once his audience had filed out, he gestured for Ben and Coldwell to join him in private. They sat opposite one another in the study, by a window over the gardens, as the Governor lit up his pipe, took a few hard-earned puffs, and rolled his head back wearily.

'What a pig's ear we've made…' he muttered between puffs. 'Do you know, we've been through five Colonial Secretaries in the past year? Every time I write back to the Cabinet, I have a new "Right Honourable" to answer to. And none of them know the first thing about our colony.'

Coldwell cleared his throat and gestured to Ben. 'Hopefully I can lighten your mood, Governor. This is Benjamin E. Canaan. He's been sent to clean up this little quandary of ours.'

Bowring leant forward to get a good look at Ben. 'Ah. So *you're* Palmerston's boy. He has been singing your praises from the spires of Parliament.'

'Pleased to hear it.'

'And you should know – not to toot my own horn, as our American cousins say…' Bowring laid a hand on Ben's arm. 'Nobody has been a champion of Jewish emancipation more than me. Though I am a follower of Christ, it gives me great pride to sing, along with my Hebrew brothers, the immortal words of Moses: *set my people free!*'

Ben smiled politely. Bowring's charm was overweening. The most that he could muster was a brisk, 'Thank you.'

'You're very welcome. I am humbled by your gratitude. But, on to more serious matters! What's your view of the present situation?'

Coldwell filled Bowring in on what he had discussed with Ben earlier that morning. By the time he was finished, Bowring's fatuous smile had disappeared and he had returned to the safety of his pipe.

'The most important thing now,' Ben said, 'is that we protect whomever we can. Ormrod, Hokoa and Halliday are still alive. And we should keep it that way. Otherwise, Governor, with the greatest of respect to your diplomatic abilities, I doubt you will be able to hold back the flood.'

'I can barely hold it back as it is.'

'In that case, I propose we liaise directly with these three men. I should meet with them at the very least to explain the situation, get any information from them that I can. We have a head start and we must take advantage of that.'

Bowring waved Ben away dismissively. 'Ormrod is off limits. He's in Macao under American eyes – and the Yanks will not touch us with a bargepole. And as for Hokoa, he's in Chinese hands, and you know what they are like: possessive, guarded, in a world of their own... The Viceroy in Canton, Ye Mingchen, has not returned a single letter of mine.'

'Well... what about Halliday?'

Bowring mulled the question. 'Halliday, we can do. He lives on an island a few hours south of Hong Kong – New Lewis, I believe. Leave it with me and I'll set up a rendezvous.'

One of Bowring's aides appeared in the doorway: the Governor had another meeting in five minutes' time. Bowring bade them farewell and bustled for the door, pipe clamped between his teeth.

'Pleasure to finally meet you, Mr Canaan,' he declared, not

bothering to look back. 'Let's see if you are all that they claim you to be!'

No sooner was he gone than Ben and Coldwell were being escorted out. Bowring's manner reminded Ben of the first time that he met Palmerston: the affectations of superiority, the breezy indifference, the lofty sense of entitlement. Where did men like him learn these pretensions? Was it hammered into them from birth? Or did it come naturally?

As he stepped out into the sunshine and the sweltering heat, he remembered his father's words – the warning murmured to him in his childhood bedroom, not one week before his departure: *you're not one of them.*

'I must dash off,' Coldwell said, checking his pocket-watch, 'but I'll be mobilising my men to conduct a search across the island for our two suspects. In the meantime, you dig into the evidence and see what you can find. And once Bowring comes back to us, we'll liaise with Halliday and take matters from there.'

They shook. Coldwell was about to take his leave, but Ben stopped him.

'I only had one question, Captain Superintendent.'

'Please – call me Sebastian.'

'Sebastian, of course. It's just…' Ben scratched his head. 'How did you realise these killings are connected?'

'It did not take immense powers of deduction,' Coldwell said with a rueful smile. 'Each of the bodies had a phrase carved into the flesh. Two words—'

Ben's heart skipped a beat. '*Black Blood.*'

Coldwell did nothing at first. He was studying Ben's features, watching a thin crack of fear rupture Ben's quiet determination. He placed a hand on Ben's shoulder: a soothing, almost paternal gesture. 'Godspeed, my boy. It's a long road ahead.'

And with that, he marched off, leaving Ben shrouded in a pall of silence – the sinking feeling that he had stumbled into something truly evil.

Coldwell was right. It was a long road ahead, and there was no turning back now.

9

Emperors of the Sea

About twenty kilometres south of Hong Kong Island, a schooner was ploughing across the open waters of the South China Sea. It was a choppy day. Waves lashed the underside of the boat and a bracing wind buffeted the sails. A sun-beaten seaman was at the wheel, the stub of a cheap cigarette pinched between his chapped lips. He was once a dockworker by the name of Zixuan, but these days he worked as Sebastian Coldwell's personal navigator and went by Zachary. Easier to pronounce for the white man, so he said.

He felt the boat surge forward, propelled by a southerly wind caught in the mainsail, and he threw his head back to shake his hair out. Even after fifty years spent sailing the archipelagos of Kowloon, the cleansing kiss of the high seas never lost its charm.

'How much longer, Zachary?'

Coldwell and his new boy were sitting opposite one another below the boom, dressed to the nines. Coldwell was looking at Zachary expectantly, while the boy was scribbling in his note-book, occasionally looking up and chewing his pencil.

'Fifteen minutes, sir!'

The boy's gaze turned to Zachary. He was staring right at him, yet he seemed a thousand miles away.

'Benjamin!' Coldwell said.

Ben returned to his senses. He had been distracted by the tattoo on the back of Zachary's hand. It was a date etched just below the knuckles: VII.I.MDCCCXLI.

'You would be wise to sharpen up,' Coldwell said. 'Halliday does not take fools lightly.'

'I haven't been sleeping well lately.'

'That's normal. It takes a few weeks to grow accustomed to Hong Kong air. The dreams are vivid, aren't they?'

Ben thought back to his vision from the previous night. An empty field in darkness, with hills that bulged like distended bellies – soughing in fathomless yawns like a great, heaving ocean. Moonlight pulsing behind plumes of smoke that rose from distant fires. And, perched on the skeletal branch of a long-dead magnolia tree, the silent form of a black crow – spreading its wings and opening its cavernous beak.

'I don't recall,' he said.

'Lucky you. And if your luck runs out, a shot of baijiu will wash it down.'

'Or *yāpiàn*,' Zachary piped up.

'What?'

Coldwell waved Zachary away. 'Focus on sailing, Zachary! Don't bother Benjamin.'

'What is *yāpiàn*?' Ben frowned.

'It's the… Chinese word for, you know…' Coldwell shrugged. 'The fruit of the poppy.'

'Opium?'

'He's not implying you are that way inclined. It's a bad joke. Isn't that right, Zachary?'

Zachary said nothing. He just lit another cigarette.

New Lewis took shape ahead of them. Like many of the islands around Kowloon, its shores were lined with beaches and picturesque bays, while the forests inland sloped up sharply to the mountain peaks. The only difference with New Lewis was the absence of trade: no commercial wharfs, no steamers, no dry docks. The greatest merchant in the South China Sea preferred his back garden nice and quiet.

They were greeted at the jetty on the northern shore of New Lewis by half a dozen armed guards, led by a hulking red-bearded Westerner. He was dressed head to toe in khaki, as though he had been plucked from the cavalry of the British Indian Army's Corps of Guides. Slung over his shoulder was an Enfield rifle-musket – one of the new models and, judging from its polish, largely unused. He wore a signet ring on a chain round his neck, bearing the graven initials 'GP'.

The man greeted Coldwell with a bear hug as they disembarked.

'You stubborn dog! Back for more, are you?' he roared, in an American accent, before turning to Ben. 'I tell you… This man will find *any* excuse to come to Mr Halliday's island. Sad to see you've been roped into it, kiddo.'

'Actually,' Coldwell said, drawing the two men closer, 'this was young Benjamin's initiative. Benjamin, this is Grant Parry – Mr Halliday's… how can I describe you?'

'I wring necks and open jam jars. Is there a word for that?'

'Right-hand man?' Ben said.

'Well, I tend to use both hands! Anyway…' Parry gave Ben a rough shove. 'I know who you are – everyone knows who you are!'

'And who's that?'

Parry took long loping strides down the jetty. 'You've come to save us, "young Benjamin". From the Bogeyman haunting the South China Sea.'

Parry led them up the hillside, following a path through the forest, while the guards trailed behind them in silence.

Halliday's abode was at the top of the hill, on a plateau looming over New Lewis. It was a castle in the Scots baronial style: granite overlaid with ivy, ringed by battlements and spired turrets. The centrepiece of the castle was a large cupola – a folly in the shape of a pineapple – under which was emblazoned a Latin motto: *in omnibus caritas.*

A man was standing in the archway of the castle's main entrance. He looked about seventy – short, rotund, with a grey Van Dyke beard and a round craggy face. He was decked out in a cream suit and straw hat, a pink rose pinned to his lapel and both hands tucked into his waistcoat pockets in an expression of cool satisfaction. Behind him, the posterns had been thrown open to reveal a majestic walled courtyard and a line of servants. He seemed at once so small, and yet so triumphant, as though he was constantly cresting a tremendous wave.

'Mr Halliday!' Parry said, coming to stand before their host. 'We have a couple of castaways on our hands.'

'Marooned, are we?' Halliday chimed, in a resounding Scottish accent.

He made no effort to step forward, waiting instead for his guests to come to him. He stayed Coldwell with an affectionate pinch to the cheek.

'I know you, fine sir. You had a bit of rough and tumble at the Easter luncheon. Packed away too much brandy! But you…'

He took Ben's hand: no shake – just a warm grip. Ben maintained eye contact.

'Benjamin E. Canaan, sir,' Ben said, matching Halliday's smile.

'You look a wee bit green, lad. Seasick?'

'Must be the anticipation of meeting a man as illustrious as yourself.'

Halliday made an amused face at Coldwell. 'My, my. Butter wouldn't melt in his mouth!'

Ben had tangoed with enough tycoons and toffs to know the game that Halliday was playing. This was a test of his manly resolve.

Halliday gave Ben a brisk nod and waved them inside. 'Come on!' he bellowed. 'Allow me to give you a little tour of Caisteal Halliday.'

The posterns rumbled shut behind them as they entered. The ambient backdrop of New Lewis – the chirruping birds, rustling canopies, crashing waves – seemed to vanish in an instant. This was Halliday's private utopia. Nature played by his rules.

They crossed the first courtyard, down an arcade garlanded with bright pink bauhinia and camellia. On either side of the colonnade was an immaculate lawn, dotted with fairy rings of white mushrooms. In the middle was an ornate cast-iron fountain, painted turquoise and studded with gold. It bore the statue of a woman, with long hair flowing in dark ringlets and an elaborate robe draped over her body. Her hands were held to her breast like a reverent Madonna. At the base of the statue was a name and a set of dates:

Emmeline Sarah Halliday
14 August 1767 – 5 February 1796

'My mother,' Halliday said, resting his hand affectionately on the statue's foot. 'She died long before this place was built. Now she gets to enjoy the view. Every single day.'

Ben looked at the statue more closely. There was something almost mournful in her absent metal eyes, like a prisoner of some story told again and again by this old man.

'And what about the pineapple?' Ben asked, pointing up to the cupola.

Halliday sucked through his teeth. 'Well… I like pineapples. Have you ever tried one?'

'Never had the good fortune.'

Halliday gestured to one of the servants and issued a command in impeccable Mandarin. The servant bowed and skipped off in the opposite direction.

Halliday led them indoors. It was not the first time that Ben had been inside a palace, but even he was taken aback by the grandeur. The chapel could easily have seated a hundred people or more – the organ large enough for a cathedral – the ceiling one enormous Italianate fresco. The drawing room had two pianofortes, including a gold Érard that would not have been out of place in Buckingham Palace. The library was on three floors, each stack with its own ladder. The gardens were many times larger than the playing fields at Lord's. Old Masters hung on the walls with the same casual indifference as cheap knock-off watercolours.

But for all the luxury and excess, there was one thing entirely absent from Caisteal Halliday: the remotest sign of a loved one. No family, no friends, not even a colleague. Just Odysseus Halliday and the echo of his footsteps as his only companion.

'Do you live here alone?' Ben asked.

'Mostly. Ingrid, my niece, works in the firm and she rattles around the island from time to time.'

'And that doesn't… bother you? All this empty space?'

Halliday gave Ben a knowing wink. 'Power is lonely, Mr Canaan.'

They ended up in his study, Halliday behind a broad desk with his back to a set of floor-to-ceiling windows overlooking the courtyard. This room was where Halliday held onto his keepsakes: a scarred cannonball mounted on a wooden frame; model ships; a spoke from a naval steering wheel; framed receipts and invoices going back to the time of Napoleon – forget-me-nots from an unforgettable life. There were no chairs for Ben and Coldwell to sit on, leaving them no choice but to stand before Halliday while he kicked his feet up on the desk.

By the time they arrived, a plate of fruit had already been laid on a side-table: freshly sliced pineapple. 'Taste, laddie,' Halliday said, 'and tell me what you think.'

Ben obliged. A burst of sweetness, then an acidic tang. 'A little sharp on the tongue. But I appreciate the gesture. Thank you.'

Halliday rubbed his hands together. 'Now,' he said, 'what's this I hear about my name on a "kill list"? They got Lalé, de Morèse, Van Hook and Lennie – and now they want little old me as well?'

'And Messrs Ormrod and Hokoa. A full deck of dead tycoons.'

Halliday gave a nonchalant shrug. 'The first thing I should say,' he said, 'is that the inclusion of these names on this list of yours is perfectly explicable. Our dear departed gentlemen and those still living, including myself, constitute a sort of informal club in the China trade.'

'What kind of club?'

'Nothing official. We are known as *The Seven Gentlemen*. It's more a badge of distinction; a marker that we seven, effectively, carry the China trade on our backs – and on behalf of our governments. Which would explain why poor Bowring is more nervous than a whore on Bargain Saturday.'

Halliday gestured to a copper-plate photograph on the mantlepiece: the Seven Gentlemen to whom he had just referred, standing side by side outside the entrance to a trading office on Victoria Harbour. They were in dark suits and bowler hats, bearing the naval jack of their respective countries, and their names were printed just below their feet. Ben's eyes trailed left to right: Lennie, Van Hook, de Morèse, Halliday in the middle, Ormrod, Lalé…

He paused. The man on the far right, who bore the name Hokoa, had a face that he recognised. The grey beard, the mutton chops, the tinted spectacles, the look of an ageing dandy. That was the man he had seen at The Floating Life – the one served by the dancer whom Ben's suspects seemed to know.

'There is more money in that image than half the population of China,' Halliday said with great pride. 'The Chinese have their Emperor – the ruler of the land. But we are a power far greater and vaster: the emperors of the sea.'

Ben turned back to Halliday with a frown. 'When we say "China trade", what are we actually referring to? What is being traded here?'

Coldwell opened his mouth to speak, but Halliday cut him off. 'It depends, really. Each firm has its own niche. I, for example, deal in raw materials: silk, cotton, metals for machine-works. Also tea. A lot of tea.'

'Imports or exports?'

'Those are exports – back to Britain, mostly.'

'And what do you import into China?'

'Whatever the Chinese want, in truth. These days, it tends to be herbal remedies, homeopathic medicine, morphine, palliatives of all sorts – be it ingestible, smokable… The trouble with these yellow types is the filth they live in. They're falling ill every other week, so naturally there's a certain demand for… substances.'

Halliday drummed the desk with his fingertips. He was waiting for Ben to say something. Perhaps to double down on Halliday's sentiment – hurl another insult at a strange people – play the game. But Ben thought back to the sight of Zachary steering Coldwell's schooner across the South China Sea, shaking out his salt-crusted hair.

'I tend to reserve judgement until I know a man,' Ben said, straightening his back.

'That is the modern way,' Halliday smirked.

'Pardon me, sir,' Coldwell butted in, 'but I did have a question. If you think back on your career, long as I know it is, do you have any idea who might possibly want you dead?'

'Have you got all day?' Halliday laughed. 'One cannot make money without making enemies, and the more money one makes, the more enemies come with it. Whether to extract a ransom, gain a commercial advantage, or simply out of jealousy – there is always someone ready to harm me. And this episode is no different. It is but a tempest in a teapot.'

'You seem rather unbothered by the prospect of a savage death,' Ben said.

'I'm still standing, am I not? See the cannonball on the mantlepiece over there? I was about your age, Mr Canaan – a naval surgeon fresh out of medical school on a godforsaken galleon sailing across the Atlantic. We had a little a skirmish with a French ship and that thing missed my head by all of six inches. Practically singed the hair off my pate. And the Frank who fired it is food for worms.'

'Lennie Glass also thought he was untouchable,' Ben shot back, 'and it didn't save him from being gored and gutted. Now, you can act as though we're over-egging the pudding, but we both know you don't believe that for one second. What man welcomes his guests with an army of bodyguards, if not a man avoiding the worst? My wager? There's already been an attempt on your life. Or on someone in your fold. I haven't had time to look properly at the evidence, but what are the chances that I'll find something to that effect?'

Halliday shot Coldwell another look – this time, perplexity. 'I assumed you would have told him, Sebastian. About our poor Bart.'

'Mr Canaan has the evidence,' Coldwell said. 'He was going to read the files on Bart in any event.'

'I'm sorry…' Ben leant in. 'Who is Bart?'

'Bartholomew Swanson.' Halliday grew sombre. 'The very best supercargo in my fleet. He vanished two months ago after completing a shipment of tea, only to be washed up a few days later, on this very island. He was… how did you put it? *Gored and gutted.*'

'Could you show me where?'

Halliday had Parry escort Ben to the south shore, while he and Coldwell talked in private. It was a ten-minute walk down the hill, until the forest opened out onto a rocky shore running the full span of the island. To the right, the shore sloped up to a cliff-edge over the lashing waves, where the remains of an abandoned Chinese naval fort stood, a dismal relic of another era.

'We found him right here,' Parry said, gesturing to a rock pool at their feet. 'Face down. Neck snapped. Head split open down the back.'

'Any boats seen nearby at the time?'

'Not a soul. If you ask me, they killed him out at sea and dumped him under cover of night, close enough to get dragged in by the tide.'

Lalé, the Portuguese magnate, had been killed out at sea as well. And according to official reports from London, the assassins on the Isle of Dogs had taken off in boats. This was classic piracy: people who knew the waters well, who could sail through the archipelago without being detected. They were probably using trading brigs too, to blend in with the fleets that regularly traversed the South China Sea.

Something – or rather, someone – caught Ben's eye. There was a woman leaning on the parapet at the top of the fort, buffeted by the sea wind. She was too far up for Ben to make out her features.

'Who's that?' Ben asked.

'That'll be Ingrid,' Parry replied. 'Old Halliday's niece. We used to have black bears on the island – but she scared them off.'

Ben's curiosity was piqued. 'Wait here a moment.'

He climbed up the slope to get a closer look. When he reached the top, he found Ingrid smoking a cigarette and staring out across the water. Her hair was long and curly, trailing to the small of her back. She was dressed entirely in black, from her lace blouse, to her chemisette, to her leather gloves, to her tall button-up walking boots.

She must have heard Ben's footsteps. Yet she made no attempt to acknowledge his presence.

'Excuse me.' Ben cleared his throat.

She responded in a mechanical monotone. 'Are you Coldwell's bloodhound?'

'I prefer to think of myself as a lone wolf.'

'Liar. Every dog has an owner.' Only now did she turn around, taking a long drag on her cigarette. 'Or at the very least craves one.'

She had almost avian features. A thin, pointed nose; large ice-blue eyes; a grey poliosis streak running up from her brow; pale, limpid skin. The smoke crept from her lips, as though trying to crawl out of her for air. Her expression was cold, yet distantly curious – off-putting, yet strangely magnetic.

'Ingrid Marshall,' she said. She did not extend a hand.

'Ben Canaan. But I'm guessing you already know that.'

'I knew who you were the second I laid eyes on you. Traipsing from the forest back there like a brave adventurous boy. All you need is a staff and a cape and you could be like Hansel.'

'What does that make you? Gretel? The witch?'

Ingrid gave a lifeless chuckle. 'Mr Halliday's niece. He and my father co-founded the firm. Halliday & Halliday, as it was known back then. Now it is in the singular.'

'I take it your father is no longer around.'

'He grew weary of the China trade and retired to Scotland.'

'And you didn't join him?'

'For what? To live out my days being rained on in the Highlands? Marrying a laird in a kilt to the sound of bagpipes and Auld Lang Syne? Women are of more value than as accessories to their fathers and husbands.'

Ingrid had mastered the art of the dispassionate sting. An indifferent tone that could cut through like obsidian. Behind her cool veneer, she had a temper.

But Ben was not deterred. 'So you're an accessory to your uncle instead?'

'My uncle wouldn't have one-fifth of his money if it weren't for me. I'm a mathematician by training, and I put it to good use. I advise him on practically every trade he makes – every acquisition – every step through the ever-shifting market. I know the shape of the China trade inside out, and he passes off that knowledge as his own native instinct. Not that I care for adulation. I just want my cut.'

'So you like the China trade, do you?'

'It's not a question of *like*, Mr Canaan. I'm thirty-five years old. I have grown up, married, divorced, fallen in and out of love several times over, made friends, lost friends, and worked until I could no longer keep my eyes open. And in all that time, the one constant in my life has been the China trade, from the day of my birth. It is who I am. For better and for worse.'

She popped open her cigarette case.

'Care for a smoke?'

'No, thank you. I don't smoke.'

'Cigarettes, you mean?'

Ben looked askew at Ingrid. She tilted her head to one side, feigning a coquettish smile. She had seen right through him.

'Come now,' she chortled, 'I know an opium eater when I see one. You're not the only one with a keen sense of smell.'

'I wouldn't call myself an opium eater.'

'What would you call yourself then, Mr Canaan?'

'Open to temptation.'

Ingrid lit another cigarette, keeping her gaze on him the whole time. 'So am I.'

Ben heard footsteps crunching the gravel behind him. It was Parry, breathless from having ascended the fort. He motioned towards the summit of New Lewis, where Caisteal Halliday stood, bathed in sunshine.

'Looks like I must be off,' Ben said. 'A pleasure to meet you.'

Ingrid removed her gloves and extended a slender hand. Ben sensed a trace in her of something sad and broken.

'Protect my uncle, Mr Canaan. He may not be concerned, but I'm smart enough to know the truth. Something wicked stalks the Pearl River. And if you cannot stop it, it will consume us all.'

It was a tense walk back to Caisteal Halliday. The day was as warm and humid as ever, but a chill ran down Ben's spine. The more people he met, the clearer it became that Bo was right: a storm was indeed coming, though nobody knew where it was coming from. All they could do was batten down the hatches and hope for the best.

Ben rejoined Coldwell at the entrance to the castle, but Halliday was not there to say his goodbyes. They were simply escorted back to Coldwell's schooner, where Zachary was sunning himself on deck, and sent on their way.

'He didn't like me, did he?' Ben said once they were on the water.

'He doesn't have to like you,' Coldwell replied. 'We just need to do our job, whether he appreciates it or not. You're a detective. If it's applause you're after, take up singing.'

Ben pulled out his notebook and jotted down a passing thought: *Coldwell angry.*

'What do you know about his niece?' Ben asked.

'Ingrid? She's a troubled soul. A genius at what she does, no doubt about it. And it has paid dividends. But… let's just say, it's been a bumpy road.'

'I'm not sure I catch your drift.'

'Well…!' Coldwell squirmed. 'I'm not sure it's my place to—'

'These are people of interest, Sebastian. I need to know what is going on here.'

Coldwell sighed and drew Ben in so that Zachary could not hear them. 'Two years ago, she married one of her uncle's sailors – a chap by the name of Ernest Marshall. She fell pregnant shortly afterwards. But six months later, she had a... spontaneous abortion. The child simply died inside her. And, unsurprisingly, the grief drove her mad. She sank into a mania – neurosis, the doctors called it – and she had to be committed. She was eventually discharged, about four months ago, but by that point her husband had broken things off and quit the firm. Leaving her to start over again.'

Ben said nothing. The spectre of Ingrid Marshall hovering over the crashing waves now made perfect sense. The mourners' black; the cold stone of the abandoned fort, itself like a barren and empty womb; that hollow, detached gaze; the dry monotone. It was all she could do now. Smoke, think, linger on the brink of the sea.

'Why do you ask?' Coldwell looked at Ben quizzically.

'Just curious,' Ben said with a shrug.

They arrived back in Victoria Harbour just as the factories broke for lunch. An impromptu bankshall had opened up on the wharf: a floating seafood market where manual labourers, sitting shoulder to shoulder over the water, haggled with Sampan-Sams for oysters and freshly brewed tea.

'I was meaning to ask...' Ben turned to Zachary and pointed to the tattoo below his knuckles. 'Is that a date? What does it refer to?'

Zachary's face, cracked like blasted desert stone from decades in the sun, was utterly still. A thousand untold memories flowed behind it.

'Battle of Chuenpi. January 1841. When the Great Qing went to war with the white man. I was in the Qing army with my brother. He was killed – shot by British. I swore to my father that I would bring him home safe. But I broke my promise. And over what?'

He splayed the back of his hand for Ben, as if to sear the date on the boy's memory.

'*Yāpiàn*,' he seethed. 'Precious *yāpiàn*. You know what they call it?'

Ben shook his head.

'*The black crow.*'

10

The Flower Girl

Ben wasted no time. That night, he took a carriage from Mount Austin to the seedy back-alleys of Wan Chai. It was intolerably humid, even at this late hour. But he nonetheless felt a sense of relief as the lights of Mount Austin faded behind the tree-line, and he was left alone with the trundling wheels and the moaning wind.

He realised, as they entered Victoria proper, that he had forgotten to write to his family as he had promised. But what could he say, beyond a clutch of platitudes and half-truths? There was little in his head that he could openly express, without fear of some breach of confidence, indiscretion, or strategic misstep. He had to be guarded these days. So unlike the Ben Canaan of old, when his mouth would routinely land him in trouble. Everything now needed to be a calculation, even with the people whom he was supposedly serving. And what he was about to do was yet another dissimulation – another clever piece of theatre that he carefully constructed as he descended to Wan Chai.

Ben had his driver wait outside The Floating Life while he made his way through those familiar lounges. He opened the red door leading into the parlour at the back, but no sooner had he crossed the threshold than he was greeted by an elderly Malay woman wearing a rather obvious black wig. He could tell from the way that she strutted about with her nose held high that she was the queen bee in this strange little hive.

'*Français?*' she rasped.

Ben shook his head. '*Anglais, s'il vous plait.*'

She looked him up and down. Ben knew that beady expression. She was trying to gauge how rich he was – whether he promised a lucrative night, or if he was just a pretender.

'I do not recognise you,' she said. 'Madame Xu.'

Ben bowed to kiss her hand, with all the gallantry that he could muster. 'Benjamin E. Canaan. I'm new in town and was looking to… sample what you have on offer.'

'And who takes your fancy?'

Ben scanned the room, searching for the face of the dancer from the other night. He spotted her in a booth in the far corner, preparing opium for a middle-aged client. She was in the same white *aoqun*, only this time her makeup was gentler, revealing more of her natural beauty in the dim light.

'Her,' Ben said, pointing in the woman's direction.

Madame Xu looked incredulous. 'She is our most valuable flower girl. And as you can see, very high in demand—'

Ben flashed his money to Madame Xu – enough to make whatever protest she was about to muster freeze on her lips.

'Whatever he's paying, I'll pay double.'

At first, Madame Xu was too shocked to remark at Ben's impudence. Then she came to her senses and thrust out an open hand. 'Deposit. One sovereign.'

'My pleasure.'

Ben gave her the sovereign and she guided him to a private booth, enclosed by three semi-translucent paper screens stretched over latticed wooden frames. On the floor in the middle of the booth were two sets of purple velvet pillows and downy mats on which to recline, separated by an unlit spirit lamp.

'Your flower girl will be but a moment,' Madame Xu said. 'Please do have a seat.'

Ben obliged as Madame Xu shuffled off. He feigned interest in his notebook while he waited, keeping one eye on the flower girl as Madame Xu approached her. They had a hurried exchange. The flower girl sized Ben up from afar, quickly adjusted her hair – arranged in a double bun – and walked towards him.

Before she had even entered the booth, Ben understood the character that she was playing: the quietly seductive ingénue. She was smiling with almost enough sweetness to make him forget why he had come in the first place. Almost.

She kneeled before him. 'My name is Sapphire,' she said. 'I have been informed that you require a flower girl?'

Ben held his tongue. This was not the average illiterate prostitute lingering in the doorways of the Buck's Row lodging houses in Whitechapel. Her English was well-schooled. It had the inflection of someone who had learned to speak the language from reading novels.

'I do indeed,' he said. 'Someone skilled with the needle.'

'Then you are in the safest of hands. I can extract the essence out of even the most impure gum. What is your preference?'

'Benares, of the Ganges variety. Mild, hot, hints of rose…'

'…Almond too. We have it in abundance. You are a man of fine taste.'

Sapphire sat cross-legged on a pillow opposite Ben, on the other side of the spirit lamp. An attendant slid a tray between them with their kit: the polished ivory opium pipe patterned with elaborate silver ornaments, two needles with pinpoints blackened from use, matches to kindle the flame, a pair of small scissors, and a wad of black opium rolled into a perfectly round pellet. She trimmed the wick of the spirit lamp by one-eighth of an inch.

'For a cleaner, brighter burn,' she said with a smile.

'I know,' Ben replied drily. 'I would have gone with one-sixth, personally.'

'I see you have experience in taking *yāpiàn*.'

'As a rule of thumb, I only indulge in the company of a beautiful woman.'

She struck a match, bathing her painted cheeks in an inviting glow, and lit the spirit lamp. 'But never a Hong Kong flower girl.'

Ben watched her take up the needles, one in each hand, and impale the ball of opium. With consummate ease, she began to knead the ball over the spirit lamp. It was as though her fingers moved entirely independently of the rest of her body, sculpting the paste into dense rubbery strands as it began to bubble – as black shimmered into that familiar tanned gold.

'You make it seem effortless,' Ben said.

'I have handled these opium needles more frequently than chopsticks,' she mused. 'It is second nature to me by now.'

'Your powers must be in high demand from all sorts of illustrious men.'

'Oh yes. No man can resist the temptation of a good flower girl.'

Sapphire began softly singing a traditional folk tune, in time with the rhythm of her needlework. There was something intensely intimate yet at the same time unknowable about this woman: eyes that concealed their own depth, lips that drew him in only to push him away.

She rolled the strands into a cone-shaped pellet. 'Take up your pipe, Mr…?'

'Canaan,' Ben inverted the bowl of his pipe over the spirit lamp. 'Ben Canaan.'

Once the bowl had heated up, Sapphire spun the pellet round the flame, softening it just enough without melting or charring it, then plunged it into the bowl. Ben tipped the pipe at a forty-degree angle – ideal for smoking – and sealed the mouthpiece with his lips.

Sapphire slid her free hand to the nape of Ben's neck. Somehow, despite working with the flame, her fingertips were icy at the touch and made his hair stand on end. 'Deep breath, Ben Canaan…' she whispered in his ear.

Ben felt the vapour creep into his mouth and down his throat, diffusing like a velvet bloom across his chest and belly. His whole body sagged as he succumbed to that familiar sensation: bitter on the tongue, then a warm sensation as his blood vessels constricted, flowering into something sweet and calm that made the salon outside their booth fade to nothingness.

They remained like that for several minutes. Ben took periodic puffs while Sapphire caressed him, breathed softly in his ear, and coaxed him into ever deeper draws. Then she lowered him gracefully onto his back, with maternal tenderness, so that his head was resting on her lap and sinking into the folds of her robe.

She smiled at his bloodshot eyes. 'Would you like to continue somewhere more… secluded?'

Ben nodded, mirroring Sapphire's radiant expression with a sleepy smile. She helped him to his feet, brushed the ash from his lapel, and guided him out with one arm linked through his. Upstairs was a corridor perfumed with agarwood and patchouli, lined with doors that led to private pleasure rooms. Sapphire unlocked one of the doors and ushered Ben in.

'Make yourself comfortable,' she gestured to the single bed in the corner of the room. 'I will be just a moment.'

Ben perched on the edge of the bed and hung his head between his knees. But as soon as the door clicked shut, and he heard the lock latch with it, his eyes snapped open. He straightened up, adjusted his collar and surveyed the room. It was seedy, stripped bare – just the bed, a sink, a stained mirror, and a bedside table with a melted candlestick.

So far, so good. Now he simply needed to wait.

He caught his distorted reflection in the mirror. A pang of nausea rippled through his gut. That was the opium at work. He would have preferred not having to take it at all, especially when he was on the job. He steadied himself with a calming breath.

Footsteps came thudding down the corridor outside. If Sapphire was there, she could not have been alone. He resumed his position at the edge of the bed, slumped forward, fists clenched.

The key slid into the lock – then a turn – a click – a creak as the door edged open. More footsteps, now tentative, and another creak as the door shut once more.

After that, there was only silence, until a throaty cough jolted the room back to life.

'Eyes up, Englishman.'

Two men stood before him: Chinese, one in a rumpled suit, the other in a hemp jacket. They were both bald and thin, with pale skin and yellowed teeth.

'So that's what flower girls look like without their makeup,' Ben chuckled.

Rumpled Suit joined in with Ben's laughter, baring a gap-toothed grin. Then he flicked open a spring-fired switchblade and raised it to Ben's face.

'Moneybags. Put the pouch on the table or I'll take the weight of the coins in flesh.'

'But lads,' Ben shot back, 'how am I going to get back home? I need a carriage.'

'You'll need a hearse if you don't do as you're told.'

Rumpled Suit took another step towards Ben, while his mute companion slid a hand into his back pocket. Ben knew that posture: a shooting stance. He had to act quickly.

'I'm sorry…' Ben shrugged. 'Maybe it's the opium, but I can't hear you. You're going to have to speak up.'

The knife was a few inches from Ben's cheek.

'I said,' Rumpled Suit hissed, 'put the money on the—'

Ben did not give him the satisfaction of finishing his threat. He grabbed Rumpled Suit by the wrist, twisted it back, and slammed the base of his palm into his elbow joint. In a flash, the knife had clattered to the floor and Rumpled Suit had joined it, curled up and clutching a broken arm. Hemp Jacket whipped out his revolver, but before he could fire a shot Ben landed a piledriver of a punch to the jaw. The man collapsed in a heap and Ben snatched the gun from him. He flipped open the cylinder, but it was empty.

Ben sighed, almost disappointed. 'Chaps! I expected more of a fight.'

The men were too busy writhing on the floor and nursing their wounds. Ben swung the door open. Sure enough, Sapphire was standing in the corridor. She was shocked to see Ben emerge unscathed.

'You,' he said, gesturing with the empty revolver. 'In.'

Sapphire obliged. Ben grabbed both men by the scruff of the neck. 'And you: out.'

Ben chucked them out and bolted the door shut. He turned to Sapphire.

'What do you take me for?' he seethed. 'I've been hanging around opium dens since I was eighteen years old. I know how you people do business. Sure, the English girls aren't as imaginative as the Hong Kong variety, but it's all the same tricks. Lure in young men who flash enough cash to make it worth your while, tease them with a bit of singsong, guide them by the manhood into your chambers, and rob them blind. But I suppose it's a convenient racket. They wouldn't dare tell their families they were mugged by a woman of the night.'

'Exactly,' she replied. 'Everybody wins. They keep their dignity; we keep their money.'

'And that's what I was banking on. What, you think I show off that kind of money for fun? No. This…' He waved his pouch of money. 'This was just bait to get you alone.'

'And what are you going to do now?'

Sapphire looked as though she was preparing for the worst. But all Ben did was take out his wallet and extract his identification papers, bearing the stamp of both the British government and the Hong Kong police department.

'I could do many things. I could have you arrested for your antics and leave you to rot in a jail cell.'

'It was Madame Xu who put me up to it—' Sapphire blurted in a panic.

'Or…' Ben silenced her with a wave of the hand, 'I ask you straight questions, you give me straight answers, and there would be no reason at all for me to put you away. Sound fair?'

Sapphire looked about in vain for an escape. But it was no use. 'The door is bolted and you're in my way,' she said. 'So it looks like I don't have much of a choice, do I?'

'Let's start with your name and age,' Ben removed his pocketbook and a pencil. 'And none of this "Sapphire" claptrap.'

'If you must know, my real name is Liang Yue. I'm twenty-one years old.'

'Family?'

She shook her head. 'No parents. Just my younger brother. And my husband.'

'And your husband is comfortable with your line of work?'

'What?' she snorted. 'A whore doesn't deserve love?'

'And how long have you been doing this?'

Liang hesitated, then pursed her lips. 'Longer than you would probably like to know.'

Any hint of Liang's previous performance had slipped away. The same face, the same makeup, the same hairstyle – but the eyes revealed an unspoken pain beneath the surface of the thinly drawn character of 'Sapphire the Flower Girl'.

'Who were those two men who paid you a visit last week?'

'You'll have to narrow it down,' Liang snorted. 'I'm paid daily and nightly visits by all sorts of men.'

'You know which ones I'm talking about. You were dancing. Then two men came in from the rain and took you to one side for a private chat. And you came out looking like you'd seen the Grim Reaper. Who are they?'

'I don't know them.'

Ben narrowed his eyes at her. Liang's lies were wearing thin. She sighed in frustration. There was no way out of this bind but to tell Ben the truth. She took a seat on the edge of the bed and Ben pulled up a chair opposite her.

The men, so she claimed, were associates of her husband. The tall one was Aiguo, and his friend with the beard was Zirui. Until that night, not a word had passed between her and them. In fact, she had seen them only once before: a stormy night the previous summer, appearing without warning at the door of the home that she shared with her husband and brother. She had offered to make them tea, but her husband outright refused. Instead, he dragged Aiguo and Zirui out into the garden, under the bough of their ginkgo tree, to talk in private. Liang had watched them from the window, but their voices were drowned out by the rain, and it was too dark to read their lips. After a short while, the two men took their leave and her husband came back inside. He was drenched, shame-faced and withdrawn.

'That was the only strange thing,' she said. 'Usually my husband tells me everything. There are no secrets between us. But that night, he refused to answer a single question. It felt as though he was hiding something – either for his sake or mine.'

'And you never saw those men again?'

'No. Not until the other day.'

'And what about your husband?' Ben asked. 'What does he do?'

'He is a lawyer. An adviser for the Board of Works. They handle construction projects: waterways, bridges, palaces. He has always liked building things.'

'Name?'

'His name is Bo.'

Ben had been scribbling down Liang's information at speed, but that name brought his pencil to a jarring halt. His eyes flicked up to meet hers. Liang flinched, but she dared not say a word, even as Ben closed his pocketbook and drew closer to her.

'When those two men paid you a visit last week,' Ben said, 'it concerned Bo, didn't it?'

Liang's throat tightened. Her lips were sealed, but Ben detected the tiniest tremor.

'Bo left for Britain five months ago,' she said, her voice quivering. 'All he told me was that he had a posting there – but never any details. He promised me that Zirui and Aiguo would accompany him, that he would be back by the summer solstice. But Zirui and Aiguo appeared that night at The Floating Life without him, and they told me… that he had vanished. That they had no choice but to leave him behind.'

The look on Ben's face was grave – like a mourner watching the coffin being lowered into the ground.

The question spilled out from Liang like an errant breath: 'What happened to him?'

Ben clasped his hands and looked to his knees. 'He is dead, Liang. I'm sorry.'

Liang's reaction was instant and visceral, as though she had known it was coming and was waiting to release the grief that had been quietly eating away at her. She buried her head in her hands and started sobbing uncontrollably.

'How…?' she choked through her tears.

Ben recounted the whole saga to Liang, step by step, blow by blow: from the killings, to their first encounter on Hopkins Street, to Bo's confession and final act of defiance. All the way through, Liang was shaking her head, as if the gesture could erase reality.

'It's impossible,' she said. 'Bo was a decent, honest, hard-working man. He is not capable of what you've described.'

'He confessed to it. He gloated over it.'

'Then that man was not my husband. Even if he had his face, his voice, his name… that was not Bo, but a devil in his form.'

'Well,' Ben said, 'devil or not, your husband and his two associates stand accused of conspiracy and mass murder. Why do you think I've come all this way? For a harmless little jaunt? Bo opened up a vortex that is slowly consuming everything and everyone in its orbit. And I'm here to put a stop to it.'

Liang's expression sobered. That glint of fiery resolve in Ben's eyes told her everything. This was no routine police interrogation. Her entire life as she knew it had changed and she was deep in uncharted waters.

'Now tell me the truth,' Ben pressed, 'Where are Aiguo and Zirui?'

'I don't know.'

'Why did Bo do what he did?'

'*I don't know!*'

Ben leant in and lifted her chin so that they were face to face, mere inches apart.

'If you're lying to me,' Ben said, 'if you're more involved in this than you're letting on, I *will* find out. That much I can promise you.'

Her makeup ran in streaks down her cheeks. Her breaths came out in shudders. Ben could practically feel her heart pounding through his fingertips. But she held firm.

'I don't care for your investigation, Mr Canaan. All I wanted was a peaceful, happy life far away from this cesspit of an island. Bo promised me that we would do it, that we were closer than ever. And now what do I have? *Nothing.* No future, no hope, no escape. And you sit there and tell me that the one true thing in my life – the man I loved – was someone that I never really knew. I'm the one who has been lied to, not you.'

Liang abruptly got up and made for the door.

'If you'll excuse me, I have to get back to work before Madame Xu gets suspicious.'

Ben grabbed her by the arm. 'We're not finished.'

She snatched herself away. 'I believe we are. And don't grab my arm like that again, Mr Canaan, or it will not end well for you.'

'Two can play at a game of threats, and mine are far less pleasant than yours.'

Liang scoffed right at him. 'You British are all the same. You walk all over us because you don't see us as people – just a means to an end. No different from the earth you dig or the seas you sail.'

'I don't fight for you,' Ben darkened. 'You're a suspect. I fight for the people whose lives have been lost, who never had a chance to stand up for themselves.'

'No, you fight for your paymasters in London – the same men who fatten themselves on our labour. You wouldn't even be here if it were not for them. Taking their marching orders. Bowing and kissing the ring, your mouth full of "Yes, my lords" and "Thank you, sirs". You're a glorified errand boy who's tricked himself into thinking that he's doing God's work.'

Ben was in half a mind to keep arguing with her, but he let her last few jabs slide.

'I have it on good authority,' he said, 'that Hokoa – the great Chinese trade baron, self-styled king of silk and tea – is one of your clients.'

'And on whose authority might that be?'

'My own two eyes,' Ben cut her off sharply. 'I saw you tending to him last week, so you can spare me the theatrics. I need a private conference with him. It's urgent.'

Liang leant back against the wall. 'Dear Hokoa is a law unto himself. I don't have that kind of power over him.'

'I thought no man could resist the temptation of a good flower girl.'

'Not when she isn't properly incentivised.'

'I'll pay you three pounds if you can secure a rendezvous,' Ben said.

'Seven.'

'Five.'

Liang stuck out her hand. 'Deal. And if I do that for you, I expect you to leave me and my brother alone for good. Understood?'

'I would like nothing more.'

'Excellent. Now what say you unlock this door and let me get on with my evening?'

Ben obliged. Before they parted ways, he gave her a card with his address at Mount Austin, telling her to notify him as soon as she had confirmation from Hokoa.

He returned to the parlour downstairs. He was about to take his leave – but something made him hesitate. He thought back to the image of Liang sitting on the edge of the bed, desperately wiping away tears that would not abate. Lost and alone, as bewildered as he was: just another solitary figure groping through the labyrinth, blind to the forces acting upon her.

He tracked down Madame Xu, who was busy flogging a flower girl to another customer. As soon as she recognised him as the young man with the pot of money in his pocket, he had her undivided attention.

'How much does Sapphire bring in for one week here?' he asked.

Madame Xu sucked her thumb. 'Five pounds and ten shillings, I would say.'

Ben knew it was likely half of that amount, but he did not quibble. He handed Madame Xu the stated amount. 'Give her the week off and her cut of the money.'

Before Madame Xu could even say thank you, Ben was out the door. He had done his part. Whether he could obtain an audience with Hokoa, for better or for worse, was now up to the flower girl.

11

The End of the Seven Gentlemen

Ben spent his nights that week trawling through the evidence. His best work always came in the small hours. Maybe it was an excuse to avoid the dreams that plagued his sleep, or a pretext to nurse the Overholt that he kept on his desk by the balcony. Maybe it was the need for a habit of any sort – for want of opium, a new poison: witness statements, sketches, daguerreotypes, autopsy reports, lurid and violent accounts of dead men.

Every document from the boxes that Fitzjohn had transported to Mount Austin had found its rightful place on the wall opposite his bed. He came to enjoy nothing more than those long meandering hours by candlelight, on his back at the foot of his bed, gazing in silence at this spider's web that he had painstakingly pieced together. He took pride in his handiwork, obsessing over it when he was alone, drifting back to it in his mind's eye when he was in company. He would begin each day by tracing his index finger around each lead, as though casting a spell to draw out their secrets.

First there was João Gilberto Lalé. Ben had been able to track down the remains of his ship *The Beatriz*, crumbling in a warehouse along the dry docks of Sai Wan. The port authority had been trying to offload the ship to a buyer, but it was not for the taking. The ship, so it was claimed, was cursed, ever since it had been found drifting like the *Flying Dutchman* across the high seas – strewn with corpses bloated from the heat and picked at by hungry gulls.

The official story ran that there were no survivors, but Ben noticed a discrepancy in the personnel logs: the body of a line cook by the name of Lucky Nelson, a freedman from Jamaica, had never been recovered. He was assumed to have slipped overboard, but a conversation with the Hakka stevedores at Sai Wan revealed that Lucky was alive and in hiding. He was determined to keep a low profile: being the sole survivor of the massacre and a black man meant that the English colonial authorities were more likely to treat him as a scapegoat than as a victim.

The stevedores directed Ben to a shelter run by the Basel Missionary Society in Stanley, on the south side of Hong Kong Island, where Lucky had apparently taken refuge. Ben found him in a lonely corner of the refectory, head down and keeping to himself. It was a convenient arrangement: Lucky had a regular supply of hot food and a roof over his head, and all he needed to do in return was feign interest in the daily sermons of overzealous preachers with dreams of turning the whole of China to Christ, one soul at a time.

It took some cajoling before he would speak to Ben, agreeing only on the condition that Ben would not reveal his whereabouts to the authorities.

'We were sailing back from Kolkata with a consignment,' Lucky explained. 'I ask no questions 'bout Lalé's business, but I heard it was one of them opium shipments. They do the big auctions in Kolkata and the merchants buy it up to sell to the Chinamen. The cargo that day was the biggest all year for the firm – real pricey stuff. So Lalé wanted to make sure it had safe passage. It vexed them supercargoes but that was just old Lalé's way.'

Safe passage, however, was not on the menu for *The Beatriz*. Not far from its landing point on the archipelago, Lucky peered out the porthole to see about a half a dozen pirate boats descend on Lalé's galleon. In a flash, they had been boarded. Lucky hid in the pantry as the pirates laid waste to the crew and scoured the ship for any stragglers. There was no bargaining, no conversation, no pleading – just summary executions, one after another.

Lucky caught a glimpse of only one of the attackers, whom he spied through the keyhole of the pantry. A man dressed all in black, with a balaclava obscuring his face and a golden armband bearing the image of a snake. Exactly the same description as the men who had firebombed the Isle of Dogs.

From start to finish, the attack lasted about twenty minutes. Then a pall of silence fell over the ship. Not a soul stirred. The attackers had not bothered to dump the bodies in the sea. Instead, they had left them where they lay in their death throes: slumped against walls, face-down in pools of blood, folded over themselves in a macabre tableau mort. They had reserved the worst for Lalé himself: stripped naked and tied to the trunk of the main mast, his throat slit open to his spine, and the words BLACK BLOOD etched with a knife into his chest.

Lucky did not tarry. He took the ship's sole lifeboat and rowed out into open waters. He landed a week later at Gaolan Island, further west along the shores of China, and made his way on foot back to Hong Kong.

'It was worse than my wildest nightmares.' Lucky's eyes were wide as the memories seemed to play out before them. 'Now I see poor old Lalé's face in the dark corner of every room, and I hear the creaking of the mast in them silences when I'm alone. I may be alive, but death follows me wherever I go.'

'Do you have any idea who might want to do that to Lalé and his men?'

Lucky looked around furtively, checking for eavesdroppers.

'Opium is a dangerous business,' he said. 'Lalé presented himself as no different from the coffee and iron merchants, but make no mistake: opium was his trade. And that puts a target on a man's back, you see.'

'So these… pirates, let's call them… they were after the opium?'

'That's what I thought at first. But the more I think 'bout it, the stranger it seems. Usually pirates take the goods for themselves, maybe a few men as ransom too. But those pirates there, they killed us down to the man and threw the opium overboard. They took nothing neither. So where's the money to be made? They had no interest in it, you see.'

Lucky grabbed Ben's arm, as though he was back on that lifeboat, searching for land. The look on his face said it all: blind animal terror – a warning.

'They didn't come for money,' Lucky whispered. 'They came with a *vengeance*, sir. They came for *blood*.'

The ferry to Macao took longer than expected. But that just gave Ben more time to drink in the sight of the Pearl River: clippers weaving round the islands that protruded from the silvery waters; the mouth of the river further north, where the estuary narrowed past the forts of Xin'an County and split off into innumerable smaller tributaries. Every few minutes, merchant ships hailing from Britain, America, Malacca, India and more would ring their bells – a signal to the stevedores manning the harbours that fresh consignments had arrived. The entire delta had given itself over to commerce, ceaseless and striving, where each sailor would look to the next as his rival.

Portugal had been using Macao as a strategic trading post with the Great Qing for centuries before the British even dreamed of acquiring Hong Kong, and it showed. The colony sported public buildings and shopfronts across the Praia Grande in the Portuguese colonial style, spilling inland into an agglomeration of terracotta rooftops and brightly coloured façades, a homage to the sun-baked shores of Lisboa. Hills protruded from the urban sprawl, topped with lighthouses and in one case the ruins of a Jesuit cathedral, its cross casting a shadow over the treetops.

Somewhere on one of these hills was the estate of Félix de Morèse: the younger brother of the late Oberon, now executor of the massive fortune that had been amassed in the Morèse name. But it was not the olive-skinned, full-cheeked uncle enjoying the fruits of the elder Morèse's labour that had drawn Ben across the Pearl River, but rather Félix's niece: fifteen-year-old Lucile, daughter of the murdered magnifico, and the sole survivor of the horrors that befell the place that she had formerly called her home. Once she came of age, Lucile was bound to be one of the wealthiest and most eligible young women in the hemisphere. But for now, she led a reclusive life under Félix's wing, seldom seen in public as she came to terms with her loss.

Ben had managed to win a private conference with Lucile after some great effort, and only with Coldwell's intervention.

Even then, it came with conditions. He had thirty minutes at most and Félix would sit by her side. If at any point Lucile became overwrought in recounting the events of that fateful night, Ben would promptly be sent on his way.

The day was already wearing on by the time he reached the grounds of Félix's estate: a green mansion house nestled behind a row of palm trees, with a tall turret attached to the side of the house where Lucile had her private quarters. He was made to wait on the veranda for an hour. It was only when the afternoon light deepened into a mellow shade of gold and the evening cicadas began their chirruping that an attendant ushered Ben inside.

He sat with Lucile in the parlour of the main house, decorated with vivid blue azulejo tiles and a Blüthner piano by the bay windows over the gardens. Lucile sat on a divan on the other side of a low glass table, hands crossed over her lap and her eyes to the floor; Félix had one hand on her shoulder, and a bodyguard stood by the door glaring a hole in the back of Ben's head.

'I remember it only in… patches,' Lucile said.

'It must be an appalling thing to have to recall,' Ben said with the utmost sympathy. 'I promise you that we will be as swift as possible.'

'And you are under no obligation, my dear,' Félix intervened, giving Ben a wary look.

'Of course. Just bear in mind, mademoiselle: what you say today may help other people avoid a similar fate.'

Lucile recounted what little she could salvage from the fog of that night. It had been a perfectly normal midweek evening: dinner with the family, along with her eldest sister Albertine's new husband, her father leaving early to work in his study as was his habit; then card games in the parlour, while Lucile went to the library down the corridor to fetch her copy of Dumas's *The Black Tulip*.

'The moment I picked up the book,' Lucile said, 'I heard an enormous crash at the front of the house. I stuck my head out the door to the library to see what was happening. At first I thought it was a silly joke by my sisters. But then… I saw them.'

'Who?'

'*The strangers.*'

Lucile retreated into herself. Ben looked at Félix, perplexed.

'The three men who broke in that night,' Félix explained, 'each armed with a short dao – those daggers given to soldiers in the Green Standard Army of the Great Qing.'

'Like horsemen of the apocalypse,' Lucile said.

She hardly got a look at the men. It all happened in the blink of an eye. Instead she just ran, as her mother's screams became more distant, until she could hear only the soft thuds of her slippers on the carpet. The family had a secret door in the chapel, in the west wing of the estate: one of the panels at the foot of the reredos behind the altar, which the Morèse children used in their games of hide-and-seek. Lucile hurried in, closed the door behind her and dropped down into the cavity below. That was where she stayed: in the crawl space under the floorboards of the chapel, peeking up through the narrowest of cracks at the glimmering candlelight of the altar.

'I thought I was alone,' Lucile continued. 'But then I heard the chapel doors open and the strangers entered, ushering the rest of my family in at knifepoint. They had them kneel by the altar, right above me. I dared not breathe.'

Lucile's mother pleaded with the men to spare the children, while her father tried to bargain by offering them money and protection from the police. For at least a minute, the men stood in silence. They were savouring the sight of the rich and powerful on their knees as they begged for mercy. These untouchables who had set themselves apart from the common man – brought swiftly back down to earth by the great leveller of the blade.

Finally, one of the men interrupted them. He spoke in Mandarin, which Lucile, a child of Macao, was able to follow in snatches.

'What did he say?' Ben asked.

'He addressed my father,' Lucile replied. 'He said there was no amount of money that could tempt them. That God was on their side and that all the riches of the world lay with Him. My father called them false shepherds: that true men of God would not harm other people, let alone in the house of God. But the men seemed… unmoved. Possessed by an unshakeable conviction. They believed that they were doing God's will – that my father was the false shepherd – that his blood had to be shed for the old world to be burned to the ground, and the new world to be born from its ashes.'

Ben thought back to Bo's words in his cell at Whitehall Place: the same messianic rhetoric – the mantras of religious fervour – the immovable dogma of faith. The one thing from which no man could be dissuaded.

'Did they say at any point why they had come? Why your family in particular?'

'I didn't understand everything… One of them said something about poison in my father's blood. A black poison infecting the land… And then they—'

Lucile broke off suddenly. She stifled a sob with her hand and doubled over. Félix spoke soothingly, reassuring her that she could stop if she wanted. But she shook her head, even as tears came streaming down her cheeks.

'That was the last thing they said…' she wept, 'before everything was lost.'

They started with the children. Lucile could not see what happened, but she could hear their sobs being snuffed one by one, each time eliciting anguished wails from her parents. Then their wailing was interrupted by a final thud as their bodies dropped to the ground.

It was only when the police arrived the following morning that the full extent of the horrors became clear. Each member of the family had their heads almost entirely severed; the children and mother ranged in a semi-circle; and Oberon slumped over the altar, stripped shirtless to reveal the words BLACK BLOOD carved into his chest. The floorboards were pulled free to reveal Lucile, curled up and shivering, her face splattered with her own family's blood. They shielded her eyes with a blanket to spare her the sight of the bodies, and carried her away.

'I have not been back to that house since,' Lucile said in a taut whisper, as though she were afraid that if she spoke too loudly the strangers would find her again, 'and I never wish to go back. I hope it is destroyed, Mr Canaan, and that nobody may ever know it existed. The more I think about it, the more I wonder whether those men may have been right: maybe this land is cursed. Maybe it is poisoned. How else could God allow such senseless violence? We here on the Pearl River are nothing more than objects of His wrath.'

Ben returned from Macao to find a letter slipped under the door to his room at Mount Austin. The envelope had already been cut open with a paper knife. The letter ran to a few terse lines:

Fitzjohn admitted to leaving the letter there, having picked it up at reception, but he adamantly denied opening it, or seeing anyone else enter Ben's room in his absence. From then on, Ben insisted on collecting his own correspondence, which he kept in the padlocked safe in his room.

He rode to Victoria at the appointed hour. The Club Lusitano sat on a quiet side-street off Caine Road, separated from the thoroughfare by a steep flight of steps hemmed between a Baptist church and a taxi rank reeking of stale horse manure. But once Ben was inside, it was as though he had entered another world: walls draped with Tyrian purple velvet, aroma lamps flavouring the air with liquorice and cedar – enfolding Ben in a warm and gentle embrace.

He gave the name 'Wellington' to the woman at the front desk and was led into the main club. A man was waiting for him in a private booth: slight, rather gaunt, with a pronounced forehead and a bushy handlebar moustache that completely covered his lips. He had set two items on the table: his bowler hat and a small glass jug of clear liquor.

'LF, I presume?' Ben asked as he sat down.

The man said nothing, not looking at Ben until the woman at the front desk had slid shut the door to their booth.

'So you are the great British detective,' the man said,

extending a hand. 'Luuk Fontaine. I was deputy chairman of Van Hook's.'

'*Was*?'

'The firm is closing its China office. I am a casualty.'

'I'm sorry to hear that.'

Fontaine waved away Ben's consolation as though it were a bothersome housefly. 'It was inevitable. Geert's death cast a shadow over the enterprise. Nobody will do business with us – not our Western counterparts, nor our Chinese clients. They consider us afflicted with ill fortune. Perhaps we are.'

'I suppose that is what these killers are banking on,' Ben replied. 'Causing enough chaos to push people away from the China trade altogether.'

But Fontaine turned his beaked nose up at the suggestion. 'I would refine your hypothesis, Detective. Certainly, it is an assault on the China trade – but, more to the point, it is an assault on *opium*. After all, opium is the backbone of our business.'

Ben was taken aback by Fontaine's candour. 'I thought it was more about tea, silk, silver and spices.'

'Don't be naive,' Fontaine smirked. 'Those markets exist to lend respectability to the enterprise. But make no mistake: the China trade is subsidised by opium. That is how the Seven Gentlemen, Van Hook included, made most of their money. They ply the Chinese with the fruit of the poppy, and in so doing create a vast and insatiable market. By any conservative estimate, ten per cent of China habitually uses opium. That is forty-five million people who would sell their kidney or prostitute their own children for a bit of dross – *yanhui*, they call it – made from the recycled ash of already smoked opium. Is it any wonder that their people, after all these years, have deemed the status quo intolerable? "The Seven Gentlemen" is the most cursed epithet in China. It was only a matter of time before it all started to catch up with them.'

Ben was reminded of his meeting with Halliday – that effortless toothy smile as the word 'substances' dripped from his mouth; of Bo's allusions to 'black blood'; of the 'poison' running through Oberon de Morèse's veins. A world with such a rotten core, with an evil so deeply entrenched, that only annihilation would suffice to fix it.

'And that's what happened to your boss, isn't it?' Ben asked.

Fontaine nodded gravely. Van Hook was a mountain of a man, as loud as he was large. Quick to anger, slow to forgive. A braggart and a bully, he brought his love for big game hunting with him into business: always looking for the kill. But the gruesome murders of Lalé and de Morèse were enough to frighten even a man of Van Hook's constitution.

'He never told me how,' Fontaine said, 'but he was able to establish contact with the killers, in hope of negotiating a truce. He always fancied himself as a grand dealmaker. The day he disappeared, he left me a note: that he was sailing up the Xi River to a rendezvous point, though he would not say where. We never heard from him again.'

After a fortnight, Van Hook's corpse was found in the forests outside Wuzhou by a local pig farmer scouring for truffles, about two hundred miles from Hong Kong. He was suspended by rope fifty feet up in the canopy overhead, stark naked, beaten to a pulp, his belly sliced wide open and emptied of his guts.

'And not long after that, I received this note on my doorstep…' Fontaine handed Ben a slip of paper. The handwriting was immaculate, almost as though it had been printed, reading:

'The blood is opium,' Ben murmured, 'the black blood that runs through the veins of the Great Qing.'

'And what we are witnessing, Detective, is the bloodletting.'

Fontaine's theory echoed Bo's own words. Disgruntled men from the rank and file of Chinese society, taking it upon themselves to tear up the established way of doing things, no matter the consequences. Ideologues motivated by the suffering of their countrymen to defy the will of commerce, to plough the field of tycoons and trading firms with salt. 'The destruction of opium, once and for all,' Ben echoed.

'Or worse, the creation of a vacuum for someone else to fill. That is my greatest fear: that these killers are seeking to drive out the British, the French, the Americans and their ilk, so as to create a new unchallenged monopoly. Different name, same beast.'

Fontaine popped open the bottle of liquor and poured himself and Ben a shot each.

'Either way,' he continued, 'it's not my problem anymore. Now that I have been relieved of my duties, I am free to go home – and that is precisely what I plan to do. I am on a boat bound for Rotterdam tomorrow morning, where I plan to live out the rest of my days with my two pups in what I hope to be a tedious retirement. So a toast is in order. Baijiu. Drink up.'

They clinked and knocked back their shots. Ben could not contain a wince. 'It's got a kick…' he said through gritted teeth, 'right back in the… oesophagus.'

Fontaine smirked. 'A putrid drink for a putrid place. I look forward to seeing the back of it. You should do the same.'

'You know, it's not the first time I've been told that. And I have a tendency, for better or for worse, not to heed such warnings.'

'And how has that worked out for you?'

Ben leant across the table and poured himself another shot. 'Fontaine, I am one of Her Majesty's government's most prized agents, trusted to solve her most intractable problems. In the course of my service, I have seen half of Europe and an ever-growing portion of the rest of the world. I move in spheres that no Jew of my station could ever dream of entering. I am sought after by the great and the good. I live over a cricket ground in a leafy suburb with my cat. I dine in palaces and clubs with patrons who would have spat at me just for coming near. And this January past, I turned twenty-three. So… I'd say it's working out alright for me so far.'

Fontaine watched Ben knock back his second shot, which the young man made a point of not wincing at again.

'Pride comes before a fall, Mr Canaan,' Fontaine said with a wry smile.

They refrained from talking about business for the remainder of their rendezvous. Instead Fontaine spoke longingly of Rotterdam; of the canals on crisp winter mornings as the echoes of the Sunday bells bounced across the water; of the scent in mid-June of the *Hollandse Nieuwe*, when the streets filled with people dropping soused herring down their gullets; of his precious Claus, a water spaniel, and Hilda, a senior Pomeranian. They forgot about this sinking island in this sinking world, two new friends staving off the darkness with a moment of quiet reflection.

It was only when Fontaine took his leave that Ben asked the question that had been burning inside him. 'If you don't mind me saying so, Fontaine… You speak of your trade with disgust. You seem ashamed of it. Yet you devoted your life to it. How do you justify the endeavour to yourself, when you're alone with your thoughts and your conscience?'

'The same way you do, Detective. You serve the interests of those who wish to continue the China trade. You're hunting the men trying to wipe it out. How do you sleep at night?'

'I can't say I thought about it that way. I'm just doing my job.'

'Exactly. You don't think about it. They stuff your mouth with so much gold that, in the end, you can only speak through your backside.' He donned his bowler hat. 'But look on the bright side: they are fashioning you into one of their own. All the better for you. Good luck, Detective. Pray we never meet again.'

Ben was left alone to contemplate the baijiu. Just as Fontaine described it: a putrid drink for a putrid place. And yet he could not help but pour himself a third shot. Like his investigation, like Hong Kong itself, its ugliness made it all the more tempting. Maybe that was why the Seven Gentlemen had met their end: they too had fallen under the dark spell of this island and, try as they might, could not tear themselves away.

He knocked back the baijiu. He was already getting used to its taste.

12

The Pleasure Boat

Ben was having breakfast in the dining room at Mount Austin when he received Liang's letter. Hokoa, against all expectations, wanted to meet him. An audience was set for the following day at noon. Ben was to be picked up from Liang's home by Hokoa's page and taken to the Hong Kong Boating Club on Causeway Bay, where a private boat would be on standby.

Liang lived at 12 Tang Lung Street. It was a modest bunga-low with a thatched roof, set back behind a small garden lined with banyan trees. The grass had been choked by the heat, withered brown, and the soil was knotted with weeds. Stray chickens roamed about, congregating around Ben to peck the tip of his boots as he approached the front door where Liang was waiting.

She looked uneasy. One hand rested on the doorframe, while the other was balled into a fist at her hip. She had ditched the *aoqun* and opted for civilian clothes: a plain mottled-brown *shanku* jacket with a high collar, the kind typically worn by com-moners, and dark *ku* trousers. She wore no shoes or makeup, and her dark hair flowed freely to her shoulders.

Ben gave a conciliatory bow. 'A fine morning to you, my lady.'

'I'm preparing tea.' Her voice was warmer than her demeanour. 'Come in. Please take off your shoes.'

The bungalow was shoddy on the outside, but neat and orderly on the inside. The walls were decorated with handscrolls yellowed by age, depicting pastoral and maritime scenes. Long-necked ceramic vases bearing plum blossoms and bright azaleas populated the shelves, separated by long lines of books. If 12 Tang Lung Street was a window into Liang's soul, then the picture it painted was of precision, restraint, depth.

Ben sat on a cushion by the unlit hearth, breathing in the smell of oolong from the kitchen stove. He cast an eye across the room. A salt print sat on the mantlepiece above the hearth. Through the vague sepia-toned blur, Ben made out a man and a woman sitting at a café table: Liang on the left, and a man on the right whom Ben instantly recognised as Bo. Liang's expression was serious and intense, but Bo had a carefree smile, as if lightly amused by something that lay just beyond the frame.

Then, a voice: 'Are you English, sir?'

Ben looked up. The sliding doors at the far end were open a crack and a boy was peeking out. He looked to be about fourteen, on the smaller side, with large round spectacles. He was holding a bundle of parchment papers rolled into tubes.

Ben nodded and the boy took a few tentative steps towards him.

'And you speak English, sir?'

'I'd be a shoddy Englishman if I didn't,' Ben replied. 'My name is Ben.'

'My name… *Tao*,' the boy pressed his free hand to his chest. 'I practise… English – yes? I show you.' He sat down opposite

Ben and unfurled his papers: a column of words in English that Tao had to translate into Mandarin.

Tao gestured to Ben. 'You help?'

Ben peered at the first word in the column: *koo-shun*. 'Well, that says *cushion*, I think. But they haven't spelt it correctly. Here…' He wrote down the correct spelling. 'Cushion, see? Like this!'

He held up his pillow and Tao wrote out the translation. They worked their way through a few more words, before Liang returned with the tea. She issued a stern word to Tao in Cantonese, sending the boy off with his tail between his legs.

'I told him to stay in his room while you are here,' Liang said, setting Ben's oolong on the table before him.

'Afraid I'll teach him a few bad words?'

'I would prefer to keep my brother's involvement with government agents and murder investigations to a minimum… if that's acceptable to you.'

'Well, he seems like a nice enough boy,' Ben lifted the teacup to his lips. 'Bloody good oolong, by the way.'

Liang poured herself a cup. She was not eager for idle chatter. After all, this was a relationship of pure convenience. To Ben, she was but a stepping stone to Hokoa; and to her, he was an interloper who had passed into her life unasked for and was destined to pass just as swiftly out.

In the end, it was Ben who broke the silence. He reached into his pocket and pulled out a wad of money. 'Five pounds, as agreed,' he said, 'assuming this isn't another trick of yours.'

'That will not be necessary, Mr Canaan. I heard about your payment to Madame Xu. I am grateful for it – it gave me the week I needed to collect myself after the news that you brought.

Anything more and I would be indebted to you. And I vow to be in debt to no man.'

Another long, strained silence. Ben pocketed the money and sipped his tea.

'You have a lovely home,' he said.

'Bo bought it. He lived upriver in Canton, but this became our home. Given the social disparity between me and him, our relationship had to remain discreet. Nobody bothered us here. We could be ourselves.'

'What happened to the rest of your family?'

'We were in Henyang, further inland. Me, Tao, our parents. My father was a fisherman and our mother was a seamstress. It was a simple, peaceful life. But it was a place ruled by opium and that attracted the wrong kind of attention. The Governor sought to clamp down on the trade and sent in the army. It was supposed to be a routine door-to-door inspection. But as so often happens when *yāpiàn* is involved, it spiralled out of control. Almost every able-bodied person in our neighbourhood was tortured, killed, or made to vanish – including our parents. And so I was left alone, at ten years old, having to care for my infant brother as though he were my own.'

'And how did you end up in Victoria?'

'By sheer chance. We lived as vagrants for a year, migrating south to be closer to the water, where the jobs were. And that's how I met Madame Xu. She took me in at twelve with promises of money, glamour, powerful friends. She moulded me into what I am today and I went along with it because I had no choice, if Tao was not to starve. She taught me English – how to dance and sing – how to seduce – how to lie sweetly. And, above all, how to prepare opium to the satisfaction of her clients. I became well-known for my skills. That is why I am able to attract men like Hokoa to such a dismal place as The Floating Life. They call me "the diamond in the dirt" of Hong Kong.'

She let out an acerbic chuckle and refilled Ben's tea.

'Bitter irony, isn't it? Opium destroyed us, yet now it is the only thing keeping us alive. Even as it slowly kills us, we cannot survive without it. That is the story of China. Though one good thing did come of it…' She gestured to the salt print. 'My Bo. Can you believe: that meek, strait-laced, softly spoken man of the law was a client of mine? But he was different from the others. He was led into my arms by loneliness, not lust. And like two streams from different sources that meet in the same shallow pond, we filled out the gaps in each other's spirits. I don't care what you claim he did. The man I knew aspired not to violence, but to a better nation with a brighter future. Not just for himself, but for *us*.'

She removed a postcard from the folds of her *shanku* and slid it across the table. It bore an engraving of a picturesque town buried in a lush forested valley, on the banks of a winding river, below a resplendent sun.

'*Shangrao*,' she said, her voice trembling at the name. 'Neither of us have seen it, Mr Canaan, not but in our dreams. Yet we made a vow to one another that we would leave this vile trade behind and start a new life there. Now, without Bo, there is no point in going. The dream was not to go to Shangrao, but to go there with him.'

There were tears in Liang's eyes: not just of sadness, but also of anger. Outrage at the dream having been snatched from her at the eleventh hour; at being given the opportunity to taste love, only for it to be taken away forever. As a flower girl, she was forced to wear a mask of breezy indifference. But she was a woman in pain, a deeper pain than Ben could imagine.

'I know we got off to an awkward start,' Ben said, 'But I share in your sorrow, Liang. I wouldn't want anyone to suffer what you have suffered.'

Liang seemed unmoved by his sympathy. Her lips contorted in a subtle sneer. 'It's your trade, Mr Canaan. If there weren't murders to solve, what would you do with yourself? It's just like opium. Nobody wants to say it's their traffic, but they need it. Whether it's to make money, or have a purpose, or simply feel alive – we profit from evil. Every. Single. Day.'

She took back the postcard of Shangrao. Not a minute later there came a knock at the front door: Hokoa's page Runchu had arrived. The boy walked Ben down to the Boating Club on Causeway Bay, where the summer regatta was in full swing. Hong Kong's rarefied elite – those well-heeled denizens of the lofty estates on Kennedy Road and the Peak – had descended to the waters for a balmy afternoon of champagne and cold meats.

A long, sleek wooden boat by the name of *Yóuchuán* was moored at the pier. Oarsmen sat at either end with their legs dipped in the water, resting after a long day of rowing like a pack of exhausted dogs. A chef manned a live stove, grilling freshly caught seafood. And in the middle was a private box ringed by half a dozen bodyguards, its curtained walls burnished with intricately painted blue and yellow dragons.

The bodyguards frisked Ben before waving him into the box. Hokoa was ensconced inside, reclining on a set of padded cushions, midway through a hit on his opium pipe as a flower girl massaged his temples. He was unchanged: the mutton chops, the dark glasses, his pink facial scar, his distinctive silver cane.

As soon as he saw Ben, his opium-induced lethargy evaporated. He brushed himself off and gestured with a puckish smile for Ben to sit down.

'Come in, Mr Canaan – don't be shy!' he bellowed. 'May I call you that? "Mr Canaan"? Or is "Detective" the preferred mode of address?'

'Either is fine by—'

'My apologies, I am just so… titillated! This is a real mystery. Ripped straight from the pages of the Gothic tales that I so enjoy by the late Mr Poe – but he was American, wasn't he? I don't suppose you've read him?'

'I'm more of a Thackeray man—'

'Never mind, never mind! I'm speaking nonsense – *piffle*, as you English might say. I shall call you "Detective". It adds to the intrigue. Are you hungry? I hope you are. A feast is underway – and not just of the culinary variety…'

He opened a golden chest to reveal the glossiest, most pristine opium that Ben had ever laid eyes on.

'This is no mere *yāpiàn*,' Hokoa said, practically salivating. 'This is the *mafen* variety, native to Guangdong. A bit of local flavour!'

He turned to his flower girl.

'My dearie, would you be so kind as to heat some up for myself and the detective?'

While the *mafen* was being prepared, Hokoa waxed lyrical about the *Yóuchuán*. It was his precious 'pleasure boat', which he took out once a month for a round trip of the Pearl River Delta, from his base in Qing-controlled Canton to Hong Kong and back again. Good for business, he claimed – a chance to cast an eye over his firms along the shores of the Pearl River and make his presence felt as the grand old man of the China trade. Though this reasoning smacked of falsity. Ben saw no indication of any interest on Hokoa's part to peer beyond the curtains of his box, more taken up with his pipe than with commerce.

Ben joined for the final leg of the journey, back to Canton. For the first interminable hour, Hokoa regaled Ben with tales of his meteoric trajectory to the top of Chinese society: from a troublesome anti-establishment malcontent, dropping out of school to work odd jobs in the Guangdong countryside; to a low-level Plain Blue bannerman in the Qing army; rising through the ranks to general by the age of just forty; and parlaying his successful military career into a wildly lucrative business as southern China's most powerful merchant.

'Now,' he said, laying a hand on his chest with a theatrical flourish, 'I am wealthier, I daresay, than the Emperor himself. Though other parts have, alas, failed me – my eyes, most notably. Deteriorated from the constant flash of gunpowder in my military days. It left me sensitive to light. Hence the protection and my… *aversion* to sunshine.'

The food arrived: a thick stew made from bighead carp fried in red chillies; clams drenched in a sticky black bean sauce; stir-fried enoki mushrooms on a bed of green onion pancakes; and rice wine flavoured with ginger and tamarind to wash it down. Hokoa was voracious, alternating between messy gulps of stew and hits of the opium pipe.

'How I have been looking forward to this little confabulation,' Hokoa declared, using a scallion pancake to wipe his lips clean. 'Every good mystery requires a few grisly murders, and by Jove we are spoiled for choice! Not to say that it isn't tragic, of course. I have spent more on consolatory fruit baskets in the last few months than in all my years. But Fate, in all her wonders, has kept me alive for a greater purpose. And our introduction made me realise what that is: *to help you unravel the mystery.*'

Hokoa's enthusiasm was endearing. Ben knew this type. Too rich, too sedate, too comfortable. A life transformed by wealth into a lazy routine: meetings here and there, numbers in contracts, leisure without purpose and without end, the gradual onset of ennui. Now, to fill the emptiness between gourmet meals and hollow flattery, Hokoa had nothing else to do but snatch at glimmers of excitement like fireflies in the dark. Ben could see it writ large on his face. This was a game, only one level above mahjong or rummy.

'You've made your fair share of enemies, haven't you?' Ben said with a smile.

'It is inevitable in my line of work.'

'Odysseus Halliday said much the same thing,' Ben stirred his stew with his chopsticks. 'After all, opium is a dangerous business…'

Ben and Hokoa stared at each other. At first, Hokoa was frozen like prey realising that it had been caught. Then he mirrored Ben's smile. 'I see the veil has been pulled from your eyes, Detective.'

'It required a little effort. Most people in these parts seem happy to dance around the fact that you and the rest of the Seven Gentlemen are opium magnates.'

'I make no bones about it. The others are – or *were* – less honest: speaking in euphemisms, winks and nudges. The China trade is all about keeping up appearances. But you are right, of course: in my world, danger emanates from every angle.'

'Above all from your own countrymen,' Ben said pointedly. 'How must they feel, seeing you make your fortune from a drug that has turned your nation into a society of addicts?'

'I am quite sure they spit poison on my name. As is their right. The Great Qing have a long and storied history of battling against the influence of opium. Take, for example, the war they fought against you British less than two decades ago to drive opium out altogether – a war they roundly lost. The only reason they haven't turned on me yet is because, much as they hate to admit it, they need me. The revenue generated by our precious *yāpiàn* flows not just into my pockets, but into the government coffers of the Great Qing, to fund its armies, build its bridges, smelt its iron. That is why they call it *yao qian shu*: the tree of ancient legend that sheds silver coins when shaken.'

Hokoa cut a relaxed figure as he casually dismissed a generation of grievances. He had the same confidence as Halliday and Lennie Glass: that money alone was enough to save his skin, by tying tongues and bending others to his will.

'But what if there are people out there who cannot be bought?' Ben asked. 'Motivated not by money, but by dogma. They don't want your riches. They want to destroy you.'

For the first time all afternoon, Hokoa grew darkly serious. 'I do not believe that such people exist, Detective. For they too have paymasters. So, even unwittingly, they act as pawns in someone else's struggle for wealth and power, to which they themselves are blind.'

Hokoa removed his glasses to reveal cloudy-grey pupils and raw skin around the folds of his eyes, cracked from years of scarring.

'It is curious though…' Hokoa purred. 'Bartholomew Swanson said almost exactly the same thing as you, when he came to see me the week before he died.'

Swanson. Ben knew that name: Halliday's supercargo, the one found washed up on the shores of New Lewis. Hokoa was bristling with enthusiasm. After an hour of digging, they had struck a seam of gold.

'What did Swanson want from you?'

Hokoa gleefully set the scene. 'It was a chilly night in late March. We were sailing up the Humen and he was sitting right where you are now. Pale, anxious, petrified. As though he had seen the face of death and knew that it was waiting for him, right around the corner. He had come, so he said, to warn me. That the waters of the Pearl River had turned against the Seven Gentlemen and the tide was swelling up to sweep us all away. That the Black Blood murders were not random, but a coordinated campaign, calculated to transform the opium trade forever.'

Ben copied down Hokoa's statement. So that was what had got Swanson killed. Like Ben, he had been piecing together the fragments of this puzzle, one lead at a time, and he simply knew too much. His knowledge was the catalyst for his death.

'Did he know anything about the perpetrators themselves?'

'Just a name. Rumours of one "Ames": someone on the inside, who had infiltrated the inner circles of the China trade and was funnelling them information.'

'"Ames"? But no clue as to who this might be?'

Hokoa shook his head. 'A ghost, Detective. Just another face in the crowd.'

Ben racked his brains for any mention of an 'Ames' in the evidence, but nothing came to mind. More likely than not it was an alias. But the implication for Ben's case made his blood run cold: not that he had never met Ames, but that he may already have met him without even realising.

'So you see, this is a war on multiple fronts,' Hokoa said. 'Nobody can really be trusted – not even the Seven Gentlemen whom you have sworn to protect. Ultimately we are all rivals in a ruthless market, vying for supremacy over the unruly dragon that is the Great Qing, and governed by one unshakeable rule of nature…' Hokoa took another hearty puff and exhaled a ripple of fragrant smoke. '*To the victor go the spoils.*'

By the end of the afternoon, the pleasure boat reached Canton harbour. There was no trace of colonial influence here: no streets named after British colonial officers, no municipal buildings modelled on fashionable European styles. Manchu bannermen loped about in plain red uniforms, armed with bows and arrows and sheathed swords, cigarettes dangling from their lips as they brushed flecks of ash from their carefully groomed moustaches. Penetrating the salty sea air was the aroma of soy sauce and fried garlic, from food stalls serving fresh shaobing flatbread to the legion of stooped and sweating sailors piling in from the crammed piers.

An entourage was waiting on the jetty where they moored. There were about a dozen or so men in yellow, blue and red robes – the ceremonial colours of the Great Qing. Leading the pack was an older man with a long narrow beard and wiry grey hair styled in a queue. He was dressed all in black with maroon beads draped around his neck, and his hands were tucked into folds over his belly.

'You'll have to excuse me,' Hokoa said to Ben. 'I have some matters to discuss with my friends.'

'Your friends being?'

'The man in black is Ye Mingchen, the Viceory of Lingguan. He was personally appointed by the Emperor in Beijing to protect Chinese interests across the Pearl River. The others are civil servants in his retinue: government officials, advisers, and the like. Give me a moment.'

Hokoa hobbled off the boat with the help of his bodyguard to greet Ye Mingchen. The two men exchanged deep bows and began talking in an undertone.

Ben leant out the side of the box to get a closer look at the entourage. They were stony-faced, tight-lipped, motionless. But one of them gave Ben pause – standing out because he alone was looking back at Ben out the corner of his eye. He was instantly recognisable. His tall stature. His gaunt, clean-shaven face.

It was Aiguo. One of the two men that Ben had tailed from London. Ben's prime suspect. And here he was, standing just a stone's throw away – embedded in the ranks of the Great Qing, with the ear of the Viceroy and by extension the Emperor. The man that Ben had been pursuing all this time was a high-ranking government official of the Great Qing.

Aiguo acted as though he had not seen Ben. But both men knew in that moment that the jig was up. Ye Mingchen led Hokoa and his entourage back to the train of carriages waiting for them on the esplanade. A boat was summoned to take Ben back to Hong Kong – a trip that he spent in tense silence, staring out across the Pearl River as night fell and plunged the watery expanse around him into darkness.

He arrived at Mount Austin just as the hotel was starting to wind down for the night. But he had no intention of sleeping. Instead, he made a beeline for Fitzjohn's door. He found his aide already in his pyjamas, nursing a hot toddy and a piece of gingerbread.

'Mr Canaan?' Fitzjohn mumbled. 'Whatever is the matter?'

'Alert Coldwell and Bowring,' Ben said, patting Fitzjohn on the cheek. 'By heaven, I think I know what's going on here!'

13
Saints and Sinners

They gathered at dawn in a boardroom at Government House. Ben stood at the head of the blackwood table with a map of the Pearl River unfolded before him. To his right was Coldwell, looking sharp as ever; to his left was Governor Bowring, still bleary-eyed and nursing a strong coffee.

'Lalé, De Morèse, Van Hook, Glass, Ormrod, Hokoa, Halliday,' Ben said, pinning each name in a semi-circle around the mouth of the Pearl River. 'The Seven Gentlemen. Our access point into the world's largest market. It is through them that our goods pour into China. And what comes pouring out? Money. Endless silver.'

Ben marked this inflow and outflow with a series of arrows. Bowring was practically salivating as he gulped down the last of his coffee. 'A beautiful trade surplus,' he said.

'Now shift the perspective ever so slightly,' Ben continued, 'and ask yourself a different question: what are they to the Great Qing?'

He turned the map on its head. Now the three of them were staring south towards the mouth of the Pearl River, which was barricaded from the outside world by those names.

'They are a steel vice with a stranglehold over the China trade. A coalition of foreign interests, flogging foreign drugs and foreign goods, at the whim of faraway empires that seek to exploit the Chinese people. They tried to fight a war against it, and what happened?'

'They lost,' Coldwell said.

'Exactly. Now opium flows as freely into China as the Asiatic monsoon. And the Great Qing is powerless to stop it. That, my friends, is the greatest and most intolerable humiliation for the Great Qing. They have effectively lost control over their borders – over their land – over their waters – over their own people. So what do they do?'

Ben leant over the map, pinched the paper bearing Lalé's name, and ripped it out.

'Rather than open warfare against the British navy, which they are destined to lose, they engage in *covert warfare*. Strike out man after man, firm after firm…' He ripped out each name one by one. 'Soon enough the field is cleared. The Seven Gentlemen are no more – amputated from the body of China like a gangrenous limb. And the Emperor is free to reassert control over not just opium, but the China trade itself.'

By the end of his speech, the names of the Seven Gentlemen had been torn off – exposing the ragged mouth of the Pearl River to the sea that lay beyond.

'So long as the perpetrators are "unidentified", or "vigilantes", or "lone hands", the Great Qing has plausible deniability. But we know now that one of the killers is a Chinese government official, and another was an adviser to a government board. And if that means what I think it means, then what we have is a plot by the Great Qing to drive us out once more, without a cannon fired or a soldier despatched.'

'This is a scandal,' Coldwell said under his breath.

'No,' Bowring shot back. 'It's an act of war.'

A chill fell over the boardroom. Coldwell and Bowring, usually composed, now seemed perturbed. Four of the Seven Gentlemen had been killed. If Ben was right, then the Great Qing was already over halfway to its objective, and the remaining targets were fragmented and disorganised. They were on the backfoot.

'One more thing,' Ben said as he folded up the map. 'Does the name *Ames* mean anything to either of you?'

Bowring shook his head. Coldwell looked puzzled.

'I knew a Thomas Ames who lost his life in Sevastopol,' Coldwell said. 'But he was just a lad from Kildare. Nothing to do with the China trade.'

Ben went straight back to Mount Austin to carry on with his report for the Wetherton Inquiry. Word of his progress was relayed to Bruckner via Fitzjohn. No doubt the gist of Ben's news would make Bruckner and the PM's Westminster clique apoplectic. But as of yet, all Ben had were threads in the web. What he lacked was proof – hard and fast, incontrovertible, a bloody rag bearing the initials of the Great Qing.

A few days later, he received an unexpected invitation: a personal note from Ingrid Marshall, Odysseus Halliday's niece. Halliday had invited him for dinner aboard his steamer *Emmeline*, anchored a couple of hours by boat from Victoria, off the coast of Lintin Island. It promised, in Ingrid's words, to be a night of business and pleasure in equal parts. Whatever it was, Halliday had something in store for him, and Ben was not about to pass up the opportunity.

Ingrid met him at Victoria Harbour. The veiled shadow of a schooner took shape like fragments of a dream coalescing into a clear picture. Ingrid was standing at the prow, in mourner's black, her hand resting so lightly on the ropes connecting the mast to the bowsprit that she seemed almost to levitate.

'Good afternoon, Mr Canaan,' she said, with that characteristic humourless charm. 'I hear you've been busy.'

'Making hay while the sun shines.'

'You have the tan to show for it.'

Ben hopped on board and kissed Ingrid's outstretched gloved hand. 'Have you come to kidnap me then? I can't promise I'll fetch a tremendous ransom.'

'If you keep it up, I may have to throw you overboard free of charge.'

She turned to the handful of sailors manning the schooner, all Hong Kong locals with matted sea-swept hair, looking as though they had been fished out from the depths of the Pearl River Delta and left out to dry. She issued a command in Cantonese and they obeyed her without a moment's hesitation.

Ben sat with her on cushions nestled in an alcove under the mainmast. Champagne was already waiting for them in an ice bucket, along with a rack of oysters and cigars.

'Veuve Clicquot,' Ingrid said, handing Ben the bottle. 'I had a crate delivered by the widow Clicquot herself. Do the honours, why don't you?'

Ben gave her a wry look as he carefully eased out the cork. 'If I didn't know any better, I'd say you were trying to seduce me…'

'It's a commercial apéritif, Mr Canaan.'

'Is that what they call it now?'

'Well,' Ingrid placed an oyster shell to her lips and knocked it back, 'apéritifs tend to be followed by something you can really sink your teeth into—'

Pop! The cork went flying free and landed in the churning sea. Ben poured a couple of flutes. 'I guess we'll just have to finish this now, won't we?'

That proved to be no trouble. By the time they crossed the bays of southern Kowloon and entered the estuary, the champagne had been drained and the oysters polished off. Ingrid removed her gloves, unpinned her hair, and lit up a cigar. Once upon a time, her father would have told her that only whores smoked cigars. Now, as if to underline the provocation, she blew the wisps of smoke right at Ben, daring him to look at her take those slow, calculated puffs. Oddly enough, they never once talked business. Bystanders on passing brigs could easily have mistaken them for bright well-to-do young things deep in courtship.

Just before sundown, Ingrid leant over the railing, cigar still clenched between her teeth, and pointed north-west. 'There she blows!'

The mist had cleared and Lintin Island lay before them. Even from a distance, Ben could see that it was heaving with activity. The shore was almost entirely blotted out by an enormous fleet of hulks, permanently moored as anchorages for the storing and trading of goods. Circling them like worker ants around the queen were 'dragons': slim, streamlined galleys designed for speed and manoeuvrability. Sailors hauled man-sized crates through the foaming surf, while merchants and smugglers haggled on the terraces of haphazardly built trading offices. Sunbaked and wind-blasted, the island itself seemed to groan and creak under the weight of commerce.

A dragon whipped past them, weaving its way upriver. Ben caught a glimpse of its cargo: brick after brick of opium tightly packed into wooden crates. That explained the early evening frenzy. This was the beating heart of the opium trade – the organ pumping out the black blood of China.

'It all begins here,' Ingrid said, marvelling at her works like a young Ozymandias. 'We have our men buy up opium at auctions in Kolkata, Malacca, Bandar Abbas and Constantinople. Then they transport it to Lintin, where the handover to the Chinese smugglers takes place. Silver is exchanged for the goods and the smugglers sail via the waterways of China into the mainland, to sell the opium directly to the Chinese people.'

'Don't you worry about resistance from the Qing?'

'And what can they do, exactly? Their border officials are paid off. Hundreds of thousands of people across the Empire find gainful employment in some niche of the trade. And nobody is more eager than the consumers themselves. The silver we receive is paid into the East India Company treasury in return for bills of exchange, which we pocket for a tidy profit. That silver is then used to finance the purchase of tea from China, which boosts productivity, generates a healthy trade surplus, and facilitates the import of higher quality goods to meet the insatiable demand for tea back in Britain.'

Ingrid leant over and slid the cigar into Ben's mouth.

'Everybody wins. Deep breath.'

'I told you I don't smoke.'

'What if I asked especially nicely?' She ran her hands through his hair. 'It's just business, after all. We are doing what any person would do in our shoes.'

Ben took one quick puff. It was a Byron Selección 1850: oak, cocoa, pepper, cedar.

'Making hay,' he said.

'And once the sun goes down…' She snatched the cigar back. 'Anyway. You don't mind if we make a quick stop? We have a friend to pick up for dinner.'

They sailed round to the north shore of Lintin. It was quieter here. Palm trees circled the glassy waters of a tranquil bay. Cliques of sailors, peeling off from the melee on the south side, had strung hammocks a few feet up in the trees and dozed with their hats over their faces. A small yacht was moored on the beach, bearing the name *Kingdom of Heaven*.

But it was the scene on the beach that caught Ben's attention. About two dozen Chinese smugglers were kneeling in the sand. Loping back and forth through the surf before them was a preacher in a navy-blue *changshan*. One hand was raised with his index finger extended as though he were Michelangelo's Adam reaching for God, while the other clutched a pocket Bible. As they approached, his voice began to penetrate the ambient rush of the tide: fluent Mandarin, rising from a drawl to a passionate roar.

Ingrid and Ben landed on the beach and watched the preacher from the margins. As soon as he had finished, a couple of his acolytes rushed forward to distribute pamphlets to his audience. One of them shoved a copy in Ben's hands: a bilingual English–Mandarin tract called *On a Stranger's Love*. A quick glance told Ben everything he needed to know. The usual screed about giving up all material things in exchange for the mercy of Christ. At the bottom was the name of its author: FINLAY ARMSTRONG.

'Good evening, my dear,' came an American-accented voice.

The preacher was walking over to them. He was exceedingly tall and spindly, with an oval-shaped face as worn as a saddle, bony fingers, and curiously extended arms that seemed almost too long for his body. His gait was uneven, caused by a scoliotic spine pulling his right side higher than his left. But his expression, despite his obvious pain, was one of warmth and welcome.

'Good evening, Reverend Armstrong!' Ingrid embraced him with a kiss on each cheek. 'You are effortlessly charismatic as always. I trust you've had a productive day?'

'Eight souls,' he said with a shaky bow.

Ingrid made her introductions. Armstrong was a Baptist priest from Georgia, in the United States, but had spent the last two decades as a missionary in southern China. He had founded a church known as the Tabernacle of New China on Po Toi, one of the southernmost islands of the archipelago. From there, he had been slowly building a loyal congregation, with the goal of bringing Christianity to all of the Great Qing.

'And how do you know Halliday?' Ben asked.

'He is a man of faith,' Armstrong replied, 'and a valuable supporter of my little flock.'

'Darling Finlay is too modest,' Ingrid butted in. 'He has successfully converted thousands, possibly tens of thousands, of the Han and Manchu people. I daresay he has saved more Chinese souls than any individual on earth.'

Armstrong gave another bow. 'I could not have done it without the patronage of you and your uncle.'

The reverend joined them on Ingrid's boat and they set sail for the *Emmeline*, which hovered further west along the estuary. They stood port-side, watching the merchant ships congregate around Lintin for a long night of bartering.

'Interesting place to evangelise,' Ben remarked.

'I preach to lost souls, Mr Canaan,' Armstrong said. 'The Chinese smugglers – they're the ones who need to hear my message the most. Their lives are steeped in sin and hardship, and each smuggler individually knows hundreds of opium-eaters who may hear the good word by proxy. Tragic as it may be, it is the most effective way to water the garden of the faithful.'

Emmeline was a luxurious steamer, more fit for a royal retinue than for the private indulgence of one man. It had five salons, each with its own grand piano; a fully stocked bar and wine cellar; a library of three-hundred volumes; and a viewing platform offering a panoramic vista of the Pearl River. Each room was named after a royal burgh of Scotland, with the centrepiece dining hall bearing the title of Halliday's native Selkirk.

They dined beneath a sentimental portrait of the boat's namesake, Halliday's mother, reimagined in an epiphany of angelic youth. Tenderloin steak was on the menu tonight, with grilled long beans, dark-skinned Yunnan potatoes, creamed water spinach, and cognac. They were joined by a trio of Halliday's colleagues: the muscle Grant Parry, stabbing at his double helping as though he were back on the battlefield with his bayonet; William Bevan, editor of the Halliday-funded *Hong Kong Register*; and John Portishead, a banker with the East India Company.

Halliday had hit the cognac a little too hard and the booze was bringing out his braggadocious side. The guests listened politely as he extolled his exploits.

'I was a young man chartering my first ship to the opium auctions on the Indian coast. Back then, the boats were leakier than an old man's bladder and even mild winds in the wrong direction could send you reeling. So when the cyclones hit the Bay of Bengal, the other merchants would hang back and wait for them to pass. And me? What did I do? Any takers?'

Ingrid laid a hand on his arm. 'You sailed straight on, Uncle.'

'Damn right I did! I sailed into the mouth of the leviathan because I knew, if I could get there first, then I could snap up all the opium, empty the coffers, and scarper on back to Lintin before my rivals could even touch Indian soil. I put myself in the hands of the Almighty and accepted my fate. If I was destined to be killed, then so be it. But I never was, my friends. Every single time, I survived without so much as a scratch. That, gentlemen, is how I made my fortune: courage, conviction, creativity.'

He knocked back his cognac. It was barely down his gullet when he slammed his fist on the table and roared: '*Another!*'

One of the servants rushed forward with a fresh bottle. Ben studied the faces of Halliday's companions. Parry and Ingrid seemed indifferent – perhaps they were used to these outbursts. Armstrong swirled his cognac, unsettled by Halliday's vulgarity but not wishing to cause offence. Bevan and Portishead, meanwhile, were vaguely amused. But nobody seemed willing to defuse the awkward silence.

In the end, it was Portishead who gave in, eagerly changing the subject. 'What do we all think of this business with the Taiping?'

'The great rebellion in the north?' Bevan said. 'I for one think it's marvellous.'

Ben's ears pricked up. 'Sorry, what is the "Taiping"?'

The party looked at Ben incredulously. Ingrid intervened with a chuckle. 'Forgive our dear detective. He is a new arrival and is not yet *au fait*. Educate him, Reverend.'

Armstrong leant in to get a good look at Ben. He spoke with a great solemnity, his long fingers silently rapping the tabletop. 'The Taiping Rebellion,' he explained, 'is a civil war being waged against the Great Qing further north. A national Christian movement intent on overthrowing them and establishing a new order of sorts, under the banner of Christ rather than traditional Chinese Confucianism. Some would say that it marks a new epoch in Chinese history: a profound and irreversible moral awakening.'

Ben studied Armstrong as he spoke. The reverend's body was frail, but his mind was made of unbending steel. He had the will of a man with God on his side.

'It may just bring about the end of the Great Qing as we know it,' Portishead remarked, 'and I must say, I find that rather appealing. They have always been a thorn in the side of our trade. Their leaders are smug and obtuse, acting as though opium is the greatest of all evils when they commit sins orders of magnitude worse upon their own population.'

'And besides,' Parry mused, 'nobody wants our product more than the Chinese themselves. If the Emperor didn't want his people to turn to opium, then he shouldn't have made life so crushingly hard for them, such that opium is their only escape.'

Bevan raised his glass. 'Allow me to propose a toast. To the splendours of opium and the riches that it brings…'

'And to its saviour,' Ingrid said. 'Our dear friend, Benjamin E. Canaan.'

Ben accepted the toast with a practised politeness. But his attention was drawn away from them and towards Halliday. He was a few feet away and yet an ocean apart – silent as he devoured his tenderloin and knocked back yet another cognac.

The guests were sent on their way as soon as dinner was over. But Halliday kept Ben behind, summoning him to the Stirling salon. The Scot cut a less polished figure as he leant on the back of an armchair by the fireplace: his voice slurred, anger strobing in his eyes.

'And it *is* the Chinese then, is it?'

'That's the working theory. Bowring and Coldwell are convinced of it.'

Halliday sighed in frustration. 'Those yellow bastards never learn, do they? They tried to force us out a few years ago and it blew up in their faces.'

'They would likely say that they have genuine grievances.'

'Such as?'

'Well… I suppose they believe that opium is eroding the fabric of their society. That, if it were up to them, it would not be permitted. That you are subjugating and exploiting them.'

Halliday seemed to harden. 'Your view or theirs?'

'I'm just playing devil's advocate, sir.'

'Well you're not a bloody advocate,' Halliday snapped, jabbing his finger at Ben. 'You work for me.'

That made Ben bristle. 'With respect, Mr Halliday, I work for the British government.'

Halliday walked right up to Ben until their faces were inches apart. 'Then why aren't we going to war with the Chinese now? Why are we padding around like a bunch of scared little pussycats, playing footsie at meetings, killing time until they kill us?'

'We need proof before we can do that. We cannot go to war without a proper justification.'

'Why not?'

'Because it wouldn't be right, sir.'

Halliday scoffed in Ben's face and a fleck of saliva struck Ben beneath the eye. But Ben did not flinch. Halliday peered down at his own clenched fists and took a deep, weary breath.

'Noble words. "Right". "Wrong". But they mean nothing at all. I have been a sinner all my life. I have mercilessly crushed my competitors. I have been vindictive and a bully and have delighted in bending people to my will. I get my way by any means necessary. I have lied for my own gain. I have used, discarded and destroyed countless men over the years. And how has the world repaid me for my sins?'

He gestured around the room, at its luxury and decadence.

'I am one of the wealthiest men on the planet. People kill each other to win my favour. I am treated with kindness, respect and gratitude by all who darken my doorstep. Not only have I never been punished, but they even call me a great man. A statue of me stands at my alma mater in Edinburgh. I give morsels to charity – build a few orphanages, set up the odd scholarship, pay off the occasional widow's debts – and I am held up as an exemplary human being. They will write books about me. And yet, I am a sinner.'

Halliday's face gleamed in the firelight. It was a kind of madness that had gripped him. But just as quickly as that flame emerged, it dampened into a look of shame and regret.

'My mother, on the other hand, was a saint. Emmeline overflowed with the milk of human kindness. She was the eldest of five children – four younger brothers who all died of consumption. She gave up what little life she had to take care of them, and when each one passed, it was like losing one of her own. She never said a bad word to anyone, even when they thoroughly deserved it. How did the world reward her for her virtue? She was forced into a marriage with a man who despised her – a philanderer who beat her into two miscarriages. Her family dismissed her pleas to be released from this union. She died alone and in excruciating pain, at twenty-six. No priest arrived to give her the last rites. Nobody attended her funeral. And now, she is forgotten. No books will be written about her. And yet… she was a saint.'

Halliday gripped Ben's arm. There were tears in his eyes.

'There is no right or wrong, Mr Canaan. There are only win-
ners and losers. And I will *not*, under any circumstances, lose. I
refuse. Do you understand?'

Ben gently removed Halliday's hands. Against his better
instincts, he felt a swell of pity for the man. For all Halliday's
crudeness, there was something pathetic about his defiance – as
though he was still the little boy powerless to stop his mother
slipping away from him.

'If it is the Great Qing behind this,' Ben said, more softly
now, 'then we need a unified strategy going forward. You and
what remains of the Seven Gentlemen must put aside your old
commercial rivalries and unite against a common enemy.'

Halliday finally relented. 'Fine. I'm meeting with Ezekiel
Ormrod in Macao in a few days. Why don't you come with me –
present your theory to him – see what he says.'

They shook on it. 'Gladly, sir,' Ben said.

Before he could let go, Halliday tightened his vice-like grip.
'But you know how I feel. If it's war we have on our hands, then
war it must be. And if you're not willing to sail into the storm,
then someone else will – and you will be left behind.'

Not a word more passed between them. Ingrid arrived to take
Ben back to Mount Austin. They sat opposite one another in
that same nook under the mainmast, and soon the *Emmeline* had
disappeared in the gloom, leaving Ben lost in his own thoughts.
There was one word rattling about in his head: *saviour*. Ben
Canaan, the saviour of opium. Is that what he had come to Hong
Kong to do? Or was that just a by-product of following orders?

Ben was expecting to land at Victoria Harbour and take a
late-night carriage back to Mount Austin. But instead, the boat
approached Hong Kong Island from the south, mooring at a
jetty by a walled waterfront estate. The lights were off and the

curtains were drawn. He looked back at Ingrid. She was holding a set of keys.

'This isn't Victoria,' Ben said.

They both rose to their feet. Before Ben could step off the boat, Ingrid came up to him, slipped her hands under his jacket and round his waist, and pulled him so close that he could smell the last woody remnants of the Byron Selección 1850 on her breath.

'No,' she whispered, tightening her grip around him. 'No, it's not.'

14

Best Laid Schemes

Ben splashed his face with cold water. He was stooped over a washbasin before a fogged-up bathroom mirror, shoulders hunched as he took deep bracing breaths. The night was unbearably humid. Even with the window open to let in the breeze, a clammy sweat clung to his skin. He wiped a clear streak through the condensation on the mirror to catch his reflection: ashen-faced, hair matted, dark rings under his bleary eyes.

He ambled to the bedroom, stifling a yawn. Ingrid was on her back in the four-poster bed, naked and lighting up a cigarette. Wispy tendrils of tobacco smoke curled around a kerosene lamp, as moonlight lifted the room from shadow. The bedroom was decrepit, just like the rest of the house – riven with cracks and damp, stripped bare as though ready for demolition. Ingrid did not acknowledge him as he sat on the edge of the bed. He studied the faded ceiling fresco and spotted the bleached outline of Icarus falling back down to earth.

'Ever considered hiring a decorator?' Ben asked, tracing his fingertips up Ingrid's belly.

'We did. But that was then. This is now.'

She slid her leg up, until her foot was pressed against his chest.

'It wasn't supposed to be like this,' she exhaled. 'I was supposed to have my hands full, fretting over a mewling boy, waking at all hours at his slightest cry or troubled dream. My uncle was of the view that a maid or a governess would do it for me. But I didn't want that. I liked the idea of caring for him. Spoiling him. Making him all mine.'

Baby Esther flashed before Ben's eyes. Her tiny grasping hands. The whimpers of excitement. He could still feel her latching onto his finger, as she had the day he left, when he made that quiet promise to himself that he would see her again.

'My little sister had a girl a few months ago,' he said with a rueful smile. 'It's hard to believe that one day she'll have regrets and fears. That she'll fall in and out of love. Makes you wonder where it all comes from.'

Ingrid scoffed. 'Don't start talking about a *soul* now…'

'Why not? Don't you believe we have souls?'

Ingrid took a long pull on her cigarette. 'I persuaded myself that the thing inside me had a soul,' she said. 'That he was already alive and waiting to be born. And then he came out and he was just a limp, half-formed creature, a mass of blood and tissue. There was no soul. Nothing divine or eternal. That's all we are, Ben. Animals in the jungle. But because we have houses, clothes, and sacred institutions, we've convinced ourselves of the impossible: that we are special.'

'Well, call me an idealist,' Ben replied, 'but I think humanity is worth fighting for.'

Ingrid turned to look directly at him. 'You sound like my father,' she muttered. 'Dipping in and out of evil, yet always insisting on the fundamental goodness of human beings. Speaking pretty and doing ugly on the sly.'

'Is that why he left the China trade?'

'He couldn't stomach it any longer. He urged me to join him. But I refused. He was lying to himself, suddenly afraid of God's judgement. I was not so naive. Though perhaps you are.'

Ingrid's words were cutting. But Ben understood from the quiver of Ingrid's lip the deep well from which they had been drawn. Loss had hardened her soul.

'How do you do it?' he asked. 'How do you turn your brain off and just… do your job?'

Ingrid leant up close to him. 'You don't. The root of your pain is that you cannot accept that no man has clean hands. You must learn to live with yours being dirty.'

'But that's not why I came to Hong Kong. I didn't come to be the "saviour of opium". I didn't come for the Seven Gentlemen. I came because I wanted to do right by those who had suffered. I looked into the eyes of a mother and child burned to death, and she was staring back at me with what was left of her – as though pleading with me to save her. I'm… I'm just trying to do the right thing.'

Ben noticed a glimmer of shame and regret in Ingrid's eyes. She reached out to him, to cradle his head in her hands.

'I know,' she whispered. 'But sometimes there is no right thing to do. Hong Kong is a cruel mistress. She teaches you this lesson one blow at a time: that we live in a lawless world where everything is a means to end. Opium leads to money, money leads to prestige, prestige leads to power…'

'And then what?'

'Death, I suppose. But satisfaction in knowing that you were the user, not the used. The eater, not the eaten.'

Ben closed his eyes. Memories cleaved to the darkness behind his eyelids. Walking through Smithfield Market, shouldering the disdain of passers-by at the mere sight of a Jew. Bobbies beating his peers back into the sordid poverty of Whitechapel. Catholic schoolboys tearing apart the stall of the florist Avraham, for sport. Generation after generation of children, who became men and women, who became fathers and mothers, who became elders, only to be lowered into the grave – all crushed, silenced, eaten. His father stripping away his airs and graces with the words: 'You're not one of them.'

Ben prised himself away from Ingrid and threw on his clothes. He was overcome with a sudden overwhelming urge to get out. Ingrid did not fight him. All he said was, 'We shouldn't be doing this.' But he knew even as he spoke that it was foolish, that it was already done.

Ingrid arranged for a carriage back to Mount Austin. It was just before sunrise when Ben returned. The hotel was still slumbering, not least the attendant at reception, whose head lolled over the back of his chair. Ben passed Fitzjohn's room on the way upstairs: dead silent.

He approached his top-floor suite, instinctively reaching for his keys. But something was off. The handle had been snapped in half and the door, which he was certain that he had locked, was ever so slightly ajar.

His room had been utterly ransacked. His web of evidence on the wall had been torn apart. The boxes given to him by the police had been emptied out. Their contents, all those reams of paper, had been ripped up and scattered across the floor. And painted across the far wall in red were three words:

GO HOME DETECTIVE

Only one item had been left untouched: the Overholt, half-drunk since Ben's arrival, left in its usual spot on his writing desk. He picked it up, popped off the cork and took a tentative sip. 'Small mercies…' he mumbled.

By breakfast, the police, including Coldwell, had descended on Mount Austin. But no clues could be found. The doormen had retired at midnight and the receptionist had been dozing since one in the morning, which left several hours for someone to sneak in unnoticed before Ben's arrival. Since Ben's suite was the only one on the top floor, nobody was within earshot of the break-in. Fitzjohn received the brunt of Coldwell's fury: after all, it was his job to keep an eye on their prized detective, and he had failed. The most that Fitzjohn could muster was a pitiful apology delivered in his customary nasal stammer.

Coldwell sat with Ben on the terrace later that morning and offered him a lifeline. A breach of this kind spelled danger for Ben – one that he was not obliged to risk if he did not want to. He had done good work, even in his relatively short time in Hong Kong. Coldwell and his men could finish the investigation on his behalf. Someone else would testify before Lord Wetherton.

It was tempting. Hong Kong disagreed with Ben on a visceral level. It nauseated him, stuck in his throat, poisoned his dreams. But then he thought of Bruckner and Palmerston in the Breakfast Room of 10 Downing Street: his vow of loyalty – the fear of disappointment – the extended hand that said, against all odds, 'We have chosen you.' And what would it say, to return to London with empty hands, empty pockets, and an empty wad of paper where his precious report should have been written?

'No,' Ben said with a shake of the head. 'I'm getting close. That's why they threatened me the way they did: *because they themselves feel threatened*. And if I back out now… it will have been for nothing.'

*

It was another balmy night on the Pearl River. Thunderstorms had been threatening all week and dark turgid clouds had swallowed up the moon, plunging the estuary into total darkness. The only light in that great gulf between Kowloon's glimmering shores to the east and those of Macao to the west was the signal lantern of the *Emmeline*, swaying back and forth with the tide.

Halliday stood at the prow alongside Ingrid and Ben, while Parry lingered behind them, polishing the barrel of his hunting rifle. Halliday was taciturn and on edge. Ben wondered whether it had anything to do with his recent tryst with Ingrid. She had assured him that she would keep their transgression to herself, but he had no guarantee of that. Then again, maybe it mattered little to Halliday. Maybe all he really cared about was the prize before him: a tête-à-tête with one of the last of the Seven Gentlemen.

They were greeted at Macao's main harbour by a troop of Portuguese colonial officials, who ushered them into a carriage bound for the Governor's Palace in São Lourenço. Macao's governor, Isidoro Francisco Guimarães, had offered it up as a neutral venue for Halliday and Ormrod. Guimarães himself was waiting under the porte cochere: a stocky man in full military regalia, festooned with medals, a stiff high collar immobilising his neck.

He greeted Halliday with a hug, Ingrid with a kiss to the hand, and Ben with a brief peremptory glance. Then he rolled his eyes up to the sky, turning his lip as if in disapproval of creation's handiwork. 'Come in. The heavens are ready to burst.'

The Ormrods were installed in the parlour. The magnate from New York, Ezekiel Ormrod, was too obese to stand and was instead planted like the Laughing Buddha in a wheelchair.

Everyone around him was fretting. Fenella, his wife, laid her hands on his shoulders as though cloaking him in a protective spell. Calvin, his middle-aged son, offered him a glass of chilled water. His granddaughter Marceline – an auburn-haired girl of eighteen in a striking turquoise dress – stared quizzically at them as they entered.

'Odysseus!' Ormrod bellowed. He grabbed Calvin by the sleeve and pointed at Halliday. 'Son, look at this fine specimen of a man! A neck like a stallion, calves like old pistons. I suppose you could bounce a bullet off that chest.'

'I suppose you'd like to try,' Halliday said with an insincere smile.

Marceline cleared her throat and crinkled her pert reddish nose with displeasure. 'Is that the detective?' she said, nodding in Ben's direction.

'Dripping with contempt, I see,' Ben replied. 'I'm starting to think I'm not wanted.'

'I simply object to a meddlesome London boy dragging Grandfather into mortal danger.'

'Marceline – *please*,' Ormrod waved her away. 'I apologise. My granddaughter inherited her grandmother's… wilfulness.'

The two firms began their parley. At Halliday's invitation, Ben presented the Ormrods with his theory about the killings. All the while, the senior Ormrod listened attentively – and by the time Ben reached the end of his narrative, he seemed impressed.

'You got yourself a good one!' he said to Halliday. 'Your boy's got a big brain on him – and even bigger stones.'

'Do you think he's right?' Halliday replied.

'It's an eminently plausible theory, which has crossed my mind more than once. After all, the Great Qing is not exactly enamoured with us. *But…* I must say, I somewhat doubt the proposed motive. All this harping on about destroying opium, purging China of its "black blood"… It feels too deliberate, too insistent. A killer does not brag of his motive. He simply kills and enjoys watching the world speculate, chatter away, obsess over his every move.'

Ormrod glanced at his wife. She gave a curt nod.

'A case of the lady protesting too much,' Ben said.

'Precisely. Perhaps these murders are less about getting rid of the opium trade, and more about shifting its centre of gravity, into the palm of some other firm.'

A pregnant silence followed as Ben quietly connected the dots. Luuk Fontaine had voiced a similar fear in the Club Lusitano: that this was a power play dressed up as a holy war. But if that were true, then anyone could be a suspect. Not just the Great Qing, but any man ambitious and unhinged enough to take on an entire industry – including Ormrod himself.

'That would be an extremely risky thing to do,' Halliday said caustically.

'But think of the spoils! Come, Odysseus, you know as well as I do that the China trade has been too crowded for too long. It's like you've got a…'

'An apple pie,' Fenella cut in.

'Exactly! A sweet steamy apple pie, jam-packed with fruit. Only now, too many people are invited to the party. So the slices are getting smaller, less filling – and soon we're all going hungry. It's the same story everywhere: trade is booming, yet revenues are going down. Why? Because Seven Gentlemen is probably… five gentlemen too many. So, whatever the motive of these nasty fellers, devilish they may be, they've done us a favour. The field has been laid waste. Now it simply needs to be replanted. And that can only be done by men with the existing infrastructure to do so.'

Halliday mulled Ormrod's proposal, letting the pause hang for as long as he could, as if each passing moment added an ounce of pressure to his American counterpart.

'You want to cut a deal?' he finally said.

'Why not? We divvy up the remains between ourselves in an Anglo-American alliance of sorts, with nobody but the Great Qing to stop us. It is a foolproof scheme. But we must act swiftly. To quote a countryman of mine, a cat in gloves catches no mice.'

'To quote a countryman of *mine*, the best laid schemes of mice and men go oft awry.'

Ormrod folded his arms over his bulbous stomach. It was this, or nothing. Fenella and Calvin were of the same disposition. Marceline stood apart: watching Ben watch her grandfather's sly, euphemistic dance with Halliday.

'You seem to have it all figured out,' Halliday said. 'If I didn't know any better, I'd say you were the one who orchestrated these killings.'

Fenella looked outraged. Halliday nonchalantly twirled his thumbs, savouring the affront. But Ormrod brushed it off, baring his teeth in an expression of vicious delight.

'Unlike you, Odysseus, I have been steeped in the business of opium from birth. My father was one of the creators of the trade that you inherited.'

'The only man in this room who inherited anything was *you*,' Halliday shot back. 'I was not lucky enough to have a father like yours born before me. I built my business from scratch.'

'Well… your brother did. And how did you repay him? By taking his daughter as your own?' Ormrod's gaze flicked to Ingrid, just in time to catch her blanch at his words.

'You clawed your way into the China trade to make a bit of money,' Ormrod continued. 'But I am the China trade, and I respect it accordingly. I would not kill our fellow Gentlemen because killing them would be… *beneath me.*'

Halliday's glee curdled into something less pleasant. He rose to his feet and gave a curt bow to the Ormrods. 'I will consider your offer carefully. And there is still the matter of the killers themselves, whom Mr Canaan is tracking down.'

Ormrod was unruffled by the suggestion. 'They don't concern me. People have wanted and always will want to kill men like us. But death is not in our destiny.'

'I met one of them before he blew his brains out,' Ben retorted, 'and he too seemed to think destiny was on his side.'

'And that, Detective, is the difference between us and them.' Ormrod raised a clenched fist. 'Those men cry out to destiny – but we are the ones who write it.'

And with that, the meeting drew to a close. The parties trailed out to the front of the estate. By that point, the heavens had opened and a deluge was pummelling Macao. The carriages were waiting in the thick ropes of rain: one for the Ormrods, one for Halliday's crew. About twenty policemen stood on guard, drenched through. The front gates were wide open. Beyond them was pitch-black: no streetlights, no moonlight, not even a lamp to rupture the veil.

Halliday, Ingrid, Parry and Fitzjohn proceeded to their carriage. Ben, meanwhile, lingered by Marceline as the attendants struggled to heave Ormrod into his carriage.

'What made you choose Halliday as a master?' Marceline said to Ben.

'He's not my master and I'm not his slave.'

'You do an awfully good impression of one.'

'I'm just doing my job. Which, before you get too lippy, involves keeping you safe.'

'We do not need you, Mr Canaan. My grandfather is an immoveable object.'

'Yes, I can see that.'

Ormrod settled into his seat opposite Fenella. Calvin gestured for Marceline to get in. Ben guided her by the hand onto the first step of the carriage.

What happened next was a blur: ten seconds passing in the blink of an eye. A shout from one of the policemen behind Ben – something incoherent and guttural, followed by the clunk of a cocked rifle. Then the sound of trampling feet. Figures emerging from the darkness of the street, through the front gates, into the courtyard. An object hurtling through the air to land with a dull thud between the back wheels of Ormrod's carriage. It was a soda water bottle, filled to the brim with powder, crooked nails and shrapnel, and a fuse burning right down to the wick.

Without thinking, Ben grabbed Marceline and yanked her back, spinning her round to wrap her in his arms. Then he heard a deafening bang – felt a rush of heat across his body – and a shockwave knocked him off his feet. He felt the blood before the pain: a warm film coating the left side of his face. The hearing in his left ear had gone, leaving only a sharp tinnitus over a cacophony of screams and gunfire.

Marceline opened her eyes. She was covered in mud, but unscathed. Ben told her to stay down and she nodded frantically, but his own voice was incomprehensible to him. He turned to find Ormrod's carriage blown to pieces and engulfed in flames. Calvin had fallen to the ground a short distance away, staring in mute horror at his right arm, torn off at the elbow and hanging by its sinews and tendons. He caught only a glimpse of the inside of Ormrod's carriage – the mangled remains of Ezekiel and Fenella, their bodies ripped open from the explosion and charring black in the fire.

It was an ambush. A dozen assassins had descended on the estate, armed with rifles and improvised grenades, now locked in a crossfire with the police. Across the courtyard, Halliday and his entourage were piling into their carriage as swiftly as they could. It was now or never. Ben and Marceline hauled her father to his feet and dragged him across the terrace to Halliday's carriage, as bullets fizzed past their heads to pock the portico of the Governor's Palace.

They reached the carriage and Ben bundled his two charges inside. He was about to join himself, but then he caught sight of one of the attackers on the far side of the courtyard. His balaclava had been pulled skew to reveal his face: *Zirui.*

Ben knew at once what he had to do. He slammed the carriage door shut.

'Go!' he yelled. 'Get them to the boat!'

'Hurry!' Ingrid screamed at the driver, who whipped the reins to send the carriage careening down the path and out the bounds of the estate.

Ben was left alone with Parry and the last surviving policemen. Men on both sides were dropping like flies. Zirui doubled back and made a break for it out the front gates. Ben and Parry took off after him, weaving through the melee until they were out on the empty street. Zirui disappeared down an alleyway heading south towards Praia Grande Bay. Ben was faster than Parry and peeled off, darting through the maze of claustrophobic backstreets until he hit the water's edge and there was nowhere left to run.

He found a breathless Zirui leaning on the esplanade over-looking the bay. He turned to face Ben. Both men knew it was the end of the line.

'Mr Canaan!' he cried out.

Ben responded with a punch square to the jaw that sent Zirui staggering.

'Do you realise what you've done?!' Ben roared.

Zirui spat out a globule mixed with phlegm and blood.

'It's… It's for the greater good – for the glory of God – to wipe away sin—'

'You've started a *war!*' Ben roared, grabbing Zirui by the scruff of the neck. 'Do you have any idea how many people are going to die now? Thousands? Millions?!'

'I – I – I did not want… war…' Zirui backed up against the railing. 'He told us it would make things pure, that the Kingdom of Heaven willed it – he promised…'

'Who?'

Zirui raised his trembling hands. 'Ames! It was Ames… We are his Horsemen…'

Ben drew Zirui close, tightening his grip around the man's collar. 'Who. Is. Ames?'

Zirui opened his mouth. But the answer never came. A gun-shot rang out, Zirui's head snapped to the side, and his body slumped over the railing. Ben took a step back, his breath trapped in his throat.

Parry emerged from the alleyway, rifle raised. 'You okay, kid?'

Ben nodded, in a daze. Parry dumped Zirui's body on the ground and fired one more round into his chest.

'Good riddance,' he spat. 'You did well to get him before he escaped.'

He offered Ben a handkerchief to wipe his face. Ben doubled over as the adrenaline waned and the pain of his injuries washed through him. Over the chorus of rain came the distant echoes of gunshots, reverberating from the Governor's Palace uphill. Ben looked across the bay, the tranquil black waters rippling in the downpour.

'No boats,' he panted. 'Nobody waiting. No escape. This was a suicide mission.'

Ben fell to his knees and began digging through Zirui's pockets. They were empty save for one item: a sepia-toned card with two Chinese characters. Ben recognised it immediately. It was the same as the one that he had found at 4 Hopkins Street back in London, among Bo's possessions. A calling card inscribed with the word *Lǎohǔ* – 'Tiger'.

'What does it mean?' Parry asked.

Ben grimaced as he pressed the handkerchief to the gash on his forehead. 'It means things are about to get ugly. And there's nothing we can do stop it.'

15

The Fog of War

It was mid-July, a month since the assassination of Ezekiel Ormrod, and a ship was coming in to moor at Victoria Harbour. She was marked out amid the trawlers and dragons swarming the waters by her gargantuan size – a triple-masted ship-of-the-line, almost two hundred feet from bow to stern, mounted with nearly a hundred cannons, fifty shell guns and fifty powder guns across the upper and lower gundecks. Two men were stationed at every gun, though not a shot was fired as she made her final approach. Rather, she drifted with the tranquillity of an apex predator, untouchable in her slumber. The only sign of her allegiance was the Union Jack fluttering at the summit of the mainmast, silhouetted against the blazing sun and casting a pall of silence over the Pearl River. She bore no name on her bulging hull, but those in the know would have recognised her as the HMS *Herakles* – a ship built for one thing and one thing alone: war.

A diminutive man stood port-side, both hands on the railing. He was one of the few aboard who was not a redcoat, instead donning a smooth black frock coat, white shirt and cravat. His Homburg hat cast a shadow over his eyes, revealing only his toothbrush moustache and fleshy lips. Gustav

Bruckner, now the most important man in Hong Kong, had arrived.

A party was waiting for him on the promenade along the harbour. Ben was at the front, sandwiched between Coldwell and Governor Bowring. They were flanked on both sides by police officers, British envoys, and a fleet of carriages, forming a protective wall between them and the hordes of civilian onlookers. This was a common sight since that fateful night. The frayed thread of peace to which Hong Kong clung had snapped: now the threat of violence lingered in the febrile air. Everyone lived with the shared anticipation that, at any moment, death would come stalking.

Coldwell gave Ben a once-over. 'You scrubbed up.'

'Couldn't hide the battle scars,' Ben gestured to the brownish scab on his left temple, where he had needed surgery to remove the shrapnel.

'I'm sure it makes the ladies swoon.'

'Speaking of which,' Bowring butted in, whispering out the corner of his mouth, 'what's this I hear about Marceline Ormrod going sweet on you? Angling for a dowry?'

Ben shrugged Bowring off. People loved to speculate. The truth was much plainer: Marceline understood that Ben's quick thinking had saved her and her father, albeit minus his right arm – and that he had come within a whisker of saving her grandparents. So her initial hostility towards him had abated and they had since struck up a correspondence, coupled with a promise that if Ben ever needed help, the Ormrod dynasty would gladly step in.

The HMS *Herakles* moored and Bruckner disembarked, trailed by a regiment of redcoats. Bowring strutted forth and, peacock-like, gave Bruckner a bow.

'By the pricking of my thumbs…'

'…Something wicked this way comes,' Bruckner said with a grin. 'Good to see you, John. Sebastian.' He turned to Ben and drew him into a warm hug. 'Benjamin. The bravest of all. I trust you are mended since Macao?'

Ben was surprised by the gesture. Bruckner had never gone beyond a terse handshake. 'Mostly. Apart from the tinnitus. I suspect Hong Kong will forever be ringing in my ears.'

'Nothing a bit of brandy can't fix! Now: let's get going. I did not double-time it to Hong Kong on that floating powder keg to indulge in mere chit-chat.'

A roundtable was hosted at the Governor's residence to bring Bruckner up to speed. The attack in Macao had wrenched the Black Blood Murders from the shadows into the public eye. The late Zirui and Bo, two of the ringleaders of the operation, were both confirmed to have had close ties to the Great Qing: Zirui as a civil servant and the protégé of Ye Mingchen, the Viceroy of Lingguan and the Emperor's representative in southern China; Bo as a lawyer working for the imperial government. The third man, Aiguo, was a fellow civil servant who had vanished the night before the attack, and a manhunt was underway to track him down.

'Are the Chinese looking for him as well?' Bruckner asked.

'That's what they're saying,' Ben replied, 'but so far – nothing.'

'Convenient.'

The other assassins in Macao were all dispatched by the police. Their identities were difficult to trace, but they all appeared to be former bannermen of the Chinese military: veteran soldiers hired for their experience in combat.

'All in all,' Ben said, 'this has the Great Qing's fingerprints all over it.'

Bruckner smiled. He plucked an almond macaroon from the pastry basket in the middle of the table and took a bite. 'Now that,' he said, 'is a damned good macaroon.'

The latest killing had left the China trade in a state of utter disarray. A gaping vacuum had been carved out of a market once jammed with competition. The countries whose representatives had once stood tall – the Portuguese through Lalé, the French through Morèse, the Dutch through Van Hook, the Americans through Ormrod – were reeling from their losses and increasingly isolated. Now only Hokoa and Halliday remained, and if the ledger left at Ben's door back in London was anything to go by, the danger had not yet passed for them.

'Thus stands the diplomatic situation – which is what I have been sent to resolve,' Bruckner said. 'Westminster is outraged, as is the rest of the civilised world. The consensus is that the Great Qing has transgressed beyond the pale and has left the PM with no option but to reassert our interests by way of open warfare. And I can tell you, from preliminary discussions, this endeavour would have the backing of all our international partners, from the Americans to the Europeans. The HMS *Herakles* is just the beginning – more are on the way. And when they arrive, if the last of the killers is not neutralised, it will not be pretty for the Great Qing.'

Ben's stomach curdled at the prospect. The very thing that he had sought to avoid – more death, more destruction – was fast approaching China. And it was because of him. He felt sick, and yet as he looked about the room, all he could see were polite smiles. The even-tempered satisfaction of a job well done.

Bruckner licked the crumbs from his fingers. 'I trust we are also tracking down this third man… Aiguo was his name?'

Coldwell motioned to Ben, who slid Zirui's calling card across the table. Bruckner inspected it in the sunlight pouring through the bay windows.

'Both Bo and Zirui had this same calling card,' Ben explained. 'It reads *Lǎohǔ* – or, in our parlance, "The Tiger".'

'Which is…?'

'We've been digging about over the past month, and we believe it refers to a hideout for outlaws and mercenaries on the Dapeng Peninsula, two hours by boat from Hong Kong. If Aiguo is holed up somewhere, it may well be there.'

'It's on Chinese soil,' Coldwell added. 'We would have to exercise the utmost caution.'

Bruckner approved. 'Very well. Sebastian and his officers will sail to Dapeng posthaste – let's see what they can find.'

'And me, sir?' Ben asked.

'You have but one job now, Mr Canaan: *finish the report for Lord Wetherton.*'

With that, Bruckner drew the meeting to an end. It was time, in his words, for him to wrangle some Chinese diplomats. But before he left, he summoned Ben for a private chat on the front terrace of Government House. It was a dazzlingly bright morning, forcing Ben to shield his eyes as Bruckner squinted up at him.

'Is it really going to be war, Herr Bruckner?' Ben asked.

'Think of it as a necessary evil.'

'To what end? Innocent people die so that we can… keep peddling opium?'

Bruckner studied Ben with his head cocked in curiosity. 'Uncertainty thrives in times of conflict, Mr Canaan. It can be difficult to distinguish strength from weakness, right from wrong, friend from foe. In German, we call it *Nebel des Krieges* – the fog of war.'

He reached into his pocket and removed a wad of banknotes.

'Now the fog has descended on the Pearl River. And we are here, you and I, to pierce through it with our greatest weapon…'

He slid £50 in cash into Ben's breast pocket.

'…*Clarity*. The PM is very impressed with your handling of the case, Mr Canaan. Consider this a token of his special appreciation – and a sign of more to come.'

Bruckner was as polished and genial as ever: with a passing smirk crinkling his moustache, he strode off to his carriage, whistling the tune to 'The British Grenadiers'.

Ben did not join his colleagues for lunch. He returned to Mount Austin alone, insensible to his cabbie's probing questions about the goings-on at Government House. He looked out the window at the swaying camphor trees, dispersed among the banks of longan and lychee – at the ever-shrinking form of the HMS *Herakles* far below him – at the islands of the archipelago studding the South China Sea like inky gems on a bed of sapphire. All he wanted, in that moment, was to be home again.

Yet, when he was back in his suite, and he sat at his desk with his pen in hand to finally write home, nothing came to him. He started and restarted a dozen times over, but every time he tried simply to say what he was doing, the words vanished. Nothing felt true anymore. It was just a story in his head, as shapeless as sand through his fingers. And in the end, he gave up, scrunching the paper into a ball.

In its place, he laid Bruckner's banknotes before him – each pristine slip in a line, tallying up the £50. A small fortune tossed his way like a bauble to a child.

'The user, not the used,' he murmured. 'The eater, not the eaten…'

He slid the banknotes into his wallet. His fingers brushed something folded up in one of the inside pockets. He removed a crumpled scrap of paper. It was the note that Bo had slipped him in Whitehall: the impenetrable code, with its blend of Latin and Chinese script.

He held it up to the light, inspecting it as an archaeologist would an unknown artefact from a bygone era. He was no cryptographer. But there was one person who might be able to help him.

It had been another gruelling day at The Floating Life for Liang Yue. Her fingers ached from relentless needlework over the flame of the spirit lamp. Long hours steeped in second-hand opium smoke had left her with a nasty dry cough. One of her clients – a French expat with a tendency to come up short – had even slapped her when she insisted on full payment.

Yet none of that seemed to matter as she laboured over the open stove in the lonely corner of Causeway Bay that she shared with her brother. Drizzle pattered on the roof. The wind chimes in the garden drifted in and out, in time with the sighing of the breeze. On nights like this, it was as though nothing else existed beyond the four walls of 12 Tang Lung Street.

Then she heard the knock at the door. Her heart instantly leapt to her throat. Ever since Bo was publicly outed as one of the Black Blood killers, she had grown suspicious of unannounced visitors – especially after dark.

She hurried the steaming dish into the living room. Tao was waiting for her at their low dinner table, cross-legged with his head buried in his latest fantasy book.

'Wait here,' she said sternly.

She picked up an axe propped against the wall, holding it out as she tiptoed towards the front door.

'Who's there?' she called.

'Your favourite Englishman,' a voice replied.

Her guard dropped. Surely not. She opened up to find Ben standing before her, damp from the rain and covering his head with a tattered newspaper. He took a step back when he clocked the axe aimed at his face.

'Is that for chopping wood, or chopping… me?'

Liang lowered the axe, though she did not let go. 'What are you doing here?'

'That is a question I have been asked many times,' he said, 'and often I don't have a satisfactory answer. Tonight, however…'

'Then you can tell me and go on your merry way.'

Ben sniffed. He had caught a whiff of dinner. 'Care to feed a hungry traveller? It's far easier to explain over rice than in the rain.'

Before Liang could rebuff him, Tao appeared behind her. 'Ben!' he cried, bursting through the doorway to give Ben a hug. 'I have more homework for us to do!'

Liang huffed in exasperation. This was a bothersome detective, with a habit of inveigling himself in her business, like a tick anchoring into the tightest cranny. But deep down she knew that this could only be about Bo – and if she had any fatal flaw to speak of, it was her curiosity.

'Best make it quick.'

They sat around the table and dug in. It was chow ho fun tonight: strips of beef stir-fried with bean sprouts, scallions and flat rice noodles, marinated in soy sauce and mixed together in a blazing-hot wok.

'I'm surprised you opened,' Ben said between mouthfuls. 'I thought you only wanted to see the back of me.'

'I thought you hoped to God for the same.'

'Clearly the devil has more in store for us both.'

He peered at Tao's book, still spread out on his lap. As Tao explained, it was Li Ruzhen's *Flowers in the Mirror*: a fantasy-adventure novel filled with tales of Tang Ao's rebellion against the cruel reign of Empress Wu; his voyage across the high seas to strange and distant utopias; the discovery of immortality at the mountain of Little Penglai. Ben was delighted by Tao's enthusiasm, responding with tales of his own, ripped straight from the *Arabian Nights*.

'You would like my brother,' he said. 'He's also mad about books and fairy tales.'

'You seem to know plenty yourself,' Liang said.

'Well…' Ben sighed ruefully. 'I was mad about them too, once upon a time.'

Ben reminded Liang in that moment of Bo. Sitting in that very spot and asking the same questions of Tao – a show of affection to a solitary, bookish boy. She half-expected Ben to remove a pipe and gaze meditatively, lost in his own little world, as Bo was wont to do on balmy summer evenings. She swallowed the jagged splinter of pain lodged in her throat and returned to her dinner.

After dessert – oolong tea and lychees freshly picked from the garden – Liang dismissed Tao. As soon as he was out of earshot, Ben's demeanour shifted. His cheery smile vanished and he linked his hands together in contemplation.

'I presume you've heard the news about your husband and his colleagues.'

Liang nodded, gazing forlornly into the dregs of her tea.

'Have the authorities been dogging you about it?'

'No. Very few people knew of my relationship with Bo.'

Ben was hiding his scepticism, but not well enough. 'Not even Aiguo?'

'He knew. But I haven't seen him – if that's what you're implying. I know as much as anyone literate enough to read a newspaper.'

Ben cleared his throat but made no reply. Liang stiffened and set down her teacup.

'Is that why you came?' she said sharply. 'Another interrogation? Sorry to disappoint.'

But Ben shook his head. 'I don't think you're complicit. But you may yet be of use.'

He handed her Bo's note and explained its provenance. Liang scanned it and was left thoroughly perplexed.

'I know this code…' she said. 'When Bo and I first met, we devised our own cipher, so that we could correspond without anyone knowing what we were saying. We did it by blending the English and Chinese alphabets, and using different keys for different months of the year.'

'So you can decipher it?'

'Well, I don't know what month this was written in. So it would take some time to identify the right key. But it is certainly possible.'

'Would you do it for me?' Ben reached into his pocket. 'I can pay.'

Before Liang knew what she was saying, she blurted, 'No.' She was sick to death of being paid by a man for some service. It was her whole life – each night giving up a little piece of herself.

'If I am going to do this,' she said, 'it will be for Bo. And if not for him, then for me.'

She laid the note down next to her teacup, smoothing it out with a tenderness reserved for sacred relics. After so long enduring Bo's absence – every day having to face the dead space at the table, at his old desk, in her bed – here was his voice, from beyond the grave. An echo that reverberated back to her, across oceans and continents and the great span of time.

'Are you alright, Liang?'

Liang looked up at Ben, her vision blurry with tears.

'I spend my whole life behind a mask,' she whispered through barely suppressed sobs. 'I paint my face with makeup. I say what men wish to hear, in a voice not my own. I hide every feeling of disgust at myself with a smile. Even my name is buried beneath a laughable cliché. The only thing that was true was Bo: a boy from a desert village in Xinjiang who, against all odds, made something of himself. Who loved and took pity on me when the world had turned its back. And now I'm supposed to accept that even this was a fantasy. That the man I loved was a murderer who has plunged our people into another war. Everything I thought was true is actually a lie. An illusion in which I'm destined to be trapped.'

Ben looked out the window. Dandelion seeds were drifting past, blown aimlessly back and forth, their fate surrendered to the impulse of the night wind.

'My grandfather used to say that everyone has their place in the world,' Ben said. 'That history chooses different people for different things. Some to work, others to have leisure. Some to live long, others to die young. Some to live by the pen, others by the sword. Some to rejoice, others to suffer. And our people, he would say – Jews, I mean – were chosen to suffer. To be an example to the world of perseverance through pain.'

'Do you believe that?'

'I don't know. If I did, I'm not sure I would be sitting here. The last thing I ever said to him was that I wanted to do things… my way. But maybe that was naive. Maybe we are all pawns in a game that we don't even know is being played, believing ourselves to be free when in reality our course is already set in stone. Maybe there is no good or evil – just destiny.'

As he spoke, Ben caught a glimpse of the sliding door behind Liang: open a crack to reveal Tao's face, sombre and silent.

16

Out, Brief Candle

So ran the headline on the front page of the *Hong Kong Register*. It was the morning after Ben's visit to Liang, and as usual he was slumped in a deckchair on his balcony at Mount Austin, poring over the newspapers between sips of black coffee.

Coldwell's mission to the Dapeng Peninsula had taken place under cover of night, supported by officers from the police department and a regiment of British soldiers. According to the *Register*, they landed at Yangtao Bay on the west coast of Dapeng, by the village of Nan'ao. This was the reputed location of 'The Tiger': a hotbed for anyone who found themselves on the wrong side of the law – highwaymen, seafaring pirates, contract killers, petty crooks running from bad debt. The British expeditionary force carried out a raid on the site, prevailing with a single casualty: Alfred Chiu, one of Coldwell's fresh-faced deputies. A comb through the hideout revealed plenty of outlaws, but no sign of Aiguo.

Ben corroborated this narrative with Coldwell himself, at Chiu's funeral. The fallen officer was given a hero's burial: his coffin draped with a Union Jack, lowered into the grave to the sound of a brass band blaring out 'God Save the Queen' and a dose of patriotic chest-thumping from Governor Bowring.

'The Chinese will not be happy,' Coldwell told Ben. 'They will no doubt treat our incursion as an act of war. Not that they have a choice in the matter. Escalation is the best defence. Or, as my erstwhile commander in Crimea would say: carry on up!'

'How should I present it in the report?'

'As it was. Self-defence.'

Ben spent several hours that evening writing up the latest developments. He found a certain comfort in the consensus that had formed around the Dapeng affair: that it was essential in the hunt for Aiguo – that, if anything, the British were doing the Great Qing's job for them. For the first time in weeks, he wrote with complete ease. He could see himself now before the inquiry, holding his own under the baleful glare of Lord Wetherton, touted in the newspapers as a British hero.

After a few hours of writing, he took a dusk walk around Victoria Peak. He followed a bridle path to a hilltop overlooking a mountain pass bisecting the ridge between Victoria Peak and Mount Gough, known as the Gap. From there, in the dying embers of the setting sun, he had a commanding view of the island: the fishing village of Pok Fu Lam tucked into a corner of Sandy Bay to the west; the racecourse and cricket clubs of Happy Valley to the east; the wooded islet of Taplichan to the south; and the great misty expanse of Kowloon to the north.

Usually the ridge was lively with people, come to take the clean air and clear their heads. But this evening was different: not a soul was out. The place had an almost unnatural stillness. Ben leant on the railing over the Gap and peered down into the gully.

'Come out!' he called.

He was met with the murmurings of nature: crickets chirping, a stream gushing down the Gap, cool gusts of air. Then the snap of a twig underfoot, and a figure emerged from the grove of plum trees behind him. It was a young man in a black *changshan*, his glossy dark hair in a queue, as was custom among officials of the Great Qing. He joined Ben at the railing.

'You have a good eye,' he said.

'I can tell the difference between a good quiet and a bad quiet,' Ben grunted. 'My name's Ben. Though you probably know that already.'

The young man gave a curt nod. 'Jun. I've been watching you since Ormrod's assassination in Macao.'

'On the orders of the Great Qing?'

'Ye Mingchen, to be precise. Viceroy of Lingguan.'

Ben picked up a handful of pebbles and dropped them one by one into the Gap, watching them disappear into the treetops.

'So when were you planning on killing me?' He smiled drily at Jun. 'Or did I interrupt you in the act?'

'I was under no such instructions. In fact, I was told to keep you safe.'

Ben could only snort. 'Safe from what, exactly? Your own men? Save it for someone who needs it. I can look after myself.'

Jun did not rise to Ben's provocation. He had been trained well in the art of diplomacy. Instead, he maintained an air of inscrutability, carefully analysing his counterpart in the silence.

'Arrogance is a vice, Detective. Above all, the arrogance of thinking that you are untouchable.' His features darkened. 'If I wanted you dead, it would be done before the first inkling of suspicion could form in your mind.'

It dawned on Ben in that moment that it was not he who had noticed Jun, but Jun who had allowed himself to be noticed.

'Why are you here?' Ben said.

'Ye Mingchen has requested an audience with you. He would go via the proper channels, but they are not to be trusted. This is a private matter, to be discussed privately.'

Ben could not quite believe his ears. Jun was asking him to throw himself into the arms of the Great Qing without the knowledge of his own allies – despite Ye Mingchen being a key suspect in the Black Blood Murders.

'I understand your hesitation,' Jun continued, as though he was reading Ben's mind. 'In your shoes, I would likely walk away. But these are exceptional circumstances, Detective. You have the Viceroy's word that not a hair on your head will be harmed. He simply wants to meet you.'

If Ben's priority was survival, he had absolutely no reason to agree. But there was something about Jun's calm insistence, that glimmer of humanity behind his humourless exterior, which reassured Ben. Besides, playing it safe had not got him particularly far in life.

He extended a hand to Jun. 'If you're lying, I will bring you down with me.'

Jun led Ben to an isolated beach on the west side of the island. A dragon boat was waiting in the shadow of the palm trees, manned by a dozen oarsmen. They made a swift journey up the Pearl River, beyond the bounds of British-controlled territory and into the belly of the Great Qing.

The boat peeled east before they reached Canton, up the Mayong River. It was here that they landed, on the edge of a bamboo grove, shrouded in a darkness so deep that everything beyond the first line of trees was an impenetrable void. Ben was escorted into the thicket, Jun leading with a sole lantern – only strong enough to illuminate the bamboo-stalks that seemed to continue endlessly in every direction.

They arrived at a clearing, where the bamboo had been cut away around a web of streams and a rocky outcrop. A network of structures had been built here: single-storey cottages with yellow roofs and crimson walls, linked by corridors to form a square around an enclosed garden. Cherry trees and haw-thorns had been planted along the perimeter, and dozens of oil-lanterns dangled from the eaves to bathe the entire complex in a blushing glow. The front entrance was adorned with door gods – elaborate engravings of deities drawn from Chinese cosmology, painted to ward off evil – and the pillars on either side bore the five-clawed dragon of the Great Qing's imperial flag. A macaque hung from a tree, clutching a freshly picked fig and watching them impishly.

Jun swung a large bronze door knocker, announcing their arrival with a thunderous rumble. Two Imperial Guards ushered them in, both in navy green and armed to the teeth. Ben was taken across the inner courtyard, past a pond swirling with fantail goldfish, and up to a sliding door.

Viceroy Ye Mingchen was waiting for him. Ben recognised him at once from his short plump stature, his oversized head, his grey goatee. He was sitting cross-legged on the floor, carefully guiding his pen along an unfurled parchment, ringed in a semi-circle by a bank of candles. The room was sparsely decorated: just a few canvases on the walls showing off Ye Mingchen's cal-ligraphy, and a gold ancestral shrine behind him.

The Imperial Guards bowed and exited, leaving the two of them alone. Ye Mingchen gestured to the shrine. Three ceramic figures resembling bearded wise men were arranged in a line on the top rung.

'Our three celestial gods,' he said. 'Fu, Lu, Shou – Fortune, Prosperity, Longevity. Tonight they watch over us, as demons rattle the gates. Come. Sit.'

He gestured to a cushion before him, on the other side of the candles.

'My mere presence is borderline treason,' Ben said.

'It is treason for me too, Mr Canaan. I am not here to waste your time, but to save it.'

Ben took a seat. Ye Mingchen turned the parchment round to show it to him.

'Do you know what this is?' he asked.

Ben shook his head.

'This is an edict that I will be issuing tomorrow morning, as ordered by the Xianfeng Emperor in Beijing. It sets out a robust condemnation of your superintendent's action on the Dapeng Peninsula. The last step before an outright declaration of war. But…'

He picked up the parchment and dangled it over the candles.

'This is not a foregone conclusion. There is still time to avoid the bloodshed.'

The corner of the parchment was tantalisingly close to that trembling lick of flame. An inch lower and it would burn to a crisp, wiping away the suffering of millions in a matter of seconds.

Ben narrowed his eyes. 'What's your game? Trying to talk your way out of a crisis of your own making?'

'My own making?' At this, Ye Mingchen smiled. He whipped the parchment back to his side of the candles and set it down. 'On the contrary: the root of this evil is you, not us.'

'Let's talk about evil,' Ben crossed his arms and leant forward. 'How about the butchering of mothers and children? Or the mass immolation of your own countrymen in a London factory?'

But Ye Mingchen was unmoved. 'The West has been immolating the Chinese people for half a century. Our civilisation is older than all your empires combined. We opened our doors to you to do business in good faith, and how did you repay us? By peddling a drug that has turned our nation into a society of addicts and beggars, panhandling for the black crow. Mothers selling their own children into prostitution and slavery for a handful of opium ash. You have descended on us like a wake of vultures, and you are blind to it – blinded by your arrogance, your self-professed superiority. Is it any wonder that the Chinese people have had enough? They have been left with no choice. A cornered rat will bite.'

Ye Mingchen's voice rose in a furious crescendo as he spoke. Ben could see the humiliation in his eyes – the burning insult of an injustice left unresolved. Yet as Ye Mingchen raged, a different question started to form in Ben's mind.

'Why have you summoned me here?' Ben asked. 'Why *me*?'

Ye Mingchen reduced his anger to a simmer. 'I know more about you than you think, Mr Canaan. I know that you are not one of them. That you are no aristocrat, but a lowly Jew who has crawled his way out of the gutter. I know that you have only recently joined their ranks, and that your soul has not yet been purchased by the great machine of Empire. That is why I summoned you. Because you are the only person who might listen to me when I say: *the Great Qing is not behind the Black Blood Murders.*'

The Viceroy presented a compelling case, full of dignity and eloquence. But Ben was not convinced.

'Zirui was in your retinue. Bo was a government lawyer. Aiguo was a civil servant. That makes three ringleaders, all in your pocket. Their henchmen – all ex-soldiers from your ranks. And the Seven Gentlemen were your sworn enemies. So every sign points to you: your men, your means, your motive.'

'I will shed no tears for the Seven Gentlemen. Nevertheless, it was not us and your compatriots are too lazy or stupid, or both, to dig deeper. They are sleepwalking into a trap.'

'A trap set by whom?'

Ye Mingchen shrugged. 'That, I cannot tell you.'

'Even if it were true,' Ben said, 'even if the whole world were wrong and you were right, there's nothing I can do about it now. It's too late. I'm just an agent.'

Ye Mingchen looked disappointed – not as the negotiator on the other side of the fence, but as a schoolmaster might look at a truant child.

'Only cowards insist on their own powerlessness,' he chided. 'I did not realise I was speaking to a coward.'

'I prefer to think of myself as a realist. I cannot stop the inevitable.'

Ye Mingchen pondered Ben's words, rolling his tongue over his lips. 'Only one thing in life is inevitable, Mr Canaan, and that is death. For most creatures, this is all that matters. They spend their days on earth cowering in death's long shadow – unthinking, unquestioning, unchanging. Simply surviving. But we, as human beings, have a unique and tremendous gift: *the ability to defy*. To wrest control of our destiny from the clutches of time.'

He leant across the bank of candles to lay his hand on Ben's arm: an unprecedented gesture of intimacy.

'I know you understand me. Else how could a man like you be sitting here? Fate would have stayed your hand before you could even conceive of your freedom. But the longer you serve your masters, the less free you will become. Soon you will be like me: girded by rigid formality – dressed in the clothes of Empire – an empty vessel for a voice that is not your own. And the person you once were will be a distant memory, like a nameless star studding the heavens. You will be a man no more. Just a cog in an infernal machine, imprisoned for eternity in a gilded cage.'

Ben bowed his head to hide the look on his face. He thought back to the very first moment that Gustav Bruckner had entered that humble tailor's shop. The promise of something more beyond the narrow walls of Whitechapel. The opportunity to become the man that he was supposed to be. Why then did he have so many questions? Why could he still not feel like himself?

'You are asking me not to believe my own eyes,' Ben said.

'No. I ask you to ask yourself: *why are you really here?* Not simply to do your job as a functionary numbed to his own conscience. Ask, Detective, and you will discover.'

Ye Mingchen reached for the candle between the two men.

'We are not your enemy. I make this oath on my soul and on the souls of my ancestors.'

He pinched the flame with his index finger and thumb and snuffed it out, leaving only a wispy trail of smoke.

'Out, brief candle!' he whispered, the gleam of the now-dead fire lingering in his eyes.

On that note, Ben was sent back to Mount Austin. The further he drifted from Chinese territory, the harder he tried to dispel Ye Mingchen's words – to reject them as mere puff. But the voice persisted. It persisted as he bathed in the middle of the night. It persisted as he lay in bed, staring wide-eyed at the ceiling. It persisted as he sipped the Overholt and continued with the report. It persisted as he listened to Coldwell and Bowring play their war games over Sauvignon Blanc and oysters.

The evening after his clandestine rendezvous with Ye Mingchen, Ben decided to take the ferry out to Dapeng. He had read enough headlines. It was time to see it for himself.

He landed at Nan'ao at twilight, the land bathed in oceanic blue. Almost immediately, he saw the remains of what was once 'The Tiger': a collection of wooden buildings, two storeys high, across the waterfront over a small private harbour. It had been reduced to smouldering rubble, loose planks of wood jutting out like old forgotten gravestones, charred as black as coal. White flecks swirled in the air, and for a moment Ben thought it was snow. But they were at the height of summer, and even in winter snow never fell here. Rather, it was ghost-white ash, pirouetting around the wreckage in a mute dance of death.

But the destruction was not limited to The Tiger: the town of Nan'ao itself lay in ruins. Fishing posts had been burnt to the ground. Shops and dispensaries had been ransacked and stripped of their goods. Homes had their windows smashed in. The eerie quiet of grief smothered the town, throttling what little life remained.

There was a bungalow near the waterfront lit up from within – one of the only in view that showed any sign of activity. The door was open and people were shuffling in and out, mostly the elderly, leaning on each other for support. Cautiously, Ben entered the property.

It was a mourning ceremony. The locals, simple fishing folk, had formed a ring in the middle of the bungalow. Isolated in the eye of the circle were three people – an old woman wrapped in a dark shawl, a middle-aged man with a harrowed and haggard aspect, and a young boy looking withdrawn and raw in the face from crying. They were standing over two bodies, laid on a bed of plum blossom and chrysanthemum and dressed in plain pauper's clothes made of sack: a young woman with an infant nestled, cold and pallid, in her arms.

As soon as the old woman saw Ben, she staggered towards him, crying out in anguish. 'English! English!'

Ben raised his hands, trying to appease her. She cut him short with a slap to the face. It barely registered, let alone left a mark, but the rage behind it stunned Ben more than any right hook at his former boxing club. The middle-aged man stepped in to guide the woman away.

'She ask if you have no shame!' he spat, pointing to the bodies with tears in his eyes. 'My wife, my daughter… You see what you have done?!'

'I am looking for their murderer…' Ben stammered.

'*You are the murderer!* You, English! Soldiers, police – you came… destroyed houses, shops… killed anyone you could find… Raped women! For what?! *For what?!*'

To this, Ben had no answer. All he could say were the words: 'I'm sorry…' He backed away, beyond the threshold of the front door, as the bodies were swallowed up behind the mourners.

A thousand unspeakable thoughts raced through his mind as he trudged back to the water's edge. He took a calming breath, trying to make sense of the horror around him, but it caught in his throat.

He covered his mouth to stifle a sob. But another came, and then another. They did not stop until he was weeping uncontrollably, unseen and unheard as the moon emerged over the endless black seas – shuddering in grief for two brief candles snuffed without reason: a woman whom he never knew, a child who never got to live.

17

A British Hero

The rain had been relentless all week. But in the verdant plain of Happy Valley, just south of Victoria, the mood was one of celebration. Across the road from the racecourse was the Queen's Theatre: newly built and named, like most places on this island, after the monarch who had never set foot inside. It was opening night – not for a performance of Shakespeare or Verdi, but for a gala dinner honouring the Friends of British Hong Kong.

It was a Who's Who of the English political elite. Diplomats clinging to prominent Whig donors like remora to the belly of a humpback whale. Colonial administrators toasting Château Lafite Rothschild with compradors of prominent mercantile interests. Rivals playing at being friends, jostling in the imperial arena for advancement and advantage. Patriotic music accompanied each course: lobster salad to 'Rule Britannia'; guinea fowl and spinach in oyster sauce to 'Fairest Isle'; peach pie and clotted cream to 'Music for the Royal Fireworks'.

Ben sat at a round table in the main hall, quietly picking at his food. He was sandwiched between Ingrid and Bruckner, with Halliday and Parry directly opposite, along with a gaggle of lower downs from the firm.

It would have been hard to guess from the revelry that this little world was teetering on the brink of war. Nobody spoke about it directly. Instead, it could only be hinted at, inferred from particular words and gestures, extracted from the repartee like a splinter from under the skin. Everything was euphemism. They talked not of the dead, but of 'sacrifice'. Not of gunboats, but of 'diplomacy'. Not of destruction, but of 'expense'. And all in one incessant voice:

'The British navy would make swift work of the Chinese.'

'They were foolish! Picking a fight that they knew they would lose. They launched a hideous campaign against us, and it must be avenged. Amply.'

'Of course, any suffering is tragic. But if direct hostilities cannot be avoided… What can be done? It is a necessity.'

'With the right kind of pressure, they will accept that our China trade is here to stay.'

'As they should. Always quarrelling with us, instead of working together! Do they not realise that the trade serves to benefit them too? In truth, we are doing them a favour that they are not willing to do for themselves.'

'Precisely! We must forge a more civilised future for China. God granting victory to the Taiping rebels in the north, I daresay all of China will join the faith. Brothers in Christ.'

'And brothers in commerce.'

'And it would not have been possible without our dear detective, of course…'

Ben broke from his trance. It was Ingrid who had said those last words. With one hand, she plucked a petit four from her plate and greedily popped it in her mouth; the other slid surreptitiously under the table and between his legs, to rest on his crotch.

'I'm… just doing my job,' Ben said, trying to mask his unease.

After dessert, the diners rose from their tables to mingle more freely. In the melee, Ben received a tap on the shoulder from Halliday. They retreated to a quiet corridor at one remove from the gala to speak in private, beneath a poster of the theatre's upcoming inaugural performance of *King Lear*. Halliday dabbed his sweaty brow with a handkerchief. He was drunk.

'You will have noticed that I have no children, Mr Canaan.'

Ben nodded politely.

'I have Ingrid, of course. A splendid niece. Very attentive. She… takes care of my every need. She always has, you know. She has loved me ever since she was a little girl.'

Still, Ben held his tongue.

'And I like it, I do. I like having people on whom I can look kindly. They give me their loyalty, and in return I give them purpose. That is power. And the same applies to you. There is *much* that you can gain from me, Mr Canaan. More than you can imagine. And all I ask for in return is your loyalty.'

Ben thought back to what Halliday had told him when they first met on New Lewis: that power was lonely. It was only now that he fully grasped what the old man meant: that the whole world looked at him, but nobody *saw* him. All they saw was what they could get from him. Halliday was nothing more than the office that he inhabited, while the man he once was – the boy staring at his mother's lifeless body – had been lost somewhere along the way.

Ben bowed. 'Thank you for your generosity, sir.'

They returned to the main hall to find Coldwell on the stage, before the orchestra, giving an impromptu speech to the crowd.

As soon as Ben entered, Coldwell pointed him out with a jolly roar: 'There he is! Come here, Mr Canaan!'

Before Ben knew what was happening, he was being propelled through the crowd and up onto the stage. Coldwell was also on the tipsy side, spilling his champagne as he linked his arm around Ben.

'This man,' he said, 'is one of our best. Thanks to his tireless work, we will finally be able to hobble the Great Qing. Our little colony will be the springboard for a new era of peace and prosperity. Let the annals of history show that Detective Ben Canaan made it happen. He is, in the truest sense, a British hero!'

The audience broke into rapturous applause and raised their wineglasses to the gods. Ben's name resounded throughout the hall, swelling with the pride of Queen and Country. In a single gesture, Ben was offered the one thing that had never been accorded to the sons and daughters of Whitechapel: *acceptance*.

He should have been happy. This was the moment that he had dreamed of in his father's dusty workshop. This was the murky fantasy that played out in his mind when he glimpsed an expensive suit, or the swinging door of a gentlemen's club, or a bewigged barrister bustling down the Strand towards the Royal Courts of Justice. This was the impossible made real, as palpable as the scent of Floris in the air and the arm around his shoulder.

And yet, he felt absolutely nothing. He smiled, he waved, he bowed. But there was nothing behind it – just a cold and desolate vacuum. It was as though he had crossed the finish line after a gruelling race to the silence of an empty stand. Even as he shuffled offstage to be embraced by his admirers, he had never felt so alone.

He made a beeline for the foyer, if only to get away from the hubbub. Loitering on his own was Coldwell's navigator Zachary, the one who had first taken Ben to New Lewis, rolling a cigarette and keeping his head down.

He offered Ben a cigarette, but Ben declined.

'So they like you now, do they?' Zachary gestured to the double doors leading into the main hall.

'Seems so,' Ben shrugged.

'You'll make a lot of money soon. They give money to their boys. Shuts them up.'

'You don't sound too fond of them.'

'For what? They take what they want. Never ask us what we think about it.'

Zachary flicked his ash to the floor and exhaled a plume of smoke into the air. He could only shake his head in impotent anger.

'Buddhist temple here once,' he said. 'Last Emperor gave them this island. They took the gold and melted it for jewellery. Called it "oriental neckwear". Scratched out Buddha's face and put *theirs*.'

He pointed to the portrait looming over the foyer: Queen Victoria and Prince Albert, looking as imperious as one would expect, in full royal garb.

'If you object to them,' Ben asked, 'why do you work for them? Why are you waiting outside to take Coldwell home?'

'Same reason as you: they make the rules, we play by them. In the end, money has loudest voice.'

The side door to the lounges swung open and a pair of young nobles emerged: a thirty-something dandy in a velvet tailcoat and beaver felt hat, wielding a silver cane; arm-in-arm with his fiancée, wearing an extravagant turquoise ballgown and a dazzling diamond on her ring finger. The man eyed up Ben and Zachary as he passed. He pointed his cane at the sailor.

'You shouldn't be here, let alone smoking. If you wish to laze about, do it outside.'

'I work for the Captain Superintendent. And it's raining outside.'

'Did it sound like I was asking? This is no place for your kind.'

But Zachary made no effort to stub out his cigarette. Instead, he took another long, indulgent pull. In response, the man took a step closer to him.

'Put it out, Ching-Chong.'

Ben intervened with a conciliatory hand. 'That's not necessary. Leave him be.'

The man looked askance at Ben. 'Oh, so we have a coolie-lover here too, do we? How about you both go off and work the rice paddies, if you're that keen on each other?'

Ben was no stranger to bigotry. But something about this man's sneering, poisonous tone made his blood boil.

'How about you keep your beak in your own business and piss off back to the pile you crawled from?'

The man looked stunned by the sudden emergence of that good old East End twang, which Ben had hidden for so long.

'My God,' he said, his lips contorting in a nasty smile. 'You're that bloody Jew! How did you weasel your way in here?'

He poked Ben with his cane.

'What next? Will they start letting monkeys in as well?'

His fiancée came over and guided him away from Ben and Zachary. 'Come, darling. These dirty beggars are beneath you.'

The man waved them away as he turned his back. 'A Jew and a Chink! I thought this was a banquet, not a barnyard.'

Ben watched them disappear into the main hall. He felt Zachary's hand on his back as the navigator murmured a quiet 'Thank you'. But all he could think about was the languid ease of that man's venom. The effortless confidence in his gait, his voice, his manner. The kind of man for whom the world was laid out on a silver platter.

Ben stormed after him and burst into the main hall. 'You!'

The people around them recoiled in shock. The man turned, and before he knew it Ben had grabbed him by the scruff of the neck.

'*Apologise!*' Ben roared.

The man tried to shake him off, but Ben reeled him in closer until their foreheads were practically touching.

'Did you hear me? Don't you have any shame?! *Apologise!*'

'What the devil is wrong with you—'

Coldwell leapt into the fray to pry them apart. 'Mr Canaan! What on earth is going on here? Don't you know who this is?'

Ben was about to explain, when Governor Bowring appeared. 'What is the meaning of this, John Charles?'

'Never mind, Father,' John Charles spat, shooting Ben a baleful glare as he brushed himself down. 'A little bit of tit for tat…'

The penny dropped. This was none other than John Charles Bowring: the Governor's pampered eldest son. No wonder he strolled around like he owned the place. This island was his birthright. Ben had just touched the untouchable.

John Charles swanned off with his fiancée. The hum of chatter returned to the main hall. Ben shoved his hands into his pockets – an old force of habit when he was trying to restrain his anger.

'Mr Canaan,' Bowring said sternly, 'I respect you greatly, but I demand an explanation.'

'It doesn't make a difference,' Ben retorted. 'He made his point, I made mine. It's done. Now I'm going home.'

'Back to Mount Austin already?'

'No – *home*. I've done my job. I want to go back to London and be rid of this place.'

Coldwell shared a momentary glance with Bowring. It was the first time that Ben had seen them genuinely taken aback.

'Ben…' Coldwell said, 'your job is not finished. We need to find the last killer. You have the report to write. This is incredibly valuable work – you must listen to me—'

'No, you listen to me!' Ben jabbed his finger at Coldwell. 'I know what happened at Dapeng. I saw it with my own two eyes. That wasn't "self-defence". That was a massacre. You used the raid on The Tiger as an excuse to go on a rampage against innocent people. For what? *Revenge?!* What am I supposed to say at the inquiry? That British troops decided to have a jolly raping civilian women?'

Coldwell looked around nervously. Ben was causing a scene in front of far too many people. The geniality that Ben knew so well evaporated, and the man that Coldwell used to be – the soldier hardened by combat and sub-zero Crimean winters – came to the fore.

'You will say what we tell you to say. Because that is what the world needs to hear.'

'The world needs to hear the truth.'

'That *is* the truth. It is the truth because we said it.'

It was just as Bruckner had said to Ben back in London: *Discretion. Reliability. Absolute loyalty.* The same nausea that he felt at Dapeng welled up in him again and he turned on his heel. If he did not get out quickly, he feared he would vomit up the evening's feast.

He exited the theatre and stood under an awning by the entrance, listening to the downpour and taking deep breaths of sweet night air. The orchestra inside began playing 'God Save the Queen', scattering its melody across the enormous swathe of darkness that smothered Happy Valley. Beyond that little halo of golden light encircling his feet was a cruel, oppressive, godforsaken place. The sordid underbelly of Empire.

He stayed there for what felt like an eternity, lost in his own thoughts. The Wetherton Report hung like a spectre before his eyes. What excuse would he give to Bruckner and Palmerston if he did leave? What would he divulge to his family? What would happen to the vast land of China, just a stone's throw across the Pearl River, when the gunships rolled in? None of it made sense to him anymore. The mysterious web that he had been drawn into was as tangled and confounding as when he had first arrived.

His thoughts were interrupted by the trundling of a carriage. A run-of-the-mill taxicab halted outside the theatre. A woman stepped out wearing a thick woollen coat, her hair damp from the rain.

It was Liang.

'Ben!' She ran across the road to join him under the awning. 'I've been looking for you all evening. I went up to Mount Austin, but the staff told me you had come here for a gala dinner.'

She was shivering, and not from the rain. Something had happened – something serious.

'What's the matter?' he asked.

Liang held out Bo's encrypted note. 'I did it. The code. Ben, it's… You have to read it to understand…'

Ben unfurled the note and scanned its contents. It was just five lines, but what he read made his heart plummet to his stomach.

'Liang…' He grabbed her by the hand. 'Are you *absolutely* sure about this?'

'I'm certain. The cipher corresponds exactly to the key that we used for letters written in December. What you are reading is the only possible translation.'

Ben turned to face the dark. Five simple lines. And now this whole affair had become infinitely more complicated.

'What does this mean for us?' she asked.

But Ben was already running back into the theatre. He found Coldwell chatting to a couple of officers from the police department.

'Sebastian,' he said, 'I want to apologise for my conduct earlier. I don't know what came over me – perhaps a pang of melancholy in this deluge. In any case, I took some air outside and already I feel greatly improved. So let me put your mind at ease: *I am going nowhere*. Rest assured, I will not leave Hong Kong until the job is done!'

18

Heaven and Hell

It was a Sunday morning. The storms had passed and the skies were clear, save for the occasional tuft of cloud. A gentle breeze softened the baking July heat. This was the only day of the week when the China trade was allowed to rest. Merchant brigs anchored offshore, weary sailors dozed in their hammocks, and the windows of the trading offices were shuttered.

But on the South China Sea, two kilometres south of Hong Kong Island, the waters were busier. A cluster of sailboats and ferries moved in a scattergun formation, all heading in the same direction: the island of Po Toi. The people aboard these vessels were a mixture of Chinese, Europeans and Americans, ranging from elderly couples to young families cradling infants. They were dressed modestly – the women in long-sleeved, high-necked white dresses, with floral bonnets to shield their faces from the sun; the men in plain dark suits and cravats.

Ben and Liang stood at the prow of one of the crowded ferries. Neither of them spoke, not wanting to draw attention to themselves. Po Toi came into view as they sailed round Beaufort Island. It was almost entirely uninhabited – just craggy cliffs and grassy plains, undulating with the rise and fall of the island's many hilltops.

Perched on a steep bluff over the western shore was a church. The bell below its tapering spire was tolling the hour as the boats landed at the jetties below. Acolytes in monastic habits ushered the worshippers off the boats, up a flight of stairs built into the cliff-face, and across a field of Hong Kong irises to the doors of the church, where its name was painted in white: Tabernacle of New China.

Ben and Liang found a space near the back and waited for the service to start, scanning the crowd for a familiar face that did not appear.

Once all the congregants were seated, the doors slammed shut and a curate – a young Chinese man, clean-shaven with his hair cut short just like Bo – took the pulpit before the altar.

'Brothers and sisters,' he said, in carefully practised English, 'I must begin with an apology. Our dear Reverend Finlay Armstrong is not here today. Indeed, he will absent for the time being, leaving it to me as his curate to deliver the sermon on his behalf. Now, our community as you know is a humble one – we subsist not on the bread of commerce, but on the milk of your kindness and good will. Ledgers will be passed around for you to inscribe a sum to donate, if you so wish, so that we can spread the word of Christ across all of China.'

The ledgers in question were passed from person to person in each row. Ben recognised the design. The emerald-green tint of the leather. The elaborate frontispiece. The same as the ledger that had been left at his door back in London – the one inscribed with the names of the Seven Gentlemen.

He snapped it shut and passed it on.

The curate thanked the congregants for their generosity and the service commenced. It consisted mostly of songs and

Bible-readings, all on the theme of sacrifice: giving up worldly temptations and material gain to partake in the spiritual wealth of Christ. The congregants were enthralled. Ben could see the soothing effect of this message play out on their faces. The stresses of daily life ebbed away, replaced with a sense of calm reassurance. It was almost as though a spell had been cast over them, suspending everything outside the walls of this church and rendering them unthinking, unquestioning.

At the end of the service, the congregants obediently filed back out. Ben and Liang, however, strode in the opposite direction, towards the curate.

'Good morning, my dear friends,' the curate said. 'I do not recognise you. Are you members of our congregation?'

'Well, I'm a Jew and she's a Buddhist,' Ben replied, 'so I'll let you draw your own conclusion.'

'And what brings you to the Tabernacle of New China?'

'We'd like to have a word with Reverend Armstrong.'

The curate gave them a serene smile. 'The reverend is absent at the moment.'

'And you have so gamely filled his shoes! Why don't we step somewhere private?'

The curate's gaze flitted to the departing congregation. 'I should really be attending to our congregants—'

Ben flashed his identification papers, complete with his government and police credentials. 'I wasn't making a request… *my dear friend.*'

The curate relented and led them to the vestry. He offered them goji berry tea, which had been left to brew over an open stove. Ben and Liang refused.

'First things first,' Ben said. 'Where exactly has Armstrong disappeared to?'

'The reverend set sail on his yacht a few days ago. He has an important engagement upriver.'

'I asked where *exactly*.'

'That is all I know. The reverend's private affairs are his business.'

'And when will he be back?'

The curate could only shrug, slightly bemused. 'Ask God. Only He knows.'

Ben did not appreciate the curate's posturing, fastidiously concealed behind a veneer of piety. He nodded to Liang. She removed three albumen prints from her pocket: photographs of the three men at the heart of this mystery.

'Do you recognise these men?' she asked.

The curate studied the prints. He let slip the tiniest flinch. 'I do.'

'What are their names?'

'This one is Zirui. This is Aiguo. And this is Bo. They are… were… members of our congregation. It was the reverend who converted them, as he did so many souls.'

Liang looked incredulous. She jabbed her finger at the image of Bo. 'This man? Converted by Reverend Armstrong?'

'Absolutely. I remember it. He was baptised almost two years ago, just out front. Soon afterwards, he brought his companions into the fold and the reverend converted them as well.'

Liang retreated into herself. This was obviously news to her: another revelation about her late husband – another side to his life that she had never witnessed.

'I'm assuming you know what these men stand accused of,' Ben said.

The curate nodded. 'We were horrified to hear it, sir. I knew very little about them. It was Reverend Armstrong who was more

closely acquainted with them. They were never prominent figures in the community – they preferred to sit on the margins.
They seemed completely peaceful to me. Which made the news
all the more shocking.'

They sat in silence. Ben leant back and clasped his hands
behind his head. He and the curate maintained unbroken eye
contact for an agonising few seconds.

'Is Aiguo here?' Ben asked.

The curate shook his head.

'Are you sure? Perhaps we should take a look around.'

'I suppose that is also not a request,' the curate mused.

'Look at you!' Ben grinned. 'Fast learner.'

They searched the church from top to bottom, including the
cellars under the nave. The curate led Ben and Liang on a brief
circuit around the island, to inspect the coastal grottos and
the outhouses dotted across the plain. But they found nothing.
Aiguo was not on Po Toi.

Ben and Liang returned to the jetties as the last ferry back
to Victoria was boarding. They were about to climb up the ramp
when one last question occurred to Ben.

'Is the reverend's yacht usually kept on Po Toi?' he called
out to the curate.

'No, sir. It is moored at one of the ports on Hong Kong Island,
though I don't know which.'

Throughout most of the journey back, Liang gazed mourn-
fully across the waters, as though the answer to her questions
lay buried full fathom five.

'He never told me that he was a Christian,' she said, trying
to make sense of it out loud. 'But then… if he was, he couldn't
have told anyone because of his job. The Great Qing would
never tolerate a Christian in their ranks.'

By the time they reached Victoria, a new working theory was forming in Ben's mind. He went straight to Coldwell and Bruckner to lay it out for them. He began by unfolding the note that Liang had given him and placing it flat on the table in Coldwell's office:

My dearest Liang,

I should never have listened to Armstrong.

I thought I was serving God, when in truth I was serving the Devil.

I wish that I could undo what I have done. But is too late for me now. Please forgive me.

Yours for eternity, Bo

'We're being led by the nose, I'm sure of it,' Ben said. 'They – whoever "they" are – want us to think that it's the Great Qing that is behind these killings. But the answer has been right in front of us this entire time.'

Coldwell and Bruckner exchanged a sceptical look. Neither of them was convinced.

'Armstrong is a lame preacher who spends his days propped up on a soapbox,' Coldwell stifled a chuckle. 'And you're suggesting *this man* is behind the Black Blood Murders?'

'Whether it's him, or someone else that he's working for – someone more powerful – I don't know. But every fibre of my being tells me something isn't right. Everything is too *convenient*. Like it's been put there for us to find.'

'You've seen these men,' Coldwell retorted. 'They were well resourced. Organised. A militia. Where would a man like Armstrong even begin orchestrating something of that nature?'

Ben frantically flicked through the pages of his notebook.

'Scattered throughout this case are mentions of this man "Ames". Someone embedded in our own ranks, working hand-in-glove with the perpetrators. And how did I meet Armstrong? *At Odysseus Halliday's dinner table.* He's a confidant of one of our closest allies. Hiding in plain sight. He has a vested interest, I'm sure of it. All this preaching about giving up your wealth – meanwhile he has his own yacht, his own island, his own church, his thousands of followers, his rich friends. The ledgers in his church are the same as the one left at my door in London. Even the names, Armstrong and Ames, they sound almost interchangeable—'

'*Enough!*' Bruckner bellowed.

Ben flinched. For the first time since he had met Bruckner, the slender and unassuming German had lost his temper. Bruckner bowed his head and took a deep breath to collect himself.

'You're a good man,' he continued, 'but you are unravelling, and you need to get a hold of yourself. This is not the Ben Canaan that we enlisted.'

'My mind has never been clearer,' Ben insisted. 'You're just too pig-headed to listen.'

'Oh really? You think I don't know about your opium addiction? Your mistress in London who brings it to you weekly? The flower girl that you've been consorting with since you arrived? The first thing you did when you came here was visit an opium den. And the sleepless nights you've been suffering, the nightmares, the alcohol… Now this. I fear that Hong Kong, as it has done to so many men, has broken you. I should have known. Even the PM had his doubts about you for this job, and I vouched for you because I had faith. But perhaps we have asked too much of you. I'm sorry. I blame myself.'

'Bo put this note in my pocket. It must mean… something!'

Coldwell placed a sympathetic hand on Ben's arm. 'It means you've been bamboozled, Ben. That's what the Chinese excel at. They can't win in open battle, so they resort to deception, to divide us from within. And look at us now: bickering on the cusp of victory. It's just more trickery from beyond the grave.'

'We are on the cusp not of victory, but of a war based on a false premise. On a mistake. How many people are going to die because of us? We have to stop it.'

'It is out of our hands!' Bruckner shot back.

Before Ben could say another word, Bruckner dismissed him with a final wave. Their meeting was over. Ben had overplayed his hand and alienated the people he needed most. As he skulked out of the police station, he could not help but feel like the outsider again. The hard-won confidence of his superiors, which he had enjoyed for so long, had quickly evaporated.

But he remained undeterred. If there was one thing that had seen him through the tightest of spots, it was trusting his instinct. That was exactly what was called for today. And if the British would not help him, then by hook or by crook he would have to honour the promise that he made to his grandfather in the living room back home: he would do it himself.

First, he drew up a list of names – all the bannermen who had been a part of the militia that carried out these killings. He spent the following day travelling around Hong Kong Island, visiting every church and searching for matches among the names on their membership records. Sure enough, each bannerman was inscribed as a recently baptised member of one church or another. Every last one of the assassins was a Christian convert.

His next stop was Zachary. He found him in a bar in Chung Wan, where sailors and fishermen were known to drown their sorrows over games of *madiao* and bowls of dried squid. Ben bought him a bottle of baijiu in exchange for his undivided attention.

'I need you to find me a yacht,' Ben explained. 'It's called *Kingdom of Heaven*. It belongs to—'

'Finlay Armstrong,' Zachary said. 'I've heard of him. Yankee preacher man. He sails around China on it, shoving pamphlets in our faces.'

'All I know is that it's kept at one of the ports on Hong Kong Island. But last I checked, there are almost fifty of those and I don't want to draw too much attention to the fact that I'm circling him. His acolytes were a little wary when I questioned them.'

'So you want me to trek around Hong Kong, going from port to port asking where it is?'

'You worked the docks and you're a sailor. It's less suspicious that way. It also means they're more likely to let you see the departure logs than they are some nosy English boy – and that's what I'm really after. I need to know where he went, as soon as possible.'

Zachary was inclined to help. He felt that he owed it to Ben for defending him against Governor Bowring's son. Ben only had one further request: Zachary was to take his findings to Liang's place, not Mount Austin. Ben wanted this off the books for now.

While he waited for Zachary to report back, Ben called on Ingrid to warn her about Armstrong. It started as a routine sit-down on the garden terrace of her waterfront estate – purely professional, though as usual with Ingrid, it did not end that way. By twilight she had him dining on miso-glazed tilapia and

Huangjiu yellow wine, as the great expanse of the South China Sea glittered with a thousand pinpricks of silver moonlight. By nightfall they had moved on to sorbet ices and hot buttered rum for dessert. And by midnight they were in bed.

But Ben could not get the case out his head. Every time Ingrid presented some distraction, he obstinately circled back to it.

'It all comes back to that letter,' Ben whispered, as though he was nervous that he might be overheard. 'The bloody rag I've been looking for. One that directly implicates Armstrong.'

Ingrid tried to shut him up with a kiss, but he pulled away and paced to the window, tracing his fingertips along the fogged-up pane.

'It was addressed to Liang, in a code only she could decipher. Yet Bo gave it to me. So the question is… *why*?'

'Ben, why don't you come back to bed—'

'The only reason he would give me the letter is if he knew that I would go to Hong Kong – that I would be led to Liang – that I could get her to decipher it for me. But how could he have known that? How could he have known my next steps before I took them?'

Ingrid had nothing for him. She could only splay her palms in a gesture of exasperation.

'*I was supposed to take them all along,*' Ben declared. 'It's just as Liang said: what if everything I thought was true is actually a lie? What if I'm just thinking what they want me to think?'

At this, Ingrid rose to her feet and came over to caress Ben's cheeks. 'Dear boy, you're starting to sound a little… paranoid.'

Ben rifled through his pockets and pulled out the note to wave it in her face. 'This is a message in a bottle, Ingrid. Cast out by Bo as a last Hail Mary to try and make things right. It's a confession that he wanted the two people who mattered most to know: Liang, as the only woman he loved; and me, as the only man who cares enough to find out the truth.'

Ingrid's features hardened. The temperature in the room seemed to plummet.

'Is it the truth you're after?' she said. 'Or are you just looking for any excuse to prevent the coming war, because you can't bear the fact that you have helped to bring it about?'

She kissed him, not out of love, but out of pity. Ben barely reacted. She pulled away.

'I told you once that you must find a way to live with your hands being dirty,' she said. 'This is one of those moments.'

She slipped on her dressing gown and slunk down the corridor to the bathroom, calling out to one of the servants to draw a bath. Ben watched all the while, clenching and unclenching his fists as he turned obsessively around the burning question of what to do – and what to believe.

Early one Friday evening Ben was in his room at Mount Austin when he heard a knock at his door. It was Fitzjohn, and from the apprehensive look on his aide's face, he had come bearing bad news.

'Communication from Bruckner.' Fitzjohn handed him an envelope and scuttled off.

It read as expected: written confirmation that the British would not pursue any further line of inquiry in relation to Armstrong and that Ben was expected to rule him out in the report. Nothing to the contrary would be accepted. The party line had been set, and Ben now had no choice but to toe it.

He spent hours installed at his desk, staring at a blank piece of paper: the start of the next section of his report. His pen hovered inches from the page, but never dared to meet it. Some inkling of the words that he had been told to say would form in his mind, only to fall apart. It felt so fake, so wrong – a half-woven story that he could no longer bring himself to believe.

Ben grabbed the Overholt, poured the remainder into a whiskey glass, and knocked it back in one grimacing gulp. Then he began writing, barely conscious of his scribbles, plunging headlong into the lie like a diver into icy waters:

The evidence pointing to Reverend Finlay Armstrong proved to be inconclusive, giving rise to no more than incidental suspicion. No further reasonable cause was identified.

No sooner had he lifted his pen to come up for air than he felt a distant rumble at his window. At first, he thought it was a thunderclap heralding a summer monsoon. But then it rang out again, preceded by a high-pitched whistle. Then another, and another, shorter and sharper than any thunder he had heard.

It was no storm. Those were explosions.

He hurried onto the balcony. Fires were erupting along the shores of Chinese-controlled Kowloon to the north, a couple of miles from his vantage point. Blinding bursts of orange flame illuminated the silhouettes of British barques sailing across the Pearl River. Bright white flashes strobed from their hulls: volley after volley of cannon. Plumes of gunpowder smoke shrouded the waters – a mist of death swallowing up Kowloon.

Resounding over Hong Kong were the first chimes of war: a naval attack designed to test the strength of China's southern defences. It was already too late to stop what was happening. Ben could only stare in helpless horror as this runaway train left him stranded at the station. How many mothers and children like the ones at Dapeng, or on the Isle of Dogs, were being slaughtered? How much blood was on his hands?

He stormed out of the hotel and made his way downhill to Victoria on foot. He found the settlement largely deserted. People had retreated indoors for shelter, for fear of retaliation by the Chinese. The streets were filled not with the sound of commerce, but with the ear-splitting shriek of cannon-fire.

He turned onto Spring Garden Lane in Wan Chai. The sign for The Floating Life materialised up ahead, rattling back and forth in the wind. But Ben had not come for Liang this time. Instead, he craved the one thing that would banish the guilt gnawing away at his guts: the black crow – *yāpiàn* – opium.

Before he knew it, he was reclining on a mattress in an isolated corner of the den. His shoes were off. The pipe was already placed against his lips. A flower girl was performing her magic at the spirit lamp, heating up the ball of paste to smoking point. She lowered it into the bowl and Ben took the deepest breath he could. He wanted to flood his lungs until every capillary was turgid with black blood. He closed his eyes, waiting for it to hit.

It started with that sinking feeling. The muscles relaxing from head to toe. The barrage of gunfire and the screams in his head fading to an ambient hum in the pit of his belly. The faces of those who had died – burnt alive, gored, raped, disembowelled – merging into a shapeless mist. The only voice left was that of the flower girl:

'Sink into Diyu, Englishman… Sink into the realm of the dead…'

It felt as though he was floating on a bottomless black ocean. He breathed a sigh of a relief. He was exactly where he wanted to be: nowhere. A place of nonexistence. No pain, no shame, no regret. He was just like the people whom he could not save – embraced by sweet, warm, loving death.

All he needed to do was keep smoking. That way, he would never have to leave.

'*Ben?*'

He opened his eyes. This was not The Floating Life. There were no clouds of smoke; no flower girl; no opium eaters. Instead, a familiar face came into view: a boy with big round glasses, peering over him with a combination of curiosity and caution. It was Tao.

As soon as he saw that Ben was awake, he leapt to his feet and ran out of the room, shouting in Cantonese. Ben sat up with a groan. He was back in 12 Tang Lung Street. God only knew how many hours had passed since the British assault on Kowloon. For now, Victoria had fallen quiet again. The cannon-fire had ceased and only the chirping of the crickets remained.

He sluggishly poured himself a cup of oolong from the pot steaming next to him and took slow, painful sips. Eventually, Tao returned with Liang in tow. She was carrying a bowl of pungent broth infused with an array of herbal remedies – ginseng root, dried red sage, buds of yanhusuo. As soon as she entered, she set the tray down and hurried over to Ben.

'Lie back!' she insisted. 'You've not yet come down from the high.'

'Or up from the low,' Ben quipped, before erupting into a fit of coughs. 'How did I end up here?'

'It was supposed to be my night off,' Liang said, stirring the broth. 'Then I received word from Madame Xu that my "English companion" was smoking himself into oblivion on cheap dross. So, fool that I am, I decided to pull you out of the hole that you had dug for yourself.'

'That wasn't necessary, Liang. I was there by choice.'

'Such gratitude. You do realise you were smoking glorified rat poison? I had a client binge *yanhui* for an evening and his heart stopped like *that*.'

Ben rubbed his bleary eyes. 'Maybe that would have been good for me.'

'Now you really sound like a madman. Here, drink up.'

She foisted the broth on him and Ben gingerly took a sip. He recoiled from the acrid taste, but Liang compelled him to continue.

'You're about the third person to call me that this week,' Ben said. 'And you know what? I think I'm starting to believe it.'

It was three hours since Ben had begun his opium binge. It was imperative that he did not fall asleep again until the opium was fully flushed from his system, so Liang stayed up with him until dawn, talking about anything and everything to keep him awake. Ben told her that she was not obliged to take care of him, but on each occasion she dismissed him: 'If I didn't think you were a good man, I wouldn't do it,' was all she said.

Shortly after the bells tolled six, there was a knock at the door – though Liang was not expecting visitors. Ben left it to her to answer while he slouched in the living room.

But then he heard her say the name of their new visitor: *Zachary*. In a heartbeat, Ben was staggering to his feet and lumbering to the front door. Sure enough, Coldwell's navigator was standing before them, cap in hand.

'I know where Armstrong went,' Zachary said, his voice a gravelly whisper. 'And it may not be what you expect...'

'That, Zachary, is just how I like it,' Ben said. 'Why don't you come in and we can all have a chat?'

19

Ghosts

It had taken Zachary the better part of a week to dig up the answer. But in the end, it was the docks at Sai Wan, a stone's throw from the British naval barracks, that yielded results. Armstrong kept his yacht, *Kingdom of Heaven*, docked in a regular spot on the marina. Eight days previously, she had set sail with Armstrong and a small crew for a town called Jintian. No expected return date was provided – Armstrong had described it as a 'flexible visit'.

'And where is this Jintian?' Ben asked.

They spread out a map of China on the low table by the hearth.

'We are here,' Zachary said, pointing to the Pearl River Delta on China's southern coast. 'Hong Kong sits at the mouth of the Pearl River estuary, which runs through Guangdong province. If you follow the estuary up and to the west, you reach the Xi River – one of the main tributaries that flows into the delta. Follow the Xi River and it branches off once more, becoming the Xun River.'

He traced his finger upstream, following this path deeper into mainland China.

'The Xun takes you into Guangxi province, and it is here – not far from the border with Guangdong – that you will find Jintian.'

His finger landed on a nondescript spot on the map, deep in a forest on the banks of the Xun. It was the kind of place one could pass without noticing its existence.

'But Jintian is no ordinary town,' Zachary continued. 'It was the birthplace, in 1851, of the Taiping Rebellion.'

Ben recognised that name. He cast his mind back to the conversation with Armstrong around Halliday's dinner table aboard the *Emmeline*. That was the civil war raging up north, between the Great Qing and the radical Christian insurrectionists seeking to overthrow the dynasty. The one that Armstrong himself had referred to as a great moral awakening.

As Zachary explained, Jintian was where the leader of the Taiping, a revolutionary by the name of Hong Xiuquan, founded his Christian sect and launched his campaign against the Great Qing. Now, after five years of bloody conflict, Jintian remained as one of the last southern outposts of what had become known as the Taiping Heavenly Kingdom. And it was this place to which Armstrong had sailed.

It could mean only one thing: Armstrong was in cahoots with the Taiping rebels. This was no plot by the Great Qing to throw off the shackles of the opium trade. This was a holy war, waged by a militant Christian insurgency against the regime that had ruled these lands for two hundred years. And they were about to play their winning hand: baiting Britain into a war with China, and in the process bringing about the demise of the Great Qing. It was just as Bo presaged in London: they would raze the old order to the ground and build a new world from its ashes.

It would take a full day of sailing to get to Jintian. Zachary offered his services, since he was not needed by Coldwell. Ben was already set on going, but Liang refused – Tao's safekeeping was more important to her.

They spent the rest of the day preparing for the voyage. Zachary pulled a few strings and got hold of a workmate's clipper – built for speed and stealth, perfect to get Ben to Jintian as quickly and inconspicuously as possible. Meanwhile, Ben sent a note up to Fitzjohn at Mount Austin, stating that he would spend a few days taking the air and recuperating at the thermal baths on Luofu Mountain, in central Guangdong.

By five in the afternoon, the clipper was ready and Ben had packed the essentials: his identification documents, his trusty penknife, and his gun. It was a nervy ride up the Pearl River estuary. The British assault had left Kowloon in a state of disorder. There was always an outside chance that a roaming British gunship might mistake them for a Chinese trading boat and blow them to smithereens. The prospect of being captured and taken prisoner by the Great Qing, on the other hand, was no less daunting.

But nobody troubled them as they ventured north. The factories and fisheries along the shores of Kowloon had been reduced to smoking ruins. Business along the Pearl River had ground to a halt; the merchant brigs and dragons were resting at anchor; and the warehouses had been shut for fear of bombardment.

'Britain is getting the war it craves so much,' Zachary muttered.

They steered west and passed up the waterways branching off the Pearl River. They were no longer in waters under British dominion. What happened next would depend entirely on how effectively they could blend in with the other Chinese trawlers. They passed a succession of quaint towns and villages, each with some distinct character: the glassmakers of Lanhe – the forts of the Ancient City in Shawanzhen – the smoky aroma of cured fish on the waterfront of Beijiaozhen. Just a short trip from the British settlements were unique cultures in miniature, untouched by the long arm of the West.

The deeper they penetrated into China, the wilder things became. The fire and steel of industry were replaced with banks of dense forest and waterlogged marshland. The grass grew taller, forming thick walls of reeds that clogged the brackish swamps. It was not long before their only companions were the shrill, chattering song of the babblers in the treetops and the quiet churning of water under the clipper.

They made a brief stop at Zhaoqing, where the Pearl River Delta ended and the Xi River began. Zachary went into one of the local taverns on Ben's behalf to buy congee and steamed mantou buns. Most people in these parts had never clapped eyes on a Westerner before and Ben did not want to draw any unwanted attention. He pulled his straw hat tight over his brow and stayed on deck, keeping his distance.

Beyond Zhaoqing, the Xi River took them into mountainous terrain, carving a path down a steep forested gorge. By then, night had fallen. Ben and Zachary were swarmed by mosquitoes, until their necks were raw-red. There were barely any lights out here: just a pale moon and the solitary lantern on deck, reflected in the waters of the Xi.

The one constant throughout this changing landscape was the presence of opium. Even the tiny fishing villages of the Guangxi countryside had been visited by the black crow. Cabins up and down the riverbank had been converted into storehouses for crates of opium. In every community were rake-thin men and women of all ages, some wandering around shirtless and others in rags, in a perpetual opium-induced stupor. Their hair had turned white and their high-pitched groans quivered in the humid air.

'*Yangui*,' Zachary said, with a mixture of disgust and sadness. 'Opium ghosts.'

The following evening, shortly before sunset, they arrived at Jintian. They were traversing the Xun River and had just entered Gui County. Suddenly, the bright yellow flags of the Great Qing, once so prevalent, disappeared – replaced with the red-and-white standard of the Taiping Heavenly Kingdom. Banners were draped from the roofs of riverside granaries and mills, bearing the same graven image that Ben had seen all those months ago in Aiguo and Zirui's room aboard the *King Kyrië*: the cross-legged man in yellow robes, in his guapi mao hat, with a gold seal of a coiled, fanged snake covering his face.

The entrance to Jintian was demarcated by a pagoda on the water, acting as a watchtower over the wood-walled buildings that sloped up the hills on either bank. The people looked noticeably different to those in Qing territory: the men and women dressed in beige silk *magua* jackets and trousers, and wore their hair at shoulder length. At every street corner were militias with modern rifles and swords sheathed at the hip. Jintian had once been full of temples, but the symbolism of the old religion – the dragons, the murals depicting the Five Forms of the Highest Deity, the statues of the mythic immortals of the Taoist pantheon – had long been torn down. In their place now stood chapels and churches, towering crucifixes and monuments to Christ.

They moored on the south bank. Jintian was a small community, and it did not take them long to find Armstrong's *Kingdom of Heaven* tethered to a jetty further upriver. Zachary proceeded to ask around the waterfront for Armstrong, while Ben pretended to be a missionary so as not to attract undue attention. Nobody recognised the name, but many knew of a

'Yankee preacher' who was paying a visit to the town. He was staying at a local inn, The Temple, built in honour of their leader Hong Xiuquan.

Zachary waited on the boat in case they needed a swift getaway. Ben, meanwhile, ventured alone into Jintian in search of The Temple. He found it at one end of a plaza built on the reputed site of the original Jintian rebellion that had sparked this civil war. The ground floor was a rustic canteen serving up a variety of seafood dishes: gelatinous fish maw soup, dried scallops and shrimp in honey-infused soy sauce, and steamed pomfret with pickled plums.

He spotted Armstrong immediately. He was seated at a table at the back of the canteen and was digging into a whole steamed grouper drizzled with hot oil, his coat-wallet on the tabletop. Opposite him, with no food of his own, was Aiguo – the selfsame 'Longshanks' that Ben had tailed to Hong Kong.

A server approached Ben and posed a question in Mandarin. Ben simply pointed to Armstrong.

'That man there – the priest – who is he?'

The server was taken aback by Ben's English.

'Priest!' Ben whispered. 'Do you understand? Who is he? His name, yes?'

There was a moment of confusion, before the server clocked Armstrong and realised what Ben was asking. 'Ah, priest… Yes. Priest… Mr Ames…'

That was all Ben needed to know. His lip curled into a snarl. *I've got you now.*

He barged past the server and approached the table at the back. He placed both hands on the table and leant in to get a good look at them.

'Space for three?'

If Armstrong was surprised by Ben's presence, he concealed it well behind a pious smile. Aiguo did not have the same self-possession and went white as a sheet. He had the air of a man on the run: haggard, unshaven, thinner than Ben remembered.

'By all means, Detective,' Armstrong replied.

Aiguo shuffled over to make space for Ben. Armstrong deftly slipped his coat-wallet into his breastpocket and snapped his fingers for a server.

'A glass of huangjiu and a bowl of yutang soup for our guest.'

'No need for the soup, but I'll take the huangjiu,' Ben cut in. 'I won't be staying long.'

Once Ben was served, Armstrong returned to his grouper. His scoliosis had all but vanished. He sat perfectly upright and displayed none of the infirmity that Ben had witnessed on the beaches of Lintin island.

'How did you find us?' Armstrong said.

'I'm a dedicated man.'

'Clearly, since you've come all this way… Commendable.'

Ben eyed up his two dinner companions. Armstrong was nonchalantly tucking into his grouper, while Aiguo, whether out of fear or shame, could barely make eye contact with Ben.

'So that was your game all along, wasn't it?' Ben said. 'The Taiping are at war with the Great Qing. But the Great Qing is stronger, wealthier, more numerous. What better way to turn the tide than to lure the world's most powerful empire into a war against your sworn enemy? So you embed Taiping loyalists within the upper echelons of the Great Qing's political elite. Then you use them to frame the Great Qing for a series of murders that would inevitably draw the wrath of the British. And just like that, the Great Qing is fighting a losing war on multiple fronts, and the path is cleared for a Taiping victory.'

Armstrong was smirking as he gulped down another morsel.

'Was it worth it?' Ben scoffed, turning to Aiguo. 'All the blood you've spilled? All your countrymen who will lose their lives because of your actions? Do you think your loved ones would approve of what you've done?'

'I need not the approval of man, but only that of God,' Aiguo replied in a flat monotone. *'If I were still trying to please man, I would not be a servant of Christ.'*

'Galatians 1:10,' Armstrong nodded in approval.

Ben stared pointedly at Aiguo. His words were defiant, but his face told another story. He was struggling desperately to believe a mantra that he had been taught to say.

'So Aiguo is a foot-soldier,' Ben said to Armstrong. 'A dogsbody who's there to take marching orders. Which makes you what? A zealot? Or just a greedy businessman who's been promised a share?'

'Greed has nothing to do with it, Detective.'

'Oh, really? Well, for a selfless man, you've amassed a respectable fortune. You preach sacrifice to your followers, but you don't seem to practise it yourself.'

Armstrong laid down his chopsticks. 'I have sacrificed everything I once was in the name of my duty – a duty that I owe to powers far greater than myself. What am I? I am but a ghost. No face, no name. Nothing but what my duty tells me to say and do. Just like that shivering boy to your right… and just like *you*, Detective.'

'I'm nothing like you,' Ben sneered. 'You've brought destruction to the gates of China, and I'm trying to stop it.'

'You can stop what's coming just as much as you can stop the rising of the sun.' Armstrong generously refilled Ben's glass. 'You sincerely believe that you – an individual, a single solitary man – can change the course of history. But it's not true. It's a story that we put down in books and poems, that we chew on before bedtime like opium eaters, so that we can sleep comfortably. Only one thing really changes history: *the systems that we build.* The great imperial and religious projects that span nations and oceans and time itself. And you are a cog in that machine – you exist to serve its needs. That's why you're here in the first place! If Aiguo is a lowly foot-soldier, then so am I, and so are you, and so is everyone. The difference between you and me is that I accept it, and you prefer to live in delusion.'

Armstrong was a natural-born sermoniser. In his speechifying, he had landed on the very thing that had been troubling Ben for so long. The feeling that he was always playing someone else's game – that he had to follow its rules rather than his own – that he was not one of the 'Great Independents', as had been said to him once by a certain Contessa in Constantinople, but a puppet bouncing limply on its strings.

'I could always go to these paymasters,' Ben shot back. 'See how they react when they find out they're being taken for a ride by a bunch of jungle Christians.'

Armstrong suddenly started cackling – so loud that half the canteen turned to look at them in confusion. He wiped his bright-red brow with his napkin and stifled a guttural snort.

'Apologies,' he said, clearing his throat. 'That was very amusing. Besides, why are you so opposed to the prospect of a Taiping victory? Have you not been paying attention? Is it daisies and rainbows out there? Look, look – think about it this way…'

He pushed two small glass bowls across the table: one filled with salt, the other with pepper.

'Let's say the salt is your vision for the future, and the pepper is the Taiping's. In your society, women are kept immiserated – glorified cattle for their fathers and husbands. In Taiping society, all men and women are equal as one great collective. Your society is degraded by a culture of rampant individualism, in which every man puts his own interests before those of his neighbour. In Taiping society, everyone is held to account by an all-loving, all-knowing State. Your society has brought decadent chaos to which the fat and indulgent elites of China have already capitulated. The Taiping give people a purpose that is larger than themselves. We are delivering China from its own collapse. And, above all, we are spreading the word of Christ.'

'The word of Christ?' Ben laughed in Armstrong's face. 'I'm no Christian, but I'm pretty sure Christ didn't teach you to butcher and lie and steal your way to the top.'

Aiguo finally spoke up. 'We are taught to do whatever is necessary to serve God—'

'Who are you trying to convince?' Ben snapped. 'I can see your guilt. I know that Bo felt the same way – it's only because of him that I found you both. Are you telling me that you never asked each other, or yourselves, whether what you're doing is right? That there was no shadow of doubt in your mind when you murdered those people? How many more need to die before you acknowledge that this has gone too far?'

To this, Aiguo had no riposte. He shrank back into himself and turned his gaze to his restless hands, picking at the dirt under his fingernails.

It was Armstrong who came to Aiguo's aid. 'On the contrary, Detective: you are the one who has gone too far. The only way to survive this game, if you do indeed wish to survive, is, as we Americans say, to look out for number one. But the way you are going, you are risking more than I suspect you are willing to lose.'

Ben was about to protest, but Armstrong silenced him.

'It's very easy. Forget all of this happened. Go back to Hong Kong. Finish your report as planned. Let history take its course, and enjoy your money, your manor and your mistress.'

Ben finally lost his temper. He seized Armstrong by his collar and dragged him to his feet. The wine crashed to the floor. All activity in the canteen broke off and a server rushed over to separate them.

'If you think I'm going to roll over like a spaniel asking for a belly rub, you are sorely mistaken. I'll stop this from happening – even if it kills me, even if I drown trying to hold back the flood.'

'Then make your peace with the Almighty—'

Ben pushed Armstrong away and stormed off, as the priest hollered after him: 'Bless you, sir! Bless your heart!'

Ben retraced his steps back to Zachary. He found his companion standing by the clipper, looking around warily at the people of this strange enclave.

'I don't like this place,' he said. 'I tried lighting a cigarette and a group of children threw my tobacco in the river.'

'Well, I've got good news: we're legging it out of here. Let's get her going.'

Zachary began loosening the ropes tethering the clipper to the south bank. While he worked, Ben saw a familiar face emerge from the masses milling past them: it was Aiguo, following Ben furtively.

Ben was instantly on guard, but Aiguo raised his hands. 'I come in peace, Detective.'

He looked over his shoulder to check if he was being followed. Then he drew Ben in close and whispered in his ear.

'Find me at the Pok Fu Lam Fishery on Hong Kong Island, two nights from now. Sha Wan Road, on the west shore. In the meantime, keep to yourself. Nobody can be trusted.'

Ben instinctively recoiled, but Aiguo clasped his hands in desperation.

'*There's still time to make things right.* Please. Promise me.'

There were tears in Aiguo's eyes. He was not lying.

'Okay,' Ben said, 'I promise.'

Aiguo was about to turn away. But then he looked at Zachary, who was staring back at him angrily, as if he knew deep down what Aiguo had done and could not forgive him.

'Bo and Zirui were my closest friends,' Aiguo said. 'We just wanted to do the right thing. To build a better world, even if it had to be forged in blood. I'm not a bad man, Detective – none of us were. We were simply… led astray.'

Before Ben could say another word, Aiguo ran back the way he came, disappearing into the crowd. Ben and Zachary sailed out of Jintian as quickly as they could, before Armstrong could alert the Taiping. Within the hour, they were cruising down the Xun, through the wilderness of Guangxi, the two men standing side by side at the helm, under the glow of the boat's sole lantern.

'I'm assuming you struck something, even if it was not gold,' Zachary said.

'You could say that.' Ben removed an item from his jacket: it was Ames's coat-wallet.

'I noticed that Ames kept this in his breast pocket. So I started a little altercation with him. After all, I needed an excuse to get up close. It was about time my pickpocketing days came in handy.'

He perused the contents: coins, a few promissory notes, a card bearing the text of the Nicene Creed – nothing of particular importance. But it was the document folded up in one of the sleeves that caught Ben's eye. He unfurled it and held it out to the light.

What he saw brought his whole world grinding to a halt.

It was a government-issued international pass-card. His name had been filled in as *F. Ames*. He had been given Clearance Level 1A – the very same as Ben's – and stamped at the top of the page was the insignia of none other than Her Majesty's government.

20

Everything is Connected

Ben strode through the doors of Mount Austin like a man possessed. He paid no heed to the people around him. Instead, he marched across the lobby, up the stairs, past Fitzjohn without so much as a nod in his direction, and into his suite. He bolted the door shut behind him.

He rifled through his papers, skimmed his report, dug through his bureau and wardrobe – looking for any sign that someone had tampered with his belongings in his absence. Nothing stood out. But his thoughts were still racing, the panic in his chest rising like a surge of bile. He needed absolute isolation. So he drew the curtains shut to block out the light and hauled his desk across the room to block the door. Only then, as he collapsed in his chair, breathless from the exertion and with his gun trained on the door, could he think straight.

His mind turned around a single question: *what did it mean?* Was Armstrong acting on the orders of the British? But if that was the case, why would Ben have been sent to Hong Kong in the first place? Why would the Executive pit one of its agents against another? Or, in allying with the Taiping rebels, had Armstrong turned renegade? But if that were true, why did Bruckner insist that Armstrong was nothing more than a lame preacher?

Or was this too a lie? Another ruse to send Ben deeper into the labyrinth, to make him think what his enemies in the shadows had always wanted him to think? He buried his head in his hands. It felt as though he had already lost his mind and had been left to scrabble around in the darkness searching for a fragment of certainty. He should have listened to his instinct all those months ago, when it told him that Pandora's Box had been opened – that this case was rotten. But now he was trapped in Hong Kong, so far out at sea that he had lost sight of land, with no place to swim to and no hope of returning to shore.

'Mr Canaan?' came a voice, followed by a tentative knock at the door. 'It's Fitzjohn. Did you have a restful stay at the Luofu baths?'

Ben held his tongue. The handle began twisting and squeaking as Fitzjohn tried to push his way in.

'Is everything alright, sir?'

Ben thought back to Aiguo's words – *Nobody can be trusted* – and he quietly cocked his revolver. 'I'm fine, Fitzjohn, thank you! Luofu was just the tonic I needed. But I must say, I've come back extremely tired and need a good night's sleep.'

The handle stopped turning. There was a long silence.

'Why don't you let me in, sir? There is a matter for us to discuss.'

'I'm *extremely tired*. What is it?'

'Well… I received word from Herr Bruckner today. You are expected at the isle of New Lewis tomorrow evening. A boat will be waiting for you at Victoria Harbour at eight o'clock.'

Fitzjohn's suspicions were clearly roused by Ben's behaviour, but he did not press any further – for now, at least. Ben dismissed his aide and withdrew back into himself, only uncocking his revolver when the last traces of Fitzjohn's footsteps had died away.

He did not rise from that chair all night, nor did he sleep a wink. He traced the shifting colours of night to dawn to sunrise as the murky shafts of light bled through the curtains to paint his wall. Nobody came to bother him, except a magpie-robin that alighted on his windowsill shortly after midnight and pecked at the glass pane.

Come morning, he bathed to wash off the dirt and hot sweat of his voyage. He donned a change of clothes – a rumpled black suit, white shirt and cravat – and had a meagre breakfast, consisting of the last few crackers that he had brought with him from the *King Kyrië*. Then, with his penknife and gun tucked into his belt, he crept onto the balcony, levered himself over the edge, and dropped down to the balcony on the floor below.

He landed with a gentle thud. Almost immediately, he heard a yelp – the elderly woman staying in the room beneath his had just got out of bed and was still in her dressing gown. 'Heavens!' she screamed. 'An intruder!'

But Ben did not hang around. He leapt down two more balconies to ground level and ran into the undergrowth of the forest abutting the hotel.

He rejoined Liang at 12 Tang Lung Street. Hong Kong had descended into terror during Ben's absence. The Great Qing had remained studiously silent about how it would respond to the recent British assault. But now reports had started filtering through Hong Kong about Chinese bannermen amassing on the coastal forts of Kowloon and military ships setting sail from Canton. Retaliation was inevitable, though nobody knew when or how it would happen.

'Once the Great Qing strikes back, it's war,' Ben said darkly. 'If it isn't war already…'

They were running out of time. Their saving grace was Aiguo: the impending rendezvous in Pok Fu Lam, the prospect of finally uncovering the truth. Ben's initial plan was to go alone, but Liang insisted on coming with him.

'My husband was destroyed by this conspiracy,' she said. 'I didn't just lose him – I lost our future. So I deserve to hear the truth. To know why he was killed, what it was all for… and who this man that I loved really was.'

It was settled. Tao was at school, so Liang arranged for one of her friends from The Floating Life – a flower girl by the name of Mei – to pick him at the end of the day and keep an eye on him. Ben laid low at 12 Tang Lung Street until early evening, and at six o'clock the two of them set off for Pok Fu Lam. By the time they had crossed the outer bounds of Victoria and were making their way through the valley between Mount Davis and the hill of Lung Fu Shan, the weather had turned and a monsoon was battering Hong Kong.

They arrived at Sandy Bay drenched through, on the headland overlooking the coast. Across the sea out west, the clouds had broken to offer a final glimpse of the sun dipping under the horizon. Below them, at the foot of the headland, was the Pok Fu Lam Fishery. The site had fallen into disrepair, reduced to a few run-down wooden shacks and storehouses scattered across a waterlogged, marshy bank. Only one showed any sign of life: a cabin on the marsh's edge, dimly lit from within.

'It could be a trap,' Liang said under her breath, as they trudged down the headland.

Ben cast his mind back to the image of Aiguo stooped before him, clasping his hands with tears in his eyes. 'I don't think so,' he replied with a shake of the head. 'I think he was being sincere. And if I'm wrong… we'll have to find a way out.'

Ben gave Liang his penknife and they approached the cabin. Inside was a single room piled high with old fishing equipment – nets gnawed away by termites, bundles of bamboo fishing rods, rusted single-action reels – and a kerosene lamp on a table. Aiguo was pacing back and forth, one hand pressed to his temple and the other on his hip, where a hunting knife was holstered. He was lost in thought, startled to his senses when Ben entered.

'This place has been abandoned since the British took control nearly fifteen years ago,' he said, looking around with disgust, 'and it still stinks of fish.'

'I brought a mutual friend,' Ben said.

He ushered Liang inside. Aiguo looked taken aback at first – then he sagged, the stuffing knocked out of him.

'Hello, Aiguo,' Liang said, in Cantonese.

'I'm sorry to see you again,' he replied, 'in these circumstances…'

'I think you have some explaining to do.'

He nodded and took a steeling breath. 'I know.'

Aiguo pulled up two chairs and sat them down on the other side of the table, with the kerosene lamp between them.

'I know the answer already,' Ben said, 'but I want to hear you say it: you, Zirui and Bo were responsible for the Black Blood Murders, correct?'

Aiguo nodded. 'We carried them out, that is true. But that does not mean that we are the only ones responsible.'

'Well, there's Armstrong, for starters. And the Taiping rebels.' Ben slapped Armstrong's pass-card on the table. 'And the British, apparently. Everyone, it seems, except the nation that is currently under attack.'

'That was the plan all along…' Aiguo murmured.

Liang's features twisted in anger. 'You have betrayed your own people. China will be destroyed because of you.'

'And then reborn. At least, that was why we did it.'

'For a messianic delusion,' Ben spat back.

Aiguo could only shake his head. 'It was a crisis of the spirit, Mr Canaan. Bo, Zirui and I had known each other since childhood. We broke our backs to rise through the ranks of the Great Qing, believing that worldly success would fulfil us. But it did not. That was why we converted, all three of us: we needed something more, something greater than ourselves. And Armstrong gave it to us. Our answer lay in Christ – in His blood, His suffering. Here was a man who sacrificed everything for humanity's sake. What better example is there than that?'

'Some example you've set,' Ben retorted. 'I've seen the horrors that you've carried out. I've seen the consequences of your actions. There's nothing holy about it.'

Aiguo began pacing once more. He was full of febrile energy – a big pulsing ball of shame bursting at the seams for an outlet.

'But it wasn't always like that. At first, we just prayed and studied and tried to grow Armstrong's flock. Of course, we had to keep it a secret – not just from our employers, but…' he glanced at Liang, '…even from the people that we loved most. Then Armstrong sat us down and gave us a new mission. One that would destroy the old China and build a new one from the ashes. A world free of the old sins and superstitions. A Christian China. And all we had to do was kill the Seven Gentlemen and their bedfellows – make it look like the Great Qing was responsible. Britain would be brought into an open conflict with China that would overwhelm the regime, allowing our Christian brothers in the Taiping to win the war. We knew going in that we would all die in the process. But we didn't care. In our minds, we were like Christ: shedding our own blood to create a better world.'

Aiguo was no longer looking at Ben and Liang. He was in another place, another time: reliving the moment when he plunged the knife into the Morèse family; when he set fire to the factory on the Isle of Dogs, knowing who was inside; when he strung up Van Hook and disembowelled him, in the forests outside Chongzuo.

'We told ourselves that the ends justified the means. Armstrong demanded our absolute loyalty and we gave it. But over time, it became harder to believe that. It was Bo who began asking questions. Whether our mission was truly pure – whether what we were doing was in fact for the greater good – whether we were just being used. And those questions led here…'

He tapped the piece of paper on the table, tracing his finger around the royal seal at the top of Armstrong's pass-card.

'What are you trying to say?' Ben said, leaning in. 'How come Armstrong has clearance from the British?'

Aiguo could only shake his head in disbelief. 'Don't you understand, Mr Canaan? It was their idea in the first place. *They wanted it to happen.* It's just like Bo said, the last night that I saw him alive in London: we were serving not God… but the Devil.'

On that last word, Ben heard a heavy thud behind him. Aiguo looked up, over Ben's shoulder.

'*No—*'

He was interrupted by an ear-splitting *bang* and a momentary flash of white, like lightning. Aiguo staggered back, his eyes wide and his breath caught in his throat as though he had just been punched in the gut, and he collapsed to the ground.

Ben spun round. A hulk of a man was standing in the open doorway to the cabin, clad in black with his face hidden behind a balaclava. He had a revolver trained on them and smoke was trailing from the barrel.

Liang rushed over to Aiguo. He had been shot in the chest – his shirt soaked deep red and bright foamy blood pouring out in thick rivulets. She applied pressure to the wound but that just made Aiguo scream in agony.

'You,' the man growled, gesturing to Ben. 'Come with me.'

There was something familiar about the man's voice, but in the heat of the moment Ben could not place it.

'He's going to die!' Liang cried.

'He made his choice,' the man replied, 'and if you don't want to go the same way, Mr Canaan, I suggest you come with me.'

'It's okay,' Ben raised his hands. 'I'll come.'

He edged cautiously towards the man. Nobody said a word: it was just the deluge outside and Aiguo's desperate gasps as his lungs failed and blood bubbled up in his throat. The man gestured for Ben to move faster, but Ben held his ground – slow, measured steps, closer and closer to the weapon.

The barrel of the gun came to rest on his chest. Ben drew to a sudden halt.

'Well?' the man barked. 'I said get a move on—'

Ben swung his palm into the side of the revolver, knocking it off kilter, and clamped the cylinder to prevent it from firing. Before the man could take a swing, Ben elbowed him in the face and twisted the gun from his grip to send it clattering across the cabin.

Ben went for his own revolver, but the man pounced on him before he could pull the trigger. A piledriver of a right hook to the jaw and Ben was thrown back onto the table, his gun flying free. The kerosene lamp spilled over the edge and smashed on the floor, igniting a blanket of yellow flames.

'Get him up and go!' Ben yelled at Liang.

Liang hefted Aiguo to his feet, linking her arm round his waist, and limped out the back door onto the marshland. The man launched himself at Ben and kicked him in the chest, knocking the wind out of him, then slammed him to the ground, shattering the floorboards.

Ben gasped for air. He was breathless, seeing stars, bleeding from the mouth. The fire was fast spreading and choking out the air in the room. If he did not act quickly, they would both be consumed in the blaze.

'Last chance,' the man said. 'Come with me and you can save yourself.'

Ben dragged himself to his feet, wincing through the pain. In a toe-to-toe bareknuckle tussle with this giant, he was out-matched. But he did not give up. He raised his fists, just as he would do when crawling back to the scratch line in the ring of the Cricklewood Green boxing club.

'You're going to have to knock me out first.'

The man clenched his fists. 'Stupid, stubborn dog.'

Ben threw a punch, but the man caught his arm mid-air and yanked him into a headbutt, then grabbed him by the collar to launch him through the back wall of the cabin. Ben went crashing into the mud, spitting out globules of blood as he shakily brought himself to his knees.

The man emerged from the cabin, which was now engulfed in an inferno that not even the deluge could quench. He lumbered towards Ben and was about to deliver a knockout blow to the head, when Liang leapt at him from behind and plunged the penknife into his back. Even that he seemed to shrug off with a grunt; instead, he swatted Liang off him and sent her tumbling to the ground next to a prostrate Aiguo.

The man ripped the penknife from his back and tossed it aside. He and Ben brawled in the thick sludge of the marsh, hammered by rain as they hammered into each other, dragged down into the mire until they were caked in it head to toe.

He knocked Ben onto his back with a knee to the gut. Ben reached out with his left hand and grabbed the handle of the penknife half-buried in the sludge. But the man drove his boot down onto Ben's hand. There was a hideous crack – Ben's fingers snapping out of place. Then the man pinned Ben to the ground and wrapped his burly hands around Ben's throat. He slowly began to tighten his grip, inexorable as a steel vice.

'I'm not supposed to kill you,' he said, 'but I will if I have to—'

He never finished the threat. The last word was lost in a guttural choke, followed by a strange frothy gurgle. A torrent of hot blood washed across Ben's face and the body above him deflated, as the air rushed out of it with an animal wheeze. Aiguo had plunged the hunting knife into his neck. The blade was long and broad, sharp enough to gouge the man's throat wide open.

The man slumped on top of Ben. Aiguo rolled onto his back. He stared at the sky. His breathing was thin. He did not have much time left. Liang helped Ben out from under the dead weight of the slain attacker, and Ben staggered to his feet. His hand was already starting to swell. Three of his fingers were bone-white and bent out of shape.

'Bastard broke my hand…' he muttered, wiping the blood from his eyes.

'L-L-Liang!' Aiguo groaned.

She knelt at his side. He was deathly pale, the blood still pouring from the gaping bullet wound in his chest. There was no saving him now, that much was clear.

'The Lord's Prayer…' he stammered. 'I need it to finally leave this place…'

'I don't know it,' she replied. 'Aiguo, I don't know the words!'

He took a deep breath, readying himself for what was to come. 'Then follow me.'

He reached out to her with a bloodstained hand, as if trying to touch heaven itself. She linked her fingers through his and squeezed tight: a moment of comfort and consolation.

'Our Father, who art in heaven…'

Ben listened to Aiguo's halting prayer that Liang echoed back to him – a man helping to administer his own last rites, comforted that it would grant his soul a safe passage.

'Hallowed be Thy name; Thy kingdom come; Thy will be done, on earth as it is in heaven…'

Ben limped over to the body of his attacker. A moment ago a preternatural force, now putrefying in the dirt.

'Give us this day our daily bread; and forgive us our trespasses, as we forgive those who trespass against us…'

He bent down and took a hold of the balaclava.

'And lead us not into temptation, but deliver us from evil…'

He pulled it back to reveal the man's face.

'Amen.'

It was Grant Parry. Odysseus Halliday's enforcer. The man who had made a living doing the Scottish tycoon's dirty work – 'Wringing necks and opening jam jars', as he had once told him. And Ben had nearly ended up as just another one of those necks.

Everything clicked into place. The last pieces of this mysterious puzzle slotted together. The centre of this confounding labyrinth suddenly came into view.

'Liang,' Aiguo murmured with his last breath. 'Forgive me. Please. Forgive me for what I did. Forgive Zirui… Forgive Bo.'

Tears were streaming down her cheeks: all the anguish that she had endured, the grief and the lies, pouring out of her as she guided Aiguo into the next world.

'I forgive you,' she whispered.

It was not clear whether Aiguo had heard her. His eyes were already glassy and his breathing had stopped. There was no relief on his face. Just the cold and quiet uncertainty that trembles on the frontiers of death.

Ben thought back to Bo's last moments – those words to which he had returned over and over again. 'Everything is connected…' he murmured.

He looked across the waters. Somewhere out there, on the isle of New Lewis, the evil that he had been chasing was lying in wait. Now, finally, the time had come for him to bring this deadly game to an end.

21

A Useful Purpose

'What do you think this is all about then?'

Herrick pinched his cigarette between his lips and struck a match. Gilbert always asked the most frivolous questions to fill the silence. The two sailors were taking shelter from the rain on their schooner, sitting next to each other beneath a narrow awning that covered the entrance to the cabin. They had been moored at Victoria Harbour for nigh on two hours now, and the night was wearing on without any prospect of them leaving.

'I don't think about it,' Herrick grumbled. He lit the cigarette and took a weary puff.

'How do you not think about it? You can't control what you think about.'

'Sure I can.'

Gilbert was a young man – twenty-two, to be precise, and a quarter of a century younger than his grey-bearded co-sailor. He had the unbridled enthusiasm and persistence to show for it. He scooted round to face Herrick.

'But nobody can really decide what they think or feel. You might have a plan and whatnot, but things still pop up in your head. Like when something gets you in a fume. Or when you feel guilty about something. You may not want to feel it, but you do.'

Herrick shrugged and took another drag. 'It ain't worth my while. Yours neither.'

'It don't matter. It's still there. I heard this story about a man who killed his wife for her money, right. And he got away with it! He had half his life still ahead of him, all the money he could wish for, and everyone felt sorry for the bugger. He got exactly what he wanted. But he couldn't get that little voice out of his head. Eating away at him. Prodding at him.' Gilbert poked Herrick repeatedly in the ribs to drive the point home. 'And in the end he couldn't enjoy any of the nice things he had, 'cos everywhere he looked was the blood what he shed. Drove him mad. He confessed. And he got banged up.'

Herrick looked askance at Gilbert. 'Where'd you get that story?'

'I heard it.'

'Where'd you hear it?'

'What do you mean "where'd I hear it"? I heard it! Point is, now it's in *my* head. So I'm thinking about, well… what I'm doing. Here we are, waiting to take some little Jew-boy to Halliday's island in the middle of the night. A little Jew-boy who's in with the government, by the way. And in those circumstances I can't help but ask myself: what's really going on here?'

Herrick sighed in frustration.

'You know what I'm thinking about, Gilbert? *Dinner.* And the fact that I'm missing it 'cos this little Jew-boy of ours couldn't be bothered to turn up on time. You want my advice? Shut up and do as they're tellin' you. Then you and I can both get off this stinking island and go back home.'

Gilbert looked wounded. He swivelled round to look out across Victoria Harbour.

'It ain't a nice world,' he said.

Herrick said nothing, opting to finish his cigarette and flick the remains into the water. Suddenly, Gilbert rose to his feet. He had seen something.

'Herrick, look!' he exclaimed, pointing. 'I think that's him!'

A young man was limping down the jetty towards them. He was drenched from the downpour, his top half was covered in blood, and his left arm was resting across his front to support a broken hand. The dour look on his face said it all: he was not having a good evening.

'Mr...' Herrick checked his notebook, '...Benjamin E. Canaan?'

Ben nodded.

'Is that... your blood, sir?' Gilbert asked with a gulp.

Ben shook his head.

The three of them stared at each other. Neither Herrick nor Gilbert was quite sure what to say next. Then Herrick clapped his hands and turned away.

'New Lewis it is, sir!'

Gilbert lingered for a moment, looking Ben up and down. Ben narrowed his eyes. 'Don't,' was all he said.

No further explanation was needed. Gilbert thought back to Herrick's warning from just a minute ago and led their passenger onboard.

They crossed the archipelago in double time. Ben dried himself in the cabin below deck. Within an hour, they had arrived at the shores of New Lewis and Ben was greeted by a fleet of armed guards who escorted him up to Caisteal Halliday – that grey tower of stone atop its gloomy promontory.

Nobody was waiting for him at the tall wooden posterns: just the familiar motto, *in omnibus caritas*, which now rang so hollow. The deluge had turned that splendid courtyard into a turgid bog. Only the statue of Emmeline, Halliday's dearly departed mother, stood tall, the rain sluicing down her cheeks like floods of tears. Banks of candles lit up the castle from within, conjuring up ghostly ember glows that wavered in the lancet windows.

Ben was taken into the entrance hall. Standing at the foot of the wide red-carpeted staircase were Halliday and Bruckner. They had been waiting for Ben, both looking bemused.

'Mr Canaan!' Bruckner exclaimed, stepping forward. 'You're in rather a state.'

'I've had a long and illuminating few days.'

'Where's Parry?' Halliday asked.

Ben produced Parry's bloodied signet ring and chucked it to Halliday. Halliday took one look at it and nodded briskly, pocketing it without another word.

'We can only apologise for having him track you, Mr Canaan,' Bruckner said. 'However, you did force our hand with your conduct of late. What of Liang and Aiguo?'

'Liang is safe. Aiguo is indisposed.'

Bruckner gave a resigned shrug. 'Well, it's something. Come on upstairs. We have much to discuss. There is no need to make a mountain out of a molehill.'

Ben was ushered into Halliday's study. There were two others waiting there: Governor Bowring, puffing on his pipe in an armchair by the fireplace; and Coldwell, standing with that impeccable military posture at the window, watching the rain streak the glass.

'A tipple?' Halliday gestured to the drinks cabinet.

There was a Hennessy V.S.O.P that caught Ben's eye. 'You know what? I think I will on this occasion. I'll take the Hennessy.'

Halliday poured Ben a double. 'Good enough for King George, eh?'

Ben took a sip. It was warming, with hints of tobacco and vanilla. The ideal fortifier for this long-awaited parley.

'I understand this may be confusing to you…' Coldwell began.

But Ben cut him off. 'Actually, I don't think I have ever seen things as clearly as I do right now.'

'I told you he was too smart for his own good,' Bowring said between puffs. 'Look at him! Wily creature. He was always going to sniff us out.'

'Please, don't talk about our dear detective so crudely,' Halliday replied, kicking his legs up on his desk as was his habit. 'Let him enjoy being the clever boots that he is.'

Ben set the brandy down on Halliday's desk and looked around at the four of them. 'Spare me your gloating. You deceived me for long enough, but I understand now. All this time I was chasing a shapeless enemy in the shadows – some secretive cabal of ruthless mercenaries acting on the orders of the Great Qing. But that's all it was: *shadows*. There was nothing ever really there. Instead, this whole time, it was you. Every last one of you.'

Bruckner folded his arms over his chest. He was thinking hard about something, but Ben could not tell what.

'You orchestrated the Black Blood Murders. You had the rest of the Seven Gentlemen picked off one by one. This whole investigation you've sent me on – it's a construct. A pantomime written by your hand, that ends with me pointing the finger at the Great Qing for a crime that you committed.'

Ben paced over to the mantlepiece, where the photograph of the Seven Gentlemen sat. The only survivors in that photo were now Halliday and Hokoa.

'The question is: *why?* Why wipe out the Seven Gentlemen and pin it on the Great Qing? Well, that's obvious. It all comes back to opium. To the China trade. The Great Qing has long opposed it and has fought to keep it from expanding. It would be much easier at this point to change the regime altogether. Get rid of the Great Qing and replace it with an entity that you can control. But for that…'

Ben turned back to his company.

'…You need a reason to go to war. A *casus belli*. And what better pretext than an all-out Chinese assault on the trade? It unites every empire, every nation, every businessman of the West with even the remotest interest in opium against the Chinese. It's the perfect excuse to destroy the Great Qing, with the unwavering support of your allies and your own people.'

'Now he's thinking like a politician!' Halliday exclaimed. 'They grow up so fast.'

Ben brushed off Halliday's mockery. 'Which means you need someone on the inside. Members of the Qing establishment who are willing to undermine it from within. That's why you brought Armstrong into the fold, right? You made him a British agent, just like me. Codename: *Ames*. And in return, he gave you three men to act as your lackeys. Aiguo, Zirui, Bo. All intimately linked to the Chinese imperial machine. All converted to the faith and under Armstrong's thumb. All fanatical enough to destroy their own government for the promise of a "better world" – a promise that Armstrong sold them, which was always going to be broken.'

'They served an essential purpose,' Bruckner said, folding his arms over his chest, 'and we greatly appreciate their sacrifice.'

'I bet you do,' Ben spat. 'They handed you your precious war on a silver platter. And you even have the ideal candidate to replace the Great Qing: your "Christian brothers", the Taiping rebels. A British assault on China would overwhelm the Chinese and clear the way for a Taiping takeover. A more compliant regime under your control. A puppet of the West. And here's the master stroke…'

He turned to Halliday, placing his good hand on the tycoon's desk and leaning in.

'By killing the Seven Gentlemen, you wipe out all the competition in the China trade. Clear the field for one man to take over and establish a British opium monopoly…' He jabbed an accusatory finger. '*Odysseus Halliday.*'

Halliday seemed unruffled by Ben's fury. There was nothing behind that mask: just brute hunger and ambition. He put his hands up with a smirk.

'Upsy-daisy.'

'You were on that list,' Ben declared, 'but you were never going to be killed, were you? It was just a red herring, designed to throw me off the scent. You knew all along that you were safe because you'd cut a deal with the British to be "their man" in this new era for the China trade. It's like Ormrod said: Seven Gentlemen is just too many. Turns out, he was correct. A scheme like that was beneath him. But not for someone as cheap and vulgar as you.'

Ben caught a trace of scorn in Halliday's eyes. He had struck a nerve. He turned away from Halliday to confront Bruckner.

'That's why you and Palmerston sent me here. Not to carry out a real investigation, but to follow the treats that you planted, like a dog being lured into its cage. That way, I would write exactly the report you need, clear you of your own crime, testify before the Wetherton Inquiry that the Great Qing is to blame, and set your narrative in stone. I'm your trump card: not just an agent lying on your behalf, but an agent who believes his own lies.'

Bruckner's expression said it all. The light had drained from his eyes. There was no humanity in him. He was an empty vessel, consumed by the office that he inhabited.

'So that's the net result of your ruse, Gustav. The unstoppable expansion of the opium trade. A regime in China under British dominion. And Britain walks away with clean hands, vaunted worldwide as the hero who saved the day. Have I got that about right?'

Bruckner clasped his hands and gave a brisk bow. 'Quite ingenious, you must admit.'

'You're throwing thousands, perhaps even millions, onto the pyre. Laying waste to an entire civilisation. And for what? Greed. Money.'

Bruckner tut-tutted and ambled over to Ben, raising his index finger like a scholar driving home his argument.

'Not money, Mr Canaan. *Prosperity*. Do you have any idea, even the vaguest concept, of how much depends on opium? The tea we drink. The silk we wear. The cotton we sleep in. The silver in our cutlery. The herbs in our medicine. The goods that we consume unthinkingly, that we blindly expect in our daily lives – financed by the cultivation, manufacture, transport and sale of opium. If the China trade were to dry up, the bottom of the British economy would fall out. We are acting not out of greed, but out of necessity. Certainly, some people will die and a few ships will sink. But in the long run, Britain will be vastly wealthier for this little exercise. And so will you.'

Bruckner lowered his voice. He gave the impression of a man trying to talk sense into a wild and ranting youth.

'Finish the report as planned. Testify before the Wetherton Inquiry that the Great Qing perpetrated these murders. I assure you, if there are any negative repercussions, you will be protected. And the rewards for your loyalty will be handsome. A knighthood. More riches than you could ever spend. Friends in the highest places. In time, perhaps even ennoblement – the creation of a dynasty in your name. And all you need to do is… play along.'

Ben instinctively shook his head, but Bruckner stayed him with a hand on his arm.

'I'm sorry for misleading you, Benjamin. It was not personal. We were simply trying to preserve our deniability in relation to the killings. You were not supposed to dredge this up.'

Ben had no words. He was exhausted, angry, betrayed. For so long he had hunted for the truth. But now that it was in the palm of his hand, he did not know what to do with it.

Halliday stood up suddenly, straightening his waistcoat. 'There remains the small matter of Hokoa. But who will dispatch him now that Aiguo is dead?'

'We'll find some other way,' Bruckner said casually. 'Isn't that right, Sebastian?'

Coldwell gave a firm nod. 'And I trust Mr Canaan will not impede us.'

All eyes turned to Ben. Bruckner patted him on the back reassuringly. 'Mr Canaan is a reasonable man. I am quite sure he will see sense.'

Bruckner led Ben out of Caisteal Halliday, down the hill to the shoreline where Herrick and Gilbert were still waiting. They had cut precisely the same pose when Ben had first walked up to them: sitting under the awning side by side, Herrick smoking while Gilbert nattered incessantly.

'Take this young man back to Victoria Harbour, please, boys!' Bruckner called out.

Herrick and Gilbert stood to attention. 'Yes, sir!'

Bruckner turned to Ben and extended a hand. 'I expect an update about that report. Until next time.'

Ben had no choice but to play Bruckner's game – for now. He shook hands with him, then tried to pull away as fast as he could, but Bruckner had him locked in.

'Remember, Benjamin: *might is right.*'

He held Ben's hand for a second longer, then released him. Ben pushed past Herrick and Gilbert into the cabin and slammed the door shut behind him. Bruckner watched the schooner sail off into the darkness, before returning to Caisteal Halliday.

Ben holed up in the cabin for the journey back to Hong Kong. Bruckner's words rattled about in his head. The man's tone was so gentle, so inviting. It worked like magic, making the greatest treachery sound reasonable, conjuring up that other life before Ben's eyes. A world where the name *Canaan* was revered. A world where he no longer needed to wander on life's margins, but would be accepted. A world where books would be written about him. It was within his grasp and the last thing left to do was to take it. But at what cost?

There was only one alternative: throw caution to the wind and defy his masters. Protect Hokoa and expose the British plot before it was too late to save the Great Qing from collapse. But again, that same question reared its head: at what cost? Either way, Ben would lose everything – either his soul or his life – with no in between.

Gilbert knocked on the cabin door. They had landed at Victoria. Ben emerged, one foot on the jetty and one on the schooner. He turned to look at the two soaked sailors, gazing back at him curiously but not daring to ask questions.

'Stay safe, gentlemen,' was all he said. He tramped off and disappeared in the rain.

Herrick rolled another cigarette and twirled it in his fingers. He glanced at Gilbert, who looked confused and despondent, and he linked his arm around his co-sailor's shoulder.

'You're right,' Herrick said. 'It ain't a nice world. Now, how about that dinner?'

22

The Black Crow

It was another sleepless night for Ben on his return to Mount Austin. It was not just his broken hand that kept him awake – above all it was the feeling of betrayal, that he had been taken for a fool by the people he trusted most. He looked back now on his service with embarrassment. His slavish bows to Palmerston and Bruckner; his constant refrains of 'Yes, sir' and 'Certainly, my lord'; his eagerness to please. Everything now smacked of idiocy. He had tricked himself into believing that his paymasters viewed him as an equal. Yet nothing could be further from the truth. He was their plaything. A gullible boy plucked from the mud and given a bit of spit and polish to add lustre.

Now he faced an intractable problem. If he did nothing, innocent people would die and he would grow fat for the rest of his days under the burden of a tainted conscience, with only alcohol, opium and death for escape. If he spoke out, he would give up all that he had gained and all that he was set to gain – condemning himself to obscurity at best and the life of a fugitive at worst, with no guarantee that his act of defiance would make even the slightest difference.

The half-finished report sat on his desk. It would be the easiest thing in the world to turn his brain off, to silence the doubt in his head, and do as he was told. The life of which he had long since dreamed would flow as freely as the ink from his pen. And if not him, it would simply be someone else reaping the rewards of compliance. What could he possibly do? He was one man. And one man alone cannot hold back the march of Empire.

Before he knew it, the sun was up and Fitzjohn was knocking at his door. 'You're wanted at breakfast, sir.'

Bruckner was waiting for him in the dining lounge downstairs. He was already tucking into a full English, mopping up a pool of runny yolk with a rasher of bacon. A humourless Coldwell was with him and was sipping a strong black coffee.

'Come join us, Mr Canaan!' Bruckner smiled. 'Why don't you order something filling? Have you tried the devilled lamb kidneys on toast? I hear it is a speciality.'

'I'm not hungry.'

'Growing boy like you? I don't believe it.' Bruckner dabbed his lips with a napkin. 'I would ask if you have had a chance to sleep on my proposal, but you look as though you have not had a wink.'

Ben was taciturn. Coldwell was glaring at him. There was no diplomatic route out of this conundrum.

'I have had a chance to think,' Ben began.

'And?'

'And…' Ben looked at his hands. His skin was mottled. Despite the heat, his blood was running cold. '… I'll do it. I don't like it and I think it's wrong. But I made an oath. And there's no point in breaking it now.'

Bruckner seemed more interested in breakfast than the conversation. He chopped up his black pudding and speared a slice on his fork.

'Do *what*, Mr Canaan? I'd like to hear you say it.'

'I'll complete the report as you instructed. I'll testify accordingly. My lips are sealed.'

Only now did Bruckner look directly at Ben, peering over the rim of his spectacles.

'You will wait for word to arrive of Hokoa's death. That will come with further instructions as to what you will say about it. Until then, sit tight.'

Bruckner polished off his breakfast and Coldwell knocked back his coffee. Ben pursued them as they rose to their feet and strode for the exit.

'How will it be done?'

Coldwell spoke up for the first time that morning. 'You have been let off the hook once already, Mr Canaan. Do not try your luck.'

A physician was summoned to treat Ben's left hand. Two of the fingers had been dislocated and needed to be snapped back into place, while a third was fractured along with a carpal bone in his wrist. It was completely immobilised, wrapped in gauze and fastened tight with a wooden splint, leaving Ben effectively one-handed.

He may have been forgiven, but he was far from being out of the woods. Locks were placed on his windows to prevent him from escaping via the balcony. Coldwell's officers were posted around Mount Austin: one outside Ben's door, four at the entrance to the hotel, and about half a dozen others patrolling the corridors and grounds. Ben could not leave unsupervised, unless it was to go for a walk around the Peak. Fitzjohn kept an eagle eye on him, going so far as to knock on his door every couple of hours. Ben had bought himself time and a modicum of trust by committing to follow orders. But his leeway was razor thin. One false step and he would be out on his backside, or worse.

He got to work that evening. He went out for a walk alone around the Peak and returned to the ridge where he had first encountered Jun. He issued the same summons: 'Come out!'

Sure enough, the agent of Ye Mingchen emerged from the treeline.

'I admire your persistence,' Ben said, shaking his hand. 'You're like a guardian angel.'

'I was told to keep an eye on you. So, naturally, I sleep with one eye open.'

'I'm sleeping with both open at the moment. I don't recommend it.'

'What is going on, Mr Canaan? There is more activity around Mount Austin than usual.'

Ben pulled Jun in to whisper in his ear. Not even the birds were trusted to hear them.

'Your master was right,' he said. 'This a put-up job. The Great Qing is the scapegoat and it's the British who are behind it. Now Hokoa's life is in danger and I want to protect him.'

'What do you need?'

'Talk to Ye Mingchen. I need Hokoa to come to The Floating Life in secret. We're going to save his life and lay bare this conspiracy. Are you in?'

'I'll do what I can and report back.'

It did not take long for Jun to yield results. By the same time the next day, Ye Mingchen had spoken to Hokoa and secured a visit that Friday at seven o'clock in the evening.

The morning after Ben received this confirmation, Fitzjohn spotted him at reception, removing a letter from his breast pocket. He hurried after Ben and bombarded him with questions.

Ben replied by flashing him the address on the envelope: *Canaan and Sons, Tailors – 82 Whitechapel Road, E London, England.*

'Writing home,' he said. 'My mum gets nervous if I don't, you see.'

Fitzjohn was dubious, but ultimately acquiesced, opting not to press the matter further.

'Say,' Ben said to the receptionist, 'you wouldn't happen to have a copy of today's *Hong Kong Register*, would you?'

The receptionist disappeared round the back to check in the mail racks. While he was gone, Ben pried open the envelope and removed the contents. It was another sealed envelope, with an altogether different address: *12 Tang Lung Street*. Inside was a letter not to his family, but to Liang, informing her of the plan and making one vital request:

Send flower girl. Mount Austin, Friday, six o'clock. <u>Must be accompanied by attendant</u> – the ones with the hats. Do not write back. They are watching. Do not let me down.

The receptionist returned with a copy of the newspaper, which he exchanged for the letter.

Then it was the waiting game. Ben made a show of writing the report to appease the British – after all, Fitzjohn was likely checking on his progress. He hardly left Mount Austin, now living as a glorified prisoner in this hillside hotel. He made no complaint, gave no sign of discontent, and cut a figure of calm resignation, as though he had made peace with his decision.

Friday evening rolled around. Mount Austin was guarded to the hilt. Ben stayed in his room, gazing out across Hong Kong Island's north shore. Smoke was rising from the Chinese forts along the Kowloon coast – once unoccupied, now populated by soldiers and artillery bearing down on Hong Kong. Boats were filtering in and out of Victoria Harbour. On one of them, Ben did not know which, Hokoa was sailing into town, behind enemy lines, for their rendezvous.

The clock struck six. Ben held his breath. He was expecting the knock at any moment to notify him of his flower girl's arrival. But nothing came. Five minutes passed, then ten, then fifteen. He started to worry that something had gone wrong – that Liang had not been able to fulfil his request – that he would have to find another way out.

At almost half-past, however, Fitzjohn knocked on his door: 'A rather beautiful young lady and her helper have come to see you, sir?'

'Quite right!' Ben feigned delight. 'Send them up, Fitzjohn.'

Fitzjohn returned a couple of minutes later with the flower girl and her attendant in tow. She was exquisitely beautiful, in a jade-green *aoqun*, with her makeup done in the same style as Liang when Ben had hired her at The Floating Life. The attendant was a man of about Ben's height, in plain dark robes – just a *magua* jacket and *ku* to cover the legs – with a broad-rimmed conical hat completely hiding his face. A bulky leather satchel had been slung over his shoulder.

The flower girl bowed and tenderly kissed Ben's fingers. 'Good evening, Mr Canaan. I… am Emerald.'

Madame Xu clearly did not have the greatest imagination when it came to the names of her girls. Ben was about to guide her and the attendant into his room, when they were interrupted by the guard stationed on his hallway.

'One moment, sir!' the guard called, striding over to them with a finger pointed at the attendant. 'We'll need to check that bag.'

'Certainly,' Ben said. 'Go on, my good man. Open up!'

The attendant unclipped the satchel to display the contents: all the paraphernalia required for an opium smoke – the pipe, the bowl, a little spirit lamp, needles and scissors, a tinder box, and of course sealed packets of the holy black paste. Satisfied, the guard gestured for the attendant to enter.

Ben hung back and drew Fitzjohn in close. 'I trust you understand why I invited them.'

'I can put two and two together, sir.'

'Naturally, my business with the lovely Emerald is rather, shall we say, sensitive. So I would appreciate it if you could refrain from knocking. I fear it would rather embarrass—'

'Not at all, sir!' Fitzjohn raised an apologetic hand. 'I quite understand. It's not to my taste, I admit – my Annabelle would surely disown me if I ever cavorted about with such an irresistibly beautiful… Well, let's leave it at that. I'll see you in the morning!'

Fitzjohn waddled off and Ben rejoined the new arrivals in his room. Emerald had already let her hair down and was sitting on the bed. 'This is going to be very boring!' she muttered.

'Take solace in the fact that I'm paying you triple for your time,' Ben said. 'Let's get going. You're running late as it is.'

'Will you at least explain what this is about? Liang wouldn't say.'

'Top-secret matters of state, I'm afraid, and I'm nothing if not professional.' Ben turned to the attendant. 'Now strip off.'

He and the attendant got undressed and exchanged clothes while Emerald averted her eyes. The disguise was complete in no time. Ben stood before the mirror and carefully placed the conical hat over his head, adjusting it to bury his face in shadow. He pulled the left sleeve of the *magua* over his hand to hide the splint.

There were no two ways about it: this was the thinnest of disguises.

'I wouldn't bet the future of China on it,' he whispered to himself, 'but it'll have to do.'

He turned back to his accomplices.

'Once I'm gone, the two of you should remain undisturbed. If you hear footsteps outside, make a bit of noise – something that suggests… intimacy. That should scare them off.'

Emerald made for the door and Ben followed with his head bowed, onto the corridor and towards the exit. As expected, the guard stopped them before the stairs.

'Mr Canaan has dismissed my attendant,' Emerald said, laying her hand sweetly on the guard's arm. 'He does not wish for anyone else to… watch us.'

It worked like a charm. The guard shot Ben a cursory glance, then stepped aside. Emerald escorted him down to the lobby and out the front doors, nobody daring to peer under his hat for fear of causing offence. The doorman summoned a carriage to take Ben to The Floating Life, and only once the carriage was well beyond the bounds of the Mount Austin estate did Ben remove the hat.

He arrived at The Floating Life ten minutes late. Madame Xu greeted him in the main parlour. He kissed her outstretched hand in a show of respect.

'Handsome boy,' she said, stroking his cheek. 'Come. They are in the private suite.'

She led him to a candlelit room at the back of the opium den. A large round table was in the middle, laden with food and alcohol. Hokoa, the man of the hour, was leaning back in his chair with his arms outstretched, letting out a yawn. Liang and Jun were with him, both white-knuckled in anticipation.

'Detective!' Hokoa said. He hobbled to his feet with the help of his ivory cane and gave Ben a warm hug. 'I knew we would meet again. This case has a dastardly habit of reeling me back in… Perhaps I simply cannot resist the bait!'

'So *that* is why you wanted an attendant,' Liang exclaimed. 'A master of disguise…'

'Mastery is perhaps an overstatement in this instance. But I've had practice.'

Ben was about to get the parley underway, when Madame Xu stuck her head in. 'Would our dear guest like his customary dose of *yāpiàn*?'

Ben was about to dismiss her, but Hokoa beat him to it.

'Well, if it is on offer, how could I say no? Liang, fetch our little stash, will you?'

'I am already ahead of you,' Madame Xu said, holding out a violet-coloured box, about the size of her palm. Then, to Liang: 'You don't mind that I took it out for you?'

'Not at all, ma'am.'

Liang prepared the opium to be smoked, while Hokoa tapped his cane repeatedly on the floor as he mused about the present circumstances.

'So it was the English after all,' he smiled. 'I underestimated your kind. I thought you were only good for wearing wigs and moving money. But you have a crafty side as well.'

'I was duped too,' Ben said. 'They wanted me to be their unwitting accomplice.'

'So that you believe the narrative that they have set. That has always been the key to good espionage: pick your favourite story and eliminate as many people as possible, even in your own ranks, who are wise to the truth.'

Liang was needling the opium over the flame of the spirit

lamp. It was already bubbling. Hokoa reclined on the floor-cushion next to the lamp and took up the pipe, ready to smoke. Liang held out the ball of opium to place in his bowl, but before he accepted it, he offered his pipe to Ben.

'Care for a smoke?'

Ben's instinct was to say yes. In any other situation, he would have done so without hesitation. But as he watched the curlicue of smoke trail from the spirit lamp, he could not help but see the faces of all those who had died for the sake of this drug – the opium ghosts floating to and fro across the barren swamps of inland China – the kernel of evil planted in that little bubbling bead pierced by the eye of Liang's needle. An evil that, for so long, he had unthinkingly consumed, filling his veins with black blood.

He raised his hands in a gesture of polite refusal. 'Not for me.'

Hokoa shrugged. 'Suit yourself.'

He took a few hungry puffs. It was a strange sight. A man with such power and influence, who commanded more wealth than most could conceive of – enslaved by the pipe, the flame, the seed of the poppy.

They spent the next hour formulating a plan. The first step, to keep Hokoa safe, would be to enlist the help of the Great Qing, using Ye Mingchen's personal relationship with the Xianfeng Emperor. Hokoa was bullish about his chances of survival, since the British had killed Aiguo not a few days earlier. But in Ben's eyes, that just made matters riskier: Britain's next move could come from any direction, in any form, by any hand. Hokoa would have to be on high alert.

Next, they had to turn the tide against the British. Her Majesty's government had all the momentum and was galloping headlong into war, buoyed by the support that it enjoyed from a coalition of other great powers who blamed the Great Qing for the Black Blood Murders. But the Xianfeng Emperor had the power, if he so wished, to summon the ambassadors of the relevant countries – the US, the Netherlands, France and Portugal – and tell them the truth. That was where Ben came in: a defector from within the British fold, laying bare the conspiracy at the expense of his former masters. If they played their cards correctly, they could bring the world onto the side of the Great Qing. It might not prevent an opium war, but it could change its course.

'Then it's settled!' Hokoa said, hobbling to his feet. His eyes were bloodshot from the opium and his skin was dewy with sweat. 'The world must hear it from the horse's mouth. And Mr Canaan will be our horse.'

'If that is a step Mr Canaan is willing to take…' Liang said, looking nervously at Ben.

Ben mulled the prospect. The consequences of publicly turning on the British were bleak to the say the least. He would likely never be allowed back on English soil, and if he were, he would almost certainly be arrested and placed before a court-martial. That meant everything he owned in his St John's Wood apartment would go, along with his only source of income, his friends old and new, the town where he had grown up, and his family – from Hesya in her armchair to precious baby Esther.

'If we go down this route, it may be unavoidable,' he said softly.

Hokoa was limping to the door. 'You will be a hero, Detective – a real hero. Not the fake ones they parade around. Now excuse me while I attend the lavatory. I'm a little hot…'

He hunched over as he grabbed the doorknob, as though he had run out of breath. Then he turned around to look at his companions and removed his spectacles to reveal his grey eyes. But his gaze was strangely absent, as though he was looking right through them, and the spectacles trembled in his hand as he lowered them to his side. He was sweating even more profusely now, and the skin around his fingers had a bluish hue.

'Hokoa, are you alright?' Liang asked. She paced over to him and laid her palm on his forehead. 'He is hot. Hokoa, sir, sit down.'

He brushed her off. 'No, no, I'm fine… I told you, I need…'

His legs gave way and he crashed to the ground, slamming his head on the wood floor. Ben ran over to him. He was choking violently, his muscles starting to spasm, bloody spittle frothing at the corner of his mouth. Ben looked over at the opium pipe, lying upturned on the ground, next to the spirit lamp and dregs of opium ash spilled across the floor.

'Poison…' he whispered.

Hokoa's spasms intensified into a full-body seizure. He could no longer blink – the pressure in his temples seemed almost to force his eyeballs from their sockets, as his cheeks went purple and his chokes turned to gurgling gasps.

'Roll him onto his side!' Ben instructed.

He tried to stick his fingers into Hokoa's mouth to force him to vomit, but Hokoa's back arched, his legs kicked helplessly, and with a final convulsion and sickening splutter he went limp. His eyes rolled back and his jaw slackened to leave his mouth drooping open.

Ben checked his pulse, but felt no trace. Liang covered her mouth with her hands. The wealthiest man in China was dead and she had inadvertently administered the poison. Tonight, the black crow – Hong Kong's very own angel of death – had visited The Floating Life.

'What do we do?' she whispered.

As if in answer to her question, the door to their suite swung open and Coldwell entered, flanked by half a dozen police officers and Madame Xu.

The Captain Superintendent snapped his fingers. Liang and Jun were promptly seized and placed in handcuffs. Ben was not. Instead, Coldwell sidled up to him and cocked his head to one side, inspecting him with relish.

'How did that turn out for you, Mr Canaan?'

23

Death Warrant

Madame Xu proved to be their undoing. As it turned out, she had been receiving bribes from the British for years – at first to provide British troops with special access to her flower girls during the war; then later to keep tabs on Liang, as the widow of their anointed assassin, and on Hokoa, as one of their targets. As soon as she found out that Hokoa was coming to see Ben and Liang at The Floating Life, she informed Coldwell. But rather than nix Ben's plot, they opted to let it happen so that Hokoa could be drawn into the open. Ben had effectively handed them their prize.

All it took was Madame Xu's sleight of hand: switching the special stash of Patna opium that Liang personally set aside for Hokoa, for a similar variety laced with strychnine. From his first puff, Hokoa was doomed. Of course, Madame Xu denied everything, even that she had handed Liang the tainted opium in the first place, with no other witnesses to gainsay her. Instead, the killing was pinned on Liang – the indignant widow of the man who had set out to kill Hokoa, completing her husband's mission. Jun's presence was used to further bolster the Great Qing's complicity. The British had the perfect scapegoats with the perfect motive.

The press ran with the British narrative. Within a day of Hokoa's death, Liang's name and the police force's sordid accusations were plastered over the front page of the *Hong Kong Register.*

Ben was kept out of it for obvious reasons and was held under even stricter watch at Mount Austin. As far as the British were concerned, he had gone beyond the pale and was no longer to be trusted. Bruckner broke off all contact with him, leaving him in the dark as to what was happening in an already fast-moving crisis. His evidence was taken away, along with his credentials and his gun. For the first time since his triumphant return to England after the Constantinople affair, when Palmerston made him that fateful offer in the hallowed halls of 10 Downing Street, Ben was on the verge of throwing it all away.

The only respite from his unofficial imprisonment at Mount Austin was his daily breakfast in the lounge with Fitzjohn. His aide retained a degree of sympathy for him, which he expressed by plying him with coffee, crumpets, and smoked haddock. One morning, he went so far as to offer Ben a word of encouragement.

'Give them a bit of time,' he said, nudging Ben. 'I am quite sure, if you correct course, that the PM would have you back in the fold in a heartbeat.'

But appeasement was at the bottom of Ben's list. He could not bring himself to forgive his paymasters for deceiving him. Hokoa was right: the genie had escaped the lamp and there was no putting it back. Now that Ben knew the truth, he could not trick himself into believing anything else. But he was powerless to stop what was coming. He may as well have been in handcuffs.

A few days after the debacle at The Floating Life, Ben received his first word from Coldwell. The Viceroy Ye Mingchen was requesting an audience with the British on neutral ground. Lantau Island, just to the west of Hong Kong at the mouth of the Pearl River Delta, had been chosen. The purpose of the meeting, apparently, was a conclave to negotiate a settlement before war broke out, which the British saw as an opportunity to force through concessions on the trade. Coldwell, Bowring and Halliday would be there – but Ye Mingchen had insisted that Ben be present.

A carriage fetched him from Mount Austin to take him to the launching point for the boat to Lantau Island. He spent the trip sandwiched between two policemen, armed with batons and revolvers, his head down and his lips sealed.

But when the carriage came to a halt and he was escorted out, he found himself at Ingrid's waterfront estate. As he was marched up the front drive, she emerged in the doorway, dressed in her customary black for an outdoor excursion: a bell-shaped dress with wide sleeves, under a woollen paletot, with a mesh veil over her face and a reticule over her shoulder. Her expression was one of sadness.

'Come in,' she said softly. Ben followed her without a word. The policemen stayed out front to give the two some privacy.

She had had the table on the garden terrace laid for them, with Earl Grey tea, caraway seed cake, scones, and sliced pineapple. She sat down, expecting Ben to join her. But he did not. Instead, he traced his finger along the tablecloth and stole a brief glance at her.

'Dressed for a ride?' he asked.

'I'm coming with you for this tête-à-tête with the Viceroy. My uncle, as you probably gather, is hazy on the ins and outs of the firm. So I need to be there for the negotiation.'

'I see.'

They both fell silent. Ben looked at her again, with a flash of anger this time. Had she deceived him too? Was that the only reason she had invited him into her life, her home, her bed – to muzzle him with desire, distract him from the truth, keep him docile?

'I assume you've read the papers,' he said.

'I have.'

'And I assume you're aware of what *really* happened.'

Ingrid took longer to answer that. Eventually, with a sharp intake of breath, she nodded.

'I'm sorry for how you've been treated, Ben. It wasn't right. And I can understand why you're angry. With all of us.'

Ben loomed over Ingrid, casting her in his shadow, silhouetting the sun behind his dark glowering face.

'Did you know?' he asked.

They both held their breath. The wind rustled her veil. Up above, a pair of bridled terns were shrieking to each other, in a language only they could understand.

'No.'

Ben usually had a good eye for falsehoods. But he could no longer tell whether Ingrid was being honest. He turned away and covered his mouth with his hand, lost in thought.

'What about Liang, Tao, Jun?' he asked. 'What's happening to them?'

'As far as I know… Coldwell is dealing with them tomorrow. At least, that's what my uncle let slip.'

'What does "dealing with" mean?'

Ingrid said nothing. But the silence told Ben all he needed to know. She rose to her feet and placed a hand on his cheek, but he pulled away. Her touch repulsed him. Affronted, she turned her back to him, removed a cigarette box from her reticule, and lit up.

'For what it's worth, I don't agree with it,' she said. 'But it's out of my hands.'

'No… you just stand to get rich from it. Convenient.'

'If we didn't do it, Ben, someone else would. This isn't about choice, it's about who is first to the gun. China is backsliding into chaos, and this will establish a new order. The truth, as hard as it may be to swallow, is that they need us as much as we need them. That's the nature of Empire. It's not merely domination. It's symbiosis.'

'It only benefits the few. The rest are cast aside.'

'You're not wrong. But I didn't ask them to bring you here for a moral debate.'

'Then why *am* I here, Ingrid?'

She laid down her cigarette. For the first time since they met, she was nervous – trying to express the mass of unarticulated feelings inside her.

'I have enjoyed your company. More than enjoyed, that sounds too formal. It has been eye-opening. And I've been thinking about, well, lots of things. About who I used to be, before the baby. About learning to smile once more. Not hiding it, or acting as though it was never there. I didn't feel quite ready. It was frightening. The world is frightening. It was easier somehow to live in darkness because the darkness is safe and never changes. But I think, finally, I'm ready.'

She took his hand in hers. Her palm was unusually hot.

'So I was wondering, just as an idea, if our occasional nightly encounters might become a more permanent fixture. I'm a powerful woman, Ben. It may induce a certain… amnesia in your superiors. Am I making sense?'

Ben nodded.

'Either way, I want you to know: if nothing else was true... *then this was.*'

Ingrid put on a poker face, but Ben knew her well enough to see that she was close to crying. Some part of him, a baser part, wanted to tear her down – to make her feel what he felt.

But he could not bring himself to do that. He did not need to break her. She was already broken.

'I'll think about it,' he said.

Footsteps tapped across the patio – one of Ingrid's servants. 'The boat to Lantau is ready and waiting, ma'am.'

Coldwell and Halliday were already aboard the schooner, accompanied by eight police officers. Ingrid was greeted by her uncle and the Captain Superintendent with cordial kisses, while Ben was given nothing more than a frigid nod. The trip across the water passed in tense silence, punctuated by the occasional hushed exchange between Halliday and Coldwell as they stood at the bow and surveyed the waters.

They landed at the bay of Tai Pak Wan. Carriages were waiting to pick them up and take them to the intended rendezvous point on Sunset Peak. The higher they ascended, the thicker the forest became, until the carriage was having to squeeze through clusters of slash pine and sweet gum, over ground that had become gnarled and rutted with roots.

Ingrid was quiet behind her dark veil. Coldwell was glaring unblinkingly at Ben, resting his elbow on the sill and cupping his chiselled cheek. Ben watched the sun through the canopy and adjusted his fingers in the splint. Only Halliday looked as though he was even remotely enjoying himself.

'Why the long faces?' he sneered. 'We won! Well, I won. I told you, Mr Canaan, I bloody well told you. I will not lose under any circumstances. I bet you didn't believe me. You were very polite, all "Yes, sir; no, sir; three bags full, sir"… But I could tell you were looking at me thinking I'm a fool, a poor deluded fool. Who's the fool now?'

He tapped his cane to underline the point. He appeared for a moment to be done, but then his lower lip twisted and he shifted uncomfortably in his seat.

'You know who else was a fool? *My brother.* My lily-livered brother. He was a weak man. He had the eye of a shepherd, but the heart of a sheep. Isn't that right, Ingrid?'

Ingrid too said nothing. She absentmindedly twirled her thumbs, replaying a memory of her father: at the opening of an orphanage to house children who had lost their parents to opium abuse. It was the only time that she had ever seen him shed a tear, but to this day she did not know for whom it was shed. For the dead? For the children? Or for himself? Whatever it was, the only feeling she could recall was one of embarrassment.

'I haven't set foot in Scotland since I left as a young man for the East,' Halliday continued. 'You know what people say? They say I'm ashamed to go back to Scotland, because there they know me only as that pathetic child sobbing by his mother's deathbed. But I'm not ashamed. The only reason I'm still out here on my island is because *I like it.* I like it too damn much. And when I stop liking it, I will return to the Highlands as a laird of good works. I will stand atop the hill overlooking my castle and sing the bonny tune that my mother sang to me as she lay dying…'

He began singing, in a throaty voice. It was an old folk tune – 'The Braes o' Balquhither' – and it spoke of fields of bountiful heather, of fountains in the wild, of moorlands perfumed with wild mountain thyme.

'Let us go, lassie, go to the braes o' Balquhither, where the blae-berries grow, 'mang the bonnie Highland heather…'

Coldwell barely contained a sigh of frustration, still staring at Ben. Suddenly, Ingrid joined in – singing in a timid falsetto, not wanting to be heard but drawn into the melody.

'Where flie deer and the rae lightly bounding together, sport the lang summer day, on the braes o' Balquhither…'

Halliday broke off and clapped his gloved hands.

'Beautiful!' he cried. Then, with a gentle nod, 'Just beautiful…'

Coldwell came to life and rapped on the window. The carriage ground to a halt. They were in a clearing a short way from the summit of Sunset Peak. 'Right,' he said, 'this is the place. Odysseus, Ingrid: you come out first. Mr Canaan, you stay here for now.'

They dismounted and assembled in the middle of the clearing. A second carriage, carrying the police officers, had stopped further ahead and the officers formed a perimeter along the treeline. Halliday looked around, breathing in the chilly air. Apart from them, the clearing was empty.

'So, Sebastian,' he said, 'what's the story?'

By the time his gaze returned to Coldwell, the Captain Superintendent had removed his revolver and was aiming it right between Halliday's eyes.

Halliday flinched. 'Oh.'

Coldwell pulled the trigger. The bang sent flocks of spotted doves fluttering from the treetops. Halliday's head snapped back and a trail of blood erupted from the back of his skull to splatter the mud. He fell awkwardly, almost vertically, landing in an uneven heap, with one arm bent round his back and his head limp in the crook of his other arm.

Ingrid gasped. Coldwell turned the gun on her – but this time it let out a dull click. It had jammed. He slapped the barrel in annoyance.

'Bloody thing was working just fine…'

Ingrid came to her senses and ran back to the carriage. She tried to open the door, but it was locked. She was on Ben's side, and he was staring at her wide-eyed through the window.

'*Help me!*' she screamed.

Ingrid started pounding desperately on the window. Spittle flew as she roared through the glass, 'Ben, please, do something – please, Ben, please!!'

'Don't open that door, Mr Canaan!' Coldwell bellowed. 'You'll be taking your life into your own hands!'

All Ben could think of as he watched Ingrid's face contort in primitive terror was that phrase she had used, all that time ago: *the eater, not the eaten.*

'*DO SOMETHING, BEN!*'

Another bang. Ingrid's face disappeared behind a mist of blood that smeared the window like paint from a spilt bucket. There was a muted thud. Then silence – a long, tortured silence.

'Alright, Mr Canaan,' came Coldwell's voice, echoing behind the wall of blood. 'Time to come out.'

Still Ben could not move. His fists were clenched and his mind was racing without going anywhere.

'Mr Canaan… Come out this instant. I will not ask again.'

Ben unlatched the door and eased it open. Coldwell was standing in the middle of the clearing, his gun hanging by his side. Halliday was sprawled at his feet. On her back in the mud by the carriage was Ingrid. She was still alive, her throat ripped open from the bullet. A stream of blood was gushing out in thick dark torrents. Her eyes were wide and all she could muster were a few gasps. Still she was looking at him, barely understanding what had just happened.

'Why did you do that?' he whispered to Coldwell.

'One moment…'

Coldwell marched over to Ingrid and peered down at her. He put another bullet in her brain. Her gasps abruptly stopped.

'Belt and braces,' he said to Ben casually. 'Now what were you saying? Why? Well. They served their purpose. Halliday was a useful ally while we were executing this rather drawn-out operation. But in truth, he was too independent to be a reliable partner in the trade. If we're going to have a man controlling the new British monopoly, it must be someone more… functional. An empty suit. A tail that wags when we tell it.'

Coldwell chuckled to himself. He seemed thoroughly amused by something.

'Halliday thought he was being ever so clever by pretending to be a target of the Great Qing. I think he enjoyed playing the part of the embattled tycoon. He always preferred trickery to the straight and narrow. But, ironically, by allowing us to inscribe his name in that ledger you were given, he signed his own death warrant. Now we can just blame it on the Great Qing.'

'You've lost your mind,' Ben said raggedly. 'You've all lost your bloody minds…'

Coldwell shut Ben up by pressing the barrel of the gun to his forehead.

'Let this be a lesson to you: *nobody is indispensable*.'

Coldwell cocked the revolver.

'On this occasion, though, I'm not going to kill you. Not because I'd get into trouble – because I wouldn't – but because scooping your brains off the floor is too much of a headache. And, more importantly… you're not a threat to me.'

Coldwell came in closer, so that Ben had nowhere to hide from his white-hot glare.

'You're a snivelling boy desperate for our approval. I mean, the way you bent over for us! I could have mistaken you for a cheap whore. That's all you people are: rats, scurrying around in your little world, begging for us to tell you that you're good enough – that you belong – that you're one of us.'

He gave Ben a playful slap on the cheek.

'So, when push comes to shove, you'll do as you're told. You may make a song and dance about your morals, but in the end you'll save your own skin. Because you know, deep down, that we plucked you from the ash-heap, and we can send you right back if we so wish. You need us. Without us, you are nothing. Now…'

Coldwell uncocked the revolver.

'I am going to give you one last chance. Go back to Mount Austin and complete the report as planned. Hokoa was killed by Liang, who wished to finish her husband's job. Odysseus and Ingrid were ambushed on Lantau Island by mercenaries working for the Great Qing. And if you don't testify as such, I will make your death infinitely slower and infinitely more painful than what you have just witnessed. Is that understood?'

'I'll do it if you spare Liang, Tao and Jun,' Ben replied. 'I know you're planning to kill them. Let them go and I'll finish your damn report.'

Coldwell looked almost disappointed at Ben's attempt to negotiate.

'Mr Canaan, I hate to have to spell it out for you, but you're in no position to be making demands. You can't even bargain for your own life, let alone someone else's! No. You will do what you must do, and I will do what I must do. And it all slots together. That's how this works.'

Coldwell traipsed back to the carriage. He prodded the bloodied window with his index finger and called out to his officers. 'Better wipe this off, boys!'

Ben hung back and knelt by Ingrid's side to study her features. Her eyes revealed nothing but the void on the other side of life. Whatever soul had been there was now somewhere else. He gently stroked her eyelids shut.

'Coldwell,' Ben said, as the Captain Superintendent opened the carriage the door. 'Did she know?'

Coldwell made a face. 'Why do you care? Get in the carriage.'

They trundled off into the forest. It was as though they had never been there. The only relic of their presence were those two bodies – once human beings, now spoil for the earth to feast on. By winter, they would be gone: pecked at, pilfered, flayed, rotted away – indistinguishable from the dust whence they came.

24

The End of the Line

Liang, Tao and Jun had spent four miserable days in the holding cells of the Central Police Station. It was a dark and bleak place. Thick stone walls sealed them off from the outside world. Dank gusts of wind from the harbour blew through the corridors in the dead of night. There was nothing to subsist on but tainted water and tasteless slop made from old foxtail millet, more fit for livestock. No candles, no lamps – just a tiny barred window ten feet overhead to let in a narrow shaft of greyish sunlight.

Their only company was Coldwell's deputy Tsung, who had been posted to watch over them. He was a young man, of about Liang's age. In another life, they may have been friends. But in this life, they were countrymen on opposite sides of a war, and no amount of pleading by Liang in Tsung's native Cantonese seemed to move him.

They started to lose track of time, as though they sat at the bottom of a deep pit and the world above them had already moved on. Liang had not seen the newspapers, she had spoken to no one, she had no window into the minds of Coldwell and Bruckner. Her last hope was Ben – the only man who knew the truth and could do something to avert disaster. But where was he? And what fate had the British decided for him? All she could do was offer scant comfort to Tao as he wept quietly in her arms.

On the morning of their fifth day in captivity, something changed. Tsung arrived with a respectable breakfast of steamed buns stuffed with pork, sweet tofu pudding, and green tea. The three of them ate ravenously. Tsung watched them all the while.

'Thank you,' Liang whispered to him, in Cantonese.

Tsung's jaw tightened. As soon as they had finished, he strode off. He returned several minutes later with Coldwell in tow. The Captain Superintendent was in official military garb – a navy-blue dolman trimmed with gold, long trousers striped blue and beige, and spotless white gloves.

'Open the cell,' he said to Tsung.

Tsung obliged. Coldwell gestured to the wall of the holding cell. 'Sit with your backs against the wall.'

Liang was hesitant. 'Why?'

'Do I have to force you?' Coldwell said, checking his watch.

Reluctantly, Liang obliged. Tao clung to her side. She gently smoothed his hair as Coldwell snapped his fingers and Tsung entered the cell. The deputy reached into his back pocket and removed a set of canvas hoods. The last thing Liang saw was Tsung leaning in, hood in hand, and yanking it over her head.

The pen lay on Ben's desk, next to his papers. But he was not looking at the pen, or the half-finished report, or the wad of blank paper waiting to be filled in. Instead, his eyes were fixed on the clock opposite his bed, as he watched the pendulum swing back and forth and the minute-hand creep by at a snail's pace.

It was just past nine-thirty in the morning. He had been awake for hours but had hardly moved. He was standing at the fork in the road – at the precise point at which the paths diverged – and he was paralysed.

There was only one chapter left in the narrative that he was expected to write. It would take him all of two hours. Then it would be done: not just the report, but everything that had transpired – from the murder at Kenwood House to the execution of Odysseus Halliday and Ingrid Marshall in the forests of Lantau Island. His word would become truth, not because it happened but because people would believe it to have happened. That was the way of the world. No truth, no falsehood, no right, no wrong. Just stories, and whichever particular story people chose to believe.

He would become everything that he had never been. Vaunted at dinner parties. Showered with adulation. His children would never know deprivation or hatred. And any nagging doubts could be washed down with champagne, drowned out at the opera, buried in the gardens of a country estate.

He picked up the pen and pressed the nib to the paper. The ink pooled in a growing spot around the nib, growing darker and darker – as dark as the blood that flowed from Ingrid's throat. The same as Liang's blood, and Tao's blood, and Jun's blood, and all the black blood that would be shed in the name of Empire. Was that the price of human life? A hat for Ascot, a bottle of Veuve Clicquot, a country manor, a coat of arms?

What would his family say when they saw him in his fine suit, on his fine piece of land, if they knew what had been sacrificed to secure it? Would they even recognise him? Or would he have become the man envisioned by his grandfather Tuvia, in the living room at 82 Whitechapel Road, when Ben saw him for the last time: one who spends his life running from himself, in pursuit of the thing that he is not?

He tapped the pen twice more, to form an ellipsis on the page. Then, with sudden decision, he set it down and opened the door to his suite.

'Excuse me!' he called after the guard down the corridor.

The guard lumbered over to him. 'What is it?'

'I have a report to send to Gustav Bruckner. He has been requesting it for some time.'

'Hand it over then.'

'It's on the desk. Do you mind picking it up yourself?' Ben gestured to his left hand, still immobilised in its splint. 'It's hard to scoop all the pages up with one hand.'

The guard entered and approached Ben's desk. Ben quietly clicked the door shut behind him and, with the guard's back turned, picked up the empty Overholt bottle on his bedside table. The guard rifled through the pages.

'Doesn't look finished to me—'

Ben cracked the bottle over the guard's head. The guard fell, out cold. He would have a nasty headache, but would live to tell the tale. Ben rolled him over and yanked the guard's revolver from its holster, and tucked it into the back of his trouser-belt.

He found Fitzjohn downstairs at their usual breakfast table. 'Mr Canaan!' Fitzjohn exclaimed, shaking with him. 'I was worried you would never come down. I can order you an omelette – onions, peppers and spinach, as you like it.'

Ben looked around to make sure they were not being overheard. 'Fitzjohn, could we talk in private for a jiffy?'

'Certainly! Something urgent?'

They retreated to a quiet part of the lobby. Ben spoke in an undertone.

'Fitzjohn, be honest with me – not as my aide but as, I hope, a friend. You are aware of what Coldwell is doing today, aren't you? With Liang, her brother, and the Chinese agent.'

Fitzjohn nodded, more than a little contrite.

'When is he completing the job?'

'About noon, sir. The Captain Superintendent is having lunch with the Governor and he wants it done by then.'

'And where is this happening?'

Fitzjohn's sympathy cooled. 'Mr Canaan, I cannot honour your request, for reasons of which you are well aware.'

'It was not a request.'

'Are you threatening me, Mr Canaan?'

'Yes, I am. I like you very much, and I really do appreciate the omelettes. I would like nothing more than for you to return to your Annabelle. But if you want to do that, then you will have to tell me where Coldwell is taking them.'

Fitzjohn squared up to Ben. 'Mr Canaan. I am an aide not to you, but to Her Majesty's government. I have made a solemn oath, and there is nothing you can do that will make me break—'

Ben removed the revolver and pressed it to Fitzjohn's forehead.

'Nanfang Fort on Bluff Head!' Fitzjohn cried out. 'On the southern tip of the island, just below Stanley! About an hour and a half from here!'

Shrieks of alarm erupted around the lobby. The other guests ran for the exit while the policemen on patrol whipped out their guns. Ben wrapped his left arm around Fitzjohn's neck, facing a line of policemen in a standoff.

'Don't take one step!' Ben roared. 'I'll shoot him, I swear!'

'Let him go and put down your gun, Mr Canaan!' one of the policemen bellowed.

Ben replied by lifting his gun in the air and firing off a shot. Clumps of plaster rained down from the ceiling.

'Get me a carriage now! *Now*, I tell you!!'

The policemen were rooted to the spot: not shooting, but not backing down either. Ben started edging towards the front doors, the gun firmly planted to Fitzjohn's head.

'Will you get the man a carriage, for God's sake?!' Fitzjohn squealed. 'I'll be damned if I die in a bloody hotel lobby!'

One of the policemen motioned for his men to lower their guns. 'Alright, fetch the man a carriage. Do it!'

Ben dragged Fitzjohn with him out the front door of the hotel. A carriage pulled up before them and the driver dismounted. Ben motioned for Fitzjohn to climb up to the driver's seat. 'Take the reins,' he said. 'You're going to drive. Fast as you can.'

'Mr Canaan, have you lost your mind—'

'You'll quite literally lose yours if you don't do as I say!'

Fitzjohn complied and Ben climbed up next to him.

'If I see anyone, and I mean *anyone* following me,' Ben said firmly, 'he gets a bullet in the brain. Got it?'

Ben jabbed Fitzjohn with the barrel of the gun and his aide whipped the reins. The carriage tore off, across the front lawns and out of the bounds of the Mount Austin estate.

It took about twenty minutes of riding at breakneck speed before Ben felt comfortable that the coast was clear. By that point, they were on an isolated dirt road somewhere at the foot of the Peak. He nudged Fitzjohn and the carriage slowed to a halt.

'Please don't kill me, sir,' Fitzjohn said, close to tears. 'I've only followed orders…'

'I'm not going to kill you, man,' Ben said, rubbing his eyes with a weary sigh. 'But for what I'm about to do – I wholeheartedly apologise…'

He shoved Fitzjohn with all his strength and sent the man careening off the edge of the carriage, into the mud. Then Ben took the reins with his good hand and whipped them as hard as he could, heading south for Bluff Head. The last thing he heard from Fitzjohn, over the pounding of the horses' hooves and the wind in his ears, was a nasal cry: 'It was nice knowing you, Canaan!'

All Liang could hear was the crashing of the waves, coming and going with the groans of the ocean tide. She was on her knees and mud was seeping through her dress. Her wrists were bound behind her back. The air was cold, as though nature herself was recoiling in horror. Then she heard squelching footsteps and voices. One was Coldwell's and the other was thinner, higher-pitched, German-accented.

'It's a delightful view,' the German man said. 'No wonder the Chinese built a fort here.'

'They're being converted soon,' Coldwell replied. 'Naval barracks. Or a seaside hotel.'

'A hotel would be splendid. A bit of leisure would do this island some good.'

A gust blew through and the two men fell silent. Then the German piped up again: 'We shall build a metropolis on this land. It is a long way from now, but it will happen. Steel girders, bridges of iron, roads wide enough for a dozen carriages, towers as tall as the sky itself. It will be a jewel, studding the South China Sea. And we sit, you and I, in the foundation pit. The dirt, the clay, the fire, the seawater. Placing one brick after another in the wall.'

He cleared his throat.

'Shall we?'

'Let's.'

Coldwell ripped the hoods off his three captives. Liang was in the middle, with Tao to her left and Jun to her right. They were kneeling on the edge of a sheer drop to the sea-swept rocks a hundred feet below. Before them was a vaulted chamber – the central atrium of an ancient fort now fallen into decay. Bruckner was standing in an archway that gave onto the cliff-edge, his hands folded behind his back as he admired the panorama of the South China Sea.

'I don't suppose I need to explain why we're here,' Coldwell said.

He removed his revolver, flicked open the cylinder, and began loading bullets into the chambers. Each dull click sent a shudder through a tear-stricken Tao.

'You three are what we in the business call *loose ends*. And loose ends tend to be cut.' He pointed to Liang and Jun. 'You two, because you tried to scupper our plans at the eleventh hour. And the boy because he knows too much.'

He loaded up the final bullet, gave the cylinder a spin, and snapped it shut.

'Most people in my shoes pinch their noses in moments such as this. Not me. I like to breathe it in.'

'Because you're a coward,' Jun said through gritted teeth. 'You live like a coward and you kill like a coward. Who knows? Maybe you'll die like a coward too.'

Coldwell gave a venomous smile. 'You first.'

He shot Jun in the head: a single shot at point blank range. Jun's body lurched back from the force of the bullet and tumbled over the edge of the cliff. Liang watched him fall, his limbs flailing in vain before his body was dashed on the jagged rocks below.

An involuntary sob escaped her lips as Coldwell turned the gun on her.

'Is this how you repay Bo?' she choked. 'He did everything you asked of him!'

'Sure, but Bo is also fish food at the bottom of the Thames. So...' Coldwell offered a matter-of-fact shrug, as if to say there was nothing he could do about it.

'Then at least leave Tao. He's just a boy. He had nothing to do with any of this.'

'If you were that concerned for his life, you should have kept your nose out of our affairs. That's what happens when you kick the hornet's nest: everyone around you gets stung.'

He shifted the revolver from Liang to Tao and back again, savouring Tao's terrified weeping and the rising tremor in Liang's voice.

'Please,' she sobbed, 'you can't do this, I beg you...'

'I can, actually,' Coldwell screwed up his face. 'That's what you people don't understand. You think that you're going to be prancing around in your robes, bowing to each other and shovelling rice down your gullets for the rest of time. But things are changing. You are already the past. And we are the future.'

Liang lifted her chin, defiant through her tears. 'You'll be the past one day too.'

'Maybe. But I certainly won't be around to see it. And neither will you.'

He cocked the revolver.

'Tell you what: because you put up a decent fight, I'll let you decide who I shoot first.'

Liang shook her head.

'Your choice, Liang. If he goes first, you will have to watch it. But if you go first… well, then the boy will die all alone. And that would be *really* sad, wouldn't it?'

There was no consolation that Liang could give Tao in that moment – nothing but the look of love with which she had greeted him every morning since their parents' death. A look that said everything would be alright, even in the darkest tunnel or the deepest valley.

'I'm not going to dignify you with an answer,' Liang said to Coldwell.

'Very well. Then the boy can die alone.'

He placed the gun against Liang's temple. She closed her eyes. In the darkness, she dug up a memory of her mother and father – the vague outline of their faces salvaged from her childhood like a long-lost shipwreck. They had never felt so close as they did now.

'Show mercy,' she whispered.

'This *is* mercy,' came Coldwell's reply.

She heard the bang of a gunshot, but felt nothing – just blood splatter her face. Is this what it felt like to die? As though nothing at all had happened? As though she had stepped out of time itself? She felt the breeze on her cheeks. She heard her brother issue a helpless scream. Cold mud was still seeping through her dress.

Then she opened her eyes. She was looking at Coldwell's feet: slim black leather Wellington boots stopping short below the knee. Her gaze moved up, from his tightly constricted waist to his broad shoulders, and finally to his face. She gasped.

The right side of Coldwell's head had been blown open: a ragged exit wound stuck with mangled scraps of skull and scalp. His right eye was pulverised in its socket. His upper jaw dangled by a thread. Only his left side was intact. The corner of his lip quivered and his one good eye widened ever so slightly, as the realisation of what had just happened dawned on him. He tottered for a few seconds before collapsing onto his side, spilling the pulpy remains of his shredded brain tissue across the ground.

Liang looked to her right. Standing at the entrance to the chamber was Ben, his revolver raised as smoke trailed from the barrel. He was looking not at her, but at Coldwell's dead body. He was trying to make sense of what he had just done.

'Benjamin?'

Bruckner had turned to face them, but Ben stopped him in his tracks with the gun. 'Don't move a muscle, Bruckner. I'm not bluffing.'

Ben rummaged for the mother-of-pearl penknife in his back pocket. He pinched it between his thumb and index finger and cut through Liang's rope-binds. She immediately got to work freeing Tao.

'You have no idea what you have just thrown away, Benjamin,' Bruckner said darkly.

'Yes,' Ben replied. 'Yes, I do.'

'And what shall I tell Palmerston?'

The anger and shame that Ben had long suppressed bubbled up to the surface.

'Two words,' he said. '*I. Quit.*'

And with that, he left with Liang and Tao in tow. As they exited the fort, he heard Bruckner's voice echoing after them: 'We'll hunt you down to the ends of the earth, Benjamin! We won't rest until we've ground you down to dust!'

But soon Bruckner's threats were lost to the wind and the waves. The carriage that Ben commandeered at Mount Austin was waiting on a dirt track up from Nanfang Fort, on the edge of a plain swaying with wild heather.

Just as Liang and Tao were about to get into the carriage, they heard footsteps crunch towards them. A young man emerged from behind a pillar. It was Deputy Tsung – ordered by Coldwell to hang back until Liang, Tao and Jun had been disposed of – and now he held the escaping trio at gunpoint.

Ben's gun was at his side. Tsung would be quicker to the trigger. Coldwell's deputy had total control over what happened next. Their lives were now in the hands of this acne-riddled adolescent, standing face to face for what felt like an eternity.

Tsung's gaze landed on Tao. The boy was covering his eyes and crying.

The deputy sighed. Without a word, he lowered his revolver and turned away. The message was clear: *I saw nothing.*

Ben hopped onto the driver's seat, seized the reins, and they set off at a mad dash. It was a race against time now. Soon the entirety of Hong Kong Island would be mobilised against him, and not long after that the rest of the British Empire would follow. With the pull of a trigger, Ben had made himself the most wanted man in the world.

'Are you alright?' Liang asked Ben.

Ben spurred the horses on – one part of him scrambling to figure out his next steps, the other obsessively replaying the image of Coldwell's body slumping to the ground.

He spoke more to himself than to Liang: 'That's the first time I've killed a man…'

Liang and Tao laid low at the Basel Missionary Society's homeless shelter in Stanley – the very same where Ben had found the sailor Lucky Nelson during his investigation. Meanwhile, Ben disappeared to set his plan in motion. He had precious few hours before news of Coldwell's death spread across the island and he intended to use them.

He returned to the shelter around dinnertime, with a leather saddlebag slung over his shoulder and a change of clothes for himself, Liang and Tao. By then, even the remote community of Stanley was awash with rumours of a mysterious British agent on the run. They would have to move in secret. They got changed and, after sundown, followed the coastline westward on foot, bound for Deep Water Bay.

Among the multitude of ships moored on the bay was a dragon – a smuggler boat ready to sail upriver into China. The captain of the boat recognised Ben and greeted him with a handshake on the jetty.

'Ten minutes,' he said.

The captain looked Liang and Tao up and down, then set about loading his boat with cargo. It was only then that Liang realised what Ben had done.

'How much did you pay?' she asked.

'Let's just say there was a substantial premium given the circumstances.'

Liang took his hand. 'I will pay you back. I promise.'

But Ben shook his head firmly. 'Liang – I only paid for two spaces. You won't see me again.'

'What do you mean? Where will you go?'

'I've got my own way out,' he said. 'It's a long shot, as they say at the races. But I fancy my chances.'

He held out the saddlebag. He had £200 left from his advance payment by the British. So he had taken a hundred of that and converted it into silver taels, about four hundred in total, for Liang to keep. She was speechless when Ben told her the sum. It was enough for her and Tao to live off for the rest of their lives.

'I can't accept this—' she began.

But Ben shushed her and shoved the saddlebag into her arms. 'Take it. It's yours now.'

There was another item left in one of the pockets of the saddlebag: the salt print that had been sitting on her mantlepiece, depicting her and Bo at a café in happier, simpler times. Ben had managed to sneak back to 12 Tang Lung Street to get a hold of it.

'It would have been a shame to leave it behind,' he said.

Liang hugged Ben tightly. Her words were lost in a sob of relief.

'Where is it taking us?' she asked.

'The smugglers are heading north-east, for Nanjing. But you're getting off before then… a little town called Shangrao. You may have heard of it.'

The paradise in the forests of Jiangxi, printed on the postcard that lived in Liang's breast pocket, pressed to her heartbeat. The dream of a future that she had believed to have died with Bo. She was overwhelmed.

'Go and live in peace. Nobody will know who you are. Nobody will know where to find you. You can start over.' He wiped away Liang's tears. 'The promise that you made with Bo is still alive. Honour it, for him, for you, for Tao. And don't look back. Especially not for me.'

The captain loaded up the last crate and waved to them from port-side. It was time for them to leave. She tried to draw it out a little longer, but Ben was having none of it. He pinched Tao's cheek affectionately and gave him a parting order to keep at his homework, then stepped back and watched the two of them board the dragon.

'Look after them!' Ben called out to the captain.

Liang and Tao remained on deck as the boat chugged upriver, their faces dappled in the dying light and becoming fainter and fainter as they drifted away. Soon they were indistinguishable from the rolling seas of Deep Water Bay and the distant twilit shadows of the mountain peaks.

They were taken care of. Now Ben just needed to save himself. And for that, he would have to rely on the kindness of his only remaining friend on this stinking isle.

It was no challenge finding Zachary. He was at his usual watering hole. Only this time, he was drinking more than just baijiu – he had thrown rum, whiskey and a couple of beers into the mix.

Ben came up behind Zachary. 'Drowning your sorrows?'

Zachary almost fell off his chair. 'Not much to do since you done me out of a job! I was making good money with Coldwell.'

'Sorry about that,' Ben said. 'I was in a bit of a bind.'

'Still are. Half the island is hunting you down.'

Ben looked around furtively. The clientele was sufficiently sozzled not to recognise him – or, if they did, not to care.

'Let me guess,' Zachary said. 'You need my help. Again.'

'Just a quick trip,' Ben said under his breath. 'One way. Then I'll be off your hands.'

By the time the bells tolled eleven, Zachary had delivered Ben to his destination: Macao. Ben stole through the city under cover of night until he arrived at the grand hillside estate that bore the crest of the Ormrod family. The bodyguards standing watch initially barred his entrance.

'Tell them it is Benjamin E. Canaan,' he said. 'They'll know me.'

Many long moments later, the guards returned to usher Ben into the estate. He was greeted at the door by Marceline and her father Calvin. Marceline shook her head at him in disbelief.

'You are a magnet for trouble, Mr Canaan,' she tut-tutted.

'A leopard cannot change its spots.'

'We've heard the news from Hong Kong,' Calvin chimed in. 'I must admit we were in half a mind to notify the British that you had come. But Marceline urged against it. We feel that you are an honourable enough man to have at least had *some* reason for doing what you did.'

'At the risk of sounding like a cliché,' Ben said with a bow, 'I can explain.'

And explain he did, over a consommé celestine, sugared lady-fingers and coffee à la Balzac. The Ormrods listened patiently as he recounted his journey of discovery over the previous few weeks. By the end, Marceline was rapt.

'It seems you have pried open a nest of vipers, Mr Canaan,' she said. Ben knew that tone. This pampered teenage heiress had quickly acquired a taste for intrigue.

'And I've damn near ruined my life because of it.'

'Which begs the question: why have you come here? What do you need?'

'In short,' Ben knocked back the last of his coffee, 'I need a way out of here. An escape route that only you can provide.'

Calvin looked a little on edge. Marceline, on the other hand, let slip a conspiratorial smile.

'I think we can figure something out,' she said.

It was nearly two o'clock when Ben retired to his room on the estate. As in his room at Mount Austin, there was a writing desk by a set of broad windows, providing a view of the Pearl River and, on the far side of the dark waters, the island of Hong Kong.

Its lights were still glimmering. At that very moment, policemen and officers of the British Army were patrolling door to door, scouring for any sign of him.

Ben had expected some part of himself to regret what he had done that day. After all, he had thrown away a lifetime of security, peace and comfort. But he felt nothing of the sort. Instead, for the first time in as long as he could remember, the knot of pressure balled up in his chest slackened and the nagging voice of doubt in his mind faded away. He was finally free.

He sat at the desk and laid out a wad of paper. He took up one of the pens left on the desktop and wrote a heading at the top of the page:

THE TRUE TESTIMONY OF BENJAMIN E. CANAAN
OF THE EVENTS LATELY TRANSPIRED ON THE PEARL RIVER

25

Family Matters

Under normal circumstances, evensong was the happiest time of the week for Montague Wetherton. The distinguished Law Lord, with his carefully coiffed grey combover and thick tortoiseshell spectacles, was a regular face at St Albans Abbey on a Sunday evening. He had never been an especially religious man, but the service had a calming effect on him. It cleared his habitually overstuffed head and allowed him, for an hour so, to well and truly relax.

But these were not normal circumstances. It was early October, one week before the long-awaited inquiry that bore his name, and it was all that he could think about. Every day some fresh spoke in the wheel, from interlocutory applications to eleventh-hour admissions of previously unmentioned evidence. It had quickly become his black dog, loitering in the corner and sucking the joy out of every waking moment. So, far from smiling, Wetherton sat through evensong with a scowl, full of dread at the prospect of returning home to trawl through the bundles stacked in his study.

He returned to Hilbury House, his grand Hertfordshire estate, at just past eight o'clock. The help had been dismissed for the night, leaving Wetherton and his wife Lady Fiona – whom he affectionately called Fifi – to fend for themselves. That was just how they liked it. Fifi went to the kitchen to put the kettle on and prepare a plate of digestive biscuits, while Wetherton went upstairs to his study, guided by the light of his oil lantern.

The room was chilly and the window by his desk was wide open. Strange, Wetherton thought to himself: he distinctly remembered closing it before he left for evensong.

'Good evening, my lord.'

Wetherton jumped. A young man emerged from the shadows and stepped into the lantern light. He looked like a run-of-the-mill highwayman: a baggy cotton shirt under a thick duster coat, complete with canvas trousers, high leather boots, and a wide-brimmed slouch hat. He was unshaven and had dark circles under his eyes.

'Thief…!' Wetherton stammered.

But the young man shook his head. 'Don't you know who I am?'

He removed a piece of paper from his pocket and unfolded it for Wetherton. It was the front page of *The Times*, with a head-line that read: FUGITIVE AND TRAITOR BENJAMIN E. CANAAN STILL AT LARGE.

Wetherton set down his lantern. The name 'Ben Canaan' had taken on an almost mythic status since he vanished two months previously: a disgraced former British agent – a turncoat who murdered a police officer in cold blood – persona non grata in England. And now he was standing a mere six feet from Wetherton, a scruffy apparition come to him in the night.

'You have a lovely home,' Ben said. 'Did you inherit it?'

Ben was as benign as could be, but Wetherton still felt a nervous sweat bead his brow. 'No. I bought it some twenty years ago.'

Ben nodded and looked around at the décor. He knew already that Wetherton had been born a commoner. Yet this place had all the grandeur of the family seat of an old landed dynasty. This Law Lord had done well for himself.

'I was nearly a barrister,' Ben said wistfully. 'But I never had the schooling. Then again, maybe it would have been too narrow for me. Eton, Oxford, the Inns of Court, the Royal Courts of Justice – a man can spend his whole life in a leafy quadrangle. Never really seeing the world, but only hearing echoes of it.'

Wetherton had gone clammy. The poor man was shaking in his boots.

'Have you… come to harm me, Mr Canaan?'

'Not at all!' Ben chuckled. 'Contrary to what the papers are saying, I'm not in fact a deranged murderer.'

'Then why are you here?'

'I was hired to do a job. Go to Hong Kong, crack the mystery of the Black Blood Murders, and give you my testimony.' Ben circled round Wetherton's desk and slid forward a document bound with red string. 'And I am a man of my word.'

Wetherton inspected the document: it was Ben's report.

'What do you expect me to do with this?'

'What do you think? Therein lies the truth. The people deserve to know what really happened on the Pearl River.'

Wetherton snapped the document shut before he read too much. He was already skirting dangerously close to malpractice. 'I cannot accept this, Mr Canaan. I would be bringing my entire role in this inquiry into disrepute. I assume you're not testifying orally?'

Ben shook his head.

'Then this is just the hearsay of a wanted man,' Wetherton said, waving the document in Ben's face. 'There will be questions.

How did I acquire this? How do I know that it is reliable? Am I implicated in the breach of procedure that this document represents?'

'You can check it against records of my handwriting. If I need to sign a statement of truth, I will. My lord, if the procedure obscures the truth… then the procedure is broken.'

'Don't be naive. This is enshrined, codified law—'

'Then the law is broken too!'

Ben was not for turning. Wetherton adjusted his combover – a little tell whenever he was at his wits' end. Just when he thought this case could not get any more maddening, he was met with some fresh absurdity.

'If I do as you suggest,' Wetherton sighed, 'then I will be aiding and abetting in a crime.'

'And if you do not do as I suggest,' Ben said, 'then you will be aiding and abetting in a far greater crime, committed on a far grander scale. One that has been perpetrated for a hundred years, and will continue for a hundred more unless we speak out. Untold millions will perish so that a callous few can prosper. I do not profess to have the answers, still less a solution to these injustices. But I believe that our highest responsibility in life is to leave behind a better world than the one that we inherited. And if we are to make good on that promise, then at the very least we must start by speaking the *truth* – no matter how much it costs us. And we do this in the hope that, one day, people will be able to speak that truth without having to sacrifice what men like us had to give up.'

Ben turned away and straddled the windowsill – one leg in, one leg out.

'You have the truth. I have done everything I can. The rest, my lord, is up to you.'

Before Wetherton could reply, Ben dropped out the window and scaled down the side of Hilbury House. Wetherton watched him take off on foot, into the depths of Heartwood Forest.

Fifi suddenly entered with a mug of tea and a plate of biscuits.

'I couldn't help but overhear you conversing with a known fugitive, lovie,' she said.

Wetherton leant on the windowsill. By the time Fifi set the evening snack down on his desk, Ben's shadow had vanished.

'Was he frightful?' she asked.

'Not especially.'

'Oh well, what drama!' She shuffled to the door. 'I suppose I should summon the constabulary. He will be tremendously peeved at being disturbed at this hour on a Sunday.'

'It can wait until morning, Fifi,' Wetherton said, slamming the window shut. 'The boy has earned himself a head start.'

Max Canaan stuck his head through the curtains of his bedroom window. There were journalists camped outside the Canaan family home at 82 Whitechapel Road – a whole mob of them, pouncing on anyone entering or exiting the place, in hope of a scoop. It had been like this for two months, ever since Ben's name headlined in the newspapers for all the wrong reasons. Suddenly, it was the Canaan clan who had been thrust into the limelight. One could not pass a street corner in the East End without hearing some murmur of the intrigue swirling around this family of humble tailors.

It was not just the reporters who had questions. Each member of the family had been interrogated in isolation by the Metropolitan Police, to test the consistency of their stories. But it did little good. The most that the Canaans could do was plead their ignorance. Ben had kept them in the dark about his work for precisely this reason: any knowledge was dangerous.

Max had been more forthright. He had looked the officer heading up the investigation dead in the eye – one Sergeant Will Hardy – and said quite candidly that he believed this whole manhunt to be a sham, and that his brother was being unfairly branded as a murderer. Hardy did not bother to argue with the youngster. Perhaps some part of him believed it too.

'Max!'

He felt himself yanked back from the window. It was his indefatigable mother. Ruth had an anxious streak at the best of times, and this latest turn of events had left her taut as an elastic band ready to snap.

'I'm just counting reporters, Mama. There's more than usual today.'

'Max, I already have one son being paraded on the front pages – I do *not* need another! They are perfect strangers and have no business prying into our lives.'

She pulled the curtains shut.

'And what's this I hear,' she continued, 'about you going around tearing down posters of Benjy?'

'What, you mean the wanted posters? "Dead or alive" with a ransom under his mug? Yes, I tore those down! They put one right outside the shop on Poppins Court.'

Ruth gripped her stubborn son by the shoulders.

'Nobody in this family believes for one second that Benjy is guilty of what he's been accused of – least of all me. But, whatever the truth may be, your brother has done what he does best and landed himself in a world of trouble. And you will too if you keep acting out like this. I can't face that, Max. It's not what Benjy would want.'

Some part of Max understood what Ruth meant. She was in just as much pain as he was, not knowing where Ben was or whether he would be alright. But his anger at the injustice of it all got the better of him and he tore himself from her grasp.

'That's the problem, Mama: everyone is giving up on Benjy because they're scared of the consequences! What's the point in saying we believe in him if we don't act like it?'

He stormed downstairs. Hesya was, as usual, knitting in her armchair. Judit sat in the corner, propping up Esther on her knee while Golda spoon-fed the baby warm carrot soup.

'They're making such a racket out there,' Hesya intoned with a shake of the head. 'What's getting them so worked up?'

'They're chickens,' Max pouted. 'A bunch of squawking chickens. I hate them.'

'Now, that's not very nice,' Hesya replied. 'They are people too, *bubbele.*'

Max scooped up his ledgers and sat down at the table in a huff. He was not allowed to leave while those journalists flocked outside and it was making him fidgety. It was like living in a zoo, confined to endless reviews of the company accounts while the world peered in.

As if on cue, a cacophony erupted on the steps of 82 Whitechapel Road. Solly had returned from Poppins Court and was shoving his way through the throng, while Jack Hauser beat back anyone who got too close to his father-in-law. They squeezed their way inside and slammed the door shut behind them. Solly came into the living room with a newspaper in his hand. There was a fire in his eyes: something had happened – something huge.

'Just when I thought that boy had run out of surprises…'

Max snatched the paper from his father. There was only one story dominating the headlines: Lord Montague Wetherton's dramatic unveiling of Ben's testimony at the inquiry into the Black Blood Murders. It was a final twist in the tale – that the British government itself had orchestrated the killings in an attempt to trigger war with the Great Qing; that they had systematically deceived their closest allies; and that Ben had refused to go along with it.

'What did I say?' Max declared, practically launching the paper into the air. 'Our Benjy, a cold-blood murderer? Tell it to the Marines!'

Solly's relief that his son was not the turncoat that the press had painted him to be was palpable. But he was still far from pleased. 'This doesn't bring him any closer to home, Max. If this is true, he won't be able to set foot on British soil for as long as he lives – at least not without being arrested, court-martialled... or worse, God forbid.'

'But, Papa... he did the right thing.'

'Did he?' Solly shot back. He was holding back the tears. 'He did right by himself. Now I must tell your mother that we may never again see our eldest son. Does that sound fair?'

Max fell silent. Solly sat down next to Judit. She leant over and kissed him on the forehead. 'It will be alright, Papa,' she said softly.

Jack tried to lighten the mood. He popped open his satchel and a bundle of letters came spilling out, each and every one addressed to the Canaan family. 'People have been coming into the shop down by Poppins Court all day to drop letters in. Thanks to the inquiry, they've got Benjy pegged as a modern-day Robin Hood.'

Max rifled through the letters. They read like odes to a folk legend, the stuff of fable and fantasy: thanking Solly for raising a man of the people, who stood up to the swells.

Max was glowing with pride. 'He's a hero…'

Ruth entered. As soon as she saw Solly slumped on the chair next to Judit, she knew that something was wrong. 'What is it?' she asked, wringing her hands.

Solly got up and put a hand around her waist to guide her out. The family sat in silence, as the two of them trudged upstairs and closed their bedroom door. A few moments later, they heard a muffled sob through the ceiling.

Shabbat dinner that night was sombre. For the first time since Ben had left for Hong Kong, the prospect of him never returning, of his solemn vow being broken, felt truly real. There was admiration for Ben. He had heeded the advice that his father gave him those many months ago: to remember who he was, not to allow himself to be twisted inside-out by his profession. But beyond that, there was only anguish and a sense of lost time.

The doorbell rang halfway through the meal. Max answered it to find a deliveryman at their front door, carrying a large wooden box. 'Canaan residence?'

'That's right.'

The deliveryman held out the box. 'Fabrics, sir. You ordered these.'

Max frowned. There was no such order in the accounts. 'Dad?' he called out, 'Did we order more fabrics?'

'What?' Solly ambled to the front door. 'No, we didn't order anything of the sort.'

The deliveryman stared at Solly, fixed and unblinking. 'You most certainly did, sir.'

He thrust the box into Solly hands. It was only then that the penny dropped.

'Oh… you're quite right,' Solly said. 'How forgetful of me. Thank you.'

The deliveryman gave him a knowing nod and marched off to his carriage. As soon as Solly closed the door, Max was all over the box. 'The plot thickens!'

They set the box on the dinner table and pried the lid off. Sure enough, lying atop a bed of fabrics was a handwritten note:

Joffe's Fish and Chips. Eastbourne. Sunday, 6.30pm – Benjy
     PS: <u>BRING MENDEL</u>

'Well, it's settled then,' Solly said, brimming with excitement. 'The Canaans are going to Eastbourne!'

The plan was set. They spent Saturday packing their belongings for a day trip, while Solly made a rare exception to the rules of the Sabbath and bought tickets for the night-train, due to arrive in Eastbourne on Sunday morning. They waited until sunset, when the journalists finally slunk home, and sneaked into the back of a hansom cab bound for London Bridge. From there, they took the train to Polegate, where they caught a connection to Eastbourne.

By breakfast-time on Sunday, the whole family was walking up the Grand Parade: Solly and Max leading the way; Judit and Jack close behind with both Esther and Mendel swaddled up; Ruth linking her arm through Hesya's to support her; and Golda riding piggyback on Uncle Herschy.

The family booked a single room at the Claremont. It would be a cramped Sunday night, but it was all that they could afford. They had the day to explore the town, but they were not the least bit interested. Instead, they sat at a long table at the back of Joffe's Fish and Chips – the only Kosher spot in Eastbourne – and waited for Ben to appear.

At six-thirty on the dot, just in time for dinner, the entry bell tinkled and Ben appeared. They saw him before he saw them. It was an unguarded glimpse of the new Ben: steely and stoic in the face of uncertainty. Then he caught sight of them and all traces of gloom disappeared behind a vintage Benjy grin. He shot a wry look at Mr Joffe, who was dredging his cuts of fish at the counter. Max's eyes sparkled: was he in on Ben's scheme too?

'I wasn't sure if you'd make it,' Ben said.

'Make it?' Ruth threw her arms around him. 'I would have travelled to Timbuktu to see you again!'

'I wouldn't advise that if I were you,' Uncle Herschy said, blowing his nose into a handkerchief. 'If there's one thing I learned from my days in Timbuktu—'

'Herschy,' Solly interrupted him. 'Now's not the time.'

Ben winked at Mr Joffe. 'Fish and chips for everyone, please!'

Solly instinctively reached for his pocket, but Ben stayed his hand.

'Dad, I've had you schlep all this way at short notice. This one's on me.'

Mr Joffe plated them up: battered fillets of freshly caught Atlantic cod, thick-cut chips doused with vinegar, mushy peas flavoured with mint and parsley, with ginger beer to wash it down. A feast of this kind was a rarity in the doldrums of the East End, and it was enough to silence the whole table for several minutes.

Ben regaled his family with the account of his escape from Hong Kong. His newfound status as a fugitive made commercial travel extremely difficult, nor could he rely on the smugglers roaming the Indian Ocean. Instead, it was the Ormrods who got him out. First, he stowed away on one of the family's trading brigs to Galle, in Ceylon. From there, it was another journey by boat to Suez; a train across the desert wilds to Alexandria; and, finally, a steamer via the Mediterranean and the eastern Atlantic to Southampton. It was a risky move on the part of the Ormrods, but it was their way of repaying Ben in his hour of need, for having saved Marceline and Calvin from certain death.

'But how are you going to survive, Benjy?' Solly asked. 'You can't live in England as a free man.'

Ben nodded sadly. 'That's why I won't be living in England at all, Dad. I'm catching a connection to New York Harbour tomorrow morning.'

'And what then?'

'The Ormrods have said they'll help me. They have an extensive network in the north-eastern states. So I'll probably end up there for the time being, until I find my feet.'

Ruth clasped Ben's hands in hers. 'So… you're going for good? To *America*?'

Ben paused. What words could soften the blow? He could only shake his head and say in a low voice, 'I'm sorry, Mum. This is the price that has to be paid.'

'When will we see you again?' Max asked.

Ben was hesitant. He was about to break their hearts. 'I don't know.'

Solly wanted to chastise Ben for being so reckless. He wanted to say anything that would lessen the burden of his own sorrow. But he had never seen Ben so shattered and bruised. And if there was one thing worse than the prospect of Ben leaving, it was the sight of his boy in such deep, abiding pain. He reached across the table and ruffled Ben's hair.

'You're a brave man, boychik. I'm proud of you.'

Ben leant into his father's hand. He had needed that touch for so long.

'Now,' Solly continued, 'let's smile and laugh together. We have all night.'

And so they whiled away the hours at Joffe's, like it was the good old days. They joked, they bickered, they ate, they shared the latest gossip from Whitechapel and news about the business. The boys went for a gander up and down the Grand Parade, while the women installed themselves in the salon at the Claremont. Then they retired to their tiny single bedroom. Judit, Hesya and baby Esther were given pride of place in bed, while everyone else had a little floormat on which to curl up.

Ben did not sleep a wink. Instead, he sat in the corner like a watchful protector, keeping vigil over his slumbering family, with Mendel nestled in his lap. He wanted to remember every impression, so that he could replay them in his mind on the lonely voyage to America.

In the dawn twilight, Ben made his way down to the lobby. He sat by the window over the Grand Parade with a lemon-water. The boat was being prepared at that very moment. In a couple of hours, England would be behind him forever.

'Can't sleep?'

Ben snapped out of his trance. A bleary-eyed Max was walking towards him and took a seat opposite him.

'No,' Ben said. 'Not really.'

Max hiked his knees to his chest. 'I don't suppose you've read the news.'

'What is it?'

'The Chinese seized a British boat in Canton by the name of the *Arrow* and took the crew hostage. Now Number 10 is saying it's an act of war. And if you ask me, they'll see this one through. So you got rid of one excuse, and they just replaced it with a fresh one. Another way to manufacture consent for the fight they're itching to start.' Max grew cold and bitter. 'Which means… you didn't change a thing. You threw it all away for nothing.'

'It wasn't for nothing.'

'Then what was it for, exactly? Because the way I see it, you're a near-penniless fugitive fleeing to another continent, leaving everyone behind, having to start your whole life over again. And the men you tried to stop are just getting richer, and stronger, and bolder.'

Max was right, of course. To the world, Ben was a sinner and the powers-that-be were saints. Lives would still be shattered by injustice. History would still take its course and he would remain bound up in its journey. Try as he might, Ben could not stop the wheel of time.

'Max, we live in a cruel and unforgiving world. A world that rewards evil. There are bad men who are never punished and good men who are never redeemed. Murderers live to old age, while children die senselessly. It would be so easy to just… give up. "If everyone else does wrong, why can't I?" But that's not the answer. All you'd do is lose yourself.'

'Then what are we supposed to do?'

'We do what we can. *We try.*'

Max sighed and gazed out the window. A gull had come to rest on the other side of the glass. A rootless seabird living day to day without a care, without memory, untroubled by thoughts of the future. Just one meal after another until the end of its life.

'I want to promise you something,' Max said solemnly. 'One day, I will be a man of means. I will have money and influence.

And I will use every penny to bring you back. Even if I have to buy their forgiveness. I promise you. I'll do it.'

Ben did not know what to say. He was not sure that he believed it, or even that Max did himself. He looked at Max, winding back through the memories of his little brother. The first word. The first step. The first joke. The first book. The first spark of originality.

Max had kept his feelings bottled up for long enough. The tears welled up and started dripping down his cheeks. 'Please don't go, Benjy. You're the only one who understands me.'

Ben came round to Max's side of the table and hugged him tight. Max wept quietly into his brother's chest, as Ben whispered in his ear that everything would be alright. The gull appeared to watch them fleetingly, before growing bored and taking flight.

By nine that morning, the ship was ready to depart for New York. It was another one of the Ormrods' barques: a three-masted trading vessel called *Sister Josephine*, manned by a small crew, with the American flag fluttering on high. The Canaan family gathered on the quay to give their boy a final farewell. Ben stood before them, tired and drained, but resolute. His whole life was crammed inside a leather satchel, and Mendel was tucked under his arm, purring softly.

He hugged each of them one last time. Jack gave him the old Good-for-Nothing handshake from their less sensible days. Uncle Herschy, having insisted that he would maintain a stiff upper lip as any true Englishman, immediately broke down in floods of tears. His mother smothered his face from forehead to chin with kisses. His father laid a hand on his chest – as understated and certain a gesture as ever for Ben to go and be free.

And then there was Esther. She was bigger than when Ben had last said goodbye. Her eyes seemed to see more of the world and of him. But even then, she would probably never recall his lips on her brow or his voice as he whispered a tender goodbye. It was just another moment that would be swallowed up in the darkness before memory.

He boarded the ship and stood at port side. His family remained on the quay, waving to him as *Sister Josephine* detached and set its course down the Channel. While they were still in view, Ben tied the scarf that Hesya had knitted for him round his neck – the one that read 'Honour thy mother and father'. The Canaans shrank, smaller and smaller, until they were mere dots on the shores of England.

And then, all of a sudden, Ben was alone. Alone with a crew of strangers, the chilly sea wind, the heaving of the ocean. He closed his eyes and briefly pictured himself at the window of his attic-room back home, watching the sun sink below the chimney-tops of the East End. A younger man with no sense of what lay before him. That man was still him – yet everything had changed.

He turned away and headed below deck, as the ship pointed its bow to the New World.

Buried in the valleys between the mountains of Jiangxi, there was a cabin overlooking a river. It had belonged for many years to an elderly spinster called Yulan. But she had passed away two years previously, without a husband or children, and it was quickly purchased by a new arrival in town: a beautiful young woman and her even younger bespectacled brother who, despite coming from nothing, seemed to always have money for something.

They had lived in this cabin ever since Yulan's passing. The boy went to a nearby school and excelled in letters. There was

even talk about him taking the prestigious civil service exams –
the kind of exams that would either drive him mad or bring him
prosperity and influence. His sister preferred a quiet life. She
was extremely adept with her fingers, though she never explained
why. Most of the locals believed it to be a gift of the gods. She
used her dexterity to become a seamstress, specialising in *aoqun*.
Soon most of the women in town were wearing her clothes and
it became a modest, though never too prosperous business.

She rarely spoke of where she came from and eventually
people stopped asking. Her stubbornness was stronger than
their curiosity. The only peculiarity that visitors to her workshop noticed was a salt print on the mantlepiece, of her in a
café with a scholarly-looking young man – the kind who would
have preferred to live inside books rather than the real world.
When asked where he was, she would always say in a bright voice:
'Why, he's right there!'

By the end of their second year, she had married one of the
fishermen. He was a simple man, and he only made a little money,
but he showed his love to her every day in small and unremark-
able ways: planting hibiscus in their walled garden because he
knew how she loved it – giving up his mild opium habit because
she never liked the smell – offering her small wooden totems
that he carved by hand while out fishing.

One morning in early autumn, when the leaves were beginning to fall from the trees, she was sitting on the terrace weaving
a golden dress. Her brother was inside memorising Confucius,
while her husband was mending his rowboat by the river. She
looked out over Shangrao, bathed in newly born light. For a
moment, she drifted back to the past.

But then she remembered what she had been told – to never
look back. So she let it go.

Epilogue: 1861

It was a crisp mid-April morning in Harrisburg, capital of the Commonwealth of Pennsylvania. Bluebirds warbled the city awake and the day's first steam trains chugged from the station, bound for Philadelphia in the east. Schoolboys squeezed in a final game of shinny on the playing fields by Paxton Creek. The cotton textile mills, blast furnaces and waterworks crowding the banks of the Pennsylvania Canal began firing up. State representatives, in their black suits and top hats, trickled into Hills Capitol – that gleaming dome with its grand colonnade, elevated above the rest of the city. At every turn, Harrisburg was filled with the smell of sawdust, horse manure, and the nutty aroma of roasting coffee.

On the corner of Market Street and Third Street, overlooking the bustling open-air bazaar of Market Square, was a nondescript two-storey building. On the ground floor was Maison Caroline Bergeret, a patisserie named after the octogenarian immigrant from Aquitaine who had been running it for the past sixty years. The upper floor was accessible by a narrow stairwell at the back of the patisserie, at the top of which was a door engraved with the title:

BEN CANAAN, DETECTIVE

On the other side of the door was a busy waiting room: all clients of Harrisburg's premier private investigator. Curled up on a fleece mat in the corner was a slumbering grey Chartreux cat. Manning the desk and mollifying the more impatient clients was Philip Summerhill: a baby-faced nineteen-year-old with a mop of jet-black hair and dark skin – the product of a Shawnee mother and a freed slave for a father. He knew that the people here looked at him with some suspicion. 'His kind' usually kept to other neighbourhoods. But he did not care. He was doing what he loved, and that was all that mattered.

The door to an adjoining office opened as Ben Canaan saw out his latest client. The last five years had changed him. His hair had grown out, tinged chestnut-brown by the American sun. He had finally abandoned his thin moustache and now sported a sharp clean-shaven look. Gone were the slim-fitting suits. These days, his workaday outfit was a chequered blue-and-white shirt under a navy-green sack coat, linen trousers, brogans flecked with reddish clay stains, and the flat cap that had become his signature. It was not a common sight on this side of the Atlantic, but it was his way of retaining at least a splash of his East End roots.

Ben clapped his hands together with a broad grin. 'Who's next?'

It was a jam-packed Monday, as Mondays typically were. Francine Carruthers, wife of a Dauphin County commissioner, was convinced that her husband was being unfaithful with her sister – though Ben suspected that it was Francine's sister herself who was fuelling the rumours, in an effort to destroy an otherwise happy union. Then there was Karl-Heinz Dittmar, a German émigré and amateur inventor whose patent for a steam-powered traction engine had been stolen by an unknown man across the Susquehanna River. To close the morning out, Ben received a visit from Walter Kennedy, an adolescent out for revenge against his schoolmate, who had broken his leg in order to have him kicked off the rowing team. Ben had to politely remind Walter that he was a detective, not a schoolmaster.

Once he had cleared the waiting room, Philip brought Ben his correspondence. It was the usual fare. A convoluted explanation from one of his clients about why his fee was not yet forthcoming. A demand for the remainder of last month's rent, which was still due. A letter from his family, informing him of the birth of Judit's third child. And a letter from Marceline Ormrod, appended with a forget-me-not that she had pressed into the paper.

Philip clocked that last letter with a smirk and left Ben to pen his responses. The letters having been mailed, Ben and Philip went to The Oyster House, their regular lunch spot on Tanner's Alley, in the heart of Harrisburg's black community. Slavery had been abolished here for quite some time, and the new railroad allowed abolitionists to ferry families of slaves from the Confederate States of the South to the Union in the North, where they could be emancipated and live as free people. The Oyster House was founded by one such family, and not even the racists could deny it served the best lunch this side of the Commonwealth.

Ben went to the service counter. Delilah, the eldest daughter of the owners, was doling out helpings of catfish, collard greens, lima beans and pound cake. As soon as she saw him, a bashful smile tugged involuntarily at the corners of her lips, blooming before she could stop it.

'Howdy,' he said.

'So you're a cowboy now?' she replied.

'Almost. All I need's a little something to lasso.'

Ben leant in. Delilah's eyes darted away as she tucked a strand of hair behind her ear – a hint of hesitation, but beneath that was a tremor of excitement.

'You look prettier every time I see you,' Ben whispered.

She glanced over her shoulder in case her parents were within earshot and tried to compose herself. 'Stop being a charmer and order your lunch!'

Ben surveyed the options. 'You know what? I'll have a bit of everything. I'm hungry.'

She plated him up a liberal helping. 'And an extra lump of greens,' she said. 'You gotta mind that belly 'fore it gets too big.'

'Thank you kindly.' Ben took the plate in one hand and reached into his pocket with the other. 'And for your generosity…'

He held out a book: *The Woman in White*, Wilkie Collins's latest novel. Delilah lit up at the sight of it, caught in a moment of sweet surprise.

'I remember you saying you wanted a copy but none of the bookshops would sell it to you. So I went and bought it. And I left a little note in there for you.'

Delilah took the book and was about to open it up, but Ben laid his hand on hers.

'Not in public. Wouldn't want them to see you blush!'

Delilah could only shake her head as a faint flush rose in her cheeks. Ben, as always, was incorrigible. 'Thank you, Ben. Best eat up while it's hot.'

Ben rejoined Philip at their table. His assistant had thoroughly enjoyed the show.

'You better not break her heart, Ben. Otherwise we'll never be able to come back here.'

'It's just a bit of playful flirting.'

'Oh really?' Philip chuckled, tearing off a piece of cornbread. 'Like the love letters you're getting from Marceline Ormrod?'

Ben was about to dig in, but that made him set down his cutlery and wag his finger at Philip. 'My relationship with Marceline is and always has been platonic. We go a long way back, we're good friends, and that's that.'

'Right, right… A beautiful heiress of marrying age is madly in love with you and you'd rather have a frolic at The Oyster House.'

Ben shrugged and popped a piece of catfish in his mouth. It was fried to perfection – good enough to put to bed all the recent squabbles between North and South.

'Philip, this lunch has everything. Fish, beans, vegetables, cake. It's filling, hearty and soulful. It brings a smile to my face. And the best part? It only cost me twenty cents.'

Philip idly speared his food with the prongs of his fork. 'So you're not tempted by that… other life?'

'What other life?' Ben frowned.

'Well… everyone knows about your past. Your involvement in high espionage. All the money you were making. Have you never thought about going back to it? Even if it was for the Americans? I mean, we struggle from week to week with bills and pressure and building a roster of clients… And they would pay handsomely for a service like ours. How hard would it be to just pinch your nose and take it?'

Ben was about to deflect with some flippant riposte, but he stopped himself. It was a serious question from a serious place, and there was something about Philip that reminded Ben of himself, in another life when he was not as wise or careful.

'Do you know who Voltaire was, Philip?'

Philip shook his head.

'He was a philosopher and satirist of the Enlightenment. A strident critic of the Catholic Church. And when he was on his deathbed, he was visited by a priest. The priest told him as he lay dying that this was his last chance to enter the Kingdom of

Heaven – to have everything that he could possibly desire – and all he needed to do was renounce Satan.'

'And what did he say?'

Ben looked at Philip with sudden solemnity, as though he was staring into the grave himself. *'Young man, this is no time to be making enemies.'*

No sooner had the words flown from his lips than the bells around Harrisburg began tolling. But they were not tolling for the hour. This was a tocsin – the sound of the alarm being raised. Then, rumbling ever closer like an approaching storm, came the trampling of horses. One by one, the diners filtered out to see for themselves what exactly was going on.

An enormous cavalry from the North was tearing down the thoroughfare of Second Street by the Susquehanna. There must have been well over a thousand Union soldiers on horseback, blitzing through Harrisburg, bound south for the Potomac River.

One of the officers was marshalling bystanders to the side of the road, to make way for the cavalcade. 'Come on, out the way!'

Ben waved down the officer. 'What's going on?!' he shouted.

'Haven't you heard? Fort Sumter has been besieged! It's war!'

'War? With who?'

'Ourselves, sir!' the officer called out over the rising stampede. 'Who else?'

THE SERIES CONTINUES IN

THE
CAT-MAN
OF
DIXIELAND

COMING 2027